For Christine, with thanks for her continuing support and encouragement.

THE TINKERMAN

AN INSPECTOR HOOD NOVEL

By

Michael G T Stokes

ISBN-13: 978-1-7394266-0-6
Thrussington Publishing

'He who maketh haste to be rich shall not go unpunished.'

Proverbs 28:20

CONTENTS

CHAPTER 1

Spring, 2000

Detective Chief Inspector Henry Hood joined Detective Chief Superintendent Tony Craven at police HQ four days after Julia Hamilton's surprise acquittal. Neither of them were looking forward to the meeting with the chief constable. Although the chief's retirement was only a few months away, they both knew that was not going to deter him from adopting his usual practice of demanding immediate answers from his subordinate officers. The rising tide of murders which Mid-Shires Constabulary was presently experiencing was skewing his statistics.

'Three murders in under a week and in the same division!' he barked, looking at Craven and then at Hood. 'Have you seen what the tabloids are saying?' He waved a copy of *The Sun* in front of them and didn't wait for an answer. 'Shottingham! That's what they're calling our fair city of Nottingham. Three victims in the city and county. All shot dead in just five days. And two of them on the heels of the acquittal of that bloody Hamilton woman! I've just had the Minister of State from the Home Office on the phone. What *is* going on?'

Craven and Hood looked at each other. Craven spoke first. He outranked Hood, whose promotion seemed to have been put on the back burner – yet again. Both men noted they had not been asked to sit and there was no sign of an offer of refreshment despite the early hour. Craven was almost standing to attention as he spoke. 'We have arrested two men for the St Anne's killing, sir. It looks like it was drug related. Dealers vying for control since we put Haydon Connolly away three months ago. It's happened before and will happen again. Haydon's gone down for twenty-two years and there's a bit of a rush to fill the vacuum. One of the two we have arrested has already coughed. The other may prove more troublesome, but we have the evidence. They both had firearm residue on their clothing and hands and we've recovered a sawn-off shotgun. It's probably the gun that was used in the hit.'

The chief nodded in evident satisfaction. 'Good. Well done. Have we identified the victim?'

'Yes, sir. Vince Cooper. He's Mickey Flynn's muscle, or he was. But we think Flynn was the real target.'

'And Flynn was moving in to take over Connolly's operation?'

'That's the word on the street, yes.'

'What went wrong?'

Craven suppressed a smile. 'Flynn drives a big American Cadillac, left-hand drive. Terrible show-off, he is. These two idiots we've picked up don't know their left from their right. It looks like they shot Cooper by mistake. Mickey Flynn always drives himself – he's known for it. It was dark and they thought they were blowing away the driver. Cooper was in the passenger seat. Unfortunately for him, he got both barrels.'

The chief flinched. 'What did Flynn do?'

'Exactly what you'd expect. He drove on and pushed Cooper's body out of the car on the Wells Road, just outside the hospital, about five hundred yards from where the incident occurred.'

'Very decent of him,' smiled the chief. 'Wanted to make sure he received treatment, did he?'

'I don't think so, sir. And Cooper was beyond saving. Just a coincidence where he pushed him out of his car.' He gave his superior a knowing look. 'And Wells Road is a psychiatric hospital. No A and E there.' The chief nodded his understanding as Craven continued. 'Cooper is not a pretty sight. He was shot at close range. Dead at the scene I suspect. We're still trying to locate Flynn and his car but he'll have gone to ground until things die down.'

'We know precisely where it happened do we?'

'We do. Flynn ran down the gunman as he made his escape. The other fellow picked up the sawn-off and ran for it. Officers found

Ricky Spencer with a broken leg and a smashed pelvis in the middle of the road. He's still in the Queen's Medical Centre. I interviewed him there after he came out of surgery. It's all on tape. He's coughed the lot. He even gave up his mate, Rod Blackwell. Plenty of form. He took some finding. We discovered him the day before yesterday, hiding in his ex-girlfriend's loft, still with the sawn-off. He's at the Bridewell. Saying nothing at the moment, but he will. I'll be seeking an extension from the Magistrates' Court if he doesn't admit his part today. I'm interviewing him again this afternoon.'

'I assume someone put them up to it?'

'Probably Connolly, trying to keep control of his patch; he and Flynn have been daggers drawn for years, but it won't be easy to prove.'

'Unless one of them implicates him?'

'Not much chance of that. Cooper's death will send out a clear message. Connolly would have any informer removed from circulation, even if they were in prison. He wouldn't be too fussy if it was one of his own boys either.'

'Where's Connolly being held?'

'Woodborough. He's in High Security. He was moved from Nottingham straight after his trial.'

The chief almost smiled. 'Connolly's appealing his conviction, isn't he?'

'Yes, sir. He's been refused leave, but he'll have a go before the full court.'

'Prospects?'

Craven grinned. 'No chance.'

'Good. And the two who were fished out of the Trent? I only heard about the woman last night. What about them? Has similar progress been made?'

Craven was content to defer to Hood. The chief inspector cleared his throat before he answered. He knew he was unable to report much progress, but he sounded as positive as he could and spoke with a quiet authority as he addressed the chief. 'It's early days, sir. And there's no connection with the St Anne's killings; that much is clear. Spencer was already in the QMC when the first murder occurred.'

'That's right,' confirmed Craven. 'Harry's is a much more difficult inquiry. The St Anne's killers are vicious bastards but they're rank amateurs compared to the people Harry's investigating. He's dealing with real professionals by the look of it.'

Hood acknowledged the chief superintendent and continued. 'There's a good chance both Dudley Manning and the woman were shot with the same weapon, probably a Beretta M9. We recovered one of the used cartridges from the Trent Bridge shooting and it's the same calibre as the bullet from the woman's body found in the river near Cromwell Lock. Dudley Manning was shot twice, the woman once. The firearms expert hasn't let us have his written report yet but I'm assured there's a distinct possibility that the same gun was used. We may be looking for a single killer.'

'May be?' said the chief. 'It's pretty obvious isn't it? If the same gun was used? Has the weapon been recovered?'

'No sir, not yet. And we can't be sure at this stage they were both killed by the same individual. You know me; I never assume anything. I like to follow where the evidence leads. These weapons get passed around, as you know, and the hit on Dudley looks very much like an execution. One bullet to the head and another to the heart. The killing at Cromwell has other features apart from the fact that she was shot only once.'

The chief grunted his understanding. He knew Hood was a good detective, not given to rushing to judgement. He heaved a sigh and invited both officers to relax and to take a seat. They glanced at each other then sat down, the tension both had felt now dissipated.

'The expert will require the gun, won't he, in order to reach a definite conclusion? He'd have to test fire it to be certain.' The chief had once led a major crime unit and had some experience of firearms. Hood, too, had some knowledge of the type of weapon used as he explained.

'The chances of finding the gun are not good. The magazine on a Baretta M9 usually packs fifteen rounds. A professional killer is not going to dispose of his weapon of choice with twelve rounds unused. If we are to recover it, we're going to have to arrest our killer with it in his possession.'

'You're proceeding on the basis that both were professional hits?'

'Yes, sir. That's what it looks like, especially if both killings were by the same person. We'll try and locate the gun, of course.'

'That's not going to be easy, Harry. I don't want any officers injured, or worse, making an arrest. But I suppose you'll have to discover whoever did this first?

'Yes, sir.'

'What about Doyle? Have you located him yet? He must be the prime suspect, surely? Two corpses in the same river within a few hours of his coming out of prison.'

Hood took a deep breath and shifted in his seat. 'No sign of him so far and it looks like he couldn't have killed Dudley Manning. He was only released from prison in Colchester about four hours or so before the shooting and he'd have had a hell of a job to get to Nottingham in time to have carried it out. It looks like he travelled at least as far as Leicester by train. We have him on CCTV at Leicester station at twenty-three-thirty hours. Besides, Doyle may be a villain, but he's never been involved with lethal firearms before.'

'There's always a first time,' murmured the chief, 'and a shotgun was used in the Charnwood robbery, don't forget that.' He paused and glanced at Hood. 'You developed a bit of a relationship with him, didn't you?'

'I wouldn't go as far as that, sir. But I think he trusts me, at least he did. And we mustn't overlook that the shotgun cartridges used at the Charnwood were loaded with salt. That suggests an attempt was made to avoid serious casualties. These killings seem deliberate. There can't be any doubt about it; whoever's responsible intended to kill.'

The chief nodded. 'Do you think Doyle's still around, or has something untoward happened to him as well?'

'We are working on the assumption that he's still alive. He could have died in the fire at Barnard House, but there's no sign of a body. That's the last place we know for sure where he was.'

Craven interrupted. 'The fire was very severe. It's not beyond the bounds of possibility that someone caught up in it might have died and left hardly a trace. His body could have been completely destroyed in the intense heat. I've read the preliminary report from the fire officer. He doesn't exactly rule it out.'

'Unlikely though,' pronounced the chief. 'There's usually something left behind in my experience. Could Doyle have started the fire, perhaps? It was definitely arson wasn't it?'

Hood nodded. 'Yes, sir. You could still smell the petrol when we got there. It was started deliberately, but not by Doyle, not in my opinion. That's highly unlikely. He left a message with the taxi-driver who drove him to the house asking him to contact the police if he didn't hear from him by five p.m. He gave the driver a big tip and, as you know, the cabbie did as he was asked. That's how we got there while the fire was still raging. It seems to me that Doyle must have been expecting trouble when he went there.'

'Sounds like he found it,' observed the chief. 'So, why did he go there? Who, I wonder, was he expecting to meet?'

'We are still trying to establish who rented the property from the developers. Whoever they were, they've gone to extreme lengths to cover their tracks and it certainly couldn't have been Doyle. Eight thousand in cash was paid just to rent it for a month and that was arranged weeks before Doyle was released. That the rent was paid in cash doesn't help in tracing the temporary tenant.'

'There must be something, surely, a receipt, an agreement of some kind? The owner must be furious that the place was burnt down. It had historical associations didn't it?' Hood shrugged his shoulders as the chief continued. 'They must have taken some precautions before renting out a place like that and done some kind of check on the tenant? And Doyle was rolling in cash before his arrest. That's why we got a decent confiscation order against him after he was convicted.'

Hood nodded. 'We did, but the owner of Barnard House is a property company based abroad. As far as I'm aware, Doyle has no connection with it although he had quite a property portfolio of his own at one time. The place was fully insured against the risk of fire and we do have one or two things to go on. The main shareholder is from the Cayman Islands, I believe, but we are looking into it with the assistance of the insurance investigator, but it's not at all straightforward. They'll be examining everything with a fine toothcomb, probably trying to find a reason to avoid paying out.' He smiled. 'Whether they'll get anywhere with it I don't know. A paperchase that leads to God knows where. And as I said, whoever rented it has been very careful to avoid being identified. But we'll keep working on it.'

'That Hamilton woman must be the prime candidate? Would Doyle have put himself at risk for anyone else?'

'She was probably at the house, yes. She may even have invited him there. I can't understand why he'd have gone there otherwise. But she can't have organised it. She was in custody herself until her acquittal last Friday. The house was rented long before then. I suspect it was whoever organised Hanlon's escape, possibly the father of her child, always assuming she wasn't telling the truth at her trial.'

The chief harrumphed. 'Well, we know for sure she wasn't telling the truth at her trial. It turned into a farce after Hanlon did his disappearing act.'

Hood agreed. 'Yes, sir. But she insisted throughout the trial that Doyle was her son's father. And she claimed she named the boy after him.'

The chief rolled his eyes. 'So, Doyle hasn't been excluded as the father? Is that what you're telling me?'

'No, sir. Quite the opposite. We have reason to believe that he has been excluded and what's more, we believe he knows it. Doyle must have had more than a suspicion he might not have been the father. He instructed solicitors to issue proceedings in the Family Court seeking a parental responsibility order but abandoned them after he discovered Hamilton had named him as the father on the birth certificate. Some sort of paternity test was also done while he was in hospital. He's unlikely to be the father, according to a letter he left screwed up in his cell.'

The chief smiled. 'Hamilton led him on for months, then?'

'And the jury, sir,' added Craven. 'Let's not forget the jury. She hoodwinked them too.'

The chief reacted by raising his voice. 'She misled everyone. But as we know, that's what she does. Why should Doyle be an exception? It wouldn't surprise me if she'd led him a merry dance throughout. Mind you, I don't suppose he'd be very happy about being cuckolded. And as you said, he must have had his doubts if he took out proceedings and had the tests done.'

Hood agreed. 'Always assuming it was he who asked for the tests to be done. And he had changed his instructions to his solicitor before any proceedings were actually issued. It was probably Hamilton telling him he wasn't the father before she gave birth which planted the seed of suspicion. It might have caused him to have himself tested to see if he had a low sperm count. On the other hand, she could have been lying.'

'I don't follow,' said the chief.

'I had a check done during Hamilton's trial – she admitted in the witness box she'd previously told Doyle he wasn't her child's father in order to make him angry, which she said she thought would help him survive while he was on remand.'

'Seems an odd thing to do?' said the chief. 'How would making him angry help?'

'I agree, sir. It's decidedly odd. But she probably knows him as well as anyone, probably better. And that's what she said in court. Doyle confirmed that she'd told him he wasn't the father when I spoke to him last year. They certainly had a major bust-up while he was in Leicester prison. And she never went to visit him again while he was there. She told the jury he would have gone to pieces had he thought she was carrying his child; he couldn't have coped, so she lied to him. But I think there was more to it than that.'

'What do you mean?' asked the chief.

'I think it was all part of her plan to distance Doyle from her scheme to blackmail the judge who was dealing with Doyle's trial. I believe she caused the row with Doyle to make sure he was not implicated in her actions. She clearly went out on a limb for him, which is why I retain the odd doubt as to the paternity of her child, whatever she may have got up to since.'

'I don't suppose she named anyone else as the father when she had the row with Doyle?'

'No, sir. Not according to what Doyle told me at the time. Hence my recent inquiry. I only got the results after Hamilton had been acquitted. There's a bit of a mystery how the tests came about and who paid for them. And while they'd only require a DNA sample to carry out a paternity test, the letter discovered in his cell stated he had a low sperm count. As I understand it, to get such a result would involve a lot more than a DNA sample.' He grinned, knowingly. 'He'd have to cooperate if you know what I mean. Incidentally, he accused us of using the DNA sample he'd given us on his arrest, which is nonsense.'

'Doyle must have known, surely, if he cooperated in such a test? Has he said anything to anyone else?'

'Not that we know of,' replied Hood. 'He certainly never told me that he'd organised any tests for himself.'

'What are you saying? That the test was faked? He could still be the boy's father?'

'I don't know, sir. Only Hamilton knows the truth of it, and whoever she's with now. I presume she must have cooperated in getting the necessary tests done so far as the child is concerned. There was no court order for the child's DNA to be obtained, so it was all done on the quiet, possibly illegally, but as you know sir, those two were once very close. To all intents and purposes they were living together. Doyle would have assumed he was the father until he was told otherwise. Our entire case against Hamilton proceeded on the basis that she acted as she did to ensure Doyle got away with the Charnwood robbery. It was undoubtedly her idea to kidnap the judge's wife and son and blackmail him into directing an acquittal. Pretty extreme when you think about it, but the plan had to originate with somebody who had the requisite legal knowledge.'

'So, it must have been her?'

'Yes. I'm pretty sure of it. She'd been involved in an earlier case –

nothing to do with Doyle – where a DNA sample had been excluded as evidence. I'm sure that's where she got the idea. If the co-accused's DNA result had been excluded by the judge, Doyle would have been home and free.'

'Thank God you intervened when you did,' said the chief. 'I have to admit, you and your team did a good job in exposing the plot. I'd never have heard the end of it had the blackmail attempt succeeded.'

Hood acknowledged the chief's implied accolade but he felt obliged to pay tribute to the courage of the judge who had disobeyed the kidnappers' demands and informed him what was happening. 'We were lucky that the judge told us about the blackmail attempt before a decision was given in the case. As you know, sir, the message that Duffy sent informing us where Mrs Campion and the child were being held didn't get through to me until well after we'd located through other means where they were being detained.'

The chief glowered. 'Don't remind me. That officer was suspended; if I'd had my way he'd have been dismissed.' He paused. 'You reckon Duffy was told to do that?'

'I can't think of another explanation why the message was sent. It appears that Gus Grayling had turned the whole thing around. He wanted the plot exposed in an effort to get Doyle and Hamilton arrested and sent down. What I can't quite get my head around is why everything seems to have gone full circle. Someone went to a hell of a lot of trouble, not to convict her, but to get her off. That was the last thing I would have expected. I thought Gus Grayling, had he survived, would have moved heaven and earth to ruin her because of her association with Doyle.'

The chief smiled. 'There was one major development, of course, between the blackmail plot being exposed and Hamilton's trial taking place.'

Hood nodded. 'Yes, sir. Gus Grayling died.'

'Exactly! Perhaps whoever took over from Grayling is Hamilton's new lover? That would explain it, wouldn't it? If she has thrown Doyle over and taken up with Grayling's successor there'd be every incentive to see that she was acquitted. She wouldn't be much use to him serving a sentence in double figures, would she? She may well have lost her appeal in more senses than one by the time she came out.' The chief laughed as Hood continued.

'I'm working on that theory, yes. Harold Cronshaw reckons that was what must have happened, too. It's the only thing that makes any sense. As I understand it, that's the reason counsel changed the indictment, to cover both possibilities.'

'Cronshaw? He prosecuted the case, didn't he?'

'Yes, sir.'

'And Judge Campion?'

'Sitting at the Old Bailey now. Well out of the way. And I believe he lives down south too. You can understand how he and his family wouldn't want to continue living in the house where the kidnapping occurred.'

The chief nodded his understanding. Hood returned to the relationship between Doyle and Julia Hamilton. 'But Doyle can't have known what she was up to. I'm pretty sure he only pleaded guilty to the Charnwood robbery when he did because he thought he was protecting her. He genuinely thought she was at risk from Grayling. And he gave us the first clue that led to us foiling the later robbery attempt near Retford. He informed on Duffy which led to Duffy being arrested. Duffy then named the rest of the gang although we had arrested most of them by then.'

'Pity Doyle informing on Duffy got out.'

'It was inevitable given the circumstances, especially after Duffy chose to give evidence against Hamilton. But it's Doyle's cooperation with us that's put him at risk. There's definitely a price on his head. Someone is out to get him. I'm sure no one knows about our other informant; the one who's on the witness protection programme up in Scotland.'

'Even I don't know who he is, and I don't want to know,' said the chief. 'But it was the information from Doyle which set the ball rolling?'

'Yes, sir. What he told me was crucial. Identifying Duffy was the key to solving the robbery attempt. That led us to the other informant. Everything else flowed from that. The same personnel were used, for the most part, in both sets of offences.'

'And it was because Doyle acted as an informer putting himself at risk that he was released early,' moaned the chief. He frowned. 'I was opposed to that, you know. I argued strongly against it. I can't see why he couldn't have been protected in prison. Letting someone like Doyle out early does not have a good look.' He shook his head. 'He's still obsessed with Hamilton is he?'

'I'm sure of it. Her feelings for him remain ambiguous but I'm still far from convinced that she's wholly abandoned him, not yet.'

The chief frowned. 'Doyle could still have arranged both killings, couldn't he? Even if he didn't carry them out himself.'

'We haven't excluded him as a suspect, not yet, but I think it unlikely. What would be his motive? What connection did he have with the woman found in the Trent at Cromwell? We have no evidence that he even knew her. And we still haven't identified her, not definitely.'

'Not definitely? So you do have some idea who she might be?'

'There's a possibility she could be the woman mentioned in Hamilton's trial, Maxine Kruger, a German national of about thirty-six. The woman pulled out of the Trent is about the right vintage and build. Kruger's know to the Garda in Limerick and Dublin. We are waiting confirmation. They don't have her DNA on record but they have some intelligence about her and the body fits the general description they gave us during Hamilton's trial. It could well be her.'

No one spoke for a minute. The chief looked briefly at the papers on his desk. 'What about the Mercedes Doyle hired?' he asked.

Hood had a wry smile on his face as he answered. 'The Mercedes someone hired in his name you mean, sir. We know for certain that Doyle didn't rent it. He was still in Colchester prison when the booking was made. We also have a statement from the employee who delivered it to his flat first thing last Saturday morning. The person who received it and signed the insurance form was not Doyle and the transaction was carried out in the rear car park. The fellow from the hire company had never met Doyle before and whoever it was who took charge of the car produced Doyle's driving licence or a very good forgery. For some reason, someone wanted it to look like Doyle had hired the car. The description we have simply doesn't fit him.'

The chief frowned. 'I thought we had his flat at Harbour Buildings under surveillance?'

'We still do, sir. But neither officer noticed the arrival of the Mercedes in the car park, or, if they did, they thought nothing of it. No one went up to Doyle's apartment. The business must have been conducted entirely in the car park. The two officers were watching the front of the building and the flat.'

'Asleep on the job, eh?'

'I don't think so, sir.' Hood paused. 'The good news is we've recovered the vehicle. The rental agreement was found in the glove compartment and the hirer's signature looks decidedly dodgy. It must have been someone using Doyle's details which were already logged in the company's computer system. He's hired many vehicles from them over the years.'

The chief gave Hood a cynical look. 'Doyle could still have organised all this from prison. He has form for doing precisely that. He could well have been manipulating events while he was inside.'

'Possibly, but I doubt it. I don't think he had any idea what Hamilton was up to. And a Mercedes of the exact model was spotted in Nottingham the morning after Hamilton's acquittal, outside her hotel, only an hour or so after the car had been delivered to Harbour Buildings. We have it on CCTV. She was seen to get into it. Doyle, on the other hand, took a taxi to Barnard House near Hungarton the next afternoon. He'd hardly have done that if he had control of the Merc.'

The chief was forced to agree. 'Anyone else in the car?'

'The CCTV camera was obscured by a van after a few seconds. Whoever was driving was not recorded but there seems to have been another passenger in the rear. Male, but again insufficient to identify him.'

'Doyle?'

'Unlikely.'

'Where's the car now?'

'It was recovered from outside the rental company's premises where it was left by… someone. Odd, that. The ignition key was put through the letter box. It had been expertly valeted, unfortunately, but we are having the rental agreement and the car tested for fingerprints and DNA. Nothing of evidential value discovered so far, but we're working on it. There's CCTV on King Richard's Road where the car was left. We might get lucky and spot whoever returned it. I have officers working on it now, but there's a lot for them to get through.'

'That is interesting,' observed the chief, stroking his chin with his left hand and adopting a more measured tone. 'Someone went to the trouble of burning Barnard House to the ground, probably to destroy any evidence they'd been there, and yet they leave the Mercedes intact? And with the rental agreement in the glove compartment? Something doesn't add up, Harry. Why didn't they burn that out as well?'

'A good question, sir. Let's hope we can build something from it. Perhaps someone was trying to frame Doyle? That might explain why the Merc is still intact.'

The chief frowned. He was not impressed with that suggestion. He continued to think aloud. 'Assuming Doyle didn't have the use of the Mercedes, what happened to him? How did he get away from Barnard House? Did he even get away from Barnard House? If the Hamilton woman had taken up with someone else, she presumably would have been there with him, whoever he was. Doyle could well have been eliminated. He would always have been a threat to Hamilton, wouldn't he? He could have turned her in on the Charnwood robbery any time he felt like it. And if she has a new lover, why wouldn't he get rid of Doyle? If he organised the Hanlon adventure he must be pretty ruthless and have significant resources to call upon.' He paused and gave Hood a knowing look. 'I reckon he's a goner, Harry.'

'Let's hope not, sir.'

'He'd know, of course, that Hamilton had been acquitted?'

'Yes, sir. He was told before he left Colchester. I think we can certainly put the acquittal down to the Irishman. The jury must have thought the entirety of Hanlon's evidence was bogus and provided to further his own interests. He also lied about Duffy's daughter. He told the jury he'd seen her at Grayling's place in Hastings on the sixteenth of March last year. Hamilton's lawyer was able to prove beyond any doubt that he was lying. Kelly Maguire was undergoing surgery at a hospital in Swansea that day. It can't have been her. It's as clear as day now that Hanlon only agreed to give evidence to facilitate his escape from Mansfield Shirebrook. That's what motivated him, not helping us to get at the truth. Some of us were not at all keen to use Hanlon, but we were overruled by the Attorney-General.'

The chief then raised an issue that had long concerned him. 'And how did Hanlon know he would be taken to that particular prison? Something must have leaked from somewhere. I'm dreading the Home Office inquiry coming to that conclusion.'

'I don't think there was any leak, not from us, anyway. I admit that I did initially, but having thought about it, I now consider it unlikely. Once Hanlon agreed to be a witness at the trial, he'd have known for certain he wouldn't be going back to Whitemoor, not after he started giving his evidence. Whitemoor is very high security. He'd never have got out of there, so he must have calculated that Shirebrook was his likely destination. A new prison, still in the course of construction, fairly close to Nottingham Crown Court; it was always the favourite. He would have guessed we wouldn't have risked placing him in the local prison.'

'I thought Shirebrook was supposed to be pretty secure, at least a section of it? And if it was that obvious, why was it selected?'

Hood dropped his head and paused before he replied. 'Hindsight is a wonderful thing, sir.' He looked up. 'There wasn't really any alternative. It's obvious now why Hanlon collapsed when he did. He hadn't completed his evidence. His timing had to be spot on. He had to make sure he was at Shirebrook over the week-end for the escape plan to work.' He shook his head. 'There was no leak.'

'I hope you're right; I really do.' The chief paused. 'And what happened to Hanlon? I suppose he's vanished too?'

'I doubt if we'll see him again. He's another problem though. He'll know that Doyle informed on Duffy. He would like to see Doyle dead but I suspect he'll be lying low for some time. He'll not want to go back inside.'

'Don't remind me, Harry. I'll never hear the end of this debacle, although it certainly wasn't down to us that he got away. The prison authorities will get the blame for that. The governor's already resigned, hasn't he?'

'He's moving on, sir, yes. Isle of Wight, I believe. But whoever organised Hanlon's escape had far more resources than Doyle could have mustered. The whole thing was expertly planned and extremely well executed. Doyle could never have managed anything like that. He wouldn't have a clue how to get hold of a helicopter for starters and a helicopter was the crucial component of the plan.'

'Hanlon was ex-IRA wasn't he?

'Yes, sir. So we believe, but I don't think they were involved. My money is on whoever Julia Hamilton is with now. We mustn't overlook that the escape had another object – to get her off the charge she faced. That could even have been its main purpose.'

'You think that Hanlon would have been expendable?'

'It's possible. Doyle would have done anything for her and whoever she's with now must be similarly captivated. Even if Hanlon's escape had been frustrated, the events leading up to it would probably have had the same effect on the jury. His credibility as a witness would have been shot to pieces.'

'As it was,' sighed the chief. 'That's undoubtedly why she walked. We need to locate Doyle, if he's still alive. Have you established any sort of chronology in respect of the shootings?'

Hood nodded. 'Manning was shot first. That's clear enough. A witness saw someone on a powerful motorcycle on the embankment just after midnight. He also thought he heard something – or someone – fall into the river, but he could be imagining that. He knew about the killing when he made his statement so he could simply have been trying too hard to help us.' He hesitated. 'The woman pulled from the river at

Cromwell was wearing motorcycle gear. And we know that Maxine Kruger was an experienced motorcyclist. Could just be a coincidence, of course.'

'Reliable witness is he? The person on the embankment?'

Hood smiled then shook his head. 'A homeless young man, unfortunately, and a bit of a druggie. He'd settled down for the night in his sleeping bag nearby. He says he hadn't been using for a few days, but he could be lying about that. He thought he heard two people talking before the splash. He can't say anything more about them. It was a quiet night. Cold but dry and not much wind.'

'Did he see anything?'

'Just the motorbike pulling away. He reckons there was only one person on it, but he could be wrong about that. He's conveniently vague about everything. We are trying to find a connection between Manning and the woman. But we won't get anywhere until we identify her for sure. The two deaths must be connected in some way apart from the fact that the same type of gun was used. We don't know what that link might be at the moment.'

'So, you're working on the basis the dead woman is Kruger?'

'Unless and until she's excluded, yes. We should be able to identify her one way or the other by the end of today. Dublin is being highly cooperative, unlike Lisbon.'

'Lisbon?'

'Yes, sir. That's where we believe Hamilton is now. Her mother has a villa in Portugal, in the Algarve area.'

The chief sat back in his leather chair and appeared deep in thought. He eventually looked up. 'If this woman is Kruger, that shows a direct link with Hanlon doesn't it, which in turn provides a link with the late Gus Grayling and Julia Hamilton? Hamilton knew her, didn't she?'

'Yes, sir. We thought they'd had contact with each other before Hamilton went to Hastings to see Grayling. Kruger could well have taken her there. But there was no identification on the body and, as I said, her DNA is not on any database. But the description does fit her. If it is her, it opens a real can of worms. As an associate of Hanlon, she'd be more than capable of looking after herself. If someone got the better of her, we could be looking at a rival organisation with more clout even than Hanlon, unless Hanlon killed her himself, of course.'

'Why would Hanlon want to kill her?'

'No idea. It's just a possibility we are keeping in mind. We have no intelligence that he left the country after he escaped. If Kruger had crossed him in some way, he wouldn't hesitate to exact vengeance; it's what he does. The man's a psychopath.'

'Was she actively involved in his escape?'

'She might have been. As you said, she was certainly involved with Julia Hamilton. We reckoned it was she who wrote Grayling's ex-directory telephone number on the brochure that was produced at the trial, which means she was trusted by Gus Grayling's organisation. She could well have been at the heart of it. We are still pursuing inquiries. I'm seeing the consultant pathologist later this morning.'

The chief nodded. He had clearly retained a working knowledge of the court papers in Hamilton's trial. 'Any idea who's taken over from Grayling?'

'No, sir. But the vacancy wouldn't have remained unfilled for long. I think we can take that as read.'

'Could it be Connelly or Flynn?'

Hood shook his head and supressed a smile. 'I don't think so. Neither of them could fill Grayling's shoes. They hardly operate outside Nottinghamshire unless it's to get hold of the drugs they supply. Grayling's organised crime group had a much wider geographical compass; it's equally ruthless but operating at a much higher level and over an extended area. It's possible it even has an international dimension.'

'Has the consultant pathologist said anything useful so far. Bit early for his report I suppose?'

'He thinks she must have been lying on a hard surface when she was shot.'

'Why does he say that?'

'He started the post mortem late last night into the early hours of today. The bullet had passed clean through her, but was found in the lining of her leather jacket. Had she been free standing, we'd probably never have recovered it. And it's clear that the gun was placed against her jacket when it was fired. There's no hiding the powder burns in the leather despite her time in the water. John Kennedy has no doubt about that. He's going to explain it to me later.'

'An execution, eh, like Dudley Manning?'

'Not quite like Manning. Apart from the single shot, there's evidence of a struggle. There are defensive and other injuries to her hands and body which must have been caused while she was still alive.'

'So, she may have put up a bit of a fight?' The chief paused for a moment. 'It's hardly likely to be a coincidence that both victims ended up in the Trent, is it? Was the killer trying to make a point?'

'I doubt it. But as you know, there's nothing like running water for getting rid of DNA evidence. Dumping them in the river could be explained simply by that. And they were a few good miles apart. Cromwell is a long way from Trent Bridge.'

The chief exhaled noisily. He stood up; the usual indication that the meeting was coming to an end. Both detectives jumped to their feet. It would not have been seemly for them to have remained seated while the chief was standing.

'We don't know where she went into the river, of course,' the chief added.

'No, sir. And the Trent has been very full of late and fast flowing. Always is this time of year.'

The chief frowned. 'I know that only too well; we were almost flooded at Gunthorpe recently.' He paused. 'Look, Harry, you know I'm retiring in three months. I don't want my successor being left with this mess. I want it sorted, understand?' He leant forward. 'And I want a result. Who attended at Cromwell when the call came in?'

'Acting Inspector Hooper, sir. He also attended the PM on the woman.'

'He was your sergeant in the Charnwood and Campion investigations wasn't he?'

'Yes, sir. I've been concentrating on Manning's murder. But as it looks like they are linked…'

The chief interrupted. 'Well, I'm sure Hooper's a good man, but I want you in overall charge of this inquiry. You're already the Senior Investigating Officer on the Manning murder and, as you say, there are obvious links between the two and probably with both the Charnwood and the Campion cases. He can stay on, of course, and assist you. You're to report directly to the ACC (Crime), Bob Gaunt. This investigation is being given category A status. That means, amongst other things, you can call on additional resources whenever you feel it necessary. I suggest you have a word with ACC Gaunt before you leave here. He's receiving intelligence you'll need to know about, although it will need checking out. You'll find him along the corridor. He'll retain overall control but you'll have full authority on the ground.' He paused for a moment. 'You'll be losing DS Knight shortly, won't you?'

'Yes, sir. She's moving to the Northamptonshire division in a month's time. She'll be a real loss. I could do with keeping her with me until this investigation is closed.'

The chief smiled. 'But you wouldn't want to stand in her way, would you, Harry? She's going places, that one. One of our best female detectives. She'll be sitting here one day. You mark my words.' He laughed.

Hood nodded. 'I'm sure she will, sir. Let's hope we can close this case quickly. Our primary task, after we confirm the identity of the dead woman, is to find Doyle. I'm sure he's the key to this. Dudley Manning was a friend of his. They were in the same prison for a while. It's clear now that Manning helped him in creating the impression that he was being targeted while he was inside.'

'But I thought you said he really was being targeted?'

'He was, sir. But later. I'm convinced the stabbing at Draycott Heath was a put-up job. The other attempts on his life look genuine enough though.'

'But he hasn't thought it necessary to come forward to clear himself? That's suspicious in itself, don't you think?'

'No, sir, he hasn't. It could be that he's too scared. It's certainly got out that he informed on Derick Duffy, but Duffy's no danger to him. He's still inside and it's common knowledge now that Duffy informed on Hanlon and his crew. He's in greater danger than Doyle. He'll probably be moving prisons yet again.'

'No early parole for him, then?'

'Not at the moment, but I believe it is under consideration. Problem is, there are rumours he doesn't want to come out. He thinks he'd be a dead man without the protection he presently receives.'

'And Doyle?'

'Recent events may have frightened him off completely, always assuming he's still alive of course.'

The chief smiled. 'But you don't make assumptions, do you Harry?'

'No, sir. Until I have evidence to the contrary, I shall proceed on the basis that Doyle is still with us. No advantage to anyone in assuming the contrary. Not yet.'

CHAPTER 2

Dr John Kennedy, the Senior Home Office Forensic Pathologist for the East Midlands, smiled as he pulled open the refrigerator drawer containing the body of the unidentified woman who had been pulled from the River Trent. Hood and Detective Sergeant Wendy Knight instinctively stepped back as the sheet was removed from her face. Kennedy had seen more dead bodies than Hood had had hot dinners. He was used to it. Hood, despite his years as a detective, was not. He much preferred reading the pathologist's report rather than viewing the cadaver. But sometimes, he had no option. This was one of those occasions.

'There she is,' said Kennedy. 'Good-looking woman, wasn't she? Do you want to see where the bullet went in?'

'That won't be necessary,' said Hood, eyeing a grateful Wendy Knight. 'I'm sure it will all be fully set out in writing. When will we get it?'

'My report? Tomorrow. Assuming it's been typed up by then.'

'And we have the bullet?'

'Yes a nine by one-point-nine millimetre parabellum. One of the most common bullets we come across in cases like this. It will be fully described in Dr Osborne's report. Now, if you can recover the gun, he'll be able to determine beyond question if the same weapon was used in both killings.'

'Osborne is the firearms expert?'

'Yes. Top man too. He really knows his stuff.'

'But we can safely proceed on the basis that the ammunition used is identical?'

'Oh, yes. No doubt about that. Problem is, it's fairly common. You really need to find the gun to be sure. Dr Osborne will be able to give you the statistical evidence in respect of the type of weapon, but you can take my word for it. They were both killed by a nine-millimetre tapered bullet. Must be odds on they came from the same gun.'

Hood sighed. 'Any identifying marks on the body?'

The consultant pathologist pulled the drawer out farther and lifted the sheet from over the lower body. 'She has a tattoo in the shape of a dolphin on the back of her right lower leg.'

Hood took a quick look, then stepped back.

'Apart from that, nothing. Her clothing has already gone to the lab. There was a label inside her leather jacket which suggests it was made in Germany. It's been photographed. Her underwear also appears to be from the continent, French at a guess.' He glanced at Knight and smiled. 'That may help you until you get a DNA match.'

'If we ever do get a match,' sighed the detective sergeant.

Dr Kennedy closed the refrigerated drawer.

'She could be German, then?' said Hood. 'Looks like it could be Maxine Kruger after all.'

'I think there's enough to work on that basis for now,' agreed Knight. 'But what on earth was she doing at Cromwell?'

'That's for you to discover, Detective Sergeant,' said Kennedy. 'Outside my area of expertise.'

'And she was definitely dead before she went into the water, was she?' asked Hood.

'That's what I told you over the phone, and there can't be any doubt about it, given the gunshot injury. She'd have died instantaneously, although I don't think she'd been in the water more than a day or so.'

'I didn't think anyone died instantaneously,' said Hood, raising an eyebrow. 'I'm sure I've heard you say as much in court.'

Kennedy smiled. 'Well, perhaps I exaggerate a little. She'd certainly have died in seconds and before she went into the water.'

'How can you tell?' asked Knight.

'What, that she was dead when she went in?'

'Yes.'

'The bullet – or to be wholly accurate – the parabellum that passed through her heart, is a bit of a clue, of course.' He gave Hood a wry smile. 'But we can usually tell if a victim was alive when put into a river like the Trent. If she were still breathing when she went in, water would have passed into the circulation from the lungs along with the diatoms which then get distributed through the body. Diatoms will be found in any tissue samples removed during the post-mortem procedure if that were the case.'

'Diatoms?' queried Knight.

'Algae to you; micro-algae found in rivers and oceans. Transparent and almost invisible to the naked eye. They don't occur naturally in the body, so if we find evidence of diatoms in the body tissues, it's a pretty good indication that drowning played a part in the death. Not the case here though. We found none, not in the tissue samples I took. She was definitely killed by the bullet we found still inside her jacket. The tip was damaged because after it passed through her body it struck something very hard; otherwise it would have presumably continued along its trajectory.'

'That's why you concluded she was lying on her back when she was shot?' said Hood.

'I'd say so.'

'And on something very hard, sufficiently dense to prevent the bullet lodging in it?'

'Quite. Rock, concrete, something like that. She could have been killed at the lock near the weir, lots of concrete about there as SOCO will no doubt confirm. As I said, David Osborne will deal with the firearms aspect in his report. David attended the post mortem, in accordance with best practice but he had to get off. He's due to give evidence at the Old Bailey first thing tomorrow morning.'

'No evidence she was unconscious when she was shot?'

'None. I'm still awaiting the report from toxicology, but I'm not expecting they'll find anything relevant. Plenty of defensive injuries though. You noticed the cut to her mouth? She had a loose tooth too. I'd say she was involved in a physical struggle before she died and took a heavy blow to the face. Two of her fingernails are broken even though she was wearing gloves and she has marks exactly where you'd expect if she'd been involved in a prolonged fight with someone. Her hair has been pulled hard too. There were several that had been removed by the roots. I photographed her hairline for you; it's quite clear as you'll see for yourself.' He paused as he ushered the two detectives towards the door. 'She was no weakling, either. She had quite an athletic and muscular body. She obviously kept herself fit.'

'So we're looking for a man?'

'I think so. She fought hard but was overpowered by someone stronger, probably male.'

'Age?'

'Thirty-six, or thereabouts I'd say. She's had a child, too, by caesarean section.'

'Has she?' Hood looked towards Knight. 'Did we get anything from Dublin about Kruger having had a child?'

'No, sir. Nor did they mention a tattoo, but everything else points towards it being her. The Irish police have never arrested her. It's intelligence only thus far, probably resulting from observations when they were tracking Hanlon. They've already confirmed they have several incident reports of the two of them being seen together socially in Dublin.'

'Any indication where she went into the Trent?' asked Hood.

'She was found about two hundred and fifty yards downstream from Cromwell Weir,' replied Dr Kennedy. 'An early-morning jogger spotted her. He thought she might still be alive so he hauled her out of the water himself then called the police from the lock keeper's cottage. He didn't have his mobile with him.'

'It must have been quite a shock for him,' said Hood.

'I suppose it was. It will be difficult, though, to say with certainty where she went in, pathologically speaking anyway. You need to have a word with my new assistant, Dr Waters.'

Knight smiled. 'Dr Waters?'

Kennedy laughed. 'I know, it's just one of those things, but that really is her name. Liz did her Masters on forensic aspects of drowning.

She's a real expert. She's examined every case where a body has ended up in a river or the sea for the last twenty-odd years. Not that the issue arises here. This woman died from a gunshot wound, no doubt about it.'

'I'm anxious to try and find out where she was put into the river, though. And it's a hell of a long waterway.'

'Third longest river in the country,' said Knight. 'I looked it up.'

'Is it?' said Hood. He looked at Dr Kennedy. 'Anything you and Dr Waters can suggest might well be helpful.'

'Happy to assist, although I'm not sure how. Liz attended at Cromwell when the call came in and assisted me at the post mortem. Come up to the office. We might even run to a cup of tea.'

* * *

'Ah, Liz,' said Dr Kennedy, as he, Hood and Knight entered the office. 'Let me introduce you to Detective Chief Inspector Hood. You'll be seeing a lot of him if you stay around these parts.'

Hood stepped forward and shook hands with the attractive young woman who walked from behind the desk to greet him. Tall and slender, with long dark hair tied back with a maroon ribbon, she smiled as she took Hood's hand. Her deep brown eyes sparkled with intelligence and not a little humour.

'I've been looking forward to meeting you, Mr Hood,' she said. 'I've heard a lot about you.'

Hood smiled and introduced Detective Sergeant Knight. 'All hearsay and therefore unreliable,' he laughed. 'And call me Harry, I like to keep on friendly terms with fellow professionals.'

'We were lucky to get Liz,' said Kennedy. 'We are experiencing a very real shortage of forensic pathologists at the moment. Not the most popular area of medicine for young medics to go into.'

'It certainly wouldn't appeal to me,' said Wendy Knight, grimacing.

'Oh, I don't know,' replied Liz. 'It's always been my ambition since I began my degree in medicine. At first, I was interested in microbiology – studying and researching infectious diseases. Then I attended my first post mortem and was hooked. I've never looked back. And our two latest cases fall right into my area of special interest.'

'Corpses in water,' said Hood pretending to shudder. 'Not everyone's cup of tea.' He glanced towards the kettle and the tea caddy and the collection of mugs on a table behind the desk. 'John says you may be able to help as to where the woman we've just looked at went into the water. The Trent is pretty long so I suppose she could have been dumped anywhere upstream. I assume a body can be carried a considerable distance in a fast-flowing river?'

Liz Waters smiled and shook her head. 'That's a myth spread by TV programmes like *Midsomer Murders.* Even in a fast-flowing river like the Trent, a dead body would usually sink fairly rapidly. The circulation would have stopped, you see.' She gave Hood a curious look. 'Do you ever go swimming?'

'Most weeks, yes, with my children. But not in the Trent, of course. Good exercise isn't it?'

Liz nodded. 'Excellent exercise. I'm a keen swimmer myself. Ever considered what it is that keeps you afloat?'

Hood looked puzzled. 'I've never really thought about it.'

'It's the air in your lungs. A living body has a specific gravity very close to that of water; that's what keeps you on the surface. And even a dead body can sometimes float a short distance if air is caught up in it or in the clothing. That might well have happened here; the motor cycle leathers could have trapped some air which might have caused her to float close to the surface before she partially sank near the bank where she was found. Near to the steps that I presume are intended for fishermen when the river level is normal. But I wouldn't have thought she'd have been carried very far though.'

'But the Trent is very full at the moment. The water is very fast flowing; wouldn't that make a difference?'

'Fast flowing at the surface, yes. But once the remaining air was replaced with water, she'd normally have sunk to the bottom pretty quickly. There's very little movement down there no matter how fast the water is flowing at the surface. It looks like she was caught up in those steps I mentioned. That's why she remained visible to the jogger who found her.'

'But we've seen floating corpses before.'

'Of course you have. They come to the surface eventually, but that can take some time, days usually. And a lot depends on the temperature of the water. In the normal way of things, she wouldn't have come up until putrefaction was well under way. The enzymes and internal organisms gradually break down the soft tissues into liquids and gases. The gases accumulate in the body's cavities and the body becomes lighter and, hey presto, it surfaces.'

'Little sign of putrefaction with this one, though,' suggested Hood. 'Not from what we've just seen.'

'I agree. That's why we can be pretty sure that she hadn't been in the water for more than twelve to eighteen hours and I'd say nearer twelve from the state of her, possibly less.'

'So we can proceed on the basis that she went in the water very close to Cromwell Lock?' said Hood.

'That's my best guess, yes. If she'd entered the Trent before the lock she could well have been carried over the weir before the body started to sink. Alternatively, she could have been put into the river to the north of both the lock and the weir. But I think it's unlikely she was dragged or carried to the weir if she were shot farther north. It's a fair distance from where she was found to the lock. There's also a line of buoys and navigation markers stretching across the river just before the weir. Probably placed there after the accident in seventy-five. Very dangerous part of the river especially when it's in flood.'

'She wasn't dumped in the lock then?'

'Oh, no. Unless someone operated the lock gates, her body would still have been there. And as I understand it, there's been no traffic through the lock since Saturday morning.'

'It sounds as if you're familiar with this section of the Trent?'

'I am indeed. I studied it in some detail when I was at Cambridge.'

'What happened in seventy-five?' asked Hood, his curiosity aroused.

A shadow passed over Dr Waters' face as she replied. 'It was in September nineteen seventy-five. The river was in flood. Ten soldiers on exercise died when their craft went over the weir at night and they were thrown out. There was only one survivor and he was a strong swimmer. A real tragedy. A power failure had caused the lights on the weir to go out. They must have come upon it unexpectedly in the darkness. A generator has since been installed. It will cut in in the event of a power failure. But only the area around the weir and the lock is illuminated at night.'

'I've never heard of that,' said Hood, a grim look appearing on his face. 'I wonder if this spot was chosen in the hope the body would disappear, permanently?'

'I doubt it,' responded Liz, 'although the river does become tidal after Cromwell Weir, you know.'

'Tidal? I wasn't aware of that,' said Kennedy.

'Me neither,' said Hood. 'Would that not make a difference?'

Dr Waters shook her head. 'Not in this case. She hadn't been in the water long enough. But the effect of the tides can be crucial when a body begins to surface. It can be moved both upstream and downstream depending on the direction of the tide. But our killer was probably unaware that a dead body inevitably sinks fairly quickly. He may have thought in his ignorance she'd have been carried out to sea with the river being in flood. But, as we know from where she was found, that could not have happened during the short time she was in the water. Putrefaction would have to have been well underway for the body to have surfaced and been carried along in the current.'

'And from what you have said, putrefaction had hardly got started.'

'Exactly. I also suspect our Jane Doe was put into the river while it was dark, although the lights on the weir were working. But as I said, they don't give off much surrounding light. Andrew Hooper told me he'd checked that the lights were working over the week-end. But I'm pretty certain she was put into the river well to the north of the lock. Very hazardous spot though. There are far easier locations the killer could have chosen.'

'I think that must be right, sir,' added Knight. 'I had a look at a map. It's not the most obvious spot to choose to dispose of a body, especially during the hours of darkness. The killer must have known the area pretty well.'

'We'll be going there shortly,' said Hood. 'SOCO are already there with Acting Inspector Hooper and his team, but I've only had a brief report so far.'

'Perhaps you should go there in the dark,' suggested Liz with a broad grin. 'You'll get a clear impression of what I mean. It's a pretty remote spot at night, although you can hear the traffic from the A1 if the wind is in the right direction. And there is a cottage there, presumably occupied by the lock keeper. I was the pathologist on call when the body was retrieved, but it was just about daylight when I attended.'

'We may well do that, after we've been there this afternoon,' said Hood. 'You agree with John that she was definitely dead *before* she went into the water?'

'Absolutely. You inevitably get some water in the lungs and down into the trachea, and she was face down in the water when she was recovered but that is fairly typical. The absence of diatoms in the body tissues, as John has no doubt explained, is the important thing. There were diatoms in the water samples from the river, but that doesn't tell us anything apart from the fact she'd been found in water where diatoms of that type exist. There are literally millions of different kinds, but the diatoms we found in the water samples taken from the body are a perfect match for those we found in the samples taken from the Trent itself. Nothing, though, in the tissue samples. So there's no doubt she was already dead when she went into the river, which is hardly surprising when you see the damage to her heart, or what's left of it.'

'Did you have a look at Manning's body?' asked Hood. 'I saw it not long after it had been removed from the river at Trent Bridge. Not much sign of putrefaction with him either.'

'Oh, yes. I assisted at the post mortem on him too. Unfortunately, David Osborne couldn't make it, but there are very distinct similarities. Like the woman, he was dead before he went into the river. And like her, putrefaction had hardly got started. He was jammed against Trent Bridge and was spotted early the next morning by some canoeists. Two gunshot wounds; the head wound made a mess of his brain. Probably fired at close quarters by an expert shot. No doubt what killed him.'

'And no diatoms?' smiled Hood.

'Not in his tissues, no. And no defensive injuries. I suspect he was taken by surprise. All the hallmarks of a cold-blooded execution.'

'We have a good idea where Manning was when he was killed,' said Hood. 'We found the casing from one of the bullets in the grass on the embankment, not far from Trent Bridge and very close to the river. It's a fair inference that he went into the Trent close to where he was shot. Doesn't help us though as to where the woman was when the bullet entered her body. I suppose she could have been shot anywhere, then transported to the river and simply dumped?'

'Can't help you there, Chief Inspector. Your department, I think. It certainly looks like she was shot on Sunday night and at a guess, I would say she hadn't been long dead before she was put into the Trent. And she certainly didn't go into the river anywhere near Trent Bridge. I can guarantee that much. If it's the same killer you're seeking for both murders, he may have followed a similar pattern. I'd examine the immediate area north of Cromwell Lock if I were you. As I say, I don't think she got very far from the point where she entered the river.'

'Already underway,' replied Hood. 'If there's anything to be found, Andrew will find it.'

'Excellent,' said Dr Kennedy. 'Now, how about that cup of tea?'

CHAPTER 3

Hood and Knight set off for Cromwell Lock in Hood's almost new Saab 9.3 estate. The arrival of his third child, Nicholas, the previous year had dictated that this Saab convertible had to go. He needed a larger vehicle to accommodate his growing family. Taking the A52 to Saxondale, they joined the A46, then headed towards Newark. The traffic was moving at a steady crawl along the single carriageway causing Hood to become more than a little exasperated. He spied the culprit three vehicles in front of him; a huge John Deere tractor pulling a large bowser, just ahead of a Jaguar and a Mondeo, the driver seemingly oblivious to the frustration he was inflicting on the motorists following in his wake. Overtaking opportunities were few and far between and Hood's patience was fast evaporating. He tried, but failed, to maintain a calm exterior.

'Just look at this, Wendy. We're hardly touching twenty-five miles an hour. We'll be here all day at this rate. This road really needs upgrading.'

'It's certainly a hell of a way to come just to dump a body in the Trent,' said Knight, sensing his irritation. 'As Liz Waters said, there must be several more convenient locations.'

'The traffic would be lighter at night, I presume,' replied Hood, with a hint of sarcasm. He took the opportunity to follow the Jaguar and Mondeo immediately in front of him and overtake the tractor and its lumbering trailer.

'And we haven't even got to Newark yet,' murmured Knight, glancing at her watch then examining the map on her knee.

Hood relaxed. 'I can almost hear that brain of yours whirling into overdrive, Wendy. What are you thinking?' He pressed the accelerator, overtook the Mondeo, and kept up a reasonable speed behind the Jaguar until they reached the roundabout on the outskirts of Newark.

Wendy Knight said nothing for some time, but she eventually broke her silence.

'Well, sir, Manning went into the Trent where he was shot, agreed?' Hood nodded. 'Kruger, assuming it is her, is likely to have been shot at Cromwell. It doesn't make sense to drive out there just to dump her body. Otherwise our killer must have risked travelling all that way with a body in the boot. And he doesn't seem the type to take unnecessary risks.'

Hood agreed. 'You're probably right. The question remains though, what was she doing at Cromwell in the first place and, for what it's worth, what was her killer doing there? It's an odd place for a meeting and it must have been pre-arranged.' He glanced out of the side window. 'That's the Trent over there is it?'

Knight nodded. 'Yes, sir. But it's a bit public around here if you're thinking of disposing of a body. Nice and quiet and well out of the way, though, at Cromwell. Do you think it could have been Hanlon she was meeting, or possibly Doyle?'

Hood continued along the Newark bypass until he pulled on to the A1 dual carriageway, accelerating hard to avoid an oncoming HGV. He then settled at a steady sixty-five. He still remained sceptical about the possibility of Doyle's involvement.

'We have no evidence she knew Doyle or he she. If it is Kruger, she had links with Grayling's mob as well as Hanlon, though who's running the show after Gus Grayling's death is anyone's guess. Duffy's out of the line of succession and Hanlon's on his toes. We also know that Duffy's daughter can't be in line; she's inside and will be for some time. As for Doyle, he was never a contender even if he thought he was. It's all gone very quiet in that department lately, apart from these two shootings, of course. I'm sure there's a connection though with our earlier investigations.'

'Or internecine warfare arising from the death of Gus Grayling, perhaps?'

Hood nodded. 'It's possible they could be part of the struggle to take over from Gus, I suppose, although Manning doesn't quite fit the role. I don't see him presiding over a major organised crime group.' He smiled. 'An ex-dentist with a conviction for fraud doesn't strike me as having the experience or the necessary degree of ruthlessness. Not that Gus ever involved himself personally in any of his criminal ventures, which was why he was never indicted. Arrested, yes, but never charged. He was a facilitator and provider. He got where he did in the criminal hierarchy by his willingness to go further than the next man. Always willing to go up to the next level. He was prepared to order to be done what others wouldn't, not that he would dirty his hands by killing anyone himself, of course. But he never thought it necessary to draw the line at anything other than illicit drugs. Odd, that. There's a lot of money to be made in the drugs business, but Gus wouldn't go anywhere near them. His successor, whoever he is, may take a different view. But he will have to possess similar characteristics of fearless determination and a complete absence of anything approaching a conscience.'

'Dudley was up to something though, wasn't he? That juror you spoke to, what was her name? She made that pretty clear, didn't she?'

'Yes. That was very odd, until you apply your mind to it. The juror – Elizabeth Duston – told me Manning had been offered a substantial sum of money to make sure Hamilton was *convicted,* not acquitted.'

'She should still have reported it to the judge.'

'I agree. My report is already on its way to the DPP, but I don't expect it to result in any action, not against the juror. She was the only one who was approached, as far as we know, and she took no notice of the attempt to suborn her. She simply didn't believe Manning and put it down to an effort on his part to reignite their previous relationship. And she did come forward.' He lowered his voice. 'They were lovers years ago when she worked for him as his practice manager; it was only that which prevented her from raising the matter with the judge. If there had been a conviction, of course, we'd be in a wholly different ball game. And with Manning dead, it's hardly worth spending a great deal of time pursuing potential jury interference.'

'But we are still investigating both deaths, aren't we, sir?'

'We certainly are. The two are definitely connected and I have fully in mind what he said to the juror, whatever Elizabeth Duston may think about it. What doesn't make immediate sense is why Manning wanted Hamilton to be convicted.' He left the question hanging in the air, looking for a reaction from Knight, adding, 'There is, of course, a pretty obvious explanation.'

Hood was suddenly forced to slow down and almost came to a halt as the traffic ahead of him braked sharply. An articulated lorry, three hundred or so yards ahead, had broken down in the inside lane of the dual carriageway, causing the line of vehicles in front of him to merge slowly into the outside lane. Hood concentrated on the road as Knight responded to his comment.

'And, as you've said many times before, the obvious explanation is frequently the correct one.'

Hood nodded. 'Go on.' He was now safely positioned in the outside lane and gradually increasing his speed.

'Some form of backup, perhaps, if it had all gone wrong?'

'Well done, Wendy. You're on the ball today. That's what the lawyers think it was. First thing Harold Cronshaw said when I told him about it. It's been done before, apparently. He prosecuted a case three years ago in similar circumstances.'

'You've spoken with Cronshaw?'

'Yes. I had to contact him over the jury matter. He had to know about it as leading counsel for the prosecution. Useful connection too. He was very helpful and advised me to report it to the DPP. He's coming up to Leicester in three weeks to sit as a Recorder. My wife and I are having dinner with him.'

'Is he thinking of going on the bench, then?'

'You mean full time? I doubt it. I think he enjoys the cut and thrust of the Bar too much.'

'And he thought what Manning was up to was some form of backup?'

'He did. I'm surprised it doesn't happen more often in major trials where the evidence is strong. It's quite simple. You set someone up to approach a juror suggesting that a conviction is what is required and if and when it comes about you throw them to the wolves, reveal what's happened, get the verdict quashed and a re-trial ordered. If you're really lucky, you might even avoid that. The Court of Appeal doesn't always order a re-trial. And if they do, there's always a chance the witnesses will be reluctant to attend a second time or something else will go wrong. Hamilton's acquittal rendered all that unnecessary, of course.'

Hood returned to the inside lane after passing the stationary lorry, its indicators flashing as the driver waited for assistance. The wail of a police siren could be heard in the distance. Knight continued with her analysis as Hood gained speed. She was quick to point out the obvious downside. 'But it left whoever put him up to it with a potential problem – Manning himself.'

'Exactly. You really are quick on the uptake today, Wendy. And Manning's death removes any possibility of the matter being investigated effectively. That, I suspect, is why he was killed – to shut him up, permanently.' He sighed. 'Poor Dudley. He probably had no idea what he was getting into. Whatever the O.C.G. offered him blunted his senses. As a struck-off dentist, he'd not have much chance of making a decent living after he was released from prison. He mentioned as much as a hundred thousand to the juror as his fee for his efforts which should have alerted him to the reality of the situation if he hadn't been blinded by greed. He'd never have been paid that much for such a minor piece of skulduggery. They really suckered him in.'

'And all he got for his trouble was a bullet through the brain and a swim in the Trent.'

'And one in the chest, don't forget.' Hood paused. 'He had to die. And they made doubly sure that he did.'

'That may explain why Manning was killed, but how does that help us with the woman found in the river at Cromwell? It looks like the same gun could have been used, but apart from that, it doesn't really help us, does it? And it also introduces a potential complication.'

'What do you mean?'

'Doyle. We've already established a connection between him and Manning.'

'But in a wholly different context. I don't think Doyle had anything to do with Manning's death. They were friends and fellow conspirators but their plan was to get Doyle released, which succeeded. Ironic, isn't it? The stabbing in the showers at Draycot Heath prison was undoubtedly a put-up job, to give us the impression that Doyle was being targeted and that his life was at risk. Then, subsequently, several genuine attempts were made to kill him.'

'You don't think they were contrived as well?'

'No, I don't. Someone definitely wanted Doyle dead. And they still do. That's why we need to find him.' He paused again and glanced towards Knight. 'Incidentally, I haven't disclosed my theory about Manning to anyone, not yet. I was asked to keep it confidential, until the DPP responds to my report on the jury interference and there's no telling how long that will take, so keep it to yourself for the moment. I told the chief we're still investigating the connection between the two, which, of course, we are. But as things stand, this explanation for Manning's death is only a theory, although the fact that it was Harold Cronshaw's immediate reaction is pretty supportive. But we still need evidence. A theory, no matter how compelling, is no good without evidence. And my theory does not go as far as identifying Manning's killer. Establishing a connection between Manning and the dead woman would be a start.'

'You don't think she could have killed Manning, sir? Perhaps Maxine Kruger thought she could move into the position vacated by Gus Grayling by demonstrating her ruthlessness, but someone of a contrary opinion wiped her out before she got into the saddle? Women are exerting their power in all sorts of areas these days. Why should serious crime be the exception?'

Hood smiled. He had huge respect for Wendy and didn't dismiss what she said lightly, but he had his doubts whether Kruger could have succeeded Grayling. 'It's worth considering. If she did blow away Dudley, she'd certainly qualify on the grounds of ruthlessness. And we shouldn't ignore the motorcycle gear she was wearing, although there's a two-day gap between the killings. But I doubt if she was in line to take over, even if she is responsible for Manning's death.'

Knight remained silent for the next half-mile. She then pointed to the sign for Norwell and Cromwell a few hundred yards before the turn-off. She looked again at the map. 'This is where we go off, sir. The Trent is still on our right, so we have to cross over the A1 to get to the weir. It's a very narrow road down to the lock. Andrew warned me about it.'

'So, he knew we were on our way?'

'Well, sir. I told him I was, but I didn't mention you would be with me. I doubt, though, if he'll be surprised to see you.'

Hood started to indicate and slowed down as he approached the turn-off. He looked around him. There were several heavy goods vehicles parked in the lay-by to his left as he exited the A1 and drove into the village before coming to a halt. 'I suppose whoever shot her must have had transport of some kind. He could hardly catch a bus home from here on a wet Sunday night.'

Knight did not disagree. 'But Cromwell Lock is miles from where Manning met his fate. As you said, she and her killer may have been together at Trent Bridge and then came here on Sunday night. Something caused a bust-up but we may never discover what it was.'

'Still doesn't explain why they came to Cromwell,' said Hood. 'Why here? Let's hope Andrew or SOCO have found something to assist.'

'Nothing so far; and I spoke to Andrew after we left Dr Kennedy, you know, while you were chatting to Liz Walters.' She raised an eyebrow. 'All he said was that the underwater search team was still combing the river near to where the body was found. And SOCO did a short stint yesterday, but found nothing. The weather was definitely against them. At least it's dry today.'

'Looking for the gun I suspect; but I doubt if it will be found. A professional wouldn't get rid of his weapon. He'd need it again.'

Hood looked about him again then set off at a slow speed, almost walking pace, and proceeded with considerable caution along the old Great North Road.

'There's the church,' said Knight. 'The road to the weir should run along the side of it. Just beyond the red telephone box.'

Following Knight's directions, Hood turned right into a narrow unmade road.

'According to my map,' said Knight, 'this track will take us over the A1 and down to the lock. Andrew says the locals call it Lock Lane, but it's described as Church Lane on my map. There's a large quarry on the other side too.'

Hood glanced to his left as his car lurched over a hump designed to encourage vehicles to comply with the somewhat worn sign restricting traffic to 5 miles per hour, which he had initially failed to notice. The chassis of the Saab shook. 'Look out for any more of those speed humps, will you, Wendy? I don't want to damage my car.' He continued slowly and carefully along the narrow track, turning sharply left and accelerating uphill to the bridge. He quickly crossed over the A1 then continued along the narrow roadway. Standing water in varying sized pools covered parts of the surface as they passed the quarry workings which had expanded to both sides of the rough thoroughfare. 'You're right about them not meeting here by chance, Wendy. You'd have to be well informed to find this place, especially at night.' The Saab splashed through one of the deeper puddles. 'We should have brought our wellington boots with us,' he added with a grin.

'Mine are in the boot,' said Knight. 'I like to be prepared. Apparently, the Trent floods intermittently at this time of the year. I looked it up. The spring tide sometimes makes this route impassable. Andrew says the lockkeeper told him it's not as bad as it was last month and it is fairly dry around the lock itself, so you might well manage without your boots.' She gave the chief inspector a perceptive smile.

Hood said nothing as the road opened up slightly. They rounded a bend close to the Trent and could see several officers examining the partially flooded grassy area between the road and the river. Several police vehicles were parked farther along the lane. The Saab slowed to walking pace as they approached the lock.

'Do you think Andrew will be made up permanently, sir?' asked Knight. She could see the acting inspector in the distance. 'I don't think he knows you've been put in charge of the whole investigation, unless the DCC has told him. I certainly didn't mention it. He's likely to be sorely disappointed that you're taking over as SIO. He thought this was his opportunity to make a name for himself.' She pointed. 'Oh, I think he's recognised your car. He's walking in this direction.'

'Can't be helped. Chief Constable's orders. The links between these killings and our previous investigation seem pretty well established, and Andrew will still be working with us. And he already knew I was investigating Manning's death.'

'He'll still be disappointed.'

Hood sighed. 'Well, I hope for his sake that he does get a permanent promotion. He certainly deserves it. But as we know, temporary rank is not always confirmed.'

He gave Knight a telling look. He was, of course, referring to his temporary promotion to Detective Superintendent which was not renewed after he solved the Campion kidnapping case. But at least he had passed the board. It was now simply a question of a vacancy arising, either with Mid-Shires or elsewhere.

'Andrew could well be more fortunate than I was. There's a lot of changes coming. You going off to Northamptonshire next month is the one I regret most.'

'Still in the same merged constabulary, though, sir. And a move was always on the cards once I was promoted. It will give me the chance to show what I can do without hanging on to your coat-tails.'

Hood smiled. 'I have to say I've enjoyed working with you. I find your contributions very stimulating, if sometimes a bit off beam! I shall certainly miss you.'

'Thank you, sir. I have learnt a lot working with you. Let's hope we can sort out this case before I leave.'

Hood brought the Saab to a halt, parking by the side of the memorial to the ten soldiers who had died on exercise back in 1975. He noticed that the Trent was still very full, the rising waters washing over the bank causing a number of deep puddles to form on the grass immediately adjacent to the tarmacadam road. He released his seat belt as Andrew Hooper approached the car.

'Afternoon, sir. I was wondering when you would turn up.'

CHAPTER 4

Hood was suitably impressed with the actions Acting Inspector Andrew Hooper had taken. The whole area had been sealed off from a point 25 yards south of the weir to a similar distance beyond the spot where the body had been retrieved close to a slight bend in the river to the north. SOCO officers, clad in white forensic suits, continued examining the immediate location where the body had been found while several uniformed officers conducted fingertip searches of a larger area. Another kept his eyes on a few nosey individuals who seemed keen to watch the proceedings. They were kept firmly behind the tapes at the bend in the road and well away from the sealed-off areas.

'How long have they been here?' asked Hood, nodding towards the small group of locals.

'They come and go,' replied Hooper. 'They soon get bored. I keep telling them there's nothing to see but it doesn't stop them coming. We keep them well out of the sealed-off area, of course. Cromwell isn't a large village – nothing ever happens here, hence the interest. The press were here earlier but they soon got fed up. No TV cameras yet. I'm told they were using library pictures on the BBC news this morning. I don't suppose they'd find it easy getting their equipment down here?'

'We should, perhaps, be thankful for small mercies,' said Hood. He was no fan of the media. He pulled his coat collar closer. It was a bleak and cold afternoon and he shivered as he cast his eyes over the still rushing waters of the Trent. 'I noticed that the underwater search team is still at it.'

'Yes, sir. But I'm about to call a halt. They haven't found anything. It's a daunting task, but I thought there was an outside chance the killer may have disposed of the gun in the river. They've been concentrating in the area a couple of hundred yards or so from where the body was found, but they tell me it's pretty murky on the bottom. I'll give them another half hour then bring them in, if that's all right with you.'

'Up to you, Andrew. I'm taking over as SIO, but I shall leave this part of the operation entirely to you. You seem to have everything well in hand.'

'Thank you, sir. I always had a feeling the top brass would want you in charge. This killing has every indication of being related to the death of Dudley Manning, especially if the same weapon was used.'

Hood smiled. He was pleased he and Hooper had made the same connection. The two detectives walked towards the white-painted house positioned several yards back from the concrete platform of the lock. Hood glanced down at the paved pathway. No chance of discovering a mark made by the bullet if the deceased had been shot while on her back at this point – there were too many chips and blotches in the surface. But like Dr Walters, he had almost dismissed the possibility that the killing had occurred at the lock.

'Anyone see or hear anything?' he asked, pointing to the house. 'There's someone living there, I presume?'

'That's the lockkeeper's cottage. He was up in the village on Sunday night. He sings in the church choir. They were having a rehearsal then went to the pub. He saw and heard nothing. I've also taken a statement from the jogger who pulled her out of the water. He's a Mr Jonathan Sampson, an accountant with one of the big firms in Nottingham. He was taken home yesterday in shock. Lives in Carlton-on-Trent just to the north of here. Understandably, he was pretty upset at finding the body.' Hooper checked his notebook. 'He called the emergency services at six fifty-five yesterday morning. So far, we haven't found any witnesses to the actual incident and I don't expect we will. The weather was pretty wild on Sunday night. Not many people about and no boats or barges on the river. But we are working on the assumption that she was shot somewhere around here on Sunday night.'

'No fishermen?'

'No, sir. It's close season for course fishing – until June the fifteenth.'

'Is it? What about the quarry over there?' Hood pointed to the extensive workings beyond the lock closer to the A1 as, keeping up a steady pace, they turned about and walked towards the area being examined by SOCO.

'No one working over the week-end. And we've completed house to house inquiries in the village. Nothing. Nobody saw or heard anything.'

'It must be pretty desolate out here at night, especially in bad weather,' said Hood. 'Were you on the scene when Dr Waters attended?'

'Yes. We arrived at about the same time. She gave me a brief report after she'd examined the deceased on the riverbank. We have it clearly marked where the body was found. And I attended the PM late last night. We are searching the whole area for the used cartridge from the gun, but chances are it went into the river with the deceased. We covered the same area yesterday and found nothing. I ordered a further search this morning, just to be on the safe side. And I managed to find more officers today. I was surprised they were provided so easily.'

'Category A inquiry, this, Andrew. ACC Gaunt made that very clear to me when I saw him this morning. He's technically in overall control, by the way, but I doubt if we'll see him out here. He'll be sticking close to his very warm and comfortable office. But it means we should have no trouble when it comes to additional resources. Makes quite a change, eh?' Hood looked northwards. 'It's a more extensive area than I imagined. The jogger must have been out very early.'

'Yes, sir. He usually runs the same route three days a week, but he hadn't jogged round here for the last month because of the flooding. There's an established official route, about five and a half miles in total. As I said, he works in Nottingham, hence the early start.'

'Rather him than me. He must be very keen – and very fit!' He frowned. 'You think this was a professional hit?'

'That's what it's beginning to look like. I could be wrong, but it has the look of an execution to me. You've seen the body, I take it? Bullet straight into the heart and from very close range.'

'Yes. I've just come from the morgue. I think you're right about when she was shot. From the state of the body, Sunday night seems to be the most likely time she died.'

'The marks on her body suggest she put up a bit of a fight, though.'

'She certainly did; unlike Dudley Manning.'

Hooper was more than keen to disclose his analysis of the available evidence. 'I reckon she was shot close to where she went into the river, and was carried downstream before she partially sank. There are a few spots with steps that go down to the river – for the fishermen I assume – but they're underwater for the most part at the moment with the river being so high. She was caught up by the steps which explains why she remained visible. There's a small piece of hard standing close by – parking for the fishermen in season – then there's the road itself which varies in quality so far as the surface is concerned.' He pointed towards the area where SOCO and several police officers were searching. 'The pathologist reckons she must have been on her back when the gun was fired and against a hard surface, otherwise we'd never have recovered the bullet.'

Hood nodded his agreement. 'No tyre tracks?'

'If there were, the rain and the flood water has washed away any traces. Whoever killed her was certainly lucky with the weather. It was raining heavily all day yesterday too. Made the search very challenging. I called it off at mid-day. Thank God it's dry today.' Hooper looked towards the Trent as a frogman came to the surface holding something in his raised hand. 'Hello. It looks like they've found something. At last.'

The two officers walked on quickly then waited for the frogman to swim to the bank. He climbed up one of the sets of flooded steps close to the sealed-off section where the body had been found and handed over a handgun which the acting inspector immediately placed into a transparent exhibit bag. He instructed a uniformed officer to mark the point on the riverbank where the frogman had emerged from the water then held the weapon up so Hood could see it. The chief inspector recognised the make of gun immediately.

'A Beretta. Just as we thought. An M9 by the look of it and with a sound moderator fitted. We need to get this to the expert as quickly as possible. I must confess, I was not expecting to find it. Good decision on your part, Andrew, to search for it.'

'Thank you, sir.'

'This just has to be the murder weapon; the silencer removes any doubt about it. Look at it, Andrew; this is an assassin's tool. It can't have any legitimate purpose outside the military.' Hood paused. There was a puzzled expression on his face. 'But surely, a professional would have kept it with him? Just check the magazine, will you?'

Hooper did as he was asked, keeping the gun with its silencer inside the exhibit bag as he did so. When released, the magazine was placed into a separate exhibit bag and handed to the chief inspector. Hood was familiar with the Beretta M9 model, of which tens of thousands had been manufactured, and he could see from the size of the magazine that it would have held at least fifteen rounds. He examined it closely. From the weight in his hand he guessed that the magazine was almost full.

'Now that really is odd. It doesn't make sense for a real pro to get rid of a gun like this with the magazine almost full. Mind you, if only three rounds have been discharged, it will go a long way to proving it was used in both killings.'

'We could check it now, sir.'

'I think not. Leave it to the firearms consultant. I doubt if we'll get any prints or DNA from the gun itself, but stranger things have happened. The bullets, however, may give us something. I got a suspect's DNA from a bullet a few years ago.'

'As I recall,' said Hooper, 'the used cartridge is discharged from the right-hand side in one of these.'

'Correct. As you know, we found one of them on Victoria Embankment near Trent Bridge.'

'Yes, sir. But I've seen this type of pistol being fired. The used cartridge can fly some distance when it's ejected. It could well have gone straight into the river. Not much chance of retrieving it if it did. It would have floated away and will never be recovered.'

'But we still have officers searching for it?'

'We do. We will continue to try and locate it, at least for the rest of today.'

Hood pointed to the almost bare branches of the trees and bushes, some of them standing in pools of water close to the riverbank. They looked like they were just coming into leaf but spring, like Easter, was a bit on the late side in 2000, and the cold weather wouldn't have helped. 'I guess it all looks quite different in high summer,' he said.

'Almost unrecognisable,' agreed Hooper, 'according to the lockkeeper. And he lives here all year round. But it's pretty bleak here at the moment. Not the sort of place anyone would hang about for long, especially at night.'

'It'll look a lot different in a couple of months,' added Hood. 'You probably wouldn't be able to see the river in late spring and summer from where we are standing. The water level would be much lower too.'

'It never gets anything like as high as this in the summer,' agreed Hooper, looking downstream. He then held up the exhibit bag containing the gun and the sound moderator. 'Odd though, fitting a silencer to a Beretta M9; they're fairly quiet when discharged. And we don't get many killings in this part of the world with a gun fitted with a silencer.'

'I'm not complaining about that. If you've read my briefing on the Manning killing you'll recall that our only witness, such as he is, thinks he heard two quick thuds rather than a louder report.' He stroked his chin. 'It intrigues me, though Andrew, why the killer left it on; it could easily have been unscrewed before he threw it into the water. If they'd been separated, we may never have found the silencer.'

Hooper smiled. 'Perhaps he wants us to catch him?'

Hood laughed. 'I don't think so. Whoever did this will be going down for a long time. Finding the gun is an unexpected bonus. And I'll make sure you get the credit for it.' He continued to examine the magazine then turned so the river was on his right. 'I suppose it will depend which way the killer was facing when he shot her, you know, where the empty cartridge would end up?' He looked around him. 'We already know it was placed against her leather jacket when it was discharged. It must also follow that the safety was off and the gun was ready to fire.'

'Will the firearms consultant be able to tell whether the silencer was actually fitted when the gun was discharged?'

'I don't know, Andrew, but I would think so. I can't recall a recent shooting with a gun with a sound moderator fitted, but there wouldn't be much point in screwing on the silencer after the killing had taken place, would there?'

'The killer must have been familiar with its operation though.'

Hood nodded. 'I realise it's not that straight forward preparing an M9 to fire. Not like a revolver. There's a bit more to it than just pulling the trigger.'

He glanced to where Detective Sergeant Knight was standing some distance to the north, close to members of the public who were loitering behind the police tape, still anxious to see what was happening. 'Let's see what Wendy is up to. She's talking to those young lads on their mountain bikes. And knowing her as I do, she won't just be passing the time of day with them.'

'I see she brought her boots with her,' said Hooper as he and Hood walked towards the police tapes. Hood grunted but did not reply as he tried but failed to avoid a shallow puddle. Wendy Knight continued speaking to two boys, seemingly in their early teens, sitting astride their mountain bikes. One of them was holding a black crash helmet in his hands, having just removed it from his head.

'It's a bit on the big size for you, isn't it?' Knight said.

'I've got a big 'ead,' said the taller of the two, a broad smile appearing on his freckled face. He paused to see how his answer was received. Knight rolled her eyes and shook her head as she produced her warrant card. The lad grimaced, realising the game was up. 'We didn't nick it, miss. Honest. We found it.'

'Where did you find it?'

Neither said anything for some time then the taller of the two acted as spokesman. 'It was in the water, just past the bend in the river. It was stuck in some reeds by the bank. I stretched down and grabbed it. Only found it this morning.'

Knight looked northwards beyond the sealed-off area. A track ran close to the riverbank which disappeared from view well outside the taped-off zone. 'What were you doing over there?' she asked. 'That's a dangerous area to be playing while the river is so full, isn't it?'

The boy appeared bemused. 'No, miss. We can both swim. I've got a swimming c'tificate.'

'Have you?' replied Wendy, adopting a friendly tone. 'Can you show me where you found the helmet?'

They looked at each other and grinned.

'What's it worth if we do?' asked the smaller one, his voice nearly an octave higher than his friend.

'You'd be helping solve a murder case,' replied Wendy. 'You'd like to help, wouldn't you?'

The two boys were evidently shocked. Their eyes widened and their mouths fell open.

'What? Was she murdered then? The woman who was pulled out the river yesterday?'

'You know about that, do you?'

'We thought she drowned. That's what me Dad said had happened. But we knew about her being in the river. It's all round the village.'

'Is it? Now, tell me your names.'

'You're not nicking us?'

Knight smiled. 'No, of course not. I just want to know who I'm speaking to.'

The taller one sniffed and wiped his sleeve across his mouth. 'I'm Tyler, he's Kyle. We go to the same school. I'm fourteen, he's thirteen. We ain't done nothing.'

'Do you both live in Cromwell?' asked Knight.

'I does,' replied Tyler. 'Kyle lives in Carlton.' He pointed northwards.

The smaller one grinned sheepishly. The two looked at each other again after Tyler handed the helmet to Knight.

'Shall we tell her, Tyler?' asked Kyle.

'Tell me what?' said Knight.

'About the bike,' said Kyle, his voice starting to break.

'We'll have to now, won't we,' snapped Tyler. 'Now you've let it out.'

'What bike?' asked Knight. Hood and Hooper were now standing close enough to hear the conversation but had the good sense not to intervene.

'What bike? This may be important. Tell me, what sort of bike do you mean? A mountain bike like these or a motorbike?'

The two boys looked at each other again, each urging the other to speak. Eventually, Tyler told Knight what she wanted to know.

'We seen a motorbike in a shed back along the lane. But we haven't touched it, well not really.'

'Where?'

'I've just told you. Back along Lock Lane. This side of the bridge though.' He waved his arm in the general direction. 'It's a shed belonging to the quarry. We play in there sometimes, until we get chased off. The door was open a bit and we took a shufty. It's a BMW Adventure.'

'No it ain't,' said Kyle, 'it's an R eleven fifty GS. My uncle's got one.'

'Yeah, but it's still an Adventure,' contradicted Tyler. 'Black, it is.'

'Can you show me?' asked Knight.

'But we found it. Don't we get a reward or sommat?' sniffed Tyler, wiping his nose on his sleeve.

'We'll see.' She turned and faced Hood and Hooper. They'd only heard the latter part of the conversation. 'Do you want me to deal with this, sir?'

'You seem to have it well in hand. Take one of the SOCO officers with you. Kyle, could you show me where you found the crash helmet while Tyler shows the officer where the bike is?'

'But I was with him when we found the bike. We didn't break in or nothing. We just pushed the door a bit. I want to show you too.'

'I'm sure you haven't done anything wrong. You've no need to worry about that.' Kyle dropped his head. 'Okay,' sighed Hood, 'we'll all go and look at the bike together and then you can both show me where you found the crash helmet. Deal?'

Kyle looked up, smiled and nodded his head vigorously. He sat up on his bike and started to pedal towards the lane.

'Wait for me,' called Tyler. 'I found it too.'

CHAPTER 5

Michael Doyle took the last train into Oakham from Melton Mowbray on Tuesday evening where he had spent the previous night at a B&B using the name Jack Rawlins. Not having shaved since his release from prison, he bore little resemblance to the photographs which had appeared in that day's edition of both the *Leicester Mercury* and the *Nottingham Evening Post*, along with an appeal for him to contact the police. He'd seen the reports but had no intention of responding. He trusted no one, not even Chief Inspector Hood. Not anymore. He would do what he had to do without any interference from the police. If he didn't, he knew he was a dead man. Grayling was not going to give up. It was Michael Grayling or him and he had no intention of letting Grayling have his way.

The three-coach train was fairly full despite the hour. He picked up from the conversations of some of the louder passengers that they were travelling to Stansted airport. They had holidays on their minds and showed no interest in the man sitting in a corner seat with his coat collar turned up and his scarf pulled close. The bruise over his left eye was already fading and the cut to his mouth where he had been punched by his would-be killer had almost completely resolved. A few copies of the *Mercury* were strewn on the seats, but no one took any notice of him. Even the conductor seemed oblivious as he mechanically scrutinised his ticket. 'Oakham next station stop,' he called as he put his biro across the ticket and returned it to Doyle then moved along, suggesting quietly to another passenger that he remove his feet from the seat opposite. The train started to slow down. Doyle stood, grabbed his bag from the overhead rack and made his way past the conductor towards the nearest door. The train drew to a shuddering halt. He waited impatiently for the door to open. Only he and one other passenger disembarked. A family with three heavy-looking suitcases climbed aboard through the door at the other end of the coach, drawing the attention of the other passengers. Doyle hunched his shoulders as he stepped down on to the deserted platform. He walked slowly to the noticeboard and pretended to read the timetable until the train pulled away and the other passenger disappeared in the direction of the town. He then strode through the unmanned barrier and headed northwards in the direction of the farm where, a year or more before, he had left his motorcycle in the safe custody of Dave Sherwood, an old school friend.

Oakwood Farm, as the Sherwood place was known, no longer engaged in agriculture. Dave, who lived there with his widowed mother and two dogs, now ran it as a storage facility. Over several years, 'Specky Dave,' as he was known because of the thick-lens spectacles he invariably wore, had turned what had been a failing smallholding of some twenty-five acres into a money-spinning and largely legitimate business. The two original barns had been supplemented by three large purpose-built hangars with numerous separate and secure sections where property could be stored for a weekly or monthly fee. It was far more profitable and required less physical effort than farming. Dave was also an accomplished technician and a real wizard when it came to modern telecoms. There wasn't a cell phone in existence that he couldn't take apart and reassemble in a matter of minutes, no questions asked. He and Doyle had consolidated their friendship in their late teens when Doyle had saved the autistic Dave from likely imprisonment by taking responsibility for a car theft which could have landed him with a short stretch in a detention centre. They were both as guilty as each other, but Doyle took the rap, knowing that young Dave would not have survived even a short period in custody. Dave and his mother had never forgotten. Doyle had drawn several times on the goodwill his altruism had created.

As the farmhouse came into view, he hoped his account with the Sherwoods had not yet gone into the red. He instinctively felt in his pocket for the cell phone he had taken from the woman who had tried to kill him. She no longer had any use for it, but he needed it. His own phone had been removed from him at Barnard House and had probably been destroyed in the fire he'd read about in the newspapers. He was relying on Dave to circumvent the password so he could use it as his own, at least temporarily. It might also hold a few clues as to who his would-be assassin had been.

Two Doberman dogs had the run of the extensive yard at night. They barked and rushed towards the fencing as Doyle approached the house, hurling themselves at the wire netting and baring their teeth. Doyle studiously ignored them. Several security lights came on as he passed by which encouraged the dogs to bark more raucously. He took no notice of the chained and padlocked vehicular entrance and made his way to the pedestrian gate which led to the front door of the old farmhouse. He hesitated and looked about him before ringing the bell. He did not have long to wait. The heavy door opened a few inches, the security chain preventing it being pulled back farther, and Doyle recognised Dave Sherwood through the tiny gap. Dave was not wearing his glasses. He blinked and narrowed his eyes, failing to recognise Doyle who took a pace back and stood under the security light so he could be identified.

'What do you want? It's late. We're closed.'

'Even to me, Dave?'

Sherwood pushed his head forward.

'Is that you, Michael?'

'It is. I need your help.'

The door closed briefly as the security chain was released, then opened fully.

'Christ, Michael. I didn't think we'd be seeing you again.'

'Well, are you going to invite me in or what?'

Dave took a step forward, glanced towards the still barking dogs, then quickly ushered Doyle into the house, closing and bolting the door afterwards.

'How's your mother?' asked Doyle. 'Still in the wheelchair?'

Dave nodded. 'Yeah. She has an electric one now. She's unlikely to improve much more. I've been telling her for years to give up the fags, but would she listen? By the way, she can be pretty lethal with it, so be careful if she appears. She's watching the telly in the back room at the moment.'

Doyle took off his coat and scarf as Dave led him into the kitchen. He placed his bag on the floor by the table.

'I suppose you've come for your bike?' said Dave, sitting down at the kitchen table. 'And the other stuff I've been keeping for you.'

'I have. Do I owe you anything?'

Dave shook his head. 'No. We're up to date. The bike's in good nick. I started it up the other day, just to check it out. I renewed the tax last month as well. Want a coffee or something stronger?'

Doyle declined. 'I'm fine thanks. Anyone shown any interest in my property while I've been away?'

'You mean the police? No, they've been here, of course. They're regular visitors in fact – every three months or so – but I give them a bit of harmless information now and then. Seems to keep them happy.'

'Did they ask about me?'

'When you were first arrested, yes. They were round here right away. But that was last year. Looking for a bike they reckoned you owned.' He smiled broadly. 'But not lately. I've been expecting them again though, since those two bodies were pulled out of the Trent. We thought one of them might have been you at first. Then we read about the fire near Hungarton. There were rumours going about that you'd been caught up in that.'

'You knew I'd been at the house that was fired?'

'Yeah. It was in the newspaper. The police were asking you to come forward, assuming you were still alive. I reckon they thought you might be involved in the shooting of that bloke on the embankment in Nottingham last week. When you didn't turn up here, we thought you must have bought it.' He smiled. 'I'd been wondering what to do with your bike. Worth quite a bit you know. It's a classic in the making. You'd get a decent amount for a ninety-eight Triumph Sprint. I did as you asked and registered it in my name. I told the police it was in storage as an investment for the future. They seemed to accept that.'

'I'm grateful but it's not for sale, not at the minute, and that killing had nothing to do with me by the way, although I did know the guy. We were in the same prison at one time. Dentist wasn't he?' Dave shrugged his shoulders. 'Anyone else asking for me?' continued Doyle.

Dave looked down and sighed. 'We did have a visitor.'

'Who was it?'

'He didn't give a name. A short, ugly Scottish guy. Built like a brick shithouse. Could hardly understand what he was saying. Mum could, coming as she does from up there.' Dave smiled then continued. 'He walked into the office like he owned the place. He wanted to know if you'd been in touch. I told him I hadn't seen you for nearly two years, which is almost the truth. Threatened us both when mum came in if we held anything back. She was worried how he knew about us. We'd never seen him before. It was only when he came here looking for information about you that we realised you must still be alive. Do you know who he is?'

'I have an inkling, yes. When was he here?'

'First thing this morning. He mentioned someone called Grayling, but he's dead isn't he?'

'Gus, yes. He's definitely gone. But there's a son. You didn't know about him?' Dave shook his head. 'Dangerous psychotic bastard but smooth with it. It was him who tried to have me killed.'

'Really, Michael? What happened?' Dave seemed genuinely shocked.

'Trust me, you don't want to know. If they sent someone here, they obviously know they failed to finish me off, but they'll try again. You can guarantee it. You're better off not knowing. I don't want to put you or your mum at risk. They were prepared to kill Dudley, so they won't think twice about doing away with me.'

Doyle produced the cell phone he'd taken from the dead woman. 'I need you to take a look at this for me, Dave. The battery's almost flat and I suspect it's password protected. Can you do something with it?'

'Where did you get it from?'

'Believe me, you don't want to know.'

Dave nodded. He knew from the press reports that the woman pulled from the Trent had not been found with a phone. Perhaps this was it? He decided not to pursue the matter further and took the phone from Doyle and examined it. 'I should be able to do something with it. A Motorola Star TAC – very nice. Latest model too. You can send and receive short messages on this, you know. Just give me ten minutes.' He picked up his spectacles with the thick lenses and put them on as the kitchen door was pushed open by a late-middle-aged woman in a wheelchair. She was smoking a cigarette as she powered quickly forward, stopping inches away from Doyle. She leant forward in the chair and looked at him. Her Glasgow accent was obvious but she was easily understood.

'Well, if it isn't Michael Doyle. And there was Dave and me thinking you were dead. I always said they wouldn't get rid of you so easily, didn't I Dave?'

Dave looked up. 'Yes, Mum, you did.'

'So, Michael, what are you doing here? You look about done in. You know they're looking for you?'

Doyle smiled and nodded. 'Seems I'm right popular, doesn't it?'

'You've certainly upset somebody, someone with real clout by the look of things. Dave's told you about the visitor we had? Nasty piece of work. I didn't take to him at all. Manky bastard.' She held out her packet of *Player's Full Strength* and offered him a cigarette. Doyle declined, but she stubbed hers out then lit another one.

'I've given them up,' he said. 'Bad for your health you know.'

'Too late for me,' she replied with a grin. 'It's my only pleasure. That and a wee dram before I go to my bed.'

'Dave says you didn't tell your visitor anything.'

'Nothing to tell. And you know us; last thing we'd do is give you away.' She smiled broadly. 'I'll never forget what you did for Dave.'

Doyle smiled. 'That was a long time ago. What about the police? Dave said they've been here.'

'Regular visitors they are. Seem to think we store stolen goods here, but they've never got anywhere with that accusation. But they'll be back. They know the history between you and Dave. They're bound to give us a pull if they're looking for you.'

'Do you think so? It was hardly that serious. I doubt if it's still on record anywhere.'

'Don't you believe it.' She looked about her. 'No one followed you here, I hope? That bastard said he'd be back if he didn't find you soon.'

'No. I was very careful. I took the train to Oakham and walked here from the station. Didn't see a soul. Only one other person got off the train and he went into the town. I made sure I wasn't followed.'

'Mother,' said Dave, his tone critical. 'Michael knows how to look after himself. He's only come for his bike and for me to fix his phone.'

Mrs Sherwood looked at the now disassembled phone on the kitchen table and continued. 'Last time they were here, that detective sergeant went through all the books, but they don't know your bike is here. They think it's Dave's. They're not as clever as they think they are.'

'They didn't even ask about you, not directly,' added Dave, smiling. 'But why would they? You were still inside when they were last here. How long have you been out?'

'Since last Friday.' He looked towards Mrs Sherwood. 'Which detective sergeant?'

'A new one; we hadn't seen him before, had we Dave? Can't recall his name. Came down from Sheffield way, though. He talked to Dave about football.'

'What's he like?'

'Like all of them. Nosey, pushy, but he seems to know his limitations and he was quite polite, unlike some of them. He knew he'd need a warrant to search the place and he had the sense to realise he wouldn't get one. Oh, and he didn't like the look of the dogs. They certainly didn't take to him. Well trained they are, aren't they Dave?' She cackled then took a drag on her cigarette. Dave looked up and nodded. 'Dave keeps everything regular and above board here. Everything's recorded, you apart, of course. And we have a good solicitor. He's expensive, but he knows his stuff. They know we'll contest it if they try and pull a fast one.'

'Got it,' said Dave, suddenly. 'Whoever had this phone before you, wasn't over careful with their password.'

Doyle smiled. 'I'll manage without one. I won't be keeping it for long.'

'I've had to put one in, Michael. But I've made it simple – four zeros.'

Doyle nodded. 'That's fine.'

'How's Jules?' asked Mrs Sherwood, changing the subject. 'I see she got off in that trial of hers. And I thought she was definitely going down; I'd have put money on it. I followed the case every day on *Central News*. They made a big thing of it. The police weren't very happy about the result. I saw the DCI's face on the TV. He looked mightily pissed off. That was the same day you were released wasn't it?'

Doyle said nothing for a few moments. His voice dropped. 'Yes, it was. The powers that be were waiting for the verdict before I was let out. She got off OK, no thanks to me, though.'

'There are lots of rumours going around about why you were released so early. You got fifteen or sixteen years, didn't you? How long were you in?'

'Including time on remand, just over fourteen months.'

'You were released very early then?'

Doyle nodded and let out a sigh. 'I suppose it's got out that I grassed up someone?'

'It has. But that's not what our visitor seemed interested in. It looked like there were other reasons why he was trying to find you. Sounded personal to me, but I could be wrong. He gave me the impression it was something to do with one of those bodies they pulled out of the Trent.'

'There's a connection all right,' replied Doyle. He paused. 'What I did, I did for Jules. And I had to work hard to get early release; it wasn't just because I gave the police a name. The guy they pulled out of the Trent in Nottingham helped me. We were in the same prison for a while.' He paused and turned the conversation back to Julia Hamilton. 'I don't suppose you've heard anything of Jules?'

'No, we haven't. But I wouldn't have expected to hear from her. She knows what I think of her.' She paused and drew on her cigarette again. 'Aren't you in touch with her, then? We thought that you might have been with her after we worked out you were still in the land of the living.'

Doyle decided to say nothing. He simply shook his head and looked down.

'Still in love with her, are you?' said Mrs Sherwood, a disapproving expression crossing her face. 'You mark my words, Michael Doyle. She's trouble, that one. Always has been. You're better off without her.'

Doyle looked up. 'That's what everyone says.'

'Well, think on then. No point in making yourself a martyr on her account. She just uses people.'

'I'll be the judge of that,' said Doyle, firmly. 'Now, can we change the subject, please?'

Mrs Sherwood desisted. She could see that Doyle was upset by her comments about Jules. Dave was concentrating on the mobile phone which he was now reassembling.

'You don't seem like your old self, Michael. Are you sure you're OK?' Mrs Sherwood gave him a worried look.

'I'm fine. I've had a lot to put up with over the last few months. To tell you the truth, I'm about wacked.'

'Do you want a bed for a night? It's a bit late to go opening things up in the barn now and the dogs would have to be brought in. You'll be safe enough here. We have a spare room you can use. But you'll have to be off first thing. Dave has three people working for him just now. He has an office and everything. They're usually in by eight o'clock or shortly afterwards.'

Doyle nodded his thanks. 'Sounds like you're doing well?'

'We get by.'

Dave stood up and walked to the kitchen cabinet, pulling open one of the drawers. He rummaged around then took out a phone charger and plugged it in. He inserted the other end into the now reassembled phone. It lit up and several messages appeared. He handed it to Doyle. 'There we are, password changed. It's all yours. You'll need to charge it up fully.'

Doyle swiftly scanned the text messages, four in number. The name "Max" or "Maxine" appeared in three of them. They were all to the same effect, demanding that she get in touch. There was no indication as to who had sent the messages, but Doyle had no doubt they came from Grayling. That was confirmed when he listened to two voice messages. He recognised Michael Grayling's voice immediately. The last one was two days old. He put the phone down on the side for the charge to be completed.

'So, that's who she was,' he whispered.

'Who was?' asked Mrs Sherwood.

'Nothing. Just thinking aloud. Will I be able to call back whoever left these messages, Dave?'

'No problem. I'll show you how when it's fully charged. But bear in mind you'll only be able to use this for as long as someone is paying the bill. Might be a month or only a day or two.'

'I'll remember that.' Doyle turned his attention back to Mrs Sherwood. 'Now, where's this bed you promised me?'

CHAPTER 6

The queue passing through arrivals at Stansted airport was moving quickly following the landing of the Aer Lingus flight from Dublin early on Wednesday morning. The elderly lady standing immediately in front of the man seemed flustered as she presented her passport, not that she needed to produce it arriving from Ireland. But some form of identification in troublesome times was deemed necessary and a passport was always acceptable and was the preferred method of identification by the airline. Had there been some incident that had caused these compulsory checks to be re-introduced? Usually, passengers arriving at Stansted from Dublin simply walked straight through. Only the occasional random check was made. She dropped her hand luggage while struggling with her spectacles which she had removed at the request of the border control officer. The man, now standing beside her, was dressed in dark clothing and about forty years of age. His passport was ready in his left hand. He picked up the bag for her and smiled as her passport was returned to her by the official.

'Thank you, young man,' she said. 'I'm all fingers and thumbs today. I'm always nervous when flying. It takes me an hour or two to get used to being on the ground again.' She then noticed the man was wearing a clerical collar. 'Oh, I'm sorry, should I have called you Father?'

'It's no matter,' replied the man in a refined but obvious accent. 'I've been called a few things in my time. You should come to my parish in Dublin. You wouldn't want to hear how I've been addressed there by some of the scallywags on the estates.' He smiled. 'I'll give you a hand with your bag if you like. I'll be picking mine up from baggage claim once I'm through here.'

She nodded her appreciation. 'That's very kind of you. I have a suitcase to collect as well.'

The man handed his passport to the official who gave it a cursory inspection.

'Are you staying long, Father?' he asked.

'No, only a few days, then I have to get back. No rest for the wicked, you know. I have a funeral to attend while I'm here. An old friend of the family, God rest his soul.'

'Sorry to hear that,' responded the official, handing the passport back. 'You have a nice day anyway. The weather here is quite good today for the time of year. Brightened up considerably since the week-end.'

The two passengers passed through the barrier and walked slowly towards baggage claim, the priest carrying the woman's hand luggage.

'Is someone meeting you here?' he asked.

'Oh, yes. My son-in-law is picking me up in his car. My daughter's family lives just outside Cambridge, so it's not too far. Where are you headed?'

'I'm taking the train to Peterborough. I'll be staying with family nearby. Then I have the funeral to conduct, but that's not for a few days. Do you live in Ireland yourself?'

'No. I've been to a reunion at TCD. Believe it or not, I was a student there fifty-two years ago.'

'Go on with you.'

'I was. It's hard to believe when you look at me now. I have a degree in modern history. My father said it would broaden my mind to study outside England. He was certainly right. I met my late husband while I was a student there.'

'At TCD?'

'Yes, do you know Trinity College?'

'I wasn't a student there myself, no. I was in Rome for several years, you know. At the Irish College. Even picked up quite a bit of Italian.'

'You would in all that time, I suppose. Well, here we are. Would you mind if I sit down for a moment? I'm feeling a little tired. The bags are just starting to appear.'

She made her way to one of the few seats available and sat down. His eyes were now fixed on the circulating luggage.

'I think I see my bag now. I'll be off then. Train to catch. Will you be OK? Should I find someone to help you?'

'I'll be fine, Father. Thank you for your help. You've been very kind.'

'God bless you now. *Arrivederci.*'

The priest picked up his bag from the carousel, waved to the elderly woman and made his way out of the airport. He rushed, unchallenged, along a short corridor and found himself in the huge foyer at the airport exit. But he didn't go down to the station below. His smiling countenance changed suddenly, his expression becoming serious. He walked past the car hire facilities, through the automatic doors and towards the car park. Near the first barrier, strategically positioned to make a quick exit, he noticed a black series six BMW with a tall, thin man of about thirty standing by the driver's door as if he were waiting for someone. As he approached him, the driver turned and looked at him, quizzically.

'Is it yourself?' he asked. 'The Tinkerman?'

'I am he,' replied the priest. 'You'll be the driver from Peterborough?'

'That's right. And where are we going?'

'Not to Peterborough, to be sure. The game is in Leicester.'

'So it is. And may the best team win.'

The priest smiled and acknowledged the driver. Satisfied that this was the person he was due to meet, the tall thin man took control of the suitcase and carefully deposited it in the boot as the other looked around him, then climbed into the passenger seat.

'Any problems?' asked the driver as he got into the car. He smiled. 'You really do look like a vicar.'

The man scowled. 'Not a vicar, a priest. There is a difference, you know. In my occupation it pays to know these things.' He paused before continuing. 'I was a bit surprised I had to show my passport on arrival here. There must be some sort of security alert.' He patted his breast pocket where his passport was secured and sat back in his seat. 'I hope it was nothing to do with me. I wasn't expecting it. That's why I came here via Dublin. No requirement to show any identification usually.' But he did not seem over concerned. He laughed. 'I shall be adopting a different persona on the return trip, but for the moment, I propose to continue in my present vocation. It should prove useful in tracking down my target.' He looked at the driver who had adopted a stern look. 'Ease up, Gerald. That's your name, isn't it?'

The driver nodded. 'It is for today. Like you, I prefer to keep things flexible.'

The man in the passenger seat laughed. 'I like it. Now I know everything will be fine.'

The driver smiled but said nothing. He turned the key in the ignition and started up the engine then drove towards the exit. He had already paid the parking charge, and headed out of the parking area towards the M11, taking care to observe the speed limit.

'You have something for me, I hope?' said the passenger.

'I have. In the glove compartment.'

'Clean, are they?'

The driver didn't take his eyes off the road as he answered.

'As a nun's conscience. The main item was in the car when I picked it up. I did a quick check. It's an H and K, P8, just like you ordered. The serial number has already been removed and there's fifteen rounds of ammunition in the magazine. It has no history that need worry you.'

The man nodded in evident satisfaction. 'Good old Heckler and Koch, but I doubt if I'll need so much ammo to eliminate this target.' He adjusted his seat and turned up the air conditioning. 'The only problem I will have is finding him. I may have to await instructions about that. He's very elusive, apparently.'

'Will you need any help?'

'No. I always work alone. Safer that way.' He fitted his seat belt. 'And the phone?'

'Good for a month. No chance of it being traced back to you or to anyone. It can be used for international calls too. You can safely destroy it when you have no further use for it.'

'Excellent.'

'By the way, any further information you may need is at the safe house. Bit of a rush job, this one. I only got my instructions yesterday. I know nothing, of course. It's better that way.' He smiled. 'I don't even know where the safe house is.'

'As a matter of interest, what do you know?'

'Hardly anything. I was instructed to pick you up and drive you wherever you want to go. Then I'm to hand the motor over to you and make contact. The codeword for everything is *Tinkerman*. I don't know who thought that up.' He laughed.

The man in the passenger seat smiled in response but said nothing. He sat back and closed his eyes. He didn't open the glove compartment for a good thirty minutes until they were travelling west along the A14 dual carriageway. He then quickly checked the weapon before replacing it and closing his eyes again. He didn't bother examining the phone or its charger.

'Let me know when we hit the A6, will you?'

'You seem to know the area well. Have you been in these parts before?'

'That's for me to know and, by the way, I don't like answering questions. I have studied the area and taken a few other elementary precautions. I shall be going straight to the safe house. That's all you need to know and I'll tell you where you'll be dropped off when we hit the A6. Have you made arrangements for when I take over the car?'

'I have. I'll be picked up from wherever you like to drop me, but the nearer to Market Harborough the better. All it will take is a quick call.'

'That shouldn't be a problem. Make sure you make your call from a public telephone. There are still a few about.' He paused. 'All the paperwork for the car is here?'

The driver nodded. 'In the file in the driver's door pocket. It's been hired for three weeks. And by the way, I'm not responsible for the upgrade. That was just a bit of luck. It was a series three that was booked.' He paused and looked towards the passenger. 'I suppose that will be long enough for your purposes? Leave it at the airport when you've finished with it. Will you need me after the job is done?'

'No. As I said, I have made other arrangements for my departure, but you can leave me a number in case I need to get in touch.' He glanced towards the driver. 'I haven't received the down payment on my fee yet. And nothing will happen until I do.' He smiled, but not in a friendly way.

'Not my department, that. Way above my pay scale.'

'Well, I need it in my account before I move. Tell your contact that when you speak with him. They have the details.'

'Will do.'

The man in the passenger seat suppressed a yawn. 'I think a little holiday is called for when this is over. I haven't yet decided where, but it will be a long way from here, I can assure you.' He became serious. 'It's important we aren't seen together again after we part. I have my own way of working, as you know. Just keep your eyes on the road and make sure you drive within the speed limits. We don't want to be attracting attention now, do we?'

CHAPTER 7

Early on Wednesday morning, just as the flight from Dublin was landing at Stansted, Michael Doyle collected his motorcycle and other property from the storage facility at the Sherwoods' farm just as it was becoming light. He had changed into his motorcycle leathers and stored his other clothes in one of the paniers. The cell phone was fully charged and Dave let him have a compatible charger; all part of the service. Doyle took the most direct route to Melton Mowbray then travelled along the A607 to the Leicestershire village of Thrussington where Jules' mother still owned a cottage on the Rearsby Road. He had retained a key to the back door amongst the property he had stored at the Sherwoods' farm. When he arrived, just before seven o'clock, no one was about apart from a milkman in the distance who gave him a curious look then went about his business. Doyle took the precaution of switching off the engine and pushing his bike the last few yards. He unlocked the back door then went through the kitchen into the garage. He opened the double doors of the garage just wide enough to get his bike inside, bolting it afterwards. He had already noted the "For Sale" sign on the front of the house. "Viewing by Appointment only." He realised he wouldn't be able to stay for very long, assuming as he did, that the agents would have a key and that potential purchasers might be arriving later in the day. He removed his helmet and placed it on the motorcycle then went back into the kitchen. As he had anticipated, the house was unoccupied and much tidier than he remembered. He knew there was no burglar alarm and was familiar with the layout from the couple of occasions he and Julia Hamilton had stayed there. The conversation he had picked up at Barnard House while pretending still to be unconscious, had told him that both Jules and her mother were probably in Portugal along with Michael Grayling and Jules' son. He figured he would be safe in the house for only a few hours. He stepped into the sitting room and looked at himself in the mirror over the fireplace. His beard was growing reasonably quickly but was not yet sufficient to alter his appearance significantly. He noted the bags underneath his eyes then sighed as he unzipped his leather jacket. He sat down briefly and removed his motorcycle boots.

Sidling towards the front window so as not to be seen from outside, he drew the curtains a fraction then collapsed into an armchair and suppressed a yawn. He had spent a fitful and disturbed night at the Sherwoods' farmhouse; in truth he had never slept well since he first went into prison and he intended to catch up on his sleep in the bed he and Jules had occasionally shared at Sycamore Cottage before he went on his way. But first, he had things to do. He needed to find out precisely where Jules was staying in Portugal.

Sycamore Cottage was close to its neighbouring property and he was careful to remain as quiet as possible as he began a thorough search for any clues that might point to Jules' exact location. A photograph of her mother's villa in the Algarve stood on a mahogany sideboard, but try as he might, he could not remember the name of the nearest town. He attempted unsuccessfully to open the top of an antique bureau. Locked. He cursed, silently. Then, carefully prising open the lock with a penknife and doing as little damage as possible, he opened the top of the desk and began his search. After going through the contents of the upper section, he discovered some paperwork together with several photographs of the villa with "*Carvoeiro*" written on the reverse. *That's it,* he said to himself, *Carvoeiro.* He now remembered the name. Jules had waxed lyrically about the beaches close to the old fishing village some fifteen minutes' drive from her mother's very private country house which stood in its own wooded grounds and was equipped with a swimming pool. They'd intended to travel there before he was arrested in 1999. The idea had been to explore the area where decades of wave erosion had carved out several attractive grottoes and islets along the extensive beaches. It had sounded like a mini-paradise as described by Jules, but his dream had been postponed by his arrest and then shattered by the arrival on the scene of Michael Grayling. *Was Grayling there now with Jules?* He felt sick to the pit of his stomach as he contemplated that excuse for a human being touching Jules, embracing her, making love to her. He slammed the top of the desk shut, forgetting in that moment the proximity of the neighbouring property.

After a minute or two, he began to look through the drawers until he found a telephone book. He flipped through the pages, alighting on the number for the villa together with the international dialling code. Should he telephone? He rehearsed the arguments and counter arguments. If he rang, suppose Grayling answered? He could hardly terminate the call. He'd have given himself away. Grayling would know he was using the phone of the woman who had tried but failed to kill him. Would Grayling know she was dead? Of course he would; those unanswered messages would at least have alerted him to the possibility that something had happened to her. Besides, a criminal of his calibre would still have people on the ground in the UK who would have seen reports in the newspapers; people who would be searching for him with a view to making a second attempt on his life. He pictured in his mind the brute of a Scotsman who had struck him on the side of the head with a cosh. That was a face he would not forget in a hurry. He had no desire to meet him again, but if he did, he would be ready for him. He took the cell phone from his pocket and looked at it. After a moment's further hesitation, he started to enter the lengthy telephone number, but stopped as he reached the last digit. He shook his head and sighed. No. He would wait. He needed to plan his next steps carefully. Not only would Grayling's henchmen be looking for him, the police would be anxious to find him too. He glanced out of the window and replaced the phone in the back pocket of his leather over trousers. What to do? He walked out of the sitting room, through the kitchen and into the garage where he removed the paniers from his motorcycle. He took them upstairs to the main bedroom, placing them on the bottom of the bed. After opening the transom window a couple of inches to allow some air into the room, he lay down and rehearsed his next moves before eventually falling asleep.

* * *

He was awakened two hours later by the cell phone buzzing. It was still in his leather trousers and he felt it vibrating as he came round from a deep slumber. He removed it and looked at the screen, recognising the caller's number immediately. It was the same number he had decided against ringing earlier – the telephone number of Jules' mother's villa near Carvoeiro in Portugal. Should he answer? The probability was that the caller was Grayling. He decided to risk it and accept the call. 'Yes,' he said, trying his best to disguise his voice. He failed. The caller recognised him immediately.

'Michael! You're still alive. Thank God for that.' The caller was Julia Hamilton.

'Jules! Oh, Jules. You have no idea what it means for me to hear your voice. Where are you?'

'At my mother's villa in Portugal. Look, Michael, I don't have much time. Grayling has gone out, but he could be back any minute. He has this habit of disappearing then suddenly reappearing. It gives me the creeps. It's as if he's trying to catch me out.'

'How did you get this number?' asked Doyle. He'd only just awakened but he was naturally cautious.

'I found it written down in a diary he left lying around. It's Maxine's number. Michael, listen to me. Grayling knows that Maxine is dead. He spent Sunday night trying to get in touch with her. He's been in the foulest of moods. He reckons you must have killed her. You didn't, did you? Tell me you didn't.'

Doyle paused before he answered. Should he tell Jules the truth? He saw no point in denying what had happened. 'I suppose it was down to me, but it wasn't deliberate on my part. She was doing her damnedest to kill me. It was her gun. It went off while we were struggling together. You saw what they were about, Jules, at Barnard House. She was employed by that bastard Grayling to kill me and dump me in the Trent.' He laughed nervously. 'But that's where she ended up. Not quite as clever or efficient as she thought she was.'

Jules was seemingly in no mood for gallows humour. 'Grayling blames you, Michael. I overheard him talking on Monday. He thought I was asleep. He'd worked out you must have killed her. He's sending a hit-man over to eliminate you, a real professional. That's why I took the chance to ring you, to warn you. I was praying you had Maxine's phone. I knew yours would have been destroyed in the fire.'

'So, he's not using his Scottish hard man? Do you know who it is, this so-called professional hit-man?'

'No.' She paused briefly. 'He wouldn't tell me something like that. Look Michael, I've made a terrible mistake. I should have listened to you. I should never have taken up with Grayling. The man's an animal. I sometimes think he'd kill me without a second thought if he thought it was in his interests. I've never felt so isolated and afraid. You have to help me get away from him. You have to. I'm sorry for what I said to you last week. I really am. You were right all along.'

Doyle suddenly felt elated. She still wanted him. She still loved him and needed his support. He couldn't help himself, his emotions almost overwhelmed him. 'How can I help? What do you want me to do? You know I'll do anything for you. I was planning to follow you to Portugal, but I won't be able to get there for a while yet. I have things to do over here.'

'No, don't do that.' The tone of her voice altered immediately. 'There's no point coming to Portugal. I won't be here much longer.' She dropped her voice. 'He told me this morning that he's planning to come back to the UK in a few days' time. He's taking me and little Michael with him. He says it's the perfect cover – a happy family taking a short break. Can you believe it? We'll be travelling under false names. He never uses his real identity in the UK.'

'What name will he be using?'

'I don't know. He refuses to tell me, but I'll find out eventually. It won't be the same name he used when we travelled to Portugal.'

'When will you be arriving?'

'I'm not sure, but it won't be this week. Probably the week after.'

She suddenly broke down and started to cry. She sounded desperate. 'Michael, you have to help me. I can't stand this much longer. I'm terrified of him. There's no saying what he might do. My mother's frightened of him too. Her boyfriend is threatening to move out if we stay here much longer. They both want us out of her villa and I don't blame them.'

'You know me, Jules. I'd do anything for you. Where will you be staying in the UK? He surely can't risk coming back to the East Midlands?'

'I don't know. It could be anywhere. All I know is that he has to meet up with the someone, probably the person he's sent to kill you.' She started to weep uncontrollably. 'Michael, I don't want them to kill you. I want you back with me.'

Nothing was said for some time as Jules continued to cry. Doyle eventually spoke. 'Jules, pull yourself together. This isn't like you.' He heard her take a deep breath as she tried to control herself. Her tone changed again, quite suddenly.

'Will you be using Maxine's phone for the next few days?'

Doyle noticed the sudden change but did not comment. He answered her question. 'I wasn't planning to, but I suppose I can if you like.'

'I'll ring you when I know more. If you get a different phone, let me have the number. Look, I'll ring you again tonight if I can, but it might be tomorrow. I have to be careful. Grayling will be playing cards with his so-called friends later. I should get a chance to phone you without him knowing.'

'I'll wait for your call. Take care.'

'You too.' She added a question. 'Michael, do you have Maxine's gun?'

He replied without thinking. 'No, I threw it in the river.'

'Have the police found it?'

'No idea. I heard on the radio that they're dragging the river. But whether they've found anything, I simply don't know.'

'How will you protect yourself without a gun?'

'Don't you worry about me. I won't be making it so easy for them next time, you can be sure of that.'

'Where are you?'

He hesitated. He was finding some of her questions just a little on the intrusive side. He remembered she was more than capable of manipulating him and his naturally suspicious nature started to kick in. He decided to err on the side of caution.

'Where no one will find me.'

She suddenly terminated the conversation. 'I have to go. He's just driven through the gates. Bye.'

Doyle looked at the phone and sighed with relief. He almost jumped for joy, throwing caution to the winds. Jules still wanted him. She still loved him. He was the one she desired. Grayling was an aberration. Oh, how he wished he could have seen her face and held her in his arms. But that was a pleasure yet to come, or so he believed. Then suddenly, he felt a cold shiver go through his body. What if she were using him? Lying to him? What if she were leading him on again? His thoughts turned to the child he'd believed was his. He recalled how she had played fast and loose with him while he was in custody. A sudden deep depression overwhelmed him. His enthusiasm waning fast, he told himself he really would have to proceed with the utmost care. Whatever his feelings for Jules, he had to put himself first. The last thing he needed was a professional hit-man looking for him, and worse, finding him.

At the villa in Portugal, Jules looked briefly at the phone as she ended the call, then at the man standing close to her. She glared at him. He was holding the extension in his right hand. He had been listening intently to the conversation. She noticed the pistol tucked in his belt. He took the phone from her and replaced it on its stand.

'Well done, my darling. You handled that really well. Almost too well. I almost believed you myself.' He smiled, his thin lips curling at the edges but his watery eyes told her his thoughts were elsewhere. 'It didn't sound like he suspected a thing. I just knew he'd be hanging on to Maxine's phone. He's such a bloody fool is Doyle. Pity he got rid of Maxine's gun. If the police find it, they'll connect her death with Dudley Manning's. That could cause me a problem.' He looked her in the eye. 'You will ring him tonight like you said and inform him where we will be staying when we travel to the UK in just over a week's time. I'll write it down for you. We don't want him trying to find you in the wrong place do we? I want him to come looking for you. And when he does…' He walked over to the desk in front of the window and replaced the extension. Jules looked at him blankly. Were those real tears forming in her eyes?

'I don't want you to kill him, Michael. He doesn't deserve to die. Can't you just leave him be? You've got what you want. You have me and your son. Why risk going back to England, just to see Michael Doyle dead.'

He turned on her, angrily. 'Because I choose to, that's why. He killed Maxine. You've just heard him admit it. He has to die. I have my reputation to consider. Besides, he knows too much and I have other business there apart from Doyle. I need hardly add it was because of him that I've lost several million pounds which others in the organisation will blame on me. Duffy may have betrayed the rest of my father's team, but it was Doyle who put the police on to Duffy in the first place and trashed my father's masterplan. He has to pay for that, and believe me, he will.'

'I don't know what he said about Duffy or its consequences but he only killed Maxine because she was trying to kill him. He was defending himself, for Christ's sake. What did you expect him to do? And he won't say anything about me to the police. I just know he won't.'

'He won't be saying anything to anyone. If Jamie had been able to find him, he'd be dead already, but he's gone to ground. He needs digging out and you are going to help me with the digging.' Grayling glowered. His tone remained cold and unemotional. 'I don't care about Doyle, understand? He's an irritation; an irritation that needs to be removed, permanently. I've made my decision and I will not change my mind.' He walked over to her and ran his hands through her long blonde hair, pulling her towards him. She laid her head on his shoulder, turning her face away from him. He pushed her slightly away so he could judge her reaction to what he was about to say. 'And I don't like this continuing concern for him that you are exhibiting, Julia. I don't like it one bit. Some of what you said to him over the phone there didn't sound to me like you were acting. For your sake, I do hope you've not retained any affection for this piece of shit. You need to forget about him.' He narrowed his eyes. 'I shall destroy him. Get that into that pretty head of yours. He is history.' He gripped her by her upper arms tightly and squeezed until she yelped in pain.

'Let go! You're hurting me.'

'Remember, too, my love, I cannot abide disloyalty of any kind, especially from the mother of my son.' A child started to cry in an adjacent room. 'Isn't it about time you fed him again?' He suddenly released his grip. She backed away from him, her eyes flashing with anger, but she said nothing as he continued to berate her. 'This time there will be no mistakes. And just to make sure, I mean to watch Doyle die. I'll have to pay extra for the privilege, no doubt, but it will be well worth it.' Jules now made for the door without saying another word. He called after her as she left the room. 'And so will you, my darling, whether you like it or not. Do you hear me? You'll look into those dead eyes of his. I'll get him out of your head if it's the last thing I do.'

CHAPTER 8

'Isn't that typical?' complained Acting Inspector Andrew Hooper to Wendy Knight when they were alone in the West Bridgford squad room early on Wednesday morning. 'There I am, camped out by the Trent on a miserable cold day from half-past seven in the morning and I find diddly squat; the boss comes along and the murder weapon appears from the river like Excalibur rising from the waters. Then to add insult to injury, the deceased's crash helmet and motorbike turn up – and he'd only been at the crime scene for five bloody minutes!'

Knight could hardly resist smiling as she squatted on the edge of Hooper's desk. 'He's always been lucky like that,' she said. 'And you mustn't get yourself into a state about it, Andrew. The gun would still have turned up if we hadn't arrived when we did because it was your decision to search for it in the first place.' She leant forward and lowered her voice. 'Between you and me, Harry didn't think there was a snowball's chance in hell of finding it. So it's really down to you that it was recovered. And I guess I was just lucky coming across the two boys. I noticed the helmet one of them was wearing was far too big for him; that's the only reason I approached them. Call it a lucky hunch.'

Hooper sighed. 'I should have noticed it. I'd shooed them away more than once. I should, perhaps, have extended the search area to include the quarry shed.' He dropped his head. 'The boss has now extended the sealed-off zone as far back as the beginning of the lane in the village. I suppose it will keep those nosey members of the public out of our way, but I doubt if anything else will be found, not now.'

Knight responded sympathetically. 'I wouldn't worry too much about not finding the bike. You weren't the only one who didn't notice it. And if you'd sealed off the area beyond the bridge, I'd never have come across those two boys.'

Hooper nodded his gratitude. 'What does he make of it?'

'Who, Harry? He's not said, and he's had to go off and speak with the ACC this morning. The top brass want a daily update, apparently. He'll be calling in later for the briefing.'

'Why is Bob Gaunt taking such an interest in this investigation? The ACC doesn't usually get involved in an inquiry at this level other than to appear at press briefings and claim any credit that's going. Is there something that's being kept from us?'

'I don't know. I suppose it's because the chief is retiring soon and he wants this sorted before he goes. Harry's also expanding the team. He certainly wants a result as soon as possible.'

'Do we need anyone else?'

'Not up to me. But I heard on the grapevine that a new DS will be joining us; Sean Smith. Have you met him? He joined Mid-Shires from South Yorkshire about four months ago. I suppose he'll be replacing me when I transfer to Northamptonshire.'

'I thought he was working with the major crime unit.'

'Harry's borrowed him. And what we are investigating is pretty major, don't you think?'

'It's certainly been given Cat A status by the ACC, which should help when it comes to additional resources. I suppose Sean Smith falls into that category, although I don't really know him. Looked a bit of a misery when I bumped into him last month.'

'What do you expect? He's a Sheffield Wednesday supporter!' They both laughed. 'Mind you, he knows what he's doing by all accounts. He's a bit of an expert on forensics. You'll have to watch him. You don't want him stealing your thunder.'

Hooper looked glum. 'What thunder is that? I can't get my head around this killing at Cromwell at all. It doesn't seem to make sense. No doubt Smithy will come along and solve it in double-quick time. Mind you, if he's such a whiz with forensics, he can give a hand going through all the CCTV. Raymond Craddock always seems to get lumbered with that job and I think he's getting a bit fed up with it. I suppose it's because he's only a temporary DC?'

'Don't be like that. We're a team, remember? And he's got that attractive young police woman helping him. Besides, Ray's got a decent track record when it comes to CCTV. He spotted a very helpful clip in the Charnwood robbery investigation which others had missed. Made quite a difference to the outcome. I suppose that's why he was pulled from general duties. He's hardly spent any time in uniform.'

'Let's hope he repeats it with this case. We could do with a decent lead.' Hooper sighed and sat back in his seat.

Wendy smiled. 'I'll tell you what I think, if you like, before Harry gets here. I was turning everything over in my mind last night while I was watching a crime thriller on TV.'

Hooper was dismissive. 'Don't let that rubbish influence you. This is real life, not fiction.' He cheered up and almost smiled. 'Go on, then. Tell me what you reckon happened.'

'Well, I don't think we'll have any problem proving it's Maxine Kruger's motorbike. Her DNA will be all over it. That helmet too, despite it being in the water for a while. It didn't sink, so her DNA profile will probably still be recoverable.'

'The bike's not registered in her name, though.'

'Given her likely occupation, does that surprise you? It's not been stolen. At least we know that.'

'The passport in the panier's in a different name, too. Same name as the registered owner. Monica King. I've already run a check.'

'Probably a fake,' said Knight. 'The photo could easily pass for her though.'

'Ray's visiting the address in Long Eaton this morning where the bike's registered. I gave him a bit of a break from analysing the CCTV. I bet that turns out to be fake too. Interesting that it's an Irish passport, though. She's supposed to be German.'

Knight hesitated. 'That must be the name she was using. Not very original is it, Monica King? Doesn't even sound Irish.'

'The initials match her real name, though, MK. That's probably significant.'

Hooper stretched his arms and supressed a yawn as he continued.

'And the ten thousand pounds?'

'Perhaps she was on her way somewhere and needed money.'

'No ticket or travel documents.'

Knight said nothing for a while. 'Perhaps the money was payment for something.'

'But for what?'

She paused before she answered. 'I know Harry thinks I'm possibly wide of the mark with this, but I think Kruger may have killed Manning. If we exclude Doyle, she's the favourite in my opinion. She also has a bit of a reputation in that regard. The money could be her fee for eliminating him.'

Hooper frowned and raised an eyebrow. 'Is that the going rate for a hit, these days?'

'No idea. But we know there was a motorcycle at the scene of Manning's killing. So it points to the possibility of her at least being there. And I don't think a debit or credit card would be considered appropriate for such a transaction, do you? Cash only, I would have thought.'

Hooper smiled. 'And the black briefcase?'

'Nothing in it apart from the passport and the money. If there's been a gun in there at any time, forensics will be able to prove it.'

Hooper scratched his head and let out another lengthy sigh. 'That would probably settle it, I suppose, but we'll have to wait several days before we get confirmation, unless we put Smithy on the job, of course.' He smiled. 'It still intrigues me, though, how she ended up in the Trent at Cromwell? It's a long way from Victoria Embankment to Cromwell Lock.'

Knight took a deep breath before she answered. 'I think she went there on her bike to meet someone; perhaps someone she was planning to finish off. She got there before him, hid the bike in that shed and waited. Whoever it was got the better of her, took her gun and killed her. She was dumped in the river along with the gun and the helmet, but her killer didn't hang around looking for her motorbike. It follows that he must have had transport of his own and used it to make good his escape. That's why the bike was still in the shed when we found it yesterday. I can't think of any other reason why it would still be there.'

Hooper nodded. 'Assuming as I do that it is her motorcycle, your theory would explain another thing that's been bothering me.'

'What's that?'

'Why the gun was chucked in the river; the boss was a bit thrown by that too. A real pro wouldn't get rid of his weapon of choice with an almost full magazine, but if it wasn't his, the opposite would apply. He'd want rid of it, and double quick.'

'And it's definitely the murder weapon is it?'

'Still waiting for a full report from David Osborne, but the odds are very strong. It fires the right type of rounds and there are only three missing from the magazine. That makes two for Manning and one for Kruger. David Osborne has already said he's pretty sure the same gun was used and that was before we'd recovered it. Forensics will be checking the bullets for prints and DNA too. Most villains are forensically aware these days and take care not to leave their DNA on guns but they sometimes overlook the bullets. The boss told me he'd come across a similar mistake before. Although this gun had been in the river before we recovered it, there's some chance that the magazine may have prevented the water removing all traces of DNA and fingerprints from the bullets.'

'So, if she did shoot Manning, who was she meeting at Cromwell? She can't have been there to get the money. She'd already had that. It was in the briefcase.'

'That's true enough. Find out who she was meeting and we find our killer.' Hooper paused. 'One other thing, though. Why didn't she leave her helmet with the bike? When I had a bike, I always left the helmet with it when I parked it up in my garage.'

'But it's a bit of a walk from the shed to the lock and a helmet like that is a great disguise with its shaded visor. You wouldn't be able to recognise anyone wearing it, especially at night. As to who she was meeting…?' She shook her head. 'Like you, I have no idea.'

'That's what we need to find out then. And it's not going to be easy.'

'Don't I know it. Dumping her in the river will have destroyed any chance of finding the killer's DNA on her body or clothing.'

Hooper sat back in his chair and placed his hands behind his head. 'There's another thing that's problematic. How did she end up being shot with her own gun? If whoever she was meeting was in the same business as her, he'd have had his own firearm, wouldn't he?'

Knight shook her head. 'But would he though? Think about it. Guns are not that common, even in Nottingham, and it's very risky to get caught with one. You can pick up a lengthy sentence just for possession. One low-life picked up ten years the other week after he was found with a loaded revolver, and he didn't even get the chance to use it. He was stopped by armed officers on his way to shoot his target.'

'Decent sentence, that.'

'Yes, the maximum I believe, for possession.' She returned to discussing the body found at Cromwell Lock. 'And the pathology suggests our Jane Doe was involved in a struggle, remember, a struggle that went on for a while. There had to be time for those cuts and bruises to form before she died. Perhaps she pulled her gun on him and they ended up in a fight to the death and her gun was discharged as they grappled together? It would explain the powder burns on her leather jacket too. They must have been in very close contact for that to have happened.'

'That's a bit speculative, isn't it? If she intended to kill whoever it was, why didn't she just shoot him on sight?'

Knight frowned. 'I don't know, Andrew, but we can't ignore the pathology. Perhaps she didn't intend to kill him initially but something developed, they fell out and she ended up in close contact with him.'

'The silencer is about five-and-a-half inches in length. It must have been a bit awkward if they were struggling to get possession of the weapon.'

'What are you saying? That it might have gone off by accident?'

Hooper smiled. 'I don't know about that. By the look of it, someone was clearly after killing someone. I don't call that an accident. On the other hand, I suppose it's always possible that whoever was involved with her didn't have a gun with him. Perhaps she was relying on that when she agreed to meet him?'

'At least we now know the approximate location where she was shot. What was the name of the officer who found the discharged cartridge?'

'PC Graham Henshaw. He found it in the mud only a hundred and fifty yards or so from where she was pulled out of the river. Dr Waters was almost spot on in her estimation of how far the body had travelled.'

'He did well to find it then.'

'He certainly did. Other officers were supposed to have searched the same area the day before.'

'And there's a piece of hardstanding just off the road at that location isn't there?'

Hooper stood up and walked to the large whiteboard displaying a detailed drawing of the relevant section of the Trent accompanied by several photographs which had been placed at key locations marked on the plan. He pointed to one of the photographs. 'Yes. That's where the struggle must have taken place with her back on the hard surface when she was shot, quite some distance from the lock itself. Henshaw did well to locate it. That area was underwater on Monday morning when the search commenced. The water level had dropped quite a bit by Tuesday though.'

'Well, that's another gold star for you, Andrew. You organised the area to be searched.' She tilted her head and looked at the acting inspector and tentatively raised a matter she thought might be troubling him. 'You're not too upset about the DCI taking over from you? I know you thought this was your opportunity to prove you're up to the mark for a permanent promotion.'

Hooper half-smiled as he retook his seat. 'Actually, I was expecting it. The two deaths must be linked and I only got this one because I was the acting duty inspector when the call came in. In fact, as I knew I wouldn't remain as SIO, I was hoping it would be the boss who took over. I'd rather have Harry in charge than some of the others. At least he listens. But even he has to report everything to ACC Gaunt on a daily basis.' A puzzled expression crossed his face. 'I still think that's a bit odd. I wonder if there's something going on in the background. Something that's being kept from us?'

'Politics, I expect. We're well out of it.'

'Perhaps you're right.'

Knight could still detect a trace of disappointment in his voice. Hooper stood up again and walked to the window as he attempted to change the subject.

'Are you familiar with the firing procedure of a Beretta M9?'

Knight shook her head. 'No. I don't know a lot about firearms. I appreciate I need to go on another course. I'm booked on one next month, before I move to Wellingborough.'

Hooper pointed to an enlarged photograph of the gun recovered from the river fixed to the whiteboard. 'You'll learn all about it then. It's a common enough piece of kit. I've come across the type several times over the years. It's fairly complicated. You don't just pull the trigger, you know. You have to set it up first, check the magazine and remove the safety. It will all be in the report, when we get it. But if the gun was discharged during a physical struggle, it must have been ready to fire before the violence started. There'd be little chance of carrying out the preliminaries unless she was knocked unconscious first, and there's no evidence of that.'

'That fits with her intending to shoot her victim and with him fighting back before she got the opportunity to kill him.'

'I don't know, Wendy. It doesn't seem to make sense to me. The Garda in Dublin have suspected Kruger of being a professional assassin for the last thirty months, but they've never been able to pin anything on her. She undoubtedly had links with Hanlon, and he was certainly involved with Grayling's outfit. How did someone as skilled as she's supposed to have been let someone get the better of her, and with her own gun? And her killer must have guessed there was a motorbike in the vicinity if he threw her helmet into the Trent.'

'What if he did? He wouldn't waste time looking for her bike. He'd want to get away as quickly as possible. It wasn't that obvious either, was it? The search team and SOCO had been there for most of the day, and the morning before, and they hadn't found the bike. She'd taken the precaution of hiding it a good distance from the lock.'

'Sounds like she planned it all with some care.'

'I agree, but something went very wrong and she ended up dead rather than her intended victim.'

Hooper shrugged his shoulders. 'Do you think her killer could have been using the Mercedes that was hired in Doyle's name? We haven't found any DNA or fingerprints anywhere because it was expertly valeted before it was returned to the hire company.'

'Anyone see a Merc at Cromwell?'

Hooper shook his head. 'No. No one saw anything at Cromwell. If anyone did, they're hardly likely to come forward given the reports in this morning's newspapers of a professional hit on the banks of the Trent.' He picked up a copy of the *Daily Mail* from the desk.

'I don't know where they got that from,' said Knight. 'The DCI refused to say anything when they approached him before we left Cromwell yesterday and you hadn't said anything to them earlier, had you?'

'Nothing beyond the agreed briefing, no. But they're already linking the two deaths. Look at the headline.'

'But Harry's not one for talking to the press.'

'Media speculation, I expect. They never let the facts get in the way of a good story. Mind you, they're probably right. And it doesn't take much working out. There's an obvious connection between the two.'

'Could it have been Doyle driving the Merc?' asked Knight. She knew she was clutching at straws.

'Come on, Wendy. How would he have got hold of it? Isn't it more likely that it was returned intact with the rental agreement in the glove compartment to make it *appear* that Doyle had been using it?'

Discussion of the case lapsed. Hooper went back to his desk and sat down, switched on his computer and scanned it for messages. He eventually looked up.

'Pardon the intrusion, but do you ever hear from Greg these days? I haven't heard a thing. Still in the States is he?'

Knight frowned. 'Greg Oldham? As far as I know, yes. I had a postcard about three weeks ago. He's thinking of moving to California. He doesn't like the climate in Boston. He's also managed to get himself engaged to some leggy American academic. They intend moving to Los Angeles together once he finds another post.'

Hooper paused. He couldn't help noticing the bitterness in Knight's voice. He knew that Wendy had been as good as engaged to Greg Oldham before he left for the States and he was already regretting raising the subject. He didn't want to open old wounds. 'Has he? I didn't know that. We used to meet up in the pub now and again, you know. I've heard hardly anything from him since he went to America, and nothing at all recently.'

'It's a phase of my life I consider to be over,' said Knight, with emphasis.

'And you're still stepping out with young Ray Craddock, are you?' said Hooper with a smile. 'He's your toyboy, is he?'

She gave him one of her looks. 'Stepping out? That sounds a bit old fashioned. Ray and I are friends – that's all there is to it. And I'm only four years older than he is; he's no toyboy.'

'Fancy a coffee,' said Hooper, realising he had struck another sore point. 'I'll make it if you like.' He got up and switched on the kettle.

Knight nodded and walked to the window overlooking the car park.

'Harry's back. He's parking his car at the moment. Better make him a cup too.'

'How does he take it? I've forgotten already.'

'Milk, no sugar.'

Hooper continued to mull over Wendy Knight's theory. 'Are you intending to tell him you think Kruger shot Manning?'

'Why not? I mentioned it yesterday, without having thought it through properly. He didn't seem over impressed – but he didn't dismiss it out of hand either. As you've just said, he does listen.'

'If you're right, it must follow that whoever killed her must have known her, otherwise, whoever he was, he wouldn't have agreed to meet up with her.'

'And she him, which puts Hanlon in the frame and her other associates.'

Hooper paused at length before replying. 'Problem is that apart from the Irishman, all the others are inside, either in the Republic or over here. And what chance do we have of locating Hanlon? He'll be long gone if he has any sense.' He concentrated his gaze on Knight. and sighed. 'There must be another explanation. But what it is, I simply don't know.'

'If we discount Hanlon, and I'm by no means sure that we should, there'll probably be others the O.C.G. can call on. For all we know, there could be people out there following orders who we have never heard of?' She paused for a moment. 'And they got Hanlon away, didn't they? Perhaps he's still around? He probably feels he owes them something. His escape was meticulously organised and this O.C.G. wouldn't carry out such an operation without demanding something in return. He'd have spent the rest of his life inside if they hadn't got him out of Shirebrook.'

Hooper did not reply. He turned and poured the now boiling water into three mugs as Hood walked through the door.

CHAPTER 9

Chief Inspector Hood returned to West Bridgford Police Station after attending a private briefing meeting with the ACC (Crime). The assistant chief constable, Bob Gaunt, had suggested running the enquiry from Newark, but Hood considered the facilities there inadequate and as it was too far from his home he had insisted on having his way. He knew he had the chief's full support and made that clear to the ACC and to the station's uniformed inspector who complained vociferously about the largest incident room being taken over by Hood's investigation. 'Chief constable's orders,' Hood told him. 'I'm sure you'll want to give me your full cooperation?'

He decided to retain the name which Acting Inspector Hooper had given to the Cromwell Lock inquiry, *"Operation Trent"*, and to apply it to the whole investigation. He took one gulp of the coffee Hooper had made then placed the mug down next to the kettle. Coffee-making was clearly not Hooper's *forté.*

'I'm surprised you haven't changed the name, sir,' said Wendy Knight, a cheeky grin crossing her face as the rest of the team began to arrive in the incident room. 'You usually choose a name of a character from Dickens or the title of one of his novels, don't you?'

Hood corrected her with a bemused smile. 'Always, not usually, Wendy. And what makes you think the word "Trent" doesn't have a Dickensian connection?' Knight shrugged her shoulders. 'Does it?'

'You've never read *The Old Curiosity Shop*?'

'Can't say I have, sir. I'm more into John Grisham or Michael Connelly.'

Hood shook his head but continued to smile. 'Well for your information, Little Nell, who's the main character in *The Old Curiosity Shop*, was one Nelly Trent. It all ended very sadly for her and her grandfather but so far as *Operation Trent* is concerned, it preserves my well-established practice of assigning a character from Dickens to all my major investigations. But if you and the rest of the team want to continue thinking it's named after the river, that's all right by me.' He paused and looked at Hooper, who gave Wendy Knight a knowing grin. He, unlike she, had read *The Old Curiosity Shop* which was why he had christened his investigation *Operation Trent*. The coincidence had appealed to him and he'd always been convinced that Detective Chief Inspector Hood would eventually take command. Knight knew when she was beaten. She sat down next to Police Constable Raymond Craddock, acting as a temporary DC, and the three uniformed officers who had been assigned to the team.

'He got you there,' whispered Raymond. Wendy, her cheeks reddening only slightly, nudged him with her elbow and pulled a face.

Hood continued in more serious vein as he called for silence and addressed his team. 'Now that little matter has been settled, I shall be introducing you, later, to Detective Sergeant Sean Smith, when he gets here.' He looked at his watch. 'He's on his way now from the lab in Leicester. He's a Yorkshireman, but don't let that put you off. Remember, that's where I started my career.' Wendy Knight pouted. Hood continued. 'I've asked him to join us because he has a particular expertise in forensic matters. In fact, he has a good honours degree in forensic science from Nottingham Trent, so we'll be making good use of him on this investigation.'

'Does that mean he'll be taking over the viewing of the CCTV, sir?' asked Craddock. 'There's still a lot of it to be examined.'

Hood frowned. 'I thought you enjoyed that sort of thing, Raymond.'

Craddock screwed up his face. Plainly, he didn't. 'Gets a bit boring, sir. It's usually easier with two or three of us doing it. And the WPC who's been assigned to assist me has gone off sick this morning, and I don't know when she'll be back.'

'Well, I'm sure he'll lend a hand, if he can find the time, but I doubt it. He'll be busy elsewhere. He's already made a start and established late yesterday that the briefcase found with the BMW motorcycle at

Cromwell has had a firearm in it at some time. There are definite traces of firearm residue. Whether it can be connected with the gun found in the river, we shall have to await further detailed scientific examination.'

'If he found firearm residue, that means the gun that was in there has probably been fired recently,' said Hooper.

'Correct,' replied Hood. 'It's a decent lead. We can also proceed now on the basis that the dead woman is Maxine Kruger. The information from Dublin has arrived together with a photograph and an unofficial fingerprint; the resemblance in the photograph is remarkable and Garda intelligence have a record of a surreptitiously obtained print of her left index finger – it's undoubtedly her. The Frankfurt police have also been very helpful. We now have a faxed copy of her birth certificate. Believe it or not, she was nearly thirty-nine years of age.'

'She was in good nick then,' said Knight, approvingly.

A low buzz went round the room as the various officers whispered their relief that a positive identification had been made. Hood continued.

'But it's the firearms residue in the briefcase that raises an interesting question. Wendy, what are your thoughts? Assuming, as I think we can, that the gun used in both killings was Kruger's, what does that tell us? Come on, now, all of you, think. Some of you had an easy day of it yesterday, but we need to move on.'

Knight put forward her previously expressed theory with new found confidence. 'Andrew and I were discussing a possible scenario this morning, sir.' She looked at Hooper, urging his support. He nodded his encouragement. 'It has occurred to us that Kruger may well be responsible for the death of Dudley Manning.' She paused, hoping for a reaction from the chief inspector, but he simply invited her to go on. 'Dublin reckons she may be a professional assassin. I know you didn't think you necessarily agreed with me when I mentioned it yesterday, but the firearms residue in the briefcase is surely supportive of what I was saying. As Andrew has just said, it's likely that the gun that was in there has been fired recently. Then there's the money; that could have been her pay-off. It would also explain how the gun ended up in the river. If it were her gun, her killer wouldn't have wanted to keep it. He'd want to get rid of it sharpish; throwing it in the river was the obvious solution.'

'But how do you account for her being at Cromwell?' asked the DCI. 'I agree with you that the fact she was in motorcycle leathers and must have travelled to Cromwell on her bike is a clear link to the incident at Trent Bridge. The gun strengthens that link. But what was she doing at Cromwell?'

Knight's enthusiasm waned somewhat. 'That's what we haven't yet figured out, apart from the fact that she must have met her killer there. Why they chose Cromwell, I have no idea. That the bike was hidden in the shed suggests that she probably arrived before her killer. Some sort of struggle must have taken place during which she was disarmed and shot. Then her body was rolled into the Trent.'

Hood turned to the whiteboard and ran his finger along the map of the River Trent. 'We can proceed on the basis that we know approximately where the deceased was when she was shot and when she was put into the river.' He pointed to the location marked on the plan. 'We also know more or less where her motorcycle helmet was found by the two boys DS Knight was speaking with yesterday afternoon – a nice bit of detective work, that, Wendy.' He smiled in her direction. 'Now, what else do we know?'

'The gun could have gone off in the struggle,' said Hooper. 'The powder burns on her leather jacket mean it must have been very close to her when it was fired and the defensive injuries indicate that the struggle must have been intense and fairly prolonged.'

'So, you think we're looking for a man?' asked Hood.

'Looks like it. From what Dr Kennedy said, Kruger was no weakling. It would have taken someone stronger to overpower her.'

Hood smiled. 'I think you're both on the right track, but there are one or two outstanding issues. Raymond, let's hear from you. Tell us what you've found on the CCTV so far.'

All eyes were on the young acting detective constable. He stood up before he began and moved to the front of the room.

'We have a short section showing the BMW motorcycle on the Newark bypass.'

'On the Sunday?' asked Knight.

'No,' answered Craddock. 'Late Saturday morning; eleven-fifty-seven hours. Heading north towards the A1 link.'

'On the Saturday?' queried Knight.

'On the Saturday. No sign of it at all on the Sunday. And I've been through hours of CCTV.'

Knight and Hooper looked at each other in puzzlement.

'She can't have been at Cromwell overnight on Saturday and all day Sunday, surely?' said Knight.

Hood said nothing. He'd spoken to Craddock earlier. He knew what was coming.

'There is something else,' continued Craddock, enjoying every second of his moment in the limelight. 'The Mercedes has been captured on the A46 on a speed camera. Whoever was driving it was well over the limit. Just under eighty miles an hour. There'll be a summons heading in his direction.'

'That's the least of his worries,' said Knight. 'Date, time and direction?'

'Same day, Saturday last, fourteen-twenty-two hours, heading south. There's a camera just past Cropwell Bishop.'

'Over two hours after Kruger's bike was spotted going north?'

'Exactly,' said Hood. 'But travelling in the opposite direction. Go on, Wendy. What does that tell you?'

She considered the details revealed by the speed camera before saying anything further. 'It's just possible that someone in the Mercedes was giving her a lift back south after she'd stored the bike in the shed at Cromwell.'

Hood was encouraged by her response. 'And?'

She frowned. 'I'm lost, sir. Why would she want to hide the bike at Cromwell and leave it there? Along with her ten grand and her passport too. Then get a lift back south?'

'Anyone else have any thoughts?' asked Hood. 'We need to look at all the evidence in the round, don't you think? We mustn't let this latest information distract us from the full picture.'

No one said anything.

'Is the driver shown?' asked Hooper, after a minute or so.

'No,' replied Craddock. 'It was a Gatso rear-facing camera. Just the back was recorded, including the number plate. There's no doubt it was the recovered Mercedes.'

'And no further sign of the bike?' asked Knight.

'Not on the Sunday, no,' said Craddock. 'Not at all, in fact. Never picked up again, not on what I've seen so far, which is hardly surprising. It never moved from the shed on Lock Lane. As you're aware, I visited the address of the registered keeper in Long Eaton early this morning. Fake. It's in a small block of flats. Number seven has been vacant for as long as anyone can remember. None of the neighbours had any idea who was supposed to be living there. I got in touch with the landlord. It hasn't been rented out for over eighteen months. He wants to demolish the building. He's waiting for the other tenancies to expire so he can redevelop the site.'

'And no one had seen her there?' asked Hooper.

'No, sir. She's just used the address and the post code to register the bike. If it was ever checked, it would then have come up legit on our systems.'

'Taxed and insured too?'

Craddock nodded. 'Yes, according to our computer records. All done by phone with one of the main internet insurers. The premium was paid by credit card in the name of Monica King.'

'Someone's been very careful. We are obviously not dealing with amateurs.'

Hood looked at the serious faces in front of him. 'Come on,' he said, showing a modicum of impatience. 'It appears the bike was never moved after it was placed in the shed in Lock Lane. What else do we know was happening over the week-end in question? Think about it.'

The officers looked at one another. Hooper eventually spoke.

'Was the Mercedes picked up anywhere on CCTV on the Sunday?'

'No,' replied Craddock. 'If it was out and about that day the driver must have kept to the speed limit. But there's still a lot of CCTV to be checked. I haven't even started on the material from Leicester City Council. It's a massive task.'

'Doyle went to Barnard House near Hungarton on Sunday by taxi, didn't he?' said Hooper.

Hood's eyes lit up. Now his team were applying their minds to the whole of the evidence. 'Yes, he did. We know that for a fact, but when and how did he leave? He wasn't there when we arrived.'

Knight was the next to react. 'That's what we don't know, sir. The cabbie called us just after seventeen hundred hours because he'd not heard from him.'

'Well, let's just think about that, shall we? It means he didn't leave in the same way that he arrived. When we arrived there later, the house was well ablaze. Julia Hamilton was nowhere to be seen; neither was her current paramour, assuming he was with her. She left for Portugal from Coventry airport in a private plane with an IC one male who we can be sure was not Doyle. Question: what happened to Doyle?'

'He could have died in the fire,' suggested one of the uniformed officers.

'I think we can exclude that as a possibility,' replied Hood. 'We have no evidence that he died in the fire.'

'He certainly wasn't about when we got there,' said Hooper, 'and we had a good look around. The whole area was carefully searched. We even used the dog team.'

'If he's still alive, he must have left Barnard House then,' said Hood. 'He had no transport of his own. How did he make his way from Hungarton? On foot?'

'In the Mercedes?' queried Knight, half-heartedly. She hadn't really thought through what she was saying. A moment's pause then she got to her feet. 'Got it!' she said. Her excitement was written all over her face. 'It all fits. Doyle was in the Mercedes, but not as a willing passenger. He was driven to Cromwell by Kruger. She intended to kill him and dump him in the Trent, just like she'd done with Manning. But

Doyle resisted, and in fighting for his life, the gun was discharged. She ended up in the river instead of him. Doyle drives the Mercedes back to Leicester, taking great care to keep to the speed limits, gets it valeted and leaves it outside the owner's premises. That also explains why her bike was still in the shed at Cromwell.'

Hood smiled. He was not in the least surprised that it was Wendy Knight who'd put all the evidence together and come up with the most likely explanation, a conclusion he had already reached himself, but with one outstanding issue.

'And the bike?' he asked.

'The bike, sir?'

'Yes, the bike. Why did she go to all the trouble of hiding her motorcycle in the shed at Cromwell? And why Cromwell?'

'And leave her passport and ten thousand pounds in the panier?' added Hooper.

'She must have required it to get away, I suppose, after she'd disposed of Doyle?' said Knight. 'And we were told when we were at Cromwell yesterday that no one was working at the quarry over the week-end, so it was pretty safe leaving the money and passport with the bike.'

'But on your theory, she had the Mercedes. Why did she need the bike as well? And what is significant about Cromwell? It's a fair way from Hungarton. Come on now, think it through.' Hood gave Knight an encouraging look.

Blank faces all round. The DCI was obliged to come to the rescue. 'Has it occurred to any of you that the plan might not have been to shoot Doyle, but to leave him, unconscious in the car with the gun that had been used to kill Dudley Manning, and to drive or push the Merc into the river with him still in it? It has an automatic gear box, remember, so it would not be a problem getting it into the Trent. It might also explain how he got his hands on the gun. Perhaps it was always intended to be found in his possession and it goes some way to explain why Cromwell was chosen. No problem pushing a vehicle into the Trent at that location while the river is in flood. There aren't that many places where you can get a car into the river without attracting attention. And the Trent was certainly deep enough at the time to make sure he would have drowned had the plan succeeded.' His thoughts turned to the ten soldiers who had been unable to save themselves back in nineteen seventy-five.

The full explanation now dawned on Knight. 'That's why the bike was there. The Merc was going in the river with Doyle, so she needed the bike for her getaway.'

'But somehow, Doyle got the better of her,' said Craddock, annoyed with himself that he hadn't come up with the now obvious explanation.

'Are you saying he shot her deliberately, sir?' asked Hooper.

'Not necessarily. The gun could have gone off in the struggle.'

'And after she was shot?'

'I don't suppose Doyle wanted to be caught with the gun, so he threw it in the river along with her helmet. She went in as well. He probably thought that's where she'd intended he should end up, so he paid her the compliment of doing the same with her.'

'Perhaps he didn't put her in the river?' said Craddock. 'It is tidal. If the water rose during the night, she could just have been carried into the water from where he left her.'

'Possibly, but unlikely,' said Hood. 'The water level has been gradually receding over the last week, according to the lockkeeper.'

'Case solved then,' added Hooper, cynically. 'Kruger murdered Manning. She tried to murder Doyle, but he got the better of her. Self-defence or accident. Case closed.' He shrugged his shoulders. 'Though I suppose we could always do him for concealing a body?'

Hood smiled. 'Hardly case closed, Andrew. This remains very much a theory and a work in progress, but we need evidence. And the first thing we need to do is to find Doyle.'

'If this is what happened,' said Craddock, 'why has he not made contact with us? If he's innocent, why not surrender himself?'

Hooper answered the question. 'He's just out of the nick. He probably thinks we wouldn't believe him. The last thing he'll want is to go back inside.'

'Hang on a minute,' continued Craddock. 'If Doyle was an unwilling passenger, he must have been restrained in some way. If he was, how did he get the better of Kruger? And how did he get hold of the gun?'

'Good question,' said Hood. 'Anyone?'

'Perhaps he was tied up, but she released him before she intended putting him in the river,' suggested Knight. 'She'd have to do that to make it look realistic.'

'That wouldn't work,' said Hooper, with a shake of his head. 'He'd have to be incapacitated in some way, or he would have tried to save himself once the Merc went into the river with him in it. He would have to have been rendered unconscious. He must have come round just in time.'

Wendy Knight was forced to agree. 'Bad timing on her part then. But if we'd found him dead in the river with the murder weapon, we'd probably have concluded he'd killed Manning. That's what Kruger must have hoped we'd believe.'

'Absolutely,' said Hooper.

'And it would certainly have removed suspicion from her,' added Knight, 'at least temporarily.'

'This can't have been her idea, though,' continued Hooper. 'Someone put Kruger up to this; someone who wanted Doyle dead. He wasn't just being used to divert responsibility for Manning's death from her. Someone wanted him out of the way, permanently.'

'I think you've hit the nail on the head there, Andrew. That's exactly what's worrying me,' said Hood. 'Whoever wanted him dead will have worked out by now that he's still alive and that it's Maxine Kruger who is no longer with us. Incidentally, her name is being released later this afternoon, so it will be all over the media pretty shortly. I wanted it withheld for the time being but I was overruled by the ACC. The top brass want it known we're making progress. They're also pleased we have located almost the exact spot where Kruger was shot, thanks to the PC who found the discharged cartridge.'

'PC Henshaw, sir,' said Knight. 'He did well; most of the others were for giving up when he found it.'

'He's an example to us all. No giving up on this one. And I mean that. With Kruger dead, Doyle is or will become a target.' He adopted a serious tone as he looked at each individual member of his team. 'I don't want any more pointless deaths and I don't want Doyle trying to sort this himself. If he's still obsessed with Julia Hamilton, as I suspect he is, he could well go after whoever arranged for him to be killed.'

'Will he know who wanted him dead?' asked Craddock.

'I should think so. I have a nasty feeling he met up with whoever has taken over from Gus Grayling when he went to Barnard House. I also suspect that this individual, whoever he is, has taken over Julia Hamilton too. Doyle's not going to like that. Unless we manage to stop it, I foresee a confrontation which will result in the death of one or the other, or both.'

'But Julia Hamilton and her new man are probably in Portugal. If Doyle goes out there, we have no jurisdiction. What can we do?'

'We stop him, Wendy. I have already instructed all ports and airports to look out for him.' He sighed. 'My gut feeling is that he's still here in the Midlands. We need to find him and fast. I want every address linked to Doyle checked, with the exception of his apartment at Harbour Buildings. That's been under surveillance since he was released. He hasn't been there.'

'Does that include addresses linked to the Hamilton woman?' asked Knight.

'Of course.' Hood smiled. 'I'll decide later whether we need to send anyone out to Portugal. No doubt there'll be plenty of volunteers for that assignment.'

Wendy Knight laughed and glanced towards Ray Craddock who looked equally keen.

'Before anyone gets carried away and starts booking any plane tickets, there's another problem we need to think about,' said Hooper.

Hood looked at him. 'Go on, Andrew.'

'As Maxine Kruger failed to kill Doyle, if he's still in the UK and the man who wants him dead is in Portugal, he'll have to use another paid assassin to carry out the execution. He's not going to give up. If anything, the death of Kruger will make him more determined. We don't generally go in for assassinations in this country, which means whoever gets the job is likely to come in from abroad. That means we're starting from scratch in finding him. We have no idea who he is or where he'll come from. The question is, how, exactly, do we go about locating him?'

'You think it must be a man?' asked Wendy Knight. 'It could be a woman. After all, Maxine Kruger was a woman.'

Hood nodded. 'I agree with you. Locating an assassin, of either sex, will be almost impossible. That's why we need to find Doyle and get him into protective custody. At least we know who we're looking for when it comes to him. He has obviously gone to ground. He'll not make his whereabouts obvious.' He paused ominously. 'A professional assassin is a whole new ball game. Doyle has managed to save himself from one attempt on his life; he may not be so lucky second time around. And we need to bear fully in mind this assassin could already be here. All it would take is a phone call for someone in the know.'

'Have we turned anything up yet from the phone number we've issued to the public?' asked Craddock. 'Apart from the usual cranks and nutters, that is.'

'Nothing, yet,' replied Hood. 'The phone is being manned twenty-four-seven. There's an outside chance someone will know something and get in touch, but I doubt we'll be hearing from either Doyle or the assassin.'

'What will you be doing, sir?' asked Knight. 'While we look for Doyle.'

'I'm going to see Derick Duffy. I shall take DS Smith with me, if he ever gets here.' He looked at his watch again. 'We need to find out who has taken over Gus Grayling's operation. I reckon Duffy's the only person, apart from Doyle, who knows. He was once very close to Gus Grayling. I'm going to have to persuade him to tell me. Andrew, I want you and Wendy to continue to organise the search for Doyle. Let me know as soon as anything turns up.'

CHAPTER 10

Detective Chief Inspector Hood and Detective Sergeant Sean Smith arrived at Woodborough Prison deep in the Northamptonshire countryside on Wednesday afternoon. Derick Duffy was detained in a separate part of the prison, well away from the other inmates. Arrangements were already in hand to move him elsewhere, not that he would be told where until the move was underway. It was with some reluctance that he walked the short distance to a carefully prepared room where he and Hood were scheduled to meet. Police officers were not exempt from the usual security procedures at Woodborough High Security Prison; both Hood and Smith were thoroughly searched, their fingerprints recorded and their photographs taken before being admitted. Duffy was lounging on one of three hard-backed chairs when the two police officers entered the room. He looked up and scowled.

'Hello, Derick,' said Hood. 'How are you?'

'How do you think?' replied Duffy. His tone was hardly friendly. 'As you can see. I'm still alive. Who's this with you?'

'Detective Sergeant Sean Smith,' replied the man who was the subject of Duffy's inquiry. He and Hood took the other two seats on the side of the table nearest the door. The table was securely fixed to the floor, as were the three chairs.

'I don't know you, do I?' said Duffy, looking at Smith.

'We haven't met before,' replied DS Smith. 'I'm fairly new in these parts. I was with South Yorkshire until four months ago.'

Duffy stood up and turned his back on the two detectives.

'I'm saying nothing while he's here, or them.' He half-turned and pointed to the two prison officers who were still in the room, standing by the closed door.

Hood sighed. 'Do you mind, Sean?' He nodded to the two prison officers. 'You can go too. I don't suppose I shall be very long. Perhaps you can get DS Smith a coffee or something? And I'll be safe enough with Derick. We are old friends.' He smiled. Duffy did not reciprocate.

Smith stood up, gave Hood a puzzled look, then left the room with the two officers. The chief inspector paused until the door closed behind them. He heard the lock turn. Nothing was said for over a minute. Duffy returned to the table and sat down, then shifted in his seat in the silence, trying but failing to get comfortable. Hood waited another few seconds before he spoke. 'You asked to see me, Derick. I hope you're not wasting my time? It's quite a long drive to Woodborough from Nottingham.'

Duffy grunted his reply. 'So I did.'

'Which is fortunate, because I was hoping you might be able to help me.'

'Help you? Why should I help you? It's because of you I'm stuck in here. Do you know, this is the fifth prison I've been in since I was arrested? And I shan't be here much longer. They'll be moving me on again soon.'

'When?'

'I don't know, do I? They'll not tell me until they start the process. Security. But it's on the cards. I've seen the signs. At least it proves that someone wants to keep me alive.'

'I thought you'd be safe enough here. It took me over twenty minutes to get through security.'

'No one's trying to kill you, though, are they? I shan't be safe anywhere, not until I'm in my grave.' He glared at Hood. 'And I'm not sure they wouldn't try and get at me there.'

The DCI shook his head. 'As I understand it, it's your decision not to cooperate with efforts to proceed with your application for early release on parole.'

'Early release? And how long do you think I'd last out there? Look what happened to Michael Doyle. He took his chance and they did for him. I'm safer inside.'

Hood was not expecting a reference to Doyle. 'What do you know about Doyle?'

'Only what I pick up from the screws. They reckon he's dead. He hasn't come forward has he? I do read the newspapers you know. There's bugger all else to do in here.'

Hood hesitated before replying. 'No, he hasn't come forward but that doesn't surprise me. But he isn't dead – I have every reason to believe he's still alive. He's simply gone to ground.' Hood leant forward and lowered his voice. 'I also believe that an attempt was made to kill him, but it failed.'

Duffy half-smiled. 'Did it? They'll get him in the end, though. They always do. If it wasn't for my file, do you think I'd still be breathing?'

'Your file? There really is one? I was beginning to think it existed only in your imagination.'

'Of course it exists. Don't think I don't know why you want my help. You want it, don't you? Well, you can whistle for it.'

He sat back in his seat and folded his arms.

Hood hardly reacted. 'If that's all that's keeping you alive, you must have some pretty useful information about this O.C.G. and the way it operates.'

'Grayling's dead but the O.C.G. is still operating. And you haven't a clue who's taken over, have you?'

'I know about Gus Grayling. I went to his funeral. Very sparsely attended for one who had damaged so many lives. Seemed to be overlooked by the media.'

'I think he put an "X" in the no publicity box.' Duffy laughed.

Hood paused for a moment. 'You were careful to make sure he was dead before you said anything to me last year, remember? Very sensible in the circumstances. And you're right. I do want to know who has taken over from him. Who's running his criminal operation now?'

'What makes you think I would know that?'

'Come on, Derick. You and Gus were as thick as thieves at one time. It was Grayling who set you up in South Wales using a false identity. We know it isn't Doyle or you. That leaves the Irishman Hanlon and…'

Duffy interrupted. 'Hanlon?' He laughed. 'No chance. I'll give you that for free. He's a fucking psychopath is Hanlon. There's no way he could run such a sophisticated operation. Gus used him for muscle, that's all. You're way off beam thinking he's your man.'

'Who else? I know we live in an age of equal opportunities, but I don't see Julia Hamilton running Gus's old empire, do you?'

Duffy scoffed. 'Hamilton has the brains, but there are more credible candidates.' He smiled. 'She certainly gave you lot the run around though, didn't she? Acquitted by a jury, even though she was as guilty as hell. I read all about it.' He looked down. 'I was telling the truth in my evidence, you know.'

Hood nodded. 'I know you were. We'd have had her if it hadn't been for Hanlon doing a runner. Taking off like he did undermined the entire case.'

Duffy gave Hood a harsh look. 'And look what it did for me. Not only am I regarded as a grass by Hanlon and some others, I gave evidence against Hamilton, which is as good as signing my own death warrant. I'm not very popular in here you know. There are at least half a dozen in this prison who'd happily slit my throat without giving me the time of day if they could get at me. I repeat, why should I help you?'

Hood pressed on. 'Do you know who's taken over from Gus Grayling?'

'I have a good idea, yes.'

'Are you going to tell me?'

'I am not. You're the detective, work it out.'

'Do you know who Julia Hamilton's new lover is?'

Duffy smiled. 'One and the same, I reckon, but I suspect you've already worked that much out.' He sighed in frustration. 'I wasn't allowed in court when she gave her evidence, you know. They'd shipped me back here by the time she was in the box. Missed Hanlon's evidence too. I only know what I read in the papers and I don't suppose they were allowed to print the whole story. Getting Hanlon away must have taken some doing. It would have taken a lot of bottle and a hell of a lot of resources to achieve what they achieved.' He paused and leant forward. 'They weren't interested in Hanlon at all, you know. It was all done to undermine my evidence and get Hamilton off. And you let it happen. You assured me she'd be convicted if I turned Queen's.'

He turned away, his continuing frustration all too obvious.

'Not down to us, Derick. We couldn't foresee what Hanlon was up to. Anyway, he escaped from prison not from the court. We had the court fully secure.'

'But you didn't see it coming, did you? I always suspected something like that would happen. I should never had agreed to cooperate and give evidence. Hanlon and Hamilton getting away as they have makes it impossible for me to accept early parole, even if it was offered. I'd be dead in no time, whatever protection was provided.'

Silence.

'Well, that's all water under the bridge,' said Hood, eventually. 'We can't do anything about it now. What about Gus's successor? If it is Hamilton's new lover, I need to know who he is.'

Duffy smiled. 'It would really be a feather in your cap if you pulled him in, wouldn't it?'

'So it is a he, is it?'

'No comment.'

'And this file of yours, where is it?'

'Where you'll never get your hands on it.' He paused, then smirked. 'It's with my solicitors – not the ones who represented me in the Crown Court – another firm – a firm that doesn't dirty its hands by representing the likes of me in the criminal courts. Why do you think I went to them?'

'And this file contains what?'

'Enough to put several villains away for good, including whoever's taken over the O.C.G. from Gus Grayling.'

'So, you do know who Gus's successor is?'

Duffy looked around him, then nodded. 'As I said, I have a good idea, although I am a bit out of touch these days. But I doubt if much has changed. It's in my file along with a lot more.'

'But you won't tell me who it is? We already know that Gus left all his legitimate estate to some charity.'

'Peanuts, I suspect. His real money will be elsewhere – well out of reach of you.'

'That wouldn't surprise me. Now, are you prepared to tell me who has taken over from him?'

'Be serious, Mr Hood. If I did, I'd be dead before supper. You've got to understand my position. Take those two prison officers who brought you in here. Do you think they're going to keep schtum about my seeing you? Of course they won't. The hard men in here will probably know before lockup that I've been talking to you. And it will get passed back. There are few secrets in this place.'

Hood could hardly dispute what Duffy had said. He was certainly putting himself at risk in talking to the police. 'Why did you ask to see me, then?'

'I want you to do something for me.'

'Oh, yes. What would that be?'

Duffy hesitated before replying. 'It's my daughter, Kelly. She's having a hard time inside and she won't make parole for at least another ten years, assuming she lives that long. She's being targeted, and you don't need me to tell you where the pressure is coming from.'

'What do you think I can do about it?'

Duffy leant forward. 'Look, Mr Hood. I don't care about myself. They'll get me in the end, just like they'll get Doyle. But Kelly is different. She's still young. She has the best years of her life in front of her. I don't want her spending those years locked up with who knows what. I want you to bring her parole forward. Don't get me wrong. I know she'll have to do a bit longer, but another ten or twelve years? That's inhuman.'

'She did fire a shotgun into the rear doors of a security van.'

Duffy shrugged his shoulders. 'What if she did? It was a security van full of armed police. It's hardly the same thing is it? It was a set-up.'

'And she took part in the kidnapping of a judge's wife and child. That is understandably regarded as a very serious offence. Not the sort of thing that should be encouraged.'

'But she didn't hurt anyone. She made sure the kid was okay. That's the only reason she was there. She's not really a serious villain. It was the excitement that attracted her.' He paused briefly. 'And me, of course. I blame myself to some extent. I needed her to case the judge's house. No one else could have carried that off as well as she did, pretending to be a potential purchaser. If the judge's house hadn't been for sale, I don't know how we would have got inside it prior to the kidnapping.'

'Well she's certainly paying the price for all that excitement now. The Lord Chief Justice thought her role was pivotal, if you remember, when you were all sentenced. He didn't shrink from sending her down for a long time. He certainly was not influenced by the fact she's a young woman with no previous to speak of.'

Duffy shrugged. 'Brought in special, wasn't he, because of what happened to the judge and his wife and the attempt to blackmail him? I nearly had a heart attack when my brief told me we were in front of him.'

'Well he certainly handed out the porridge. And you got nowhere on appeal either, as I recall.'

Hood raised an eyebrow. He had been very pleased with the sentences imposed.

Duffy looked away. 'Refused leave, not that I was expecting we'd get anywhere.' He paused at length then cleared his throat. 'Look, Mr Hood. If you help her, I'll let you know where my file is.'

'And give me access?'

Duffy looked about him and whispered his reply. 'Not until I know you've kept your side of the bargain. I want a letter personally signed by the Home Secretary undertaking that my daughter will be paroled within the next, say, three years.' He paused. 'I'm not daft. As I said, I realise she'll have to do longer than she has. She's been moved to a new prison because of the threats she's had to endure. I don't want her going through what I've had to put up with. It's never ending, you know. Makes life hardly worth living.'

Hood drew in his breath. 'That may not be as easy to bring about as you think, Derick.'

'Up to you, Mr Hood. Someone managed it for Doyle; they can do the same for my Kelly. My solicitor cannot give you access to my file without my consent. I understand enough law to know that.'

'I could always get a warrant.'

'Just you try. You know as well as me it would be set aside. My solicitor is an expert on this sort of thing. He knows what he's doing or I wouldn't have gone to him. You have no grounds. This conversation isn't being recorded. I'll deny I said anything to you. You can't get a warrant for something you can't even prove exists. And even if you could prove it exists, you have no idea what it contains. Reasonable grounds, Mr Hood? I don't think so.'

Hood exhaled. He knew Duffy was right. 'What if something happens to you?'

'My solicitor has instructions to send the file to the Home Secretary. Those who want me dead know that. That's why I'm still around.'

'Is there only the one copy?'

'Yes.'

'Isn't it risky not to have taken copies?'

'There are no copies. That's the way I want it.'

Hood paused. He stood up and walked around the table before resuming his seat. 'You'll have to give me more than that if you want me to approach the Home Office. They'll do nothing without some hard evidence that this file of yours actually exists. And they'll be wary of doing another deal about parole. The arrangement with Doyle has hardly turned out to be the success we hoped for.'

Duffy gave Hood an angry look. 'I don't care about Doyle. I don't want my Kelly stuck inside for the next twelve years. Is that clear enough? And I know these threats are genuine. She tried to keep it from me but she was in tears during our last but one phone call while she was still in Stafford. Someone's put the word out. She wasn't safe where she was. That's why she's been moved. Much safer where she is now. She'll be much happier.'

'Who was responsible for the threats while she was at Stafford?'

Duffy sighed. 'Who do you think? The same lot who want to finish me off.'

'What sort of threats?'

'They want my file.'

Hood nodded. 'It's in her interests that you help me then.'

Duffy shook his head. 'Oh, no. Give me some credit, Mr Hood. Once I lose control of that file, you could stitch me up like a kipper. I'd have nothing left to bargain with.'

Hood lowered his eyes before looking up. 'I can't just accept your word that this file exists. I have to have more. Be reasonable, Derick.'

'It exists all right.' He paused. 'I suppose I could get my solicitor to confirm it.'

'Does he know what it contains?'

Duffy gave Hood a condescending look and shook his head. 'Of course he doesn't. What do you take me for? And only the senior partner knows anything about it.' He frowned. 'I had to pay him enough for him to agree to the arrangement.'

'That's lawyers for you,' sighed Hood. 'But I can't see the Home Office doing anything to help Kelly unless you give me something solid. Michael Doyle has created an unfortunate precedent. They'll need some persuading to repeat the exercise.'

'It will all be revealed once I know she will get early parole. It'll mean the end of me, but I might as well be dead, living like I do. My only concern is for Kelly. It's the least I can do for her. I wasn't much of a father to her when she was growing up. I was inside for most of her childhood.'

Hood let out a lengthy sigh. 'We seem to be in a Catch-22 situation, Derick. You won't reveal anything without a parole decision and I can't progress any such application without evidence. These things are given very careful consideration, you know. Doyle was a special case. Kelly does not fall into the same category.'

Duffy stood up and turned away from Hood. 'You'd better get her into the same category or I'll be going back to my cell. We are obviously wasting each other's time.'

'Sit down,' ordered the chief inspector. 'We haven't finished yet.'

Duffy glared at him but retook his seat. He swallowed hard then looked Hood directly in the eye.

'So, you can't or won't help me.'

Hood pondered the position. He just had to get hold of that file. If it contained only half of what Duffy claimed it would accelerate his investigation and would lead to the identification of Grayling's successor. 'Look, I'll speak to the relevant assistant chief constable, Anne Davies. She's our liaison officer with the Home Office. I can't promise anything, not yet. And it isn't my decision anyway, or hers. But I should be able to find out if it's worth taking the matter further.' He leant forward. 'But it would help if you could give me something. Anything to prove this isn't another wild goose chase.'

Duffy breathed out heavily. 'I was right about what I told you before, wasn't I? I put myself at considerable risk. And I gave evidence for you against Julia Hamilton. You owe me, Mr Hood.'

'That was then. This is now.'

Duffy paused at length. 'All right. But you keep this to yourself. My solicitor is William Worth. His firm have offices in Leicester, Nottingham and Derby. He's usually found in the Leicester office. Worth, Ambler and Partners; that's what they call themselves. He'll confirm they have my file and the instructions I gave him. I'll phone him later and give him permission to reveal that the file exists. But to you, and only to you. I want that clearly understood. I don't want this being the subject of gossip amongst the police generally. But I'm not giving my consent for you to have access. Not yet. You do your bit first.'

Hood smiled. 'Thank you, Derick. That, at least, is a start. I'll visit him. tomorrow.'

He stood up and banged on the door, then turned towards Duffy. 'I'll be in touch.'

'You'd better be.'

* * *

'You told him, I hope?' asked the escorting prison officer, Brian

Logan, as Duffy began the short walk back to his cell.

'I did as I was told,' replied Duffy. 'You make sure your contact gets to know.'

'He will. Should keep you alive for a bit longer, I shouldn't wonder.'

Duffy grimaced. The officer, a heavily built man in his middle forties, smirked as they turned the corner in the corridor and headed towards Duffy's cell. Duffy was still not sure he had done the right thing. He couldn't for the life of him figure out why he had been ordered to do what he just had.

'I haven't given him access, you know. I've only told him the name of my solicitor. Nothing more.' He paused then added, cynically, 'And your people already knew that. I don't know how they found out and I don't understand why they insisted I had to be the one to tell Hood.'

'Don't you worry your head about it.'

'But why involve me? They could have got the information to Hood some other way if they'd really wanted to.'

'Ours not to reason why, Derick.'

Duffy stopped and looked the officer in the eye. 'And my daughter will be safe, will she?'

'No one will lay a finger on her. That was the deal. Shows you what a bit of cooperation can do. And she's in a much better place. Brampton Hall is more like a holiday camp than a prison. I reckon she's half-way to parole already.'

'But why did they want me to tell Hood where my file is? I can't get my head around that at all.'

'I don't know, do I?' replied Logan. 'I don't know any more than you. I don't even know who "they" are. I'm just the messenger. I do as I'm told. I'm no different from you when it comes to it except I can go home at the end of my shift. Anyway, you'll have plenty of time to figure it out. You haven't got anything on tonight have you?' He smiled broadly. 'Not going anywhere are we?'

Duffy frowned. 'You'll remember asking me that question later and you won't be smiling. I can promise you that.' Logan gave him a puzzled look before Duffy continued. 'I also need to phone my solicitor. I have to give my consent so he can confirm that he has my file.'

'I'll arrange that for you. You'll have to use the phone in the wing office. We can't have you queuing up with the others, can we? That wouldn't be safe.'

The officer grinned. Duffy said nothing more. They walked on in silence until they reached his cell. Duffy continued to lead an increasingly isolated existence in Woodborough. His only contact was with prison officers, apart from his monthly meeting with the governor and the occasional telephone call with his daughter. Hood had been his only visitor since he arrived at Woodborough two months before. The officer remained at the door and ushered his prisoner inside.

'Where am I being moved to?' asked Duffy, collapsing on his bed.

'How should I know? You think they'd tell me that? What makes you think you're about to be moved?'

'Just a feeling I have. I never stay anywhere more than a few months. You could find out where and when if you wanted to. I need to know.'

'Why? Planning to escape are we?' The officer laughed.

Duffy looked away and scowled. 'That'll be the day. There's only one way I'll get away from all this.' He spun round and faced Logan, raising his voice in anger. 'I can't take much more, you know. I'm warning you. I've just about had enough. Moved from pillar to post and seeing no one, apart from the likes of you bastards. I need to know where I'm going next.'

The officer appeared shocked. 'Calm down, Derick. You'll be fine. Just do as they say and everything will be okay.'

Duffy turned over on his bed and faced the wall.

Logan sighed then relented. 'All right. I'll see what I can do. I'll see if I can get a look at your paperwork, but it will take time. I have to be careful. Sweet dreams. I'll be back when I've organised that phone call.'

The cell door clanged shut.

CHAPTER 11

Michael Doyle woke with a sudden start. He hadn't intended to fall asleep again. He looked at his imitation Rolex watch and silently cursed. It was almost four o'clock. The front door bell of Sycamore Cottage was ringing intermittently. *Was it the agent with a potential purchaser?* He got up from the bed and crept silently to the bedroom window which overlooked the front of the cottage. He was careful to remain hidden behind the curtain as he looked outside. He observed a black BMW parked immediately opposite on Rearsby Road. He was sure that it had not been there before. Confident he would remain concealed behind the curtains, he focused his attention on a man dressed in dark clothing standing close to the front door as the bell rang yet again. The man had dark brown hair and appeared to be about six feet tall. Whoever he was, he certainly seemed impatient. Doyle remained calm. He started to think and realised it could not have been the agent; he'd have had his own keys. Could it be someone looking for Julia or her mother? He took a closer look. The visitor suddenly stepped back and looked up at the first-floor windows, prompting Doyle to move quickly back and to the side. The man shrugged his shoulders and about-turned as if to return to the BMW, when the neighbour from the adjacent house came out into the street. She must have heard the doorbell ringing. Doyle moved to the side window to get a better view. The transom was open just enough for him to hear what was being said. He could now see the man's features and noticed he was wearing what appeared to be a clerical collar.

'Can I help you?' asked the woman. She sounded suspicious until the man took a few steps towards her. She, too, then noticed his collar.

'Is this the Hamilton residence?' smiled the man.

'Yes,' replied the neighbour. 'But Mrs Hamilton isn't here. She's in

Portugal. As you can see, she's put her cottage up for sale. I don't think she has any intention of returning. I promised to keep an eye on things for her until a sale is agreed.'

'Is that so?' said the man. He sounded friendly enough. 'Well, it was her daughter's partner I was after seeing. I have some news about his mother in Ireland. She's not been at all well.'

Doyle froze as he heard those words.

'I wouldn't know about that,' said the neighbour. 'The only man I've ever seen Julia with more than once is a rascal by the name of Michael Doyle. He stayed here with Julia a couple of times. But that was some time ago. He got himself involved in a serious robbery a year or two back and was sent to prison. It was in all the papers. But I think he's out now.'

The man appeared surprised. 'Is that right? I didn't know about any robbery. His mother never mentioned it, but I suppose she wouldn't. But he's the man I'm looking for, Michael Doyle. That would definitely be the same man would it?'

'I wasn't really on speaking terms with him, but that was his name. I remember Peggy – that's Mrs Hamilton – mentioning him. I don't think she was very keen on him, to tell you the truth. And I don't think you'll see him round these parts again. He'll have gone to Portugal with Julia.' She paused. 'I can give him a message if he does turn up here again.' She dropped her voice and looked about her. 'I believe the police are looking for him, according to what I read in the *Mercury*.'

'Now, why would that be?'

'I have no idea, but he's trouble, that one. You mark my words.'

'Well, I wouldn't know about any trouble. I came over here on church business. I saw Michael's mother last month. She wanted me to ask after him, that's all. This was the address she gave me. She's been in hospital in Dublin, you see. That's how I came to meet her. I do some part-time chaplaincy work at the infirmary there. She's anxious that her son should get in touch with her. That's all.'

Doyle relaxed. He knew his mother had not been in hospital recently. The reference to Dublin was bogus. His mother lived miles away from there.

'You're a vicar, are you?' asked the woman, eying his collar.

'A priest, yes. My parish is back in Dublin though.'

The woman glanced at the BMW.

'You must be doing very well in your parish back in Dublin. That's a very expensive-looking car you have.'

The man laughed. 'Don't you be taking any notice of that. It's hired. I booked a Series Three, but they upgraded me for some reason. But I have to confess, it's sweet to drive. I have an old Escort back home. The difference is amazing.'

The woman seemed satisfied with the explanation. 'If I see him, I'll pass on your concerns, but I don't think he'll come here again, and I shall be away for a couple of days from tomorrow. Visiting relatives in London.'

'Any sign of this place selling?' asked the priest, glancing at the sale board.

'Oh, yes. There have been a number of people looking the place over. It's only been on the market for about ten days. It'll go pretty quickly. Thrussington is a very popular village, you know.'

The man looked up at the cottage again.

'I don't suppose Mrs Hamilton left you with a key?'

'I'm sorry. No, she didn't. The agents have the only keys. Perhaps you should get in touch with them. Their phone number is on the sign. A young couple looked at the cottage only yesterday. They seemed very keen.'

The man nodded and sighed. He took another look at the signboard but didn't take down the telephone number.

'Well, I'd better be on my way. There's obviously nothing for me here. But thank you for your help. And God bless. You'll remember what I said if Michael should make an appearance?'

'Should I mention your name to him, if he does happen to turn up?'

The man hesitated. 'Father O'Brien. Gerry O'Brien.'

'I'll do that,' said the woman. 'I hope his mother gets well soon.'

'She's on the mend.'

The woman smiled and nodded. With that, the man turned and

walked towards the BMW. As he reached the driver's door, he turned and took a final look at the cottage, then climbed into the driving seat and started the engine. He waved to the woman before accelerating slowly away in the direction of the A46.

Inside the cottage, Michael Doyle let out a deep sigh of relief as he observed the BMW pull away. *If that man's a priest, I'm the Archbishop of Canterbury.* He smiled to himself and sat down on the bed. An Irish priest driving an up-to-the-minute BMW did not ring at all true. And he didn't believe a word about the upgrade. Besides, he knew his mother had not been in hospital in Dublin. He'd spoken to her over the phone a few days before he was released from Colchester Prison. She was not in the best of health, but the farm where she lived was near Adare in County Limerick. If she'd needed medical treatment, there was a much nearer hospital. The man was definitely not a priest. Doyle calculated he was someone sent by Grayling to find him; to find him and to kill him. He'd been expecting Grayling to send someone, but not so quickly. The man was a probably a professional hit-man. Clever, that, disguising himself as a priest. Doyle smiled again. The game had moved in his favour. He now had the advantage. He knew what the assassin looked like. His features were now firmly fixed in his mind. He'd know him again if he saw him, however he was dressed.

There was no time to waste. He had to move and quickly. He started to pack his paniers then tidied the bed. It was time for him to hit the road. He grabbed his motorcycle boots and started to pull them on.

The man in the BMW reached the junction with the A46 and turned towards Leicester and the safe house. He had not expected to find Doyle at the cottage in Thrussington, but he had thought is sensible to check it out. He mentally crossed it off his list of premises associated with his target and relaxed as he accelerated quickly towards the city.

CHAPTER 12

It was late on Wednesday afternoon when Doyle arrived in the village in Derbyshire where his former solicitor, Trevor Parker, resided. Parker had retired from practice but had continued to deal with Doyle's financial affairs until shortly before he was released from prison on parole. He had negotiated a settlement with the Revenue and VAT authorities and managed the sale of all of Doyle's properties with the exception of the farm in Ireland which remained in Julia Hamilton's name. Harbour Buildings, where Doyle had occupied the penthouse suite, had been sold for over £4 million and Parker had maintained a rent-free lease on the penthouse for five years as part of the deal. He had wisely anticipated that Doyle would somehow manage to obtain early release from his fifteen-year prison sentence. But Doyle could not risk going there. He guessed, rightly, his apartment would still be under continuous surveillance by the police.

He already knew that he was due just under one million pounds which was all that remained to him after the unpaid taxes and associated penalties had been settled. Doyle had also been required to account for a significant sum in costs, fees and compensation paid out to the bank which had been the victim of the Charnwood robbery. This had further reduced his available assets considerably. Parker had telephoned him while he was still in prison in Colchester with the news. Disappointed as he was with the amount left to him, he was now desperately in need of cash; he required access to his account if he were going to go in pursuit of Jules. He still had over fifty thousand pounds in sterling which he had never disclosed to his solicitor, but that was stashed in a secure hiding place at the farm in Ireland and presently out of his reach. Parker had paid the balance of his legitimate funds into Doyle's bank account. Doyle now needed the card and cheque book that would give him access.

He had telephoned his former solicitor before he left Sycamore Cottage in Thrussington. Parker was not exactly happy to receive the call. 'I don't want you coming to my home,' he had insisted. 'My wife is here. If she spots you, my life won't be worth living. She has no idea I continued to act for you after you went to prison. I don't want her finding out.'

Parker reluctantly agreed to meet Doyle in the village churchyard, some distance from his home. Doyle was pleased to learn that his former solicitor was also bringing five thousand pounds in cash which he had kept back before paying the balance into Doyle's bank account. That would save Doyle having to go into the bank and risking the police discovering his whereabouts. He assumed they would be using every device to locate him including monitoring movements in his bank account. When the two men met, Parker was taken aback by Doyle's appearance. It wasn't just the embryo beard which Doyle was now sporting. When he removed his crash helmet and looked directly at Parker, the retired solicitor winced.

'You've lost weight, Michael. I hardly recognised you. Are you sure you're okay?'

'I'm fine,' Doyle assured him, patting the dog Parker had brought with him. 'Apart from someone attempting to kill me and the bloody government relieving me of over four and a half million quid, I've nothing to complain about.'

Parker smiled at Doyle's cynicism. 'At least you're free. That counts for something, more than money, surely?'

Doyle frowned. 'And you've retired just as you said you would. Got a dog, too, I see. Very nice. What's his name?'

'Her – she's a bitch.' He smiled. 'I was thinking of calling her Jules, but we settled on Tess.'

Doyle scowled. 'Very funny.'

'You should try it yourself, Michael. I mean it. Settle down with a nice woman who you can trust. The trust bit is very important. Oh, and a dog, too. There's nothing quite like it.'

'And how long would that last? The police want me to turn myself in, if you believe what you read in the newspapers.'

'I know. I've seen the reports in the press, as has my wife, incidentally. There's a number you can ring too. You could at least confirm you're still alive. There's been some speculation you might have died.'

Doyle shook his head. 'As you can see, they've got that wrong. I'm alive and I mean to stay that way.'

Parker frowned. 'Those bodies they pulled from the Trent is what interests them, I suppose? They don't have anything to do with you, do they?'

'I think the general idea was that I should have been one of them, Trevor. Fortunately, things didn't quite go to plan. But I'm still in danger. They'll try again. They've already got a professional assassin here looking for me.'

Parker appeared shocked and looked about him. The shadows of evening were lengthening and he was immediately concerned for his own safety. 'What, here?'

Doyle laughed. 'I don't mean here in your village. You're safe enough. No one knows I'm here. At least, I hope not.'

Parker visibly relaxed but still kept an eye out for anyone coming into the churchyard.

'Who's they?' he asked.

'You remember Gus Grayling?'

'I never met the man, I'm glad to say, but I know of his reputation. He was involved in that massive mortgage fraud years ago, wasn't he? The one you were dragged into.'

'He was arrested, yes, but never prosecuted. And they eventually dropped the case against me, if you remember? We never went to trial.' He paused and sighed. 'That was also when I first met Jules.' The words almost died on his lips.

'Yes. She was working for me full-time back then, more's the pity. Still, we certainly got a result. We were fortunate to find out about that non-disclosure by the prosecution. They were too embarrassed to carry on. I always suspected Grayling had something to do with that, you know. He had contacts everywhere, including, I suspect, in the police. But he's dead isn't he? He died last year.'

'He's dead all right. But he has a son – you didn't know that?'

Parker shook his head.

'Well, he has. Same name as me, Michael. He's taken over from his father. He's crazier than his old man too, and he wants me well out of the way. That woman they pulled out of the Trent at Cromwell; she was supposed to do for me, but she failed and ended up where she intended to put me.' He paused, giving Trevor Parker a wry grin. 'I've actually seen him.'

'Who?'

'The assassin. He called at Jules' mother's cottage in Leicestershire earlier this afternoon. He had no idea I was there, but I got a good look at him. Dressed like a priest he was. Dog collar and everything.'

'You're sure he didn't see you?'

'I'm sure. I'm also sure he doesn't know I saw him. I'll be ready for him if it comes to anything.'

Parker shook his head. He again appeared nervous and looked around the churchyard keeping his eyes on a middle-aged man carrying a bunch of flowers who had just walked through the gate. 'You should hand yourself in, Michael. It's the only sensible thing to do.'

Doyle shook his head. 'No way. How long do you think I'd survive inside? Grayling's tentacles get everywhere. They attempted twice to finish me off when I was in Colchester. They'll try again, if given the chance. They're not going to give up. And the police will try and pin both killings on me if they get hold of me. That's what they do. Take the easy option. All nice and tidy with remarkably little effort on their part.'

'Well, I don't know what else to advise, Michael. I really don't.'

'I don't want your advice, Trevor. I'll deal with Grayling myself. You know he's got Jules in tow. She's in Portugal with him now.'

The ex-solicitor heaved a sigh. 'You're not still pursuing that relationship are you, Michael? She's no good for you, that one. You've surely learnt your lesson by now? And I know her, don't forget. I grant you she has the looks, but she's only out for number one. You should give her up. She isn't worth it.'

Doyle dismissed his former solicitor's comments. 'As I said, I don't need your advice, Trevor. I'll deal with things from now on.' He handed Parker an envelope which he took from inside his leather jacket. 'All I want from you, apart from access to my money, is for you to keep this in a safe place. If anything happens to me – and you're sure to read about it if it does – I want you to take this to DCI Hood and give it to him, personally. You to him; no intermediaries, understand?'

Trevor Parker paused before replying. 'I suppose I can do that for you.' He opened the bag he'd brought with him and placed the envelope inside, then removed a larger brown envelope and handed it to Doyle. 'These are your bank account details and your new bank card. I was concerned the bank would close your account when you were sent down, but they haven't, not yet. There's five grand in cash in there as well, together with the keys to your apartment at Harbour Buildings in Leicester. The locks have been changed since you were last there. There's a copy of the lease in there too. It's got another four-and-a-half years to run.'

Doyle took the envelope and nodded his appreciation. 'I don't think I'll be going there for a while. That's the first place the police will look, and anyone else whose after catching up with me.'

'I still think you should go to the police. DCI Hood is an intelligent officer. He'll not have you down for killing anyone.'

'But I did kill someone, Trevor. The woman who they pulled from the Trent did her level best to kill me. Her gun went off in the struggle and she died.'

Parker appeared startled, swallowed hard and looked around the churchyard again. The man with the flowers had placed them on a grave and was walking out of the cemetery. The dog pulled on the leash. Parker partially relaxed. 'That sounds a lot like self-defence or accident to me, Michael.'

Doyle did not dissent. 'And you think I'd be able to prove that, with my record? Even if I could, they'd still try and pin something on me. And I'm not going back inside. That's a definite. I'd be a dead man within the week.'

'But if you find Jules, what good will that do you? If she's gone in with what's left of the Grayling mob, there's only one place you'll end up – on a mortuary slab! Give it up, Michael. Take your money and go and find somewhere pleasant to live well away from all this. Go abroad. Never mind your parole conditions; not that I should be advising you to breach them, of course. You've enough money to enjoy what's left to you of life. And there are other women, you know. Looks aren't everything. It's the only sensible thing to do, if you're determined not to go to the police.'

Doyle smiled. 'Well, that's me all over, isn't it Trevor? Never could do the sensible thing. Bit late to start now.'

* * *

Trevor Parker didn't go directly home. He walked to the nearby playing fields and gave Tess a run while he thought about what Doyle had told him. By the sound of things, his former client was still obsessed with Julia Hamilton. It would all end in tears. He was certain of it. But it was no longer any business of his. He no longer acted for Doyle. He no longer acted for anyone. As a retired solicitor he was no longer licensed to give anyone legal advice. He watched Tess as she tore around the playing field while he weighed up the risks he would be running if were to inform the police about the hit-man Doyle had described. Then there was Michael Grayling. He was now running the O.C.G., according to Doyle. Parker was sure the police would like to know that. Calling to Tess, who initially ignored him, he continued to turn matters over in his mind. An anonymous call perhaps? He took a deep breath, thought better of it at least for the time being and called for Tess a second time. On this occasion she ran back to him and calmly submitted to being put back on her leash.

'Good girl,' he said, ruffling the hair around her neck. 'Let's go home.'

Ten minutes later, Parker was heading down the drive of his large, detached home. He walked around the side of the house into the extensive rear garden. Closing and bolting the gate, he let Tess off the leash and went into the house through the back door. Placing his bag on a chair, he noticed some of the best china sitting on the kitchen table. He called to his wife. 'I'm back. Have you made some tea?'

Mrs Parker bustled into the kitchen. 'There you are, Trevor. Where have you been? You're not usually this late back. There's someone here to see you.' She dropped her voice to a whisper. 'He wants to know about Michael Doyle. I've told him you no longer act for him, but he's keen to get in touch. Doyle's mother is ill, it seems. He wants to speak to you personally. Bring an extra cup in with you. We are in the sitting room.'

Parker froze and swallowed hard. Glancing at his bag, he picked it up and concealed it in a cupboard before following his wife into the sitting room. He completely forgot to bring the additional cup and saucer with him. A tall man dressed in black and wearing a clerical collar stood up as Parker entered the room. His wife introduced him.

'Trevor, this is Father Gerry O'Brien. He's come all the way from Ireland.'

'To see me?' said Trevor, the words catching in his mouth.

'Not at all,' replied the visitor, stretching out his hand in friendly greeting. 'I happened to be over here on church business. I saw Michael's mother when she was in hospital in Dublin. She asked me to look him up. She's pretty desperate to see him. She's not been at all well.'

Parker felt the hairs on the back of his neck standing up. This man must be the assassin Doyle spoke about. He was certainly no priest.

'I thought his mother lived in County Limerick?'

'Ah, she does,' said the visitor, retaking his seat. 'But she was taken to Dublin for a scan to be done, at St Vincent's. It's a top hospital, you know. She's on the mend now, but anxious about her son. As I was over here I said I would look him up, but he seems to have disappeared since he came out of prison.'

'You know about that, do you?'

'I do. Mrs Doyle gave me a few details about his recent difficulties. But he's out now. He must have had a good lawyer to come out so quickly. I understand you acted for him?'

Parker sat down in the armchair nearest the door while his wife fussed about with the tea things. How did this man know he once acted for Doyle? 'I don't think that was down to me. He pleaded guilty, you know. I'm not at all sure how he managed to get early parole.'

'Will you have another cup, Father?' interrupted Mrs Parker.

The visitor declined. 'You're very kind, but I must be off. I was hoping your husband might give me a steer as to where Michael might be. That was all.'

Despite refusing more tea, the visitor remained seated. Parker had now recovered from his initial shock. He was quick to disassociate himself from his former client. 'His getting early parole had nothing to do with me. You'll need to have a word with Detective Chief Inspector Hood about that. I haven't seen Doyle for several months, although I spoke to him three weeks ago while he was still in Colchester Prison.'

His wife glared at him. 'You never told me that.'

'I didn't want to upset you, my dear. I know how you feel about Doyle.'

'Could I ask what it was about?' asked the visitor. 'Or would that be a breach of client confidentiality?'

Parker glanced towards his wife and took a deep breath. 'I don't suppose there's any harm in telling you. It's already in the public domain following the court hearing. Doyle chose not to attend when the consent order was made. It was left to me to inform him of the settlement with the Inland Revenue and Customs and Excise. All his properties were sold while he was inside. Most of the proceeds have gone in unpaid tax, penalties and confiscation. That was my last contact with him. Although I was in the course of retiring, I felt obliged to sort out his financial affairs. I no longer act for him now. I no longer act for anyone.'

'Good,' said Mrs Parker. 'He was nothing but trouble, that one.'

'So, you've retired have you?' asked the visitor.

Parker forced a smile. 'I have. Just back from taking the dog for a walk. I do that every day at this time. Very relaxing.'

Mrs Parker felt obliged to comment. 'Thinks more of that dog than he does of me. I hope you haven't left her running wild in the back garden, Trevor. She'll be digging up my vegetable patch again.'

'She'll be fine,' said her husband. 'I gave her a good run out on the playing fields.'

'Tell me,' interrupted the visitor, 'do you happen to have an address for Michael?'

Parker's reply was firm. 'No, I do not. Not since he was sent down. The last address I had for him was Colchester Prison. I got the impression when I last spoke to him that he intended to go abroad. I had to point out to him that it would amount to a breach of his parole licence after he was released, but he didn't seem too bothered about that.'

'I suppose he's pretty skint is he? Having had to pay all that tax and compensation.'

'I wouldn't go as far as that,' replied Parker. 'There were a few pounds left over. He'll not starve. And he could go anywhere in the world if he wanted, I suppose. There's nothing to keep him here that I know of.' Parker was keen to give the impression that Doyle had already gone abroad.

'The farther the better,' grunted Mrs Parker.

The visitor suddenly stood up. 'I suppose I should be off. Thank you for your hospitality. You've been very kind.' He shook Parker by the hand.

'I'm sorry I could not be of more help,' said Parker. 'I know that Michael does worry about his mother.'

'That's understandable,' said the visitor. 'She's a good woman. Goodbye now, and God bless.'

CHAPTER 13

After leaving Trevor Parker, Doyle rode on his motorcycle to a bed and breakfast establishment he knew just outside Hopwas, near Tamworth in Staffordshire. It was still light when he arrived at the small but friendly house ruled by a widow, Mrs Edna Ramsdale. What she said went – no argument. He felt he would be safe enough under her jurisdiction for a few days. There was only one other resident, an elderly man visiting his daughter in the village. 'You'll hardly know he's here,' assured Mrs Ramsdale. 'He's as quiet as a mouse. Breakfast sharp at eight o'clock, remember. No stragglers. You snooze, you lose.'

She took the eighty pounds from him in advance for two nights. Cash only. She didn't believe in credit cards and had only a passing acquaintanceship with the Inland Revenue. Having settled in his room, Doyle awaited the call from Jules. He glanced at the clock on the wall and checked the time with his watch. Six fifty-seven. That meant it would be nearly eight o'clock in Portugal; he would not have long to wait, always assuming Jules got the opportunity to phone. He unpacked the paniers he had brought up to his room and stripped off for a shower. Placing the mobile phone where he could hear it when it rang, he stood under the gushing hot water for ten minutes, contemplating his next move. He had just finished drying himself when the phone rang. He looked at the number on the screen. It was Jules. The connection was not the best but he could make out what she was saying without too much difficulty.

'Michael. I can't speak for long. He hasn't gone out. He and his friends are in the next room playing cards. We are coming to the UK next week-end.'

'This Saturday?'

'No. We'll arrive a week on Saturday. We are travelling to Dublin on

Friday. Grayling has things to do there for the next few days, or so he says.'

'Where will you be staying in Dublin?'

'We'll be in a hotel in the centre of the city. Very luxurious. The Gresham in O'Connell Street.'

'And very expensive, no doubt. But you're still travelling to Wales next week-end?'

'Yes.'

'Where will you be staying in Wales?'

'He's rented a house in North Wales. Just outside Abersoch, towards the coast.'

'Abersoch? Where the hell is that exactly?'

'It's in Gwynedd, if that's how you pronounce it. You'll have to look at a map.'

'And the house?'

'It's called White Gables, just outside the town on the Llanengan Road. It's pretty remote from what I can gather. Ideal for his purposes.'

'And I can just imagine what his purposes will include. Can you spell that for me? These Welsh names are a real bind.'

'Double L, A, N, E, N, G, A, N.'

Doyle made a note on the back of his hand with a biro.

'You want me to come there?'

'Yes, I suppose I do. But be careful, Michael. He'll have that brute of a Scotsman with him. You know, the one who knocked you out at Barnard House. He's meeting us with the Range Rover when we arrive in Wales.'

'Is he? You mean Jamie?'

'Yes. Jamie Wallace. That's his name.'

'Wallace, eh? I won't forget him in a hurry, I can tell you. He's already been trying to locate me, but he hasn't succeeded.'

'Where are you? Please tell me you're safe.'

'I'm fine. Don't you fret. He'll not find me. I'm moving about. Never stay in one place for long. But my present accommodation isn't up to your Dublin standards, I can tell you that much.'

'Grayling won't forget you, though, Michael and neither will Wallace. He's very dangerous is Jamie.'

'I know. I still have the lump on the side of my head. But he'll not have it so easy next time.'

'Then there's the hit-man to worry about. Be careful, Michael. They really mean to kill you. This isn't a game. Grayling says one or other of them is bound to find you.'

'I'll take care, don't you worry. How will I get in touch with you?'

'I'll ring you when we are on the ferry.'

'The ferry?'

'Yes. He says we are taking the ferry to Holyhead from Dublin. It makes things easier. There's not much of a check between Ireland and the UK for ferry passengers.'

'When will you arrive?'

'On the Saturday evening. At about six-thirty. If the ferry's on time.'

'What name will you be using?'

'I don't know; he hasn't said. He's kept control of the passports. But you can guarantee it won't be our real names.'

'See if you can find out. It's bound to be on the ticket or something. But I'll be there keeping an eye out for you; you can count on it. You won't see me, but I'll be about.'

'I know you will. But be careful.' Her voice dropped to a whisper. 'He's meeting up with the man he's hired to kill you, but I still don't know who he is. If they find you, there'll only be one outcome. Please, don't take any risks on my account. I don't deserve it, not after what I did to you.'

'Don't you bother your pretty little head about me. You let me worry about Grayling and his hit-man.'

'Look, I have to go. I'll ring again later in the week. Take care.'

She put the phone down and looked directly at the man standing next to her.

'Well done, my love,' said Grayling, a sarcastic grin crossing his face. 'You're learning fast. That should get him out of the shadows. With any luck, my man will be all lined up to do the job by the time we arrive.

We'll have front-row seats too. Then all we'll have to do is identify the body and, by the way, I mean both of us.'

'I don't want anything to do with it,' said Jules, shaking her head and whimpering her response. 'Just leave me out of it.'

'You have no choice in the matter.' Grayling grabbed her upper arms and glared at her, pushing his face close to hers. 'I need you to draw him out. He's not going to walk up to me and surrender himself, is he? He's not that much of a fool. There's no other way of doing this. Jamie has had no luck trying to find him. But he'll come out of wherever he's hiding to see you. He's besotted.' He paused briefly then continued. 'Yes, we'll have to find a nice quiet place for him to be despatched. My man already has somewhere in mind and we'll both be there to witness it. Get used to it, Julia. It's going to happen whatever you think about it.' He pushed her away and walked out of the room.

CHAPTER 14

Castleton street in the business quarter of Leicester consisted of a number of late Georgian and early Victorian properties with the occasional modern eyesore disfiguring the otherwise harmonious setting. The legal firm of Worth, Ambler and Partners was situated in the conservation area a stone's throw from the cathedral. With its visually complex stonework resplendent in the morning sunshine, it contributed in no small part to the character of the area. Housed in what had once been the city's main branch of Martin's Bank, it was one of several professional offices lining the road which had been laid with cobblestones in an attempt to preserve and enhance the historic charm of the neighbourhood.

Hood noticed the single yellow line immediately in front of the solicitor's office as he pulled to a halt on Thursday morning. Where to park? A traffic warden was patrolling the street at the city end and he noticed a uniformed police officer checking what appeared to be a broken window to the left-hand side of the premises. Hood called him over, producing his identification and at the same time noting shards of broken glass extending along the pavement for a considerable distance.

'What's been going on here?' he asked the officer who recognised Hood and almost saluted him.

'Hooligans, sir. There's quite a few broken windows along this side of the street. Not much damage opposite though. A trail of destruction almost to the end of the road on this side. Must have happened late last night or in the early hours after the nightclub turned out.' He pointed to a large brick building some distance away in an adjacent street, its upper floors and roof protruding into the skyline. 'That'll be the culprit, sir. The parking restrictions in this street end at eight p.m. A lot of the punters park along here. We've had complaints before about them leaving a mess in the street and urinating in the office doorways, but it's really down to the council to do something about it.'

Hood frowned. 'Might be an idea to keep the parking restrictions until after midnight?'

'I doubt if the council would have the staff to enforce them, sir, and we have better things to do.'

'Has CID attended?'

'No, sir. It's not considered serious enough. I'm making a note of all the damage so we can give those affected a crime number, for insurance purposes. Not much chance of finding those responsible. No CCTV in this street.'

Hood nodded. 'Speaking of parking, I have an appointment with the senior partner of this firm of solicitors in three minutes. Police business, not personal.' He glanced at his watch. 'I'll have to leave my car here. Make sure that traffic warden doesn't book me.' Hood pointed to the warden who was busy noting stationary vehicles in the limited parking at the far end of the street.

'I will, sir. How long will you be?'

'Not more than thirty minutes. You should be able to keep him at bay for that length of time. I've placed a police identity notice on the dashboard.'

Hood switched off his engine and exited the Saab. He waved to the traffic warden who had noticed the presence of his car. The warden picked up speed and walked towards the chief inspector, his notebook in his hand. The uniformed officer intervened. As Hood arrived at the entrance of the solicitor's office, and was about to walk through the open door, he noticed the warden turn about and stroll off in the opposite direction. Five minutes later, Hood was introduced to the senior partner of Worth, Ambler and Partners and took a comfortable seat in his impressively furnished office on the first floor which overlooked the street below.

'I don't suppose you've come about the criminal damage to two of our windows and our front door, Mr Hood? Not important enough for a chief inspector, I imagine?' William Worth smiled. He was a middle-aged man with greying hair and a friendly enough disposition. He fitted perfectly Hood's idea of a successful and senior member of the legal profession.

'No, I haven't,' replied Hood. 'But there's a PC out in the street looking into it. Tell me, has this sort of thing happened before?'

Mr Worth shook his head. 'Not to this extent, no. They make a bit of a mess in the street from time to time, leaving their take-away rubbish lying about and we did have a window cracked a year or two ago, but nothing on this scale. It's the customers from the night club in the next street. I've complained to the city fathers about it but nothing has been done.'

'I'll have a word with the duty inspector if you like, sir. See if we can't have a couple of police officers patrolling the area when the club turns out.'

'I'd be grateful if you would. It's usually worst at week-ends. The club only opens a couple of nights during the week, last night being an instance. Never had so much trouble mid-week before. And it's going to cost over a thousand pounds to replace those damaged windows. They'll be boarded up later this afternoon. But enough of that.' He placed his hands together and cleared his throat. 'I had a call from Mr Duffy late yesterday afternoon. He warned me you'd be paying a visit. I take it that's why you made an appointment to see me?' The solicitor looked at his watch. 'I have another appointment in twenty-five minutes, a major commercial client, so we must get down to business. It's about his file, I presume.'

'You do have a file of Duffy's, do you?'

'I do. More of a package then a file, though. As far as I'm aware it contains his personal papers. Rather unusual instructions came with it. I'm to keep it under lock and key and send it to the Home Secretary in the event of Duffy's death. Whether the Home Secretary will be interested in the contents I have no idea. I don't have any details of what is inside it, but that in itself is hardly to the point. He declined to tell me, insisting on absolute confidentiality. It's too bulky just to be his will, although he did tell me his will is one of the documents in there. I also have my own copy of that. I drafted it for him.'

'Are you prepared to show it to me?'

The solicitor looked over the top of his spectacles. 'The will? Perhaps, but my instructions are simply to confirm to you the file's existence, which I have done. Nothing more.'

'I have reason to believe this file may contain valuable information about a major organised crime group possibly relevant to a murder inquiry I am conducting.'

The solicitor sat back in his leather chair and smiled. '*May* contain valuable information, Chief Inspector? *Possibly relevant* to your inquiry? Is that the best you can do? On what evidence do you base this interesting proposition?'

'Duffy tells me his file is the only thing that's keeping him in the land of the living. If certain individuals got hold of it, he'd be a dead man, or so he reckons.'

Mr Worth frowned. 'I suspect he's exaggerating or simply bluffing. Our strongroom holds a number of boxes and packages belonging to clients. I must confess, I don't think our instructions from our other clients are quite as dramatic as his. But whatever property we keep secure is personal to our clients. It would be a serious breach of professional confidentiality if I were to consider acting inconsistently with any of their instructions. And I must treat Mr Duffy in exactly the same way as any other client, despite his background.'

'You are aware that he is a convicted robber and kidnapper? He clearly has intimate knowledge of serious criminal activity.'

'I'm aware of his antecedent history, yes. But I don't see how that affects the issue. I've only met him once and that was while he was on remand. He was in Nottingham Prison at the time.' He smiled. 'The only time I've ever been inside the place. My firm does not deal in criminal work, you understand. The package was handed to me by the solicitor who conducted his defence in the Crown Court, before he was convicted. I was assured the contents had nothing to do with the charges which he faced and subsequently admitted. That was the single question upon which I insisted on an answer. Given that he pleaded guilty, whatever is in there must be irrelevant to any issue arising from that criminal activity.'

'I agree. But the contents may be relevant to other matters.'

'Do you really think so? My own view is that the contents is more likely to concern his daughter. He's very upset about the sentence she received. He told me that much. He wants her parole date brought forward. Were you aware of that?'

'He said as much to me,' replied Hood. 'But I suspect there's more to it than that.' He paused and almost chuckled. 'I could apply for a warrant, you know.'

The solicitor smiled his response. 'Come now, Chief Inspector. You and I both know any such application would be refused. You have no evidence as to what is in there; this is all mere speculation. The law requires much more than that before countenancing an interference with personal property. This would simply be regarded as a fishing expedition, and the courts don't like that. The likes of Duffy are entitled to the same consideration as anyone else. We have his human rights to bear in mind, you know. And if your application were granted by a District Judge, I have every confidence it would be set aside by the High Court. We both know there is no basis for granting a warrant to seize Duffy's property. There are no outstanding criminal charges against him to which the contents can possibly be linked.'

Hood sighed. He realised he would not persuade the solicitor or a court to hand over the package. He turned to his other concern. 'And it's safe enough here, is it? I do wonder why Duffy didn't place it in a bank security vault if the contents are as important as he makes out.'

Mr Worth smiled. 'I suppose he wanted to make sure his instructions were put into effect immediately should his worst imaginings come about. In any event, our safe is as secure as any bank. This place used to be the regional headquarters of Martin's Bank you know, until forty-odd years ago. Would you like to see our strongroom?'

'That won't be necessary. I'm sure it's secure.'

Hood then had a sudden thought. 'This damage to your office which occurred last night. Is there any indication that anyone attempted to get inside?'

The solicitor seemed surprised. 'Burglars? I think not. At least, I've seen no evidence that anyone has been in here. Nothing has been stolen, as far as I'm aware. And the place is securely alarmed.' The solicitor frowned. 'Let me ask my secretary.' He pressed a button on the intercom. 'Mrs Benedict. Could you step into my office for a moment? Thanks.'

Mr Worth appeared suddenly serious. 'Mrs Benedict, Vivienne as I usually call her, has been with the firm for over eighteen years. I couldn't manage without her. If anything has been interfered with or moved, she would know. Very little gets past her.'

Moments later Vivienne Benedict was in the room. Mr Worth introduced the chief inspector who stood up and shook hands with the slim and smartly dressed secretary seemingly in her middle forties. Her red hair was streaked with the occasional touch of grey and her intelligent hazel eyes seemed to drill into his. He certainly felt she was someone whose word he could accept.

'Are you here about the damage to the office windows?' she asked.

'Not really,' replied Hood. 'But I noticed it as I arrived. Quite a mess.'

'It's not just us,' replied the secretary, her indignation apparent. 'There's a trail of broken windows all down the street. Several other offices have been affected. The accountants next door had five windows broken. It will have been the people from the nightclub in the next street. I don't understand why the city council ever gave permission for it to open so close to what is supposed to be a conservation area. They seem to be wholly uninterested in alleviating the problem.'

'You may well be right,' said Hood. 'I shall upgrade the level of the inquiry when I get back to the station.' He paused. 'Mr Worth and I were wondering whether there was any sign of a break-in having occurred during the night? The damage in the street might have been a distraction.'

Mrs Benedict shook her head. 'You think someone may have got in here? Not that I have noticed, no.' She paused and swallowed hard then looked towards Mr Worth and frowned. 'There is one thing I feel I should mention, though. It's probably nothing, but when I walked into my office earlier this morning, I had a feeling that someone had been in there, someone who shouldn't have been. Odd really. I've never felt anything like that before.' She noticed a look of concern on Mr Worth's face. 'Please don't misunderstand. It wasn't anything in particular that caught my eye. I just had a feeling that things had been moved, as if someone was looking for something.' She smiled broadly and shook her head. 'I'm no doubt imagining it. If anything had been moved, it was probably one of the cleaners or a member of staff. It was almost certainly the damage in the street that I encountered on the way in that brought on my concerns.'

'What do you mean, exactly?' asked Hood, his curiosity aroused.

'Nothing I can put my finger on,' she replied. 'Just an impression I had when I arrived for work this morning.' She looked at Hood. 'But nothing is missing. I'm sure of that. I did mention it to Mr Farmer. He obviously thought I was imagining it and wasting his valuable time but he said he would check with other members of staff and look at the strongroom to ascertain if there has been any interference with it.'

'Mr Farmer?' asked Hood.

'He's our office accountant,' said Mr Worth. 'His office is adjacent to the strongroom, on the lower ground floor. He's been with us for over thirty-five years. It was my late father who appointed him. As you would expect, we keep anything of value or importance in the strongroom.'

Hood considered for a moment whether he should take the matter further. 'Perhaps I should take a look at this strongroom of yours after all, if you have no objection, Mr Worth.'

'No problem,' said the solicitor. 'I'll show it to you myself. I have a little time to spare before my next appointment. Thank you, Vivienne. That will be all.'

CHAPTER 15

Hood followed the senior partner down the main staircase and along a wide corridor until they reached the office of the firm's accountant. Mr Frederick Farmer welcomed them outside the entrance to the strongroom in the basement. The senior partner had phoned him before setting out from his own office and informed him of the object of the visit. Farmer was a man clearly past retirement age, almost bald with a small grey moustache. He was smartly dressed in a three-piece suit and bow tie. He pointed towards the strongroom, a huge, cavernous space positioned behind an intricate metal gate of substantial size. The door of the huge safe seemed to be at least two feet thick, pushed open as it was to one side. It's original function – the secure vault or strongroom of a major bank – was quite evident. It had clearly been given a second life as the walk-in safe of a successful firm of solicitors. Hood took hold of the gate's metalwork to satisfy himself as to its strength. It did not budge.

Farmer was wholly confident that the strongroom was completely secure and had not been subject to any interference. He explained that any miscreant wishing to get into it outside working hours would have first to pass through the gate and then open the strongroom door which was protected by a double lock. No fewer than three keys would be required, all of which were kept overnight in a second small safe built into the wall of his office.

'With all due respect to Mrs Benedict,' said Farmer, giving Hood a languid look, 'I think Vivienne has let her imagination get the better of her. There have been no intruders. I'd stake my pension on it! And there is definitely nothing missing from this safe. My assistants and I spent over an hour and a half checking the main contents. The strongroom is also alarmed – with a direct line to Central Police

Station. If anyone forced an entry, the police would have known about it instantly.'

'Would the alarm sound here if the strongroom were entered at night?' asked Hood.

'Only if the door was forced. And not immediately, no. It's silent for five and a half minutes, to give the police time to get here before alerting the intruders. It's tested regularly. And there are no marks anywhere to suggest an attempt to force an entry has been made. But we have a dual alarm system. The main alarm which is separate from the strongroom security system is designed to sound within a few seconds of anyone getting into the building outside working hours. Given where the strongroom is situated, that alarm would go off well before anyone could possibly get down here.'

Hood thanked him for the information and stepped through the gate after Farmer turned a large key in the lock. With the strongroom door wide open, he could see into it without difficulty. A florescent strip light illuminated the interior which was fitted with shelves, filled with boxes and packages. Against the back wall, several black deed boxes, with the names of their owners inscribed in fading gold lettering, stood on top of each other in a rickety pile. Hood was informed the strongroom door was kept open during the working day, but the metal gate remained closed and locked. Only if the key to the gate were obtained from Mr Farmer or his assistant could anyone enter the secure area. Anyone wanting to enter the safe had to sign for anything they removed.

'It all seems very well organised,' said Hood.

'I should hope it does,' replied Mr Worth. 'We've never lost anything, not in the ninety-seven years of the firm's existence. My grandfather started the business back in the reign of Edward the Seventh, you know, although we have only been in this building since nineteen eighty-one.' He smiled. 'If he were to come back to life, he'd hardly recognise the place or the way we do business. Almost everything is computerised these days.' He smiled and shook his head. 'But I really can't imagine anyone busting into our strongroom. Shall we return to my office?'

'Could I first see the safe where the keys are kept overnight?' asked Hood.

Mr Farmer nodded and led the way up several steps into his office. It was like walking into another century. Computers and other electronic devices filled the room. Three clerks were busy producing schedules, reconciling accounts or otherwise occupied. Farmer immediately pointed to the safe, a modern contraption fixed securely into the wall and operated by a digital code. He entered the code and opened the safe. He then produced the two huge keys which opened the strongroom. Hood looked at them, briefly, then nodded.

'They look like the originals.'

'I suppose they are,' replied Farmer. 'I wouldn't want to have to get them copied. They're well looked after. Locked in my safe every night.'

'How widely known is the code for this smaller safe?'

'Only by the two of us,' said Mr Worth. 'When Fred here goes on leave, his assistant is informed of the current code. It changes every few days. Random numbers are produced by the computer. It's as safe and secure as anything could be.'

Hood sighed. 'I think we are done here.' He thanked Mr Farmer again and followed the senior partner back to his office.

'Satisfied, Chief Inspector?' asked Mr Worth, taking his seat behind his desk.

Hood raised one matter that had occurred to him on the way back to Worth's office. 'Bit of a slog, isn't it, having to go down to the lower ground floor and all the way to Mr Farmer's room just to get something out of the strongroom?'

The solicitor shook his head. 'Doesn't happen very often, Mr Hood. If I need anything, which I rarely do, I send Mrs Benedict or ask Mr Farmer's clerk to bring it up. I rarely go down there myself.'

'And you're sure Duffy's file is safe?'

Mr Worth smiled. 'Of course it is.'

Hood hesitated before raising his next query. 'I couldn't help noticing you didn't check if it was still in the strongroom when we were down there.'

The solicitor gave Hood a knowing look. 'There was no need to, Mr Hood. Duffy's file isn't there – not at the moment.'

Hood appeared momentarily perplexed. 'It isn't? Then where is it?'

Mr Worth hesitated for a moment then leant forward and smiled. 'I suppose there's no harm in my telling you this. I have a very secure little safe here in my office, for ease of access you understand.' He pointed to a mahogany cabinet against the side wall. 'You see that? It looks innocent enough, don't you think? I keep some sherry and glasses in there. I still have the odd client who expects to be served with a good *amontillado* when he comes in to change his will, for the umpteenth time. But the cabinet is in fact a small safe. Watch carefully.'

He stood up, took a key from his pocket and opened the door of the cabinet. The interior lit up and appeared for all practical purposes to be a fairly standard cocktail cabinet. A mirror reflected the cut-glass crystal glasses and a half-filled sherry decanter. Mr Worth pressed a button and the glasses and decanter moved to the left. Revealing a small but solid-looking steel door.

'This is my personal safe, Chief Inspector. If I have cause to remove anything from the strongroom, it is retained here until it is returned downstairs, always assuming I can fit it in. I have some highly personal items in there too. By happy chance, Mr Duffy's package is in there at the moment. After you made an appointment to see me, I naturally checked it out. So, I was never concerned that the main strongroom might have been entered. Not that it has been, of course. You'd have a better chance of breaking in to Fort Knox than getting in to our strongroom.'

He pressed the button again and the glasses and decanter re-appeared. He then locked the cabinet and replaced the key in his waistcoat pocket.

'It's fixed firmly to the wall, Mr Hood, and is weighted down at the base. I keep the only key.' He patted his pocket. 'If anything were to happen to me, God forbid, the necessary instructions appear in my will so my executors will be able to deal with the contents.'

'Doesn't seem to be quite as secure as the downstairs strongroom,' said Hood. 'If you don't mind my saying so.'

Mr Worth smiled. 'Oh, I don't know. Why should anyone suspect that there's anything important in there? It was my late father's idea – he had the cabinet made – and I was unaware of its principal purpose until he retired. He kept it a secret. Just like I have done. Only Mrs Benedict knows about it – and my son – he's a partner here too. None of my other partners are privy to what it actually is. To them, this is just a cocktail cabinet. Only myself, my son and my secretary – and you, now, I suppose – know its other function and I'm sure you'll not break a confidence. I think my secret is safe enough, don't you, Chief Inspector?'

CHAPTER 16

Chief Inspector Hood was bringing Friday morning's briefing to a conclusion when the uniformed station inspector entered the incident room.

'Sorry to disturb you, Harry,' he said, looking around him, 'but I've just had the Deputy Chief Constable on the blower. She wants to see you right away. It sounded very urgent.'

Was that a faint smile Hood detected on the inspector's face? Was Hood in some sort of trouble?

'Did she say why?' asked the chief inspector, checking the time on his watch.

'No, just that it was urgent and she wanted to see you at HQ as soon as. You are to drop whatever you're doing. She sounded very insistent.'

Hood wondered why the DCC wanted to see him and why she had not contacted him directly on his mobile. He was already attending an almost daily briefing with the ACC (Crime) who could have provided an up-to-date report on the progress of the investigation had she asked. Their respective offices were on the same floor at HQ. 'Ring her back and tell her I'm on my way, will you?'

'No problem.' The inspector left the room. Once in the corridor he broke into a smile. Perhaps *Operation Trent* would be moving elsewhere. He'd then have his station back. He could but hope.

Hood gave his final instructions to his assembled team. Wendy Knight was assigned together with Raymond Craddock to visit the Hamilton cottage in Thrussington and ask a few questions of the immediate neighbours. A drive past the day before had revealed nothing of interest but she had made an appointment with the selling agents to gain access to the property at 12 noon. The agent's willingness to cooperate in a murder investigation avoided the need for a search warrant. DS Sean Smith had already set out to visit the firearm expert in London. David Osborne was still waiting to give evidence in Court One at the Central Criminal Court. The trial had been delayed by the illness of a juror. It meant that he had additional time to continue his examination of the firearm recovered from the Trent, using the facilities at the Met's forensic science laboratory in Lambeth.

'You take over, will you, Andrew? I don't know what can be so urgent that I have to travel all the way to HQ now. I'm already due there on Monday. I'll ring you as soon as I know anything.'

Andrew Hooper nodded. 'I'll continue liaising with Dublin. I reckon if there is an assassin looking for Doyle, that's where he'll come in from.'

'Why do you say that?' asked Wendy Knight.

'Just a hunch, but there's a common travel corridor between the UK and the Republic. No real checks on arrival in the UK, unless there's a specific reason or a security alert.'

'I have asked for ID checks to be made on passengers arriving from Ireland, but they're not as intensive as they would be for someone flying in from, say, the States,' added Hood. 'But most people will use their passport as an easy form of identification. Most airlines require it.'

'So our assassin could fly in from the US, say to Dublin, then travel over here in comparative safety?' said Knight. 'Without his ID being given anything other than a superficial examination?'

'Correct. But we might pick something up. Whoever it is, he'll be using a false passport. You can guarantee that.' He paused. 'Look, I must get off. I don't want to keep the DCC waiting.'

Hood left the room and headed for the car park.

'Perhaps his promotion has come through at last?' whispered Knight to Andrew Hooper. 'I can't think of any other reason why the DCC would want to see him. Let's hope that's the case. He's been waiting long enough. It might well assist you in being made a permanent DI?'

* * *

When Hood arrived at Mid-Shires Constabulary HQ in Leicester, he was immediately shown into the DCC's room on the fourth floor. He was surprised to see a man in his middle forties, whom he did not recognise, standing on the DCC's side of the desk. The Deputy Chief Constable, Margaret Knowles, who seemed unusually formal in her manner, introduced him.

'This is Detective Chief Superintendent Charles West, from Professional Standards.' Her embarrassment was clear. 'I'm afraid a problem has arisen, Chief Inspector. I thought it best to bring Charles in at the outset, in a purely advisory capacity at the moment.'

Hood recognised West's name and position although he did not know him personally. What could the head of Professional Standards want with him? His reply disclosed a degree of concern.

'A problem? Concerning me? Some kind of complaint? I'm afraid you've lost me, ma'am. I don't know what you're talking about.'

Knowles appeared uncomfortable. 'It hasn't reached the point of a formal complaint, not yet. But the circumstances are potentially troubling. If you take a seat, I shall ask Chief Superintendent West to explain.'

Hood looked behind him then sat down. West followed suit, taking a seat immediately next to the DCC on her side of the desk. He adjusted his tie and cleared his throat before he began his questioning. 'Yesterday, I understand you visited the senior partner of a firm of solicitors in Leicester?'

Hood frowned, his reply indicating a degree of concern. 'Yes. I saw Mr Worth, the senior partner of Worth, Ambler and Partners, at eleven-thirty yesterday morning, on police business I might add.'

'This was in respect of the murder investigation of which you are the SIO?'

'Yes. The two bodies that were pulled out of the Trent last week-end. Dudley Manning and Maxine Kruger.'

'What was the purpose of your visit to Mr Worth?'

Hood was becoming increasingly worried about the direction in which the questions were headed but he answered with his customary frankness. 'I had discovered that he was holding a file on behalf of Derick Duffy, a convicted offender presently serving his sentence at

Woodborough High Security prison in Northamptonshire.'

'Did you see the file?'

'No, I did not, but Mr Worth confirmed that he held it. He declined either to show it to me or to reveal its contents. Client confidentiality prohibited it, or so he said. He confirmed that he, too, was unaware of what was in there other than Duffy's will.'

'He mentioned Duffy's will?'

'He did.'

'How did you find out about the file?'

Hood was now feeling more than uncomfortable. 'As DCC Knowles is aware, we have known about the possible existence of such a file for quite some time.' Hood glanced towards Knowles who nodded her agreement. 'Duffy told me about it, off the record, when we were investigating the Campion kidnapping case and the subsequent robbery attempt in North Nottinghamshire. Until yesterday, we didn't know where it was located. Duffy flatly refused to say. Some of us even doubted its existence. It was always possible that Duffy could have been bluffing in an attempt to protect himself from those he informed against. We gathered that if it did exist, it was likely to contain information that could implicate those who have threatened Duffy's life. He's had to move his location several times, such is the seriousness of the threat he faces.'

'How did you find out this file was being held at Mr Worth's office?'

Hood exhaled. 'Duffy told me two days ago when I visited him at Woodborough. He was concerned not for himself but for his daughter, Kelly Maguire.'

'She's serving a lengthy sentence herself, isn't she?' said the DCC.

'She certainly is, ma'am. Longer than her father. Twenty-four years, if I recall correctly. Duffy wanted me to broach the subject of early parole for his daughter in exchange for giving us access to his file.' He paused and looked directly at West. 'I have already sent a report of my conversation with Duffy to the ACC (Crime).'

'Have you, indeed?' responded West 'You didn't waste much time.' He raised an eyebrow and looked towards the DCC who could not resist a wry grin. She was, of course, well acquainted with Hood's professional reputation for religiously observing established police protocol. It did not surprise her that he had acted with such alacrity, as Hood went on to explain.

'I like to deal with matters as professionally as possible, sir. I wanted my conversation with Duffy properly logged before I met with Mr Worth, although my report could not have been seen by the ACC before yesterday. I prepared it after I got back to the station on Wednesday evening while matters were still fresh in my memory. I thought that was the sensible thing to do.'

'You were very careful, Chief Inspector.'

'Do you think so, sir? These are uncomfortable and potentially hazardous circumstances for any police officer. I was acting outside standard operating procedures. There is no record of what passed between Duffy and me other than my notes, made after I left him. Although I took a detective sergeant with me, Duffy wouldn't say anything in the presence of another officer. Neither should we overlook the fact he's been involved in extremely serious criminal activity over a lengthy period. Logging what occurred between the two of us seemed necessary. Simple self-protection as far as I was concerned.'

'You didn't think of taping your conversation with him?'

Hood shook his head and smiled. 'No. He would never speak to me on the record. He never has. There was no point even suggesting it.'

'But he had asked to see you?'

'Yes, he had. But I should, perhaps, make it clear that I wanted to see him anyway. He was once a close associate of the late Gus Grayling. Since Grayling's death, we have not been able to establish who has taken over this O.C.G. There are a number of possibilities, but Duffy is one of the few individuals whom I believe knows for sure who is now running the organisation.'

'You were hoping he would tell you?'

'I was. He as good as admitted he knows who has taken over. I believe whoever it is, is likely to be named in his file. And that person is clearly in the frame for ordering at least one of the murders I'm investigating.' Hood dropped his head and examined his hands which were beginning to show just the slightest signs of sweating. 'Hence my interest.'

The DCC looked at West. 'I think we need to tell Harry, I mean Chief Inspector Hood, what has happened. Bring him up to date.'

Hood raised his head. 'Have there been developments?'

'There certainly have,' said the DCC. 'There was a burglary at Mr Worth's offices last night or in the early hours of this morning. Duffy's file has been stolen.'

Hood could not disguise his astonishment. 'Where precisely was it stolen from?'

'From Mr Worth's personal safe in his own office. It's quite obvious from the surrounding circumstances that whoever stole it knew what they were looking for and also knew where to find it.'

'Mr Worth had not returned it to the main strongroom?'

'It seems not.'

'I wonder why?'

Hood now realised why he was sitting in the DCC's office with the head of Professional Services looking on. 'I understand now why I'm here, ma'am. According to what Mr Worth said to me, the only person apart from himself who knew Duffy's file was in his personal safe yesterday was me. Am I right?'

'That seems to be the top and bottom of it,' said the DCC. She appeared suitably uncomfortable.

'So, I'm under some kind of suspicion, am I? You think I told someone where it was?'

'You see how it looks, Harry.'

Hood tried but did not succeed in hiding his anger. 'Of course, Mr Worth could not possibly be responsible, could he, or a member of his staff?' He let out a prolonged sigh. 'Has anyone asked him why the file was still in his private safe? I was shown the main strongroom during my visit yesterday. I was given to understand that this file was normally secured in that strongroom. There is no way any burglar could have got into there.'

West shrugged his shoulders. 'We are still waiting for a report from the OIC. It appears as things stand that Mr Worth hadn't got round to replacing it in the strongroom. And we must remember, he is Duffy's solicitor, and a man of the highest professional reputation. Why should he come under suspicion?'

Hood raised his voice in response. 'And I'm a Detective Chief Inspector of umpteen years' unblemished service. What exactly is being alleged against me?'

The DCC intervened. 'No one is accusing you of anything, Harry.' She paused ominously. 'Not at the moment. But it doesn't have a good look. This could be very embarrassing for us. Mr Worth has reported the burglary as you would expect, but he contacted me this morning because of the sensitive nature of the stolen property.'

'Who is investigating?' asked Hood.

'Central in Leicester. DS Barbara Grant is in charge. Mr Worth has not revealed the potential significance of the file that is missing, not even to her. I would have sent a higher ranking officer as OIC, but I wanted to keep it very low key at present for obvious reasons.'

'Nothing else was stolen?'

'Not according to Worth, no. And there was a cash box with over two hundred and eighty pounds in his private safe too. That wasn't taken. It's obvious what the thieves were after.'

Hood paused while he considered his response. 'And the alarm system?'

'Circumvented, it seems. It does not appear to have been triggered. There was no additional alarm on the safe in his office.'

'So, we are dealing with real professionals? Someone has gone to a great deal of trouble to get his hands on that file and, by the look of things, to try and implicate me in its disappearance.'

West sounded surprised. 'You think a deliberate attempt has been made to implicate you?'

'Undoubtedly. That, I assume, is why I'm here? I suspect someone wants me off the case.'

'What would that achieve? Another officer of similar seniority would take over.'

'But not anyone with my depth of knowledge.' He paused, his indignation obvious. 'And what would I achieve, exactly, by passing information on to an O.C.G, always assuming I knew who to contact?' Neither the DCC nor West replied. 'Tell me,' continued Hood. 'Did Mr Worth mention what happened on Wednesday night or early Thursday morning?'

The two senior officers looked at each other blankly.

'Wednesday night?' asked the DCC.

'Yes,' replied Hood. 'A trail of damaged doors and windows all down Castleton Street including the offices of Worth, Ambler and Partners. It was put down to drunken punters from the nearby nightclub but that could well have been a blind. I raised the question when I was with Mr Worth whether any unlawful entry had been made into the solicitor's office. I was told there was no evidence of a burglary and nothing had been stolen.'

'What are you suggesting?' asked West.

'I'm not suggesting anything,' replied Hood, 'other than that it might be a good idea to investigate the matter more thoroughly before jumping to unsubstantiated conclusions. It's too much of a coincidence for my liking that all that damage was caused the night before a burglary of this gravity. Pretty good cover, don't you think? You can bet your life that whoever has Duffy's file now will have used very sophisticated techniques both to locate it and to steal it. They may well have been inside Mr Worth's office the night before. My team should be investigating this. There could well be a connection with my murder inquiry.'

'You think that, do you?' said the DCC. Hood nodded. She looked directly at West. 'I am proposing to speak to Mr Worth myself at later today. Pouring oil on troubled waters.' She then addressed Hood. 'Did Mr Worth mention anyone else who might have known about his personal safe?'

'Only his secretary – and she's been with him for nearly twenty years – and his son, but whether they knew the precise location of Duffy's file I have no idea. The son is a partner in the firm, but I suppose it's always possible some other members of staff may have known about it. Office gossip and all that.'

The DCC pondered the situation before reaching a conclusion. 'Unless Worth makes a specific complaint, it seems to me there's nothing like enough evidence here to suspend any officer, let alone an officer of Harry's standing and reputation. There may well be another explanation for this information leaking out.'

West appeared uncomfortable as he replied. 'It's standard practice, ma'am, for an officer under even the slightest suspicion to withdraw, no matter how senior he may be.' He shook his head. 'I'm not suggesting DCI Hood should be suspended; I'm not suggesting that at all, but a few days' gardening leave away from the investigation might assist with PR while things settle.'

Hood was quick to disagree. 'With respect, ma'am, it's important that the full circumstances of this burglary, always assuming there has been a burglary, are thoroughly investigated and that inquiries are carried out by my team under my leadership. The chief constable put me in charge for a reason. And as I have said, I had reported my conversation with Duffy to the ACC. I would respectfully suggest that ACC Gaunt should be spoken to before any decision is made about my position. He has overall control of the investigation. And I'm sure there's a connection with the Trent killings. Neither do we want it becoming generally known that Duffy's file has vanished. That is crucial. Central should be taken off the inquiry and a forensic team brought in under the control of my officers.'

'I'm sure Central can manage,' said West. 'DS Grant knows what she's doing and SOCO are already there…'

Hood interrupted. 'I'm sure she does. But she won't have the breadth or depth of knowledge my team has built up over the last two years. The organisation we are delving into has connections going back to the Campion kidnapping case and the attempted robbery in North Nottinghamshire in which some of the same offenders were involved. Duffy was a major source of information in cracking both cases.'

The DCC could hardly disagree. 'I think there might be something in what Harry says, Charles. When Mr Worth telephoned me, it struck me as very odd why he should have revealed the details of his personal safe to Harry on such short acquaintance.'

'That was a thought which passed through my mind too,' said Hood. 'I'd only known him for twenty minutes when he disclosed what he did. He also told me his own partners, save for his son, were unaware he had a private safe in his room.'

'Perhaps he trusts the police,' said West, 'and doesn't trust his partners. I'm glad that someone has confidence in us. We don't get a very good press much of the time these days.'

The DCC stood up and walked to the window, looked out than turned and faced the two men. 'I spoke with the chief and ACC Gaunt earlier this morning. They're both very keen for Harry to continue to lead the investigation into these murders if at all possible. They both agree with me that these killings may well be connected with Harry's previous inquiries. And if this is an attempt to get Harry off the case, it's important we don't fall for it. As I said, I shall speak to Mr Worth. For the time being, Harry continues to lead the investigations which will now include this burglary. I'll get a message to DS Grant.'

Charles West shrugged his shoulders. 'Whatever you say, ma'am. It is certainly worth looking into why Worth said what he did to the DCI.'

'That's the main reason I want to speak to him. It will come better from me, at least initially.'

Hood sighed with relief then smiled. 'And I suppose I'm going to have to tell Derick Duffy his file has disappeared, am I?'

'You'll be spared that,' replied West, dryly. 'Duffy was found hanged in his cell at Woodborough Prison early this morning.'

CHAPTER 17

'Duffy's dead?' Wendy Knight shook her head in dismay and disbelief as Hood gave her the news. 'And he killed himself? Was there a note?'

'It's certainly been made to look like he did,' replied Hood, 'and, no, he didn't leave a note. Not from what I've been told. Hanged using his bedsheet. But I doubt very much if this is suicide. He's been under threat since he first went into custody and has been moved as many as five times to make sure he stayed alive. I simply don't believe he would have taken this easy way out, not after he revealed the whereabouts of his file. He wanted to use what it supposedly contains to help his daughter to get early parole.'

'It doesn't make sense then for him to have hanged himself.'

'No, it doesn't. I suspect someone gave him a helping hand. That was always the risk he was running. Once they got hold of his file, I suppose there was no longer any reason to let him live.'

'But he was under secure guard, wasn't he?'

'He was. Someone's for the high jump if it turns out he was murdered.'

'Who's investigating the death?' asked Knight. 'Surely it should be us?'

Hood shook his head. 'Superintendent Kingston from Northampton division has been given the task. The Coroner has been informed and the Home Office notified. Duffy's death will be rigorously investigated. A full forensic post-mortem examination has already been authorised and has probably taken place by now.'

'But we are not involved, in the investigation, into his death, I mean?'

'No, not directly. Superintendent Kingston will liaise with me as and when necessary but I propose to visit the prison and inspect his cell.

Our main job is to find out how his file was stolen; oh, and there's also the little matter of establishing with certainty who killed Dudley Manning and Maxine Kruger, of course. Don't forget that. At least we now have the firearms report. We can be sure now that the same gun was used in both killings.'

'And with the silencer attached,' grunted Andrew Hooper. 'Plenty to get on with then. It supports our theory that Doyle overpowered Kruger and used her own gun on her.'

'Which underlines our need to find him,' added Hood. 'Once again, Doyle is the key to our investigation. We have to find him. How did the visit to the cottage in Thrussington go, Wendy?'

'The agent was sure someone had been in the house since his last visit with a prospective purchaser on Tuesday. And the lock on the desk in the sitting room had been forced.'

'Anything missing?' asked Hood.

'Not that he could tell,' replied Knight. 'He's been in touch with the vendor and informed her what has happened. She didn't seem too bothered about it. Unfortunately the neighbour who gave evidence in Hamilton's trial was not in. But we did speak to Tony, the local milkman. He reckons he saw someone on a motorcycle very early on Wednesday morning in the vicinity of Hamilton's cottage, but he can't say whether whoever it was actually went in. He was too far away and engaged with an elderly customer who was in need of urgent medical attention.'

'Doyle,' murmured Hood, grimacing. 'And on a motorbike. It has to have been him. Trying to find out where Julia Hamilton is, I assume. He'd have no other reason for being there. He probably had a key to the cottage but not for the desk.' He sighed audibly. 'When will the neighbour be back? She may have seen or heard something?'

'I don't know, sir. Ray and I called into the Blue Lion just down the road. We were told the neighbour was in London for a couple of days, visiting a relative. I'll try again over the week-end.'

'You do that.'

Hood moved on and produced his notes of the conversation he'd had with Duffy two days before. He read them out, almost in full, to his assembled team then asked for their comments.

'Sounds as if he didn't think he had long to live,' said Hooper, 'though I agree it doesn't look like he was planning to kill himself.'

'He certainly recognised he had problems,' replied Hood. 'Serious problems. He expected attempts would be made on his life. He told me as much after he informed on the others last year. He thought it was only his file and what it was thought to contain that was keeping him alive. But I find it very difficult to believe he killed himself, no matter how carefully it's been made to look like he did.'

'It can't be a coincidence that he ends up dead so shortly after his file had been stolen, can it?' said Raymond Craddock. 'Perhaps its contents was not what whoever organised the burglary expected to find?'

Hood nodded. 'A good point, Raymond. Perhaps Duffy was bluffing all along and there was nothing of significance in the file so he was simply eliminated?'

'I take it we have no idea what was in there?' said Knight.

'No, apart from his last will and testament. And I've been provided with a copy of that. It's very simple and straight forward. He appointed Mr Worth and his daughter as executors and left everything to her.'

'But there are no copies of the rest of the file?'

'Not according to what Duffy told me, no. His solicitor certainly has nothing apart from his will.'

'But if he wanted to use the contents of the file to assist his daughter to get early parole, there must have been something of substance in there. Otherwise he was just wasting everyone's time and putting himself at serious risk for nothing.'

'Unless he had hidden the information somewhere else?' suggested Craddock. All eyes turned towards him.

'You think Duffy might have been lying about the file?' said Hood.

'If he felt under threat to the extent that he did, perhaps the file he placed with the solicitor was a ruse and the real file is located elsewhere?' continued the junior officer. No one else had considered such a possibility. Had young Craddock been reading too many detective novels?

'What made you say that, Raymond?' asked Hood. He looked at him with increasing regard.

Craddock smiled and shrugged his shoulders. 'Just something that occurred to me. Duffy was given to that sort of thing wasn't he? He lived successfully for many years under a false identity. He deceived no end of people. Why should he change his ways now?'

Hood did not dismiss what Craddock had suggested. In fact, the more he thought about it, the more he considered it was not such a wild idea. There might well be something in it. At one time, Duffy had been regarded by police intelligence as the natural successor to the late Gus Grayling, but his turning informer and the prison sentence of 20 years he'd received must have removed him from the succession, always assuming he'd been in line. His sentence was markedly shorter than the periods of imprisonment imposed on his companions in crime because he had chosen to inform on the rest of them in return for a more lenient disposal. The usual brown envelope and senior officer's statement had been delivered to the judge before sentencing took place. Understandably, this did not go down well with his former associates. His later decision to give evidence against Julia Hamilton in an effort to enhance further his prospects of an early release would have served merely to increase the price on his head. Only the file and what it was thought to contain had kept him alive. And Hood did not overlook that when he'd seen Duffy the previous Wednesday he had seemed much cooler about leaving custody on parole or at all. He felt safer inside. Presumably, he must have considered the level of threat had increased? But Hood remained convinced that Duffy had known who had taken over the major crime group after Gus Grayling died and that he would have placed that information somewhere if not in the file lodged with his solicitor.

'If he had deposited the file with his solicitor as a ruse and had stored what he knew elsewhere, where do you reckon he might have hidden it,' he asked Craddock.

The young officer hesitated before replying. 'No idea, sir, but if he wanted to use it to help his daughter, we could do worse than have a word with Kelly Maguire. If he's left everything to her, wherever he's concealed the information, it will presumably come to her in some form or other?'

Hood nodded his agreement. 'I think you're right, Raymond. A very sound suggestion. Find out which prison she's in at the moment. I believe she was moved from the Staffordshire women's unit to Foston Hall during the Hamilton trial but wasn't returned there after she'd given evidence.'

Hood's mobile phone buzzed. He looked at the screen. It was the DCC. He answered promptly.

'Are you alone, Harry?'

'No, ma'am.'

Hood paused then moved out of the incident room, indicating for Hooper to take over. 'I am now.'

'I've spoken with Mr Worth. He isn't suggesting you disclosed where Duffy's file was, which is a relief. He's blaming himself for not replacing it in the strongroom. I've also spoken to DS Grant. There have been developments which cause me some concern. SOCO have found what appears to have been part of a tiny microphone secured to the underside of Mr Worth's desk. Preliminary tests suggest it's pretty high-powered. Whoever removed it did so in a hurry and carelessly left part of it behind. It's beginning to look like you and Worth were overheard. You were right, Harry. Someone must have got into Worth's office the night before and planted it. I think you should get over there again, pronto.'

'DS Smith is already there liaising with SOCO. I'll speak to him before I set out.'

'You do that. This was a very sophisticated operation. We are up against seasoned professionals.'

'Not very professional to leave part of a bug behind, ma'am.' Hood couldn't resist sounding cynical.

'We deserve a bit of luck now and again, don't we?'

Hood did not respond. His doubts about what had really happened at Worth's office were growing but he was more than happy if the DCC thought the presence of a bug under the solicitor's desk acquitted him of any suspicion relating to the theft of Duffy's file. 'So, I'm cleared of any involvement am I?'

The DCC tried her best to soothe Hood's ruffled ego. 'You were never under suspicion, Harry, not from me.'

'Thank you, for that. I'm glad to hear it. No reason I shouldn't share this with my team?'

'No. They'll need to know.' She paused before continuing. 'It's not looking like Doyle could have been behind this. He wouldn't have the resources.'

'Or the knowhow, ma'am.'

'No trace of him yet, I assume?'

'No, ma'am, but Dr Osborne's initial report has been received. He's carried out the usual tests. The same gun was definitely used in both killings.'

'Same killer then?'

'I don't think so. They also found a partial fingerprint on one of the bullets in the magazine. Only nine characteristics but consistent with being Kruger's. We shall have to wait a few days to see if DNA confirms it, but I'm sure the gun was hers. We are working on the basis that Doyle was meant to be the victim on the second occasion. He must have fought back and turned the tables on his would-be killer. I'm also pretty sure that Kruger killed Dudley Manning, probably on the orders of the O.C.G. responsible for the death of Duffy.'

The DCC seemed surprised. 'You don't think Duffy killed himself? I understand that's Maurice Kingston's preliminary view.'

'No, I don't buy that; not for a minute. Not pending a full investigation, anyway. I'm speaking to Maurice Kingston later today for an update, but I think I'm going to have to see Duffy's cell for myself and speak to the officers who were supposed to be keeping him safe.'

'If you think that's appropriate I suppose you should, but please be discreet, Harry. Maurice won't want you poking your nose too deeply into his investigation. It's important we keep some distance between your inquiry and the investigation into Duffy's death.' She paused again.

'You also need to know this. I'm told there was unrest in the prison at lockup on Thursday night. They had to get the riot squad in. The fact that there was trouble has been kept under wraps for the time being, but it will all come out eventually. There'll be serious criminal charges against some of the inmates. It could well be that the officers who were supposed to be keeping an eye on Duffy were diverted.'

'Diverted, ma'am? There could well be more to it than that.'

'Don't say that, Harry. That's the last thing we need. It's possible, I suppose, that the riot could have been organised in order to give someone the opportunity to get at Duffy and there are certainly some vicious criminals in there. It looks like this thing is bigger than even you thought.'

'But how could anyone get into Duffy's cell without a key? Someone had to let his killers in, assuming he was murdered. He didn't associate with the other inmates.'

'I've been informed that two officers were overpowered and their keys removed. More than a dozen prisoners are being moved elsewhere, some of them to Whitemoor.'

'That might explain it then. No doubt Maurice Kingston will be able to identify the officers concerned?'

'Yes, he should. One of them is still in hospital – he was badly beaten up but their names are known. Maurice will have all the information you need. It's aways possible, I suppose, that you're right. One or more of the officers could have been involved. But according to what I've been told, there is no way Duffy's cell could have been entered. Those keys were kept in a locked key-safe and they had to be signed for every time they were required. They were still there this morning and his cell was still securely locked immediately before he was found. There will certainly be a big push from the prison service to uphold a verdict of suicide at the inquest.'

'Hardly surprising. They'll not want to be landed with the blame.'

Hood hesitated. If the keys had not been taken, it would advance the likelihood of Duffy being responsible for his own death. He could not disguise his frustration. 'But someone must have got hold of the keys.

If we can't establish the keys were used, it's going to be very difficult to prove foul play. Unless, of course, the post mortem shows up something. Who's the consultant pathologist?'

'Guy Romney.'

'He's a good man. If there is anything, he'll find it.'

'I'll leave it with you then, Harry. Keep me informed of any further developments.'

'I will, ma'am. Any idea when the PM report will be made available?'

'You'll have to ask Maurice Kingston about that. He attended the post mortem. He and Guy Romney should have all the details.'

CHAPTER 18

Detective Chief Inspector Hood set out for HMP Brampton Hall on the Leicestershire/Northamptonshire border. He was heading to the women's prison to which Kelly Maguire had been transferred shortly after completing her evidence at Nottingham Crown Court in Julia Hamilton's trial. He took Detective Sergeant Knight with him, thinking the presence of a female officer might induce greater cooperation from the sullen daughter of Derick Duffy. He was aware that Kelly had only recently been told of her father's death but he felt it necessary to speak with her as soon as possible. It had been reported that she had taken the news badly, understandably in the circumstances, and had refused to leave her room. She had not eaten anything all day.

Hood and Knight called in at Worth, Ambler and Partners as they passed through Leicester on their way to Brampton. The senior partner readily made himself available, anxious as he was to assist the investigation as much as he could. His personal office had now been designated a crime scene and he was obliged to work in a different room as SOCO completed their examination of what remained of his private safe and the area immediately around it. The senior scenes of crime officer pointed to where the bug had been secured. The remnants had already been removed but some of the glue that had been used to keep it in place remained so Hood could identify where it had been secured. He shook his head. Someone had been very careless, or so it seemed. He then spoke briefly with the mortified solicitor in the boardroom. Mr Worth couldn't hide his embarrassment as he tried to explain why he had not returned Duffy's file to the main strongroom after Hood had left him on Thursday morning other than to indicate that his secretary leaving early that day to attend a dental appointment together with pressure of work had meant he didn't have the opportunity to replace it in the strongroom. His appointment with a major commercial client had been prolonged. Unforeseen complications in the business in hand meant that the meeting went on well into the evening. Mr Farmer and his staff had all left for the day and replacing the file proved impractical. Intending as he was to return the file to the strongroom first thing on Friday morning when Farmer returned, he had been horrified to discover when he walked into his office that his safe had been forced open and the file gone. He could not fathom how anyone could possibly have known that the DCI was visiting him on Thursday morning or that their conversation would turn to the precise whereabouts of Duffy's file. Only his trusted secretary was aware of Hood's appointment and no one could have foreseen what their conversation would have been about. Hood had his suspicions, but kept them to himself until he and Knight were well on their way to Brampton Hall.

'How could anyone have known you were going to see Mr Worth yesterday?' asked Wendy as they travelled in Hood's Saab 9.3 estate towards Brampton. 'You didn't even tell me.'

'I kept it to myself deliberately,' replied Hood. 'I was rather going out on a limb speaking to Duffy as I did. He refused to say anything when Sean Smith was present. I had to ask him to leave the room. But now I come to think about it, I have a nasty suspicion that Duffy himself was the source. No one else knew what I was intending to do. I didn't tell anyone I was proposing to visit the solicitor. I didn't even disclose it to Sean.'

'But why would Duffy want to tell anyone what he'd disclosed to you or what you proposed to do?'

'I don't know, but he may have been put under considerable pressure by someone; someone who wanted to get me off the case, perhaps? He could even have been ordered to tell me about the file to make it appear I had revealed where it was located. If it hadn't been for the discovery of the remains of that bug under Worth's desk, I'd probably be on gardening leave right now.' He smiled to himself before continuing. 'That's why we have to see Duffy's daughter. He told me she'd been having a hard time in her previous prison, which is why, I assume, she was moved to the gentler regime of Brampton Hall after Hamilton's trial.'

Knight hesitated before saying anything in response. She was already having doubts about the listening device placed under Worth's desk. 'I may be on the slow side, sir, but do you really think the bug was left behind accidently? Seems very careless given what we know about this O.C.G.'

Hood acknowledged Knight's suspicions. 'I have concerns about that too, but at least finding it where we did got professional standards off my back. I should be grateful for that, I suppose.'

'But if they really wanted to implicate you, they'd have been very careful not to leave something like that behind, wouldn't they? Why would they give you such an easy way out?'

'An excellent observation, Wendy. I suspect it was left there for another reason; perhaps to mislead us into thinking an unlawful entry had been made into the solicitor's office?'

Knight smiled. She was pleased that her doubts about a burglary having taken place were shared by the DCI. 'It has certainly crossed my mind that it could have been an inside job.'

Hood nodded his agreement. 'You could well be right, but I don't think we should rush to judgement, not at the moment. I've asked Sean to look into it in more detail. The alarm was not triggered. That's probably significant. It would have been relatively simple for someone who worked in the office to place part of a bug under Worth's desk in order to mislead, then to gain access to the safe in the senior partner's absence.'

'But there are over seventy people who work there. It might be impossible to prove who was responsible.'

'Don't I know it.' He paused before continuing. 'We'll have to give it some serious thought – after we've seen Kelly Maguire and heard from Sean. I'm concerned about Kelly. Duffy knew she was due to be moved and she probably told him where she's now detained which will mean others who might do her harm also know where she is. Duffy was genuinely worried about her; I think we should be too. This organisation seems to be able to infiltrate even the most secure of establishments.'

'So, she might not be safe even where she is now?'

'That could well be the case. Although I doubt whoever's taken over from Grayling will have established the sort of influence at HMP Brampton Hall that he was able to bring to bear at Woodborough. It takes time to corrupt someone on the inside. And some of the inmates at Woodborough would be only too willing to dirty their hands if offered a suitable inducement. That will be much more difficult to achieve at Brampton, at least in the next few days. There's a higher staff ratio there and fewer prisoners. All the women are designated as vulnerable, although there are a few killers there approaching the end of their tariffs, domestic killings in the main. Kelly can hopefully look after herself in such a regime.'

'I suppose we should be checking on any new staff at Brampton, just to be on the safe side?'

'I've already got that in hand. I've arranged to speak to the Governor after we've seen Kelly. She should be able to let us know the identities of anyone who has been taken on or transferred to Brampton in the last month. That will include inmates as well as staff. I wouldn't put it past this O.C.G. to organise someone to be transferred there as a prisoner just to get at Kelly. Trouble is, it may make us late for our appointment with Guy Romney. Happily, the prison is conveniently close to Kettering General Hospital and we need to see him to discuss the results of the PM.'

Knight let out a lengthy sigh. 'And there was I wondering how she wangled a transfer to Brampton Hall. She's serving a long sentence for armed robbery and kidnap, isn't she? She wouldn't usually qualify for Category D until she was well into a sentence of that length. And when I looked up Brampton it sounded more like a holiday camp than a prison.'

Hood smiled. 'I don't think it quite falls into that category. But, you're right, she is serving a lengthy sentence and, as things stand, won't get within sniffing distance of parole for another ten years or so.

But as I said, she's highly vulnerable, essentially because of her father. She's being treated as an exceptional case for that reason. It's fortunate she was transferred when she was. Now that Duffy's dead, if Craddock is right and the stolen file doesn't contain what the O.C.G. thought it did, she may have suffered the same fate as her father had she remained where she was. She's already being given what passes as additional security at Brampton from this morning just to be on the safe side.'

HMP Brampton Hall, originally a large but undistinguished country house, was built in the reign of William IV for a wealthy shoe manufacturer anxious to establish himself in the style of a country gentleman. It had a far from illustrious history. Several later Victorian additions had served only to ensure Historic England would never list it as being of architectural merit or importance. Occupied by the military in the later stages of World War II, half a dozen bungalows had been thrown up, very cheaply, behind the main building to house military and administrative staff. No longer required after hostilities ceased, the whole estate was transferred to the Home Office in the mid-sixties and used as a centre for training higher-grade civil servants. Both the main house and its more modern extensions along with the extensive parkland deteriorated significantly over the years and it was eventually deemed unsuitable for educational purposes. Taken over by the prison service in 1987, it became a secure detention centre for under eighteens before transforming into its present role as a category D prison for female prisoners approaching the end of their sentences. Considerable refurbishment had taken place and very real efforts made to disguise its present function. It certainly bore little resemblance to most people's idea of what a prison should look like. The perimeter fence began only several hundred yards down the lengthy gravelled drive and it was only at that point that the usual prison notices appeared describing its function and warning visitors that the prison rules were now in force. Anyone driving past on the main road would not have appreciated that there was a prison at the end of the drive. The only drawback was that visitors frequently had difficulty finding it. Public access to the wooded parkland was also generally discouraged save for the farmers who grazed their sheep on the grasslands at the edge of the park.

The residents (referring to them as prisoners was discouraged) were lodged in rooms, not cells, and the regime was one of rehabilitation and treatment rather than simple incarceration. Detainees were allowed to wear their own clothes and given extended visiting rights, most granted week-end parole in the weeks before their final discharge. There were only one hundred and five inmates, many of whom had suffered in the past with serious psychological problems. A number of them had killed their abusive partners and needed additional care and therapy. But Brampton Hall was not a hospital. It remained part of the prison system and its inmates were aware that a failure to follow the rules could mean transfer back to a much stricter environment.

After negotiating the traffic in Market Harborough, Hood turned off the A6 and headed east on the Corby Road. He managed to drive past the gates of his intended destination, silently cursing when he realised he had gone too far. He then turned and retraced his steps until he spotted the entrance. "Brampton Hall" was carved in the left of two stone pillars, but the surface was worn and the letters hardly visible.

'You'd think they have put up a sign that could be seen,' complained Knight, 'even if they didn't want it to be generally known there was a prison here.'

Hood nodded but said nothing. He drove for about three hundred yards along the gravelled drive until he reached a barrier where the perimeter fencing began. A security officer emerged from an adjacent hut and checked the registered number of Hood's vehicle against a list on his clip-board. He smiled, nodded, then raised the barrier, pointing to the rear of the main building. Hood, noting the CCTV cameras, thanked him, then swung his Saab around, passing a number of vehicles which he assumed belonged to staff before entering a small tarmacadamed area where he carefully parked in a designated visitor's space. He and Knight remained in the car until they were approached by a female officer. Hood wound down the driver's window then produced his warrant card. The officer examined it, nodded her head and pointed to a couple of semi-detached cottages at the bottom of the car park. His arrival had obviously been anticipated.

'Kelly is in the bungalow on the left. There's an officer there who will take you to her room. We are keeping a weather eye on her at the moment given the circumstances.' She smiled. 'It looks pretty casual, but there is CCTV and a boundary fence., although that's designed to keep others out rather than to keep our ladies in. We rely on trust. No one has attempted to leave us early, not in my time here anyway.'

'You obviously know why I'm here to see Kelly Maguire,' said Hood.

The officer nodded. 'The governor informed me earlier today. Kelly's taken the death of her father very badly. The governor would have greeted you herself, but she's in a meeting at the moment with her deputy and someone from the Home Office. This place is under strict monitoring by the powers that be, you know. There are some highly placed people in London who would like to close us down, but I think we are doing a good job. Most of our ladies do not re-offend once they are discharged.'

'It's certainly more pleasant than many prisons I've visited,' said Hood, looking around him. He noticed two women he took to be inmates working in a vegetable garden on the other side of the parking area. A third was feeding some chickens in a run surrounded by a mesh fence. The officer waited before continuing.

'If you come to the governor's office in the main building when you've finished with Kelly, Mrs Ledbury will see you then.' She pointed towards a side door. 'The officer will unlock that door for you and show you where her office is. By the way, although Kelly is still very upset, she's gradually bearing up.'

'You know what happened to her father, do you?' asked Hood.

The officer's response indicated that she knew more than Hood had anticipated. 'Only what I've been told. He was found in his cell, hung apparently; that's what Kelly was informed. But she doesn't believe he killed himself. She made that very plain to the governor when she was told about his death this morning. She reckons he was murdered, but she hasn't said anything else, not to me anyway. As you would expect, she's rather upset. She doesn't feel he was looked after properly at Woodborough. She spoke to him over the phone recently.' The officer paused and then questioned whether it was wise for Hood to interview Kelly so soon after she had been told of her father's death. 'You don't think it's a bit early to interrogate Kelly, sir? She's not long known about her father's death.'

'I shall be as gentle as possible, I assure you. But a great deal may turn on what she may be able to tell me. Her own safety may well be compromised. We can't delay matters.'

Hood thanked the officer as he and Knight got out of his car. He looked around him again, then locked the Saab. No point in taking the risk of someone gaining access to it. After all, despite appearances, he and Knight were in a prison and although the inmates were vulnerable, they would include a goodly number of thieves amongst them.

CHAPTER 19

Hood knocked gently on the door of Kelly Maguire's room, the young officer who accompanied the two detectives explaining that it was part of the culture of the place to indicate one's presence by knocking. Staff were not permitted simply to open an inmate's door and enter except in case of an emergency. The internal doors in the bungalow where Kelly resided were never locked and the three other inmates who shared the kitchen facilities with her were free to come and go into each other's rooms until 8 p.m. The outside door was then locked and each was trusted to remain in her own room. Occasional checks were made to ensure the rules were followed.

Kelly eventually opened the door and the officer withdrew. It was obvious to Hood that she had been crying. She looked him over, recognising him as the police officer who had interrogated her the previous year. 'I was expecting you'd show up,' she said, standing back and allowing Hood and Knight to enter her room. 'I suppose you want to talk to me about my dad?'

'That's right,' said Hood. He introduced DS Knight then expressed his condolences. 'I'm sorry for your loss, Kelly. I know you were very fond of your father and he of you. You have my sympathy.' He looked at her intently as her eyes filled with tears and she started to weep. Knight tried to comfort her as Hood looked around the room. The accommodation provided bore little resemblance to a typical prison cell. There were no bars visible and the room was decorated in two shades of pastel yellow. Brightly coloured curtains framed the window and the floor was for the most part carpeted. A small ensuite shower room and lavatory was situated behind an open door to the right. Apart from the bed, covered with a duvet which almost matched the colour scheme, there was a comfortable-looking armchair, a table with two hard-backed chairs, a bookshelf containing several volumes and a wall-mounted TV. There were papers and a couple of books on the table and a music centre against the far wall. Hood picked up one of the books and glanced at it. Kelly, who was gradually recovering her composure, noticed his interest.

'I'm doing a degree in English Literature with the Open University,' she explained, wiping the tears from her eyes.

Hood put the book down. 'Middlemarch,' he observed. 'George Eliot. Very good.' He looked at her. 'I have a degree in English Literature myself, but I prefer Dickens to Elliot.'

Kelly seemed unimpressed. 'Fills the time, and that's one thing I have a lot of, stuck in here.'

Hood took another look around the room. Overall, it was certainly cosier than the accommodation he had endured as a student in his university hall of residence back in the nineteen-eighties. Kelly then invited Hood and Knight to sit down at the table while she sunk into the deep cushions of the armchair. She now seemed in control of herself but Hood noticed she hugged herself like a child as she curled up in the chair. But he was surprised when she spoke that she adopted a quite hostile tone. Knight took out her notebook and pen.

'I hope you haven't come here to try and persuade me that Duffy committed suicide, because I don't and won't believe it. He wouldn't do that. He just wouldn't. So don't you try and convince me that he did. And the governor told me he didn't leave a note.'

Hood spoke as sympathetically as he knew how. 'I haven't come here to persuade you of anything, Kelly. As you would expect, whatever happened at Woodborough is now subject to a full investigation. We shall have to await the outcome of that before coming to any firm conclusions, but if you want my take on it, I agree with you. I saw your father on Wednesday. He certainly didn't give me the impression he was thinking of taking his own life. Quite the contrary. Tell me, when did you last speak with him?'

Kelly did not respond for some time. When she did her tone remained unfriendly and cold. 'He was only allowed one phone call a week with me. We last spoke on Wednesday, late afternoon, I think? I lose all track of time in here.' She sighed, sat up in the armchair, then explained further. 'I have to go into the main building to make or receive a phone call and that has to be at a specified time so it will be logged somewhere. We aren't allowed mobile phones, more's the pity.'

'He was aware you had been moved here, I believe?' She nodded. Hood looked around the room again. 'This certainly seems much more comfortable than the prison in Staffordshire where you were detained before.'

'It's OK, I suppose, but it's still a prison. I can't leave and I can't do what I want to do.'

'What do you want to do?' asked Hood. He was hardly prepared for the answer that came.

Kelly's tone hardened. 'What do you think? To kill the bastard who did my dad in.'

'I wouldn't advise that,' said Hood. 'It will only lead to more trouble for you.' He paused to let his advice sink in. 'So, you think you know who might be responsible, do you?'

'I have a good idea who ordered it, yes.'

'Care to share it with me?'

'No I wouldn't.'

Hood waited before continuing. 'What did you and your father say to each other when you last spoke?'

'Nothing in particular. I told him what it was like here and he was pleased it was an improvement on my previous prison. Mind you, anything would be an improvement on that dump. Stafford was almost as bad as Holloway. Foston Hall wasn't bad but I was only there during Julia Hamilton's trial.' She paused briefly as if considering whether she should say anything further, then thought better of it. Was she leaving it to Hood to make the running? The chief inspector introduced the question of early release with some trepidation.

'Have you been told when you'll be allowed to make your application for parole? You're usually given that information during your first session with the probation officer immediately after sentence.'

Kelly gave him a fierce look before replying. 'Not before two thousand and eleven, always assuming I live that long. I'll be nearly forty by then.'

Hood continued in sympathetic mode. 'As I said, I saw your father on Wednesday. He wasn't very forthcoming, but he did ask me if I was prepared to help you with your parole date, you know, to get it brought forward.'

'He told me he was going to do that when we spoke early last week, just before I was moved here, but no doubt you wanted something from him in return? You lot never do anything unless there's something in it for you.'

Hood shifted in his seat. This was not going to be an easy interview. 'Did your father say anything else to you?'

'You mean the last time I spoke to him?'

'Not just on that occasion. Anything he may have said at any time may assist in establishing his state of mind.'

Kelly glared at him. She spoke sharply. 'There was nothing wrong with his state of mind. I've told you, he didn't kill himself. He wouldn't have left me alone to cope with my sentence, not now.' Her eyes filled with tears again. 'Twenty-four years – that's what I got! Twenty-four fucking years, and I didn't hurt anyone.' She turned away and started to sob. 'Murderers get less than I did.'

Hood looked at Knight and waited until Kelly had recovered her composure. 'I agree. Twenty-four years is a long time. But you have to admit, they were very serious offences you got yourself embroiled in.'

'I only went along with them to make sure the kid and the woman came to no harm.'

'That's as may be,' replied Hood, 'but you also fired a loaded shotgun into the rear doors of a security van out Ollerton way, remember?' She half-smiled as she remembered the excitement of that moment, then looked down. 'Anyway,' continued Hood, 'there's no point going over old ground. I'm as keen as you are to discover how your father died. Look, I admit I did ask for his help, yes, and he for mine. *Quid pro quo.*' He paused as he changed the subject. 'You probably know that Gus Grayling died some time ago?'

'Yes. What of it? He'd been ill for a long time, according to what Adam told me. It wasn't exactly unexpected.'

'That would be Adam Leckie?'

'Yes, my then boyfriend. He got me involved in all this; not that we are in a relationship any longer. He picked up even more than me.' She let out a lengthy sigh. 'I don't even write to him anymore.'

'You knew Grayling, of course, didn't you, before he died?'

'Did I?'

'Come on, Kelly. We know you were involved with Julia Hamilton. You gave evidence on her behalf. You knew she went to Hastings to see him, didn't you?'

'Did I? I heard that the jury gave her a not-guilty. Had they been certain she'd been to see Grayling, they'd have convicted her, wouldn't they? And it couldn't have been me who took her there. I was in hospital in Swansea having my appendix removed. Remember? It was just a coincidence she went there on a motorbike. I think Duffy did see her there like he said.'

'We have a good idea who took her to Hastings to see Grayling, as I suspect do you. You knew Maxine Kruger too, didn't you?'

'Kruger? She's dead, isn't she? It was in all the newspapers. She was pulled out of the River Trent.'

'That's right. She'd been shot. Did you know that?'

Kelly shrugged her shoulders as Hood continued. 'You and Julia Hamilton certainly associated with some very dangerous people. We have reason to believe Kruger was part of Grayling's organised crime group.'

'I've heard the name. Adam mentioned her once. But I don't know what she or Julia Hamilton got up to. I was asked, well told really, to give evidence that I didn't take her to Hastings, which was the truth. I didn't see any harm in telling the truth.'

'I think if you had told the whole truth when you gave evidence in court the result might have been different. You'd hardly have been called as a witness if you hadn't been minded to side with her.

Remember, I was there at the trial. I saw you in the box.'

She almost laughed. 'You don't really believe that anything I said made any difference, do you? Joseph Hanlon escaping from prison in the middle of his evidence must have really buggered up the prosecution case. I don't think anything much turned on what I said.'

Hood could not resist a smile. 'Hanlon's disappearance certainly didn't help. You knew that was going to happen did you?'

Her response was immediate. 'Of course I didn't. I knew he'd done a runner before I gave evidence, but everyone did. It was all over the media. I knew nothing about it before it happened. My contact with Joseph Hanlon was minimal. I was scared of him, as was everyone else. Even Adam gave him a wide birth.'

'Your father told me you certainly knew Hanlon.'

Kelly scowled. 'Hanlon was in charge of the kidnapping, as you know; he was Grayling's muscle, so I suppose I did know him, but I'd never met him before we went to the judge's house. And that's the truth. It was Duffy who organised things. He was the planner; Hanlon's just a thug and a liar.' She gave Hood a critical look. 'And you let him escape, didn't you? There's no saying what he'll get up to now.'

Hood felt there was no point in trying to explain he was not responsible for Hanlon's escape. Kelly continued. 'But I'm sure it's because he foolishly gave evidence against Julia Hamilton that my dad's now dead. I didn't want him to. I told him no good would come of it. Looks like I was right.'

Hood shook his head. 'Possibly. But your father was a marked man well before then. He'd already fingered the kidnappers and the team that carried out the attempted robbery near Ollerton long before Hamilton's trial. He included you, of course. It was your father who told me who you were. You refused to say and we didn't have anything on record at that time to identify you. No fingerprints, no DNA. Mind you, he did ask me to go easy on you.'

'He didn't tell you anything about me that you didn't already know or wouldn't have found out. I was caught red-handed, as you said.' She raised her voice and flared her nostrils. 'Someone grassed us up, and it wasn't Duffy. He only made his witness statement *after* we'd all been arrested. The police were waiting for us. We never stood a chance.'

Hood gave her a wry grin. 'You'll appreciate that's not something I can go into with you.'

Unable to cope with the silence that followed, Kelly felt compelled to continue talking. It was now clear to Hood that having been told of her father's demise she needed to talk to someone, anyone, and he was quite content that he should be that person. He fully appreciated he was taking advantage of her distressed condition, but felt he had no option. Lives depended on it. She continued to talk about her father.

'And someone grassed him up as well. He'd been living in South Wales for years. No one knew his real identity, apart from Grayling – and Michael Doyle, of course. Dad reckoned it was Doyle who informed on him. It couldn't have been anyone else.'

There was no way Hood was going to confirm Doyle's part in exposing Duffy. He continued to push Kelly hard, perhaps too hard. 'It wasn't just Gus Grayling and Doyle who knew about your father. You knew too, didn't you? You were spending a lot of time in South Wales. You knew all about his background and his true identity. He told you everything. Am I right?'

Kelly reacted furiously. 'Are you suggesting I grassed him up? You can do one if that's what you think. This conversation is at an end.' She stood up and walked to the door, opened it and stood there seething. 'Go on. Fuck off! I'm saying nothing more to you.'

Hood remained where he was. Perhaps he had gone in too hard? 'Don't be like that, Kelly. I'm not suggesting for a moment that you grassed up anyone, least of all your father. If you had, you'd have been informing on yourself at the same time. Believe it or not, I came here to help you. I'm genuinely worried about your safety. Grayling's mob had been after your father since his arrest last year. What worries me is that they may now turn their attention to you.'

She narrowed her eyes, hesitated, then closed the door. 'Me? Why should they want to do anything to me? I did exactly what they told me. I know where my interests lie.'

'We believe they've already attempted to kill Michael Doyle.'

She smiled. 'That doesn't surprise me. That's what happens to people like him who grass. Did they succeed?'

Hood did not respond. He had no intention of disclosing what he knew about Doyle, not that he knew very much. Kelly smiled, cynically. 'He has the luck of the devil, that one. He must have grassed someone up big time to get paroled when he did. And that someone was Duffy! It wouldn't surprise me if he's been done away with.'

'You tell me.'

She smirked. 'You won't be seeing him again, not with Hanlon out there free as a bird. And there's nothing Hanlon would like more than to see Doyle dead. He enjoys hurting people. Mark my words.'

'Do you have some idea where Doyle might be or what's happened to him? It's in your interests that we find him as much as ours.'

'How the hell should I know? It may have escaped your notice, Mr Hood, but I've been inside for almost the last twelve months. I've heard nothing from anyone. All I know is what I read in the papers and what the screws in Stafford told me.' She sighed deeply. 'If he's still alive, he'll have gone abroad. That's what he and Julia always intended, or so my dad told me.'

'I understand that you were threatened in Stafford?'

'I made a few enemies at Stafford, not that that's unusual on the inside. There are some nasty people in prison, you know, even in this place.'

Hood could hardly disagree. 'Your father was very concerned about you. He clearly thought that he was putting you in danger by refusing to cooperate with whoever has taken over from Grayling.' The mention of her father again caused Kelly's eyes to well with tears. Hood continued. 'He felt he'd let you down while you were growing up. That's what he told me. He wanted to make it up to you, to help you to get out of places like this well before your present parole date.'

She wiped her eyes and looked directly at Hood. 'And how, exactly, was he proposing to do that?'

'Do you know who has taken over from Gus Grayling?'

Her response was too quick for Hood to consider credible. 'How would I know that? I was just an extra brought in to assist with the kidnapping. It was my boyfriend who got me involved. Duffy wasn't keen I should take part other than to case the judge's home. That's all I was going to do, at first. Then he wanted to make sure nothing happened to the judge's wife and the kid, which is the only reason he let me join in. Grayling couldn't have cared less about them. He was only interested in money. The money he was supposed to get for making sure Michael Doyle got off.' She looked away again. 'Duffy wasn't like Grayling.'

It had not escaped Hood's notice that Kelly frequently referred to her father by his surname. But he was aware that Kelly only got to know him in her late teens. Duffy had spent several years in prison as she was growing up and she and her mother had had little to do with him; he was just a name to her until he moved to South Wales and their relationship was renewed. The chief inspector continued to press her. 'Neither, I suspect, is Doyle. I don't think he knew anything about it. Hamilton never told him what she was up to. She seems to have gone in with Grayling's mob for her own reasons. Someone certainly pulled a lot of strings to make sure she was acquitted.'

'She's abandoned Doyle then, has she? He certainly couldn't have done anything for her. Not while he was inside. She obviously went in with someone who could. Makes sense to me.'

'That's what it looks like. And I suspect you know who.'

Kelly said nothing for several seconds. That she did not immediately repeat her denial intrigued Hood. When she did eventually speak it confirmed to Hood that she knew more than she was letting on. 'And I thought those two were definitely an item. She certainly never gave me the impression that she was interested in anyone else. I always thought she'd have done anything for Doyle.' She paused, then added cynically, 'but she was always interested in number one was Julia, not that I blame her. We all have to look after ourselves.'

'So, you did know her?'

Kelly did not reply.

'Did you know she's had a child?'

'That's what I read in the papers. She said the kid was Doyle's when she gave evidence. That's according to what I read in the *Sun*. Named the boy after him too, so it said.'

Hood hesitated. He was in two minds whether he should say anything further about Hamilton's child. He decided to take the risk. He was convinced Kelly knew more than she was prepared to disclose. 'We have reason to believe that Doyle is not the father. That distinction belongs to whoever's taken over from Grayling. We believe Julia is with him in Portugal.'

Kelly seemed sceptical. Her eyebrows shot up. 'Portugal? I don't know about that. I'd heard she wanted to have a child. But she wanted Doyle to be the father. She was madly in love with him. That's what everyone said. And he was besotted with her. That's why she organised the kidnapping – to get him off. Who else would have thought of doing what she did? Kidnapping a judge's wife? You'd have to be pretty desperate to do something like that, or insane.' She paused and let out a lengthy sigh. 'I wish I knew someone who would do something like that for me. There's no way I'll be having a child if I'm stuck in here for the next eleven years.'

'When did she tell you that?' Hood gave her a severe look. 'You did know her, didn't you?'

Kelly smiled. 'No comment.'

The chief inspector decided to turn to the issue of Duffy's file. Knight would now take over the questioning. He thought the detective sergeant might be more successful than he in prising useful information from the daughter of Derick Duffy. Knight got straight to the point. She put down her note book and pen on the table and turned and faced Kelly.

'Your father told the DCI that he had a file lodged with a firm of solicitors in Leicester, a file that contained highly damaging information about Gus Grayling's organisation. We believe it was that file and the fact that it couldn't be got at that kept him alive – until yesterday. They couldn't take the risk of killing him because he'd left instructions for it to be delivered to the authorities in the event of his death.'

Kelly did not react other than to suggest that as her father was now dead, she assumed any such file would make its way to the authorities in accordance with his instructions. She was obviously not yet prepared to reveal what she knew. Hood was beginning to get the impression that she was toying with them. She was certainly playing her cards very close to her chest.

'There's a problem with that,' said Knight. She glanced towards Hood who nodded for her to continue. 'It appears that the file was stolen just a few hours before your father was found dead in his cell. We think the two events are connected. It's too much of a coincidence to believe otherwise.'

Kelly looked blankly at Hood then dropped her head. She said nothing for over a minute. When she looked up a cynical smile crossed her face. 'I thought you said this file couldn't be got at?'

Hood and Knight exchanged glances. 'You knew about this file, did you?' asked the chief inspector.

Kelly scowled but did not reply. She was still reluctant to give anything away. Was she sizing Hood up, deciding whether she could trust him? He sighed in frustration as he indicated for Knight to continue. The detective sergeant stood up and moved closer to Kelly. 'If you did know about it, it's very important you tell us. You will need protecting from whoever killed your father. They could be coming for you next. If he didn't kill himself, he was probably murdered because the file didn't contain what he'd claimed was in there. He was either bluffing or he has the information stashed somewhere else. Did your father say anything more to you about this file?'

Kelly stood up to put distance between herself and Knight. She walked to the window, then turned and faced Hood and Knight. 'How do I know if I can trust you? My dad wasn't at all sure whether he could risk telling even you the full story. And he's ended up dead.' She bit her lower lip in an effort to maintain control of her emotions.

'Did he tell you about this file?' insisted Knight. 'We really need to know.'

Kelly did not answer immediately, but she was showing signs of uneasiness when she eventually replied. Even then she did not mention the file. 'Perhaps he was killed because they were no longer afraid of what he had on them? And giving evidence against Julia Hamilton wouldn't have helped. That must have really pissed them off.' She paused and looked directly at Hood. 'Anyway, if they've got what they wanted, why should they bother me?'

Hood took over the questioning. 'But we don't know whether they did get what they wanted. That's the point. It depends what was in the file. If it wasn't what they anticipated, in my professional opinion, their next port of call has to be you. They're bound to think you know where your father really placed the information he had about Grayling's organisation. They won't give up easily. Don't forget, Kelly, your father was once very close to Grayling. He probably knew everything there is to know about this O.C.G. He was part and parcel of it for years. He could even have been Grayling's designated successor at one time.'

She scoffed. 'I don't think so. I've already told you, Duffy wasn't anything like Grayling. You'd have to be one hell of a ruthless bastard to take over from him.'

Hood hesitated. 'Why do you sometimes refer to your father as Duffy?'

She shrugged her shoulders. 'That's what my mother called him. I suppose I got into the habit when I was younger. I hardly knew him then. And he didn't seem to mind except when we were in company. I had to be careful to use his adopted name when I was with him in South Wales though, Lafferty, that's what he was known as. Why he chose such a name I've no idea.'

'I think the name was chosen for him – by Grayling.'

She did not respond. Hood returned to the question of the file. 'He must have placed the information he had on them somewhere. He could hardly keep it with him in prison. Perhaps there's another file hidden away somewhere?'

Kelly sat down on the edge of her bed, heaved a sigh, then looked at Hood. 'There isn't another file.'

Hood tried not to react. He threw a concerned look towards Knight. 'There isn't? Are you saying there was nothing in the file at the solicitors? It was all a ruse? Duffy was bluffing all along?'

She gave Hood a harsh look. 'I didn't say that. The file at the solicitors contained Dad's will and some other papers, but they were of no account. The real information he had on Grayling and his mob is stored elsewhere.'

'Where?'

She did not reply for over a minute before smiling broadly and tapping her forehead. 'A lot of it is in my head but the rest is safe enough.'

Hood appeared puzzled. 'What do you mean?'

Kelly seemed relieved to unload what she knew. 'Duffy gave me chapter and verse when you allowed me to speak to him when we were first arrested. Remember? He realised he was going to become a target after he informed on everyone. He thought he could have been killed at any moment. And he continued to reveal things whenever we spoke right up to when we were sentenced. I had the full story by then.'

'Nothing is written down? There are no documents?'

She nodded. 'He thought it was safer that way. He didn't trust anyone except me. There's some paperwork and accounts, but they relate in the main to Grayling setting him up in Wales. They are safe, where no one will find them. He used the same accountant as Grayling, you know.'

'I didn't know that, but it doesn't surprise me. The haulage business seems to have been basically legitimate. I suppose you will inherit it?'

Her reply was full of bitterness. 'A lot of good that will do me, stuck in here.'

Hood continued. 'What does surprise me is that your father trusted you with details of the O.C.G. He cooperated with me almost immediately after his arrest. You didn't. You only pleaded after he dropped you in it. Why should he have put his trust in you?'

Kelly smiled. 'Think about it, Mr Hood. He wasn't stupid, you know. It was all part of his plan to protect me. He warned me that I had to keep in with Grayling's mob until I was released from prison and that won't be for years as things stand. He wasn't expecting me to get such a long sentence, not after he cooperated with the police. That came as a bit of a shock, I can tell you. But he told me the O.C.G. wouldn't hesitate to have me killed if I didn't follow their orders. That's why I gave evidence at Hamilton's trial. I don't mind telling you I was dreading it. I couldn't understand why they wanted her to get off. I thought they wanted her to be convicted. Something had definitely changed. Then, after Hanlon escaped, I didn't think they'd want me anymore. But her lawyers decided to call me, or so I was told. I was actually surprised I was brought to court. It was only because Hanlon lied and said I had taken Julia Hamilton to Hastings on my bike to see Grayling that they needed me to give evidence.'

Hood reflected on what Kelly had said. She obviously appreciated that Grayling's object had been to frustrate Julia Hamilton's plan. But something had changed and changed dramatically. Someone clearly wanted Hamilton to be acquitted, not convicted. And that someone must have been Grayling's successor. He needed to find out how much Kelly really knew. 'Why did your father choose to tell me the name of the solicitor who held his file? He'd refused to say anything about it before then. And I'd asked him on several occasions.'

'I don't know, Mr Hood. But I think he had his reasons or someone did.'

'What do you mean? What reasons?'

She almost smiled. 'I may as well tell you. It's quite amusing when you think about it. Duffy had been ordered to tell you which firm of solicitors held his file. That's why he asked to see you. They promised him they would leave him be if he did what he was told. He didn't believe them, of course. He didn't trust them an inch, but he did what they demanded. He also knew that they'd already discovered that his file was with the solicitors in Leicester, so he wasn't telling them anything they didn't already know. And he also knew that the file didn't contain what the O.C.G. wanted.'

'How could they know where the file was?'

'Someone must have said something.'

'But who else would know where the file was?'

'No idea, but someone obviously did.' She gave Hood a knowing look.

'How did the O.C.G. communicate with your father? He was under tight security, or was supposed to be.'

'One of the prison officers was on the take; that's what Dad told me, but he didn't name him.'

'But why was he ordered to tell me where the file was if they already knew?'

She shrugged her shoulders. 'That's what Duffy couldn't work out to begin with. It took him some time to get his head round why they wanted you to know and why he had to be the one to tell you. But he figured it out in the end. He told me what he thought was going on Wednesday when I last spoke with him.' She paused and was no longer able to conceal a smile. 'The object, you see, Chief Inspector Hood, was to get you off the case. You must have been getting too close for comfort. That's what Duffy thought, anyway.'

'But how could they get me off the case?' Hood was now very interested in Kelly's response. He already knew the answer to his question, of course, and if it hadn't been for someone's apparent carelessness, they might well have succeeded. He would never forget the twenty minutes he'd spent with the DCC and the Head of Professional Standards. But did Kelly know? Her answer quickly revealed that she did.

'By stealing the file and making it look like you had revealed where it was. They always assumed it would have been kept in the main strongroom. No chance of getting at it while it was there. Duffy thought the solicitor would take it out of the strongroom when you called to see him. Possibly even show it to you. Much easier to steal it while it was in his office.'

'But how could anyone predict the solicitor would remove it from the strongroom just because I went to see him? And he could always have returned it to the main safe after I had left him.'

'I don't know, but it seems someone did, because it can't have been returned to the strongroom, can it? Perhaps someone just took a chance once they knew you were going to see the solicitor and hoped he would keep it in his room for a while.'

Hood had his doubts about that. Did someone else working at Worth's office know the file had been removed from the strongroom? He had no intention of revealing the discovery of the partial bug under the solicitor's desk and he was already starting to question why professional criminals would have left it where it could so easily be found. Perhaps Duffy's analysis of the situation was wrong? Hood was now becoming sceptical whether a traditional burglary had really taken place. The bug could well have been left there to disguise the fact that the theft of the file was an inside job, although its presence had the beneficial effect of undermining any suspicion that he had disclosed what Duffy had told him. He decided to close down discussion on the subject.

'But as you can see, I'm still on the case.'

Kelly shrugged her shoulders. 'Well, they can't have it their own way all the time, I suppose.'

'And another thing, Kelly. You obviously knew the file had been stolen before we told you. The theft hasn't received any publicity. Have these people been in contact with you? Come on, Kelly. You knew about the file, didn't you, and where it was located?'

She laughed. 'You're not seriously suggesting I told these people about the file? What would be in it for me? I've had no contact with anyone except Duffy.' She paused and gave Hood a superior look. 'And as for knowing it's been stolen, you're here aren't you? Duffy said you would be round to see me if the file vanished, especially if anything happened to him. And here you are. Just like he said. That's right isn't it? You wouldn't be here otherwise, now, would you?'

Hood was forced to agree. He exhaled at length. 'Your father told you all this, did he? He seems to have been very confident that things would develop as he anticipated.'

'He was very shrewd was Duffy. Don't underestimate my dad, Mr Hood. People were always doing that. He was much cleverer than most people thought, and I include Gus Grayling in that. And he certainly wasn't as third-rate as Hanlon considered him to be. His analysis so far has proved to be spot on.' She paused and became slightly emotional. 'Apart from the fact that someone decided they didn't need him any longer. He didn't foresee that… or perhaps he did?' Her voice strengthened. 'That's why I know he didn't kill himself.'

'Hardly assists you though, does it?'

'What do you mean?'

'Surely you've worked it out? You're obviously as least as intelligent as your father. All they have to do to make sure none of this comes out is eliminate you. And they're certainly ruthless enough to do exactly that. Look what happened to your father.'

Kelly did not answer immediately. When she did, Hood realised she and her father had tried to accommodate every eventuality.

'But he thought of that too.' She smiled again. 'He put what he wanted to say on tape. He thought that would be safer. If anything happens to me, it will come to you. Dad specified you rather than anyone else because he thought you were at least honest, unlike some police officers he's been involved with, although he did have the occasional doubt as to whether he could trust even you completely. You see, Mr Hood, I have someone looking after me too. By the time I pleaded guilty, my dad had recorded everything. He didn't miss out anything. He discussed the final shape of it with me while we were waiting to be sentenced. I also have a very good memory, so I can remember quite a bit of what is on there, not all the details, but enough to shock you if I were to tell you.' She smiled broadly. 'I am, after all, my father's daughter.'

'And this tape; where is it?'

'What about my parole?'

'The tape.' Hood held out his hand in a symbolic gesture. 'Who is this person looking after your interests?'

Kelly smiled and gave the chief inspector a shrewd look. 'It seems we have rather a lot to discuss, Mr Hood, before I let you have anything. *Quid pro quo.* A favour for a favour. You see, I know what it means. Please don't judge me on my performance in the witness box. It was in my interests then to give the impression I wasn't very bright.'

Hood shook his head and let out another lengthy sigh. 'But how can you be sure that Grayling's mob will leave you alone? They don't know there's a tape in existence. But they'll assume you know where your father stashed the information he said he had on them, unless they conclude he was bluffing. That may be a more rational explanation for why they killed him. Nothing in the file for them to worry about so he was eliminated.'

Kelly was quick to contradict. 'Oh, but they do know there's a tape, Mr Hood. At least they should. That was the other precaution we took.' Hood, for once, appeared baffled. She continued. 'Perhaps I should explain. There was a photograph of a tape and more than a hint of what it contains in the file they stole from the solicitor's office. It wasn't the actual tape, but they won't know that. The actual tape with the recording is, eh, somewhere safe.' Her voice strengthened. 'I told you, Duffy wasn't a fool and neither am I. We'd worked everything out with great care. You see, he knew they'd get hold of the file at his solicitors eventually. I think he secretly wanted them to. He thought at one point they had someone working there on the inside, but I'm not so sure about that. That's why the two of us arranged everything in the way we did.'

Hood rolled his eyes. 'You know who's running the show now, don't you? Come on, Kelly. Your father must have known. And he's bound to have told you.'

She smiled but gave nothing away. 'Duffy certainly did know. And I'm afraid you'll get nothing further out of me on the subject until my parole is in motion. And before you ask, there's nothing in the stolen file to suggest that I have the tape or knew where it might be. Remember, Mr Hood, they think I'm still loosely associated with them. I haven't said anything to anyone. As far as they're concerned, I've been very loyal. I haven't turned Queen's evidence and I haven't informed on anyone. I took the sentence that was handed out without trying to do a deal. Why should they come after me?'

Hood sighed. 'I don't think you've thought this through, Kelly. You need to think about it some more. You'll inherit your father's property. You are his sole beneficiary. I've seen his will.' He paused and produced the copy the solicitor had given him. 'This is it. His house in South Wales and everything else he owned will come to you, including all his shares in his haulage business. He has no other relatives. The O.C.G., when they find out about the tape, will assume you know what it contains and where it is hidden. Disclosing there's a tape in existence which could possibly expose the organisation could prove to be very high risk. You mustn't overlook the fact that your father had made it clear that *you* were all he was concerned about. They'll obviously work on the basis that you know something if they have nothing else to go on. Let me have the tape, and I'll be able to ensure your safety.'

She gave Hood a contemptuous look. 'Like you did my dad? No thanks.'

'I'm sorry about what happened to your father. I really am. But he wasn't frank with me. I don't want you making the same mistake,'

But Kelly seemingly had only one thing in mind; early release. 'What about my parole? If I'm that much at risk, it puts me in the same category as Michael Doyle, doesn't it? He was paroled after he'd only done a year inside. I want to be treated the same.'

Hood sighed. 'I'll see what I can do.' He hesitated. 'But I'll need access to the tape.'

'When my parole is brought forward, and I mean guaranteed in writing, I'll produce the tape. But not before.'

'You'll have to give me something or the Home Office won't even begin to consider you for early parole.'

Kelly said nothing for quite some time. When she eventually spoke, a wry smile appeared on her lips. 'I'm not playing that game, Mr Hood. I have the means of giving you everything you need to crack open this criminal organisation. You have the ability at least to progress my parole. There's really nothing else to discuss. I hope I make myself clear.'

Hood nodded then glanced at Knight. He looked kindly at Kelly but he was far from convinced she was being wholly truthful. 'I hope you're not giving me the run around, Kelly. That will do you no good at all.'

'I've said all I propose to say.' She smiled, stood up and walked towards the door. Was she reading Hood's thoughts? 'You'll be in touch then? Don't be too long about it, will you? This place may be better than Stafford but it's deadly boring.'

Hood said nothing further as he and Knight left Kelly's room. She watched through the window as they walked accompanied by an officer towards the main building. She waited until they disappeared inside then lifted the pillow on her bed and picked up an envelope which she had secreted there. She opened it, took out a letter and started to read. She choked back her tears as she studied each line of the last reflections and advice she would ever receive from her father. Putting the letter back into the envelope, she moved slowly to the shower room, ripped up the envelope and its contents into tiny shreds and flushed them away. She took a deep breath then adopted a determined expression. It was up to her now. Duffy was dead. Only she could bring about the legacy he intended for her.

CHAPTER 20

Francis Maddison ran a medium-sized accountancy firm in Kettering. Outwardly respectable, a married man with three children, governor of a local school and an all-round good egg, he harboured a very guilty secret. For over twenty years, he had acted as Gus Grayling's *consigliere*, book-keeper and money launderer. He was careful to keep well away from Grayling's more gruesome criminal activities; he abhorred violence of any kind, but chose never to question the source of the funds he managed. He had quickly developed the facility of closing his eyes and his mind entirely to the nefarious pursuits of his most important client. Admiral Lord Nelson was a mere amateur when it came to not seeing what he didn't want to see. Over the years, Maddison had diverted massive criminal funds into all manner of seemingly legitimate investments, mainly abroad, taking a small commission for himself, of course. He had, in truth, become a very rich man, not that anyone had the slightest notion what he had been about. That included his wife, who chided him continuously about what she regarded as her miserly and frequently inadequate housekeeping allowance. In truth, she and Maddison were living increasingly separate lives. Their children were grown up and only their daughter still lived with them. She shared her mother's frequently expressed wish to move to Canada where Mrs Maddison's two brothers had settled years before. The daughter had already made an application to attend the university in Toronto, giving up a firm offer at Durham, anticipating as she did, that her excellent grades at A level would more than suffice.

It was certainly true that the family's lifestyle in Kettering was modest. Maddison assiduously avoided any sign of fast living or ostentation. His motor cars were always second hand and changed infrequently and family holidays, while the children were still at school, were usually spent at Scarborough or sometimes in Scotland at a far from salubrious B&B on the Isle of Arran. He nevertheless maintained the image of middle-class respectability. Indeed, he counted amongst his legitimate clients the local VAT inspector whose wife ran a chain of hairdressing salons, a Crown Court judge and the local Methodist minister. But he wanted out. Gus Grayling dying when he did offered him an excellent opportunity to retire, but Grayling's successor had other ideas. There was no way out, not yet. There could be no question of his giving up the reins until the transition from father to son was accomplished and a few niggling irritations sorted. The most pressing was the question of Duffy's file. Maddison had a keen personal interest in recovering it and had reluctantly played a far from minor role in its retrieval. He had figured that Duffy must have been aware of his relationship with Grayling. It was, after all, Gus Grayling who had insisted that Maddison should act as Duffy's accountant when the business in South Wales was first set up. On the few occasions he and Duffy had met, their talk had been of capital allowances and tax-deductible expenses; neither had said a word about Grayling. After a couple of years, as Duffy's essentially legitimate haulage business became established, Maddison had delegated the company's accounts and tax returns to an assistant who was equally ignorant of the firm's involvement with a major criminal organisation.

But Maddison's qualms persisted. Duffy was no fool. He could well have worked out for himself the Grayling connection. The elderly Grayling had been considering retirement too. He wanted to spend more time at his villa in Antibes. He too, had just about had enough. The serious crime squad in Sussex was starting to pay him far too much attention. And as he had accumulated a huge fortune, most of it held off-shore, there was no pressing need for him to continue taking risks, save for the real enjoyment he derived from outwitting the police and his rivals. The ageing criminal mastermind had also mentioned to his accountant, some 18 months before his death, the possibility of Duffy taking over the UK end of the O.C.G. The wary Maddison had not thought that wise. Sensitive though he was about the more brutal aspects of Gus Grayling's activities, he'd always regarded Duffy as lacking the necessary guile and ruthlessness but had followed instructions and made the necessary arrangements. Then Grayling's illness struck. Pancreatic cancer was diagnosed. And the prognosis was poor. Retirement was now postponed, indefinitely. But at the same time, there were indications the old man was losing his touch. Neither had it gone unnoticed. His richly deserved reputation for calculated violence, no longer terrified his rivals sufficiently, or so it seemed. The vultures were hovering having smelt weakness as Grayling's ill health became more generally known. His grip on his organisation was fading fast. Michael Doyle's successful raid on a security van at the Charnwood Centre had exposed Grayling's limitations. He was beside himself with anger when he discovered Doyle was responsible. He regarded him as nothing less than a traitor. Had he not helped him financially when the banks had refused to lend Doyle money following his acquittal in a mortgage fraud years before? Grayling had put considerable funds at Doyle's disposal, at a more than commercial rate of interest, of course. Doyle had employed the money to acquire his property portfolio. He still owed Grayling a significant sum, so his organising his own raid on a security vehicle at the Charnwood without first obtaining Grayling's approval rankled. Grayling's obsession, until his death, became the punishment of Doyle while ensuring at the same time the survival of his organisation and the preservation of his contacts. Any prospect of Doyle taking over was never under realistic consideration. So, in the absence of any other candidate, the grooming of Duffy as his temporary successor had begun pending a rapprochement with his son in Australia. Progress was slow, but not long before he died, Grayling and his son were reconciled and the younger Grayling anointed as his father's successor, a wise decision given Duffy turning informer shortly afterwards. But the business in Australia was not doing as well as young Grayling had pretended and the dying Grayling had been unaware that his son had been engaging in some seriously underhand activities with the hard men of Sydney. His import/export company had gradually become a cover for organised crime. Taking over his father's territory had come at exactly the right time as did the massive inheritance which he believed would eventually come to him once the legal proprieties had been completed in the various tax havens where the funds were invested. The UK operation would seamlessly merge with his Australian interests and the contacts in the UK and elsewhere which his father had built up would enhance his standing in New South Wales amongst those who had previously regarded him as something of a lightweight.

Maddison had endured many sleepless nights since he'd heard that Duffy had placed a tell-all file with an ultra-respectable firm of solicitors. The relief after he scoured through it and found nothing relating to him was immense. But there were other issues which he would have to raise with his new boss. No point putting off what would inevitably emerge. Maddison realised he was playing a dangerous game, putting his own interests before those of anyone else – and that included Michael Grayling. He was a good judge of character and he was convinced that the son had not inherited either the intelligence or the acumen of his father but he nevertheless waited anxiously in his office on Friday afternoon in expectation of the call he knew was coming.

'Did we get the file?' Michael Grayling telephoned from Terminal 1 at Humberto Delgado Airport in Lisbon, as he and Julia made their way to the gate for their flight to Dublin. Julia was carrying young Michael in her arms. The child was starting to play up, much to Grayling's annoyance. The accountant did not relish receiving a call at his office during business hours. He closed his office door before replying and told his secretary that he was not to be disturbed for the remainder of the afternoon.

'We did. Went without a hitch. And Rebecca played a blinder. She'll be a useful addition to the team.'

Grayling sounded delighted. 'Was I right? Duffy was bluffing? There was nothing in the damn file, like I always suspected?'

'Not quite, no.'

Grayling's confidence cooled rapidly. 'Explain. And make it quick. I have a plane to catch.'

'I've had a good look through it.' The accountant, like all good accountants thought long and hard before continuing. He weighed in his own mind how much he should disclose. He concluded that there was nothing to be gained by pretending all was well. After all, he had his own interests to serve. And those interests he well knew were no longer the same as Michael Grayling's or the organisation's. 'There was a photograph of you and the old man.'

'Me, and my father?'

'Yes. When you were much younger, of course. I doubt if anyone would recognise it as you, unless they knew you pretty well.'

'Hmm. That's hardly critical. Duffy knew about me and he knows what I look like. He saw me with my father on several occasions, but that was years ago. He probably left it there to make that very point. Any mention of you, Francis?'

'No mention of me.'

'That's good. That's very good. Is there anything else I need to know? I don't have much time. We are almost at the gate.'

Maddison hesitated before replying. 'There was a photograph of something else; a cassette tape. And a note in Duffy's handwriting. I recognised it as his straight away. My firm prepared the accounts of his haulage business in South Wales, remember, so I saw his handwriting frequently. The note suggests that everything he knew about the syndicate has been placed on the tape; names, details, everything… including the Australian connection.'

It was Grayling's turn to react to what could only be seriously worrying news. He stood out of the queue at the gate, pulling Julia away and allowing other passengers to pass in front of them. He dropped his voice to a whisper. 'And this tape? Where is it?'

'It wasn't with the file. He's obviously hidden it somewhere else, assuming it exists and it isn't another piece of bluster by Duffy.'

'We need to find it. Any clues as to where it might be?'

'There was a name written on the back of the note.'

'What name?'

Maddison hesitated again. He appreciated that once he mentioned the name there was no going back. 'Doyle, Michael Doyle.'

Grayling swore loudly, drawing the attention of the other passengers. 'You're joking! What would Duffy have to do with Doyle?'

'I don't know. And I'm not joking. I never joke about serious matters as you know. Perhaps he has the tape? Duffy and he could have been collaborating with each other. And Doyle has some knowledge of the organisation's business. They're both police informers too, as we know to our cost. They could have pooled their knowledge.'

Grayling cursed. He moved away from flapping ears, taking several steps from Julia and the other passengers, some of whom were looking at him in an increasingly disapproving manner. He kept his voice low. 'I don't believe it. This is Duffy playing with us. He's put Doyle's name there simply to cause irritation. It was Doyle who grassed up Duffy. I don't see those two going in with each other, against the organisation. And they were never in the same prison. Look, get Logan on to it. Duffy needs to learn the hard way that I won't be messed with. If that bastard thinks he can play games with me, he's in for a very painful awakening. I want that tape, understand? Logan has my permission to do whatever is necessary. I've run out of patience with Duffy.'

'I'm afraid that won't be possible, Michael.'

'Don't you start, Francis. Why is it not possible? Has Logan been transferred or something? We pay him enough for his very limited services. I'm not having the bastard lollygagging around the prison when he should be watching out for our interests.'

Maddison cleared his throat. He dreaded the reaction to what he was about to disclose. 'Duffy is dead. He hanged himself in his cell last night.'

Maddison could only hear a long, drawn out sigh before Grayling spoke again. He sounded increasingly agitated.

'Hung himself? Duffy? That doesn't make sense. Why would he do that?'

'Perhaps we pushed him too hard. Logan did warn us that he was becoming very fragile.'

'Suicide, or had he made enemies in there we don't know about?'

'According to Logan, it's looking like suicide, although there's no sign of a note. He was found early this morning in his locked cell. He'd been dead for hours, apparently. He was rushed to the nearest hospital here in Kettering but nothing could be done. The preliminary view is that he took his own life. There'll be an inquest, of course.'

'And a Home Office inquiry. There always is with a death in custody. This could be very awkward for us, Francis. But what do we do about this tape?'

'Logan searched the cell before he called for assistance. No sign of it. Nothing.' Maddison hesitated. 'This could all be another bluff, Michael. Perhaps there isn't a tape? This could all be a wind-up.'

'Logan knew what he was looking for, presumably?'

'Yes. He'd already been told to look out for a tape after we had analysed the contents of Duffy's file. Duffy had a music centre and some cassette tapes in his cell, but they were all commercially produced; nothing out of the ordinary. He was going to have words with him about it this morning. That's why he went to Duffy's cell earlier than usual.'

'Too fucking late!'

Maddison did not reply. The final call for the flight to Dublin sounded over the tannoy as he considered whether he should say anything further. He decided there was no point in holding anything back.

'Be fair, Michael. Logan couldn't have anticipated what Duffy had in mind. Duffy had done as he was told and given the information about the file to Hood. We also know Hood was at the solicitors on Thursday morning. He was seen to go in.'

'So, the team did their job.'

'So it appears, with my assistance of course. I didn't like becoming involved as I did, though. It was very high risk. Hood might well make the connection between my firm and Duffy, especially as I had to use my real identity. William Worth knows me; we've worked together before. But I did as you asked. I only hope that neither he nor Hood catch on.'

'You did well, Francis. And I won't forget it.' Grayling let out another lengthy sigh. 'And Hood is still on the case?'

'He is. I always said leaving that bit of the bug behind might clear him of suspicion, important though it was for other reasons. We haven't heard anything yet from our source in Mid-Shires, who, by the way, is becoming very nervous. He's also due to retire in a few months.'

Grayling harrumphed. 'This is getting out of hand, Francis. You need to take back control. Hood is getting too close. I can't risk having my UK contacts exposed. The Australians are relying on me. They have tons of the Chinese merchandise ready to import. It's our contacts they're really interested in.' He paused. 'What do you reckon? Does this tape exist, or is this another of Duffy's little games?'

'We can't assume it doesn't exist. You know me. I always work on the basis of the worst possible outcome.' He tried to laugh. 'That's why I've lasted so long.'

'You think it's possible that Doyle could have the tape?'

'I don't know. If he had it, I can't see why he wouldn't have handed it over to the police. He'd have no reason to keep it.' He paused. 'There's a more likely candidate, always assuming it exists.'

'Who's the alternative?'

'Duffy's daughter, Kelly Maguire.'

Grayling whistled through his teeth. 'But she's been loyal enough. She didn't even flinch when she picked up a twenty-four-year sentence. She didn't do a deal, unlike that bastard father of hers.'

'But we've done nothing for her. She could easily turn. She's looking at spending at least the next ten or eleven years inside. She'll know that Doyle managed to get out by informing on her father; she could well think she can do the same by informing on us.'

'She knew the score – they all did. She knows she'll be looked after when she gets out.'

'She may not be prepared to wait that long.'

Grayling's tone hardened. 'If she doesn't, she knows what will happen to her.'

Maddison ignored the implied threat. 'We need to find out where she stands. And she may have some idea where this tape is. Duffy left everything to her. I have a copy of his will. That was in the file too.'

'Did he? So, wherever he's hidden it, she'll know where it is, or be able to find out. We'll have to get someone to see her, someone we can trust. Someone like you, Francis. Do we know where she is?'

Maddison sounded reluctant to become involved. 'I don't know about that. You know I don't like getting too close. I've already put myself at risk with Worth.'

'Can't be helped, Francis. You'll have to go and see her. It shouldn't be a problem if she's inherited Duffy's property. Do you know where she is? She's been moved from Stafford, hasn't she?'

'Yes. They moved her a few days ago – to HMP Brampton Hall, category D.'

Grayling caught his breath. 'Now that does make me suspicious. She's hasn't even done a year yet, has she?'

'Not quite, no. They moved her because of Duffy. She was under threat at her previous prison, or at least she made out she was. She got involved in a fight with other inmates and claimed it was because of pressure being put on her father.'

'But we had nothing to do with that. We only put pressure on Duffy.'

'Well, she got her way. She's in much easier conditions now.'

'I suppose we can't blame her for taking advantage of the situation. Shows she has a brain. But perhaps she's not as loyal as we thought?'

'She's Duffy's daughter. Her ultimate loyalty will be to him. His death might well have affected her in ways we can only guess at. That's what worries me; the information on this tape could be used to advance her parole date. For all we know it could already be underway. Don't forget, it worked for Doyle when he informed on Duffy.'

'I don't know, Francis. There was more to it than that. Doyle got out early because we were trying and failing to kill him. Anyway, I can't see Doyle and Duffy getting together. I don't see that at all. It doesn't make sense.'

'You could well be right.' He paused ominously. 'Kelly might even think we had something to do with Duffy's death? She'll not want to believe he killed himself. She could turn.'

'But what does she know? Nothing, unless Duffy has told her what he has on us?'

'They've definitely been in contact with each other. Logan arranged the phone calls. They spoke to each other for twenty minutes last week and again on Wednesday afternoon, the day before he did himself in.' He paused again. 'Then there was the letter.'

'What letter?'

'Duffy wrote a letter to his daughter which Logan smuggled out for him on Tuesday night. It was addressed to one of the other inmates at Brampton so that it wouldn't be checked. Any letters from Duffy direct to his daughter were opened and read.'

'Did Logan open it and read it?'

'He hasn't said, but knowing Logan, I suspect he did, although he'll have taken money from Duffy and agreed to keep it confidential.'

'More fool Duffy. So, Logan's been playing both ends against the middle, has he?'

'Looks like he has. At least he admitted he'd posted the letter. It wouldn't surprise me if he'd read it first. He's got huge gambling debts. He's desperate for money. I suspect he'll probably tell us what's in the letter if we offer him enough, otherwise he'd be a fool to have mentioned it.'

'You'd better have words with him again, Francis. If he's holding out on me, he needs to learn the basics again.'

'I don't want to get involved in anything like that.'

Grayling sighed. 'I'm afraid you'll have to organise it, Francis. Speak to Jamie. He can deal with Logan. But you will have to visit Kelly. If she's inheriting Duffy's haulage business, what could be more natural than for Duffy's accountant to visit the new owner?'

'It's a bit early, isn't it? He was only found dead this morning. And it will take time to arrange a visit.'

'By the end of next week, Francis. Sort it. I need an answer before next week-end. And I don't want any loose ends, understand?'

A brief silence followed until Grayling raised the question of Kelly Maguire again. 'Category D you say? Open conditions?'

'More or less, yes. But getting her out wouldn't be a problem, if it came to it. Very low security. More Jamie's department than mine, of course.'

'Jamie's going to be very busy by the look of things. Have a think about it, Francis. I need your take on all this. I'll ring you again when I arrive in Dublin. I'll be staying there for just under a week before travelling to the UK. I suppose if we got her out, she'd let us have the tape?'

'Assuming she has it, yes.'

Grayling and Julia started to re-join the remnants of the queue, Grayling with his mobile still to his ear. He handed the passports to Julia. She took a quick look at the names before preparing to hand them to the airline attendant. Grayling was still concentrating on the call with Maddison who sounded anything but keen on Grayling returning to the UK.

'You're still coming, Michael? Police activity will intensify now that Duffy's dead and Hood is still in the saddle. You need to be careful. My advice is that you stay in Ireland. And, please, don't ring me on this number. Use the mobile. I won't be in the office over the week-end.'

'But I have to come over, Francis. It can't be put off. I'll have to deal with you know who. It's personal now. He did for Maxine. And we need to put a marker down in respect of Hood. Time he was given a warning. Get Jamie on the job. Nothing too drastic, but he needs to understand the consequences if he keeps digging.'

'You know my views about that, Michael. I want nothing to do with threatening a police officer. As for Doyle, you'll have to find him first. He didn't turn up for his second meeting with his probation officer. He's gone to ground. Hood and his team are still looking for him. They've asked him to surrender himself. It's been in all the newspapers. And they haven't found him. If you want my advice, I say leave it. You have other import business to deal with. Don't risk coming over here, not now, not just to deal with Doyle.'

'I don't want your advice, not on this subject, Francis. Doyle has to be taken out. The police are not looking hard enough. He'll be seeing me sooner than he thinks.'

'I would strongly advise you against it, Michael. Doyle isn't worth it, and you'll be putting yourself very much at risk. You shouldn't let personal issues interfere with business or, more importantly, your safety. Your father would have understood that. He and I had almost completed turning everything he had into legitimate investments. This Doyle business risks exposing everything. Leave him be. The syndicate won't like it if it all goes wrong.'

'Too late,' replied Grayling, coldly. 'It's none of the syndicate's business. This is personal. Anyway, it's all in hand. Doyle has to go. And my father hadn't given up altogether. Why else did he go after the money from Retford?'

'That was just for a bit of fun. He wanted to see if he still had it in him. Anyway, thank God he didn't live long enough to see what a cock-up the whole thing became.'

'That's because someone grassed us up. Another reason why Doyle has to be dealt with.'

'That was nothing to do with Doyle.'

'Can't be sure about that. You stick to your books, Francis. Leave everything else to me.' He switched off his phone and walked past the desk with his extended family, retrieving the passports from Julia and placing them in his inside pocket.

'Everything OK?' asked Julia.

'Everything's under control,' replied Grayling. But the expression on his face suggested otherwise. Julia smiled to herself but said nothing more.

CHAPTER 21

'What do you reckon, Wendy? Do you think she was telling us the truth?'

Hood and Knight were travelling to Kettering General Hospital to meet up with Guy Romney and Detective Superintendent Kingston. They had spent thirty minutes with the Governor of HMP Brampton Hall after seeing Kelly Maguire and time was getting on. Hood appreciated that it was unusually late for an appointment with the consultant pathologist and the SIO leading the investigation into the death of Derick Duffy, but Brampton Hall was conveniently close to the hospital and Hood was keen to discover if anything of significance had been discovered at the post-mortem examination. His conversation with Kelly had reinforced his view that Derick Duffy had probably not committed suicide.

Knight hesitated before replying. 'I don't know, sir. She certainly wasn't telling us the whole truth. She knows a great deal more than she's letting on. And the governor didn't sound at all keen that she should remain at Brampton Hall when you filled her in with some of the details about Derick Duffy's past. It doesn't appear that she received anything like full disclosure about her new charge. Cat D hardly seems appropriate given the risks Kelly faces.'

'I agree. Duffy's death changes everything, especially if this tape she mentioned actually exists. It certainly makes sense for the governor to contact the Home Office with a view to moving her to a more suitable location, with greater security, but that will take time. The bureaucratic wheels of the prison service grind exceedingly slowly in my experience.'

'Even in these circumstances?'

'Even in these circumstances, Wendy. Additional security at Brampton will be quicker to arrange. I'll ask the DCC to speed things up and beef up protection for Kelly while she's still there. Having an additional prison officer keeping an eye on her just doesn't cut it.'

'I suppose she could always go back to Stafford?'

Hood raised an eyebrow. Was Knight being provocative? 'Now, that would not go down at all well with Kelly or the Home Office. It might put her at greater risk. Whoever has been threatening her at Stafford will probably still be there. And the pressures placed upon her would inevitably increase once her return became generally known. No, I think she'll have to be moved to another part of the country altogether, where she hopefully won't attract so much attention.'

'What do you think about this tape, sir? Do you think it really exists? It all seems unnecessarily complicated. Why didn't Duffy simply reveal what he knows directly to you? If he really wants to help his daughter, that was the obvious way of doing things. What was he up to?'

'I'm not sure, but I suspect he liked to think he was keeping some degree of control over the situation. And now he's gone, perhaps he's arranged things so he retains a degree of posthumous control.' He smiled. 'And I don't think he trusted us. Not anymore. If he had disclosed what he knows neither he nor Kelly would have anything left to bargain with. He said as much to me when I saw him on Wednesday.'

'And you think Kelly knows as much as she implied?'

'No reason why she shouldn't. Possibly more.'

'She did slip up in one respect, though.'

'You think so?'

'She said her father used the same accountant as Gus Grayling. That might be worth following up?'

Hood nodded. 'Grayling did have some legitimate business interests. Like many major crooks before him, he was attempting to turn his criminal empire into something approaching a legitimate business. But I doubt if he needed much of a contribution from his accountant in respect of his remaining criminal activities. And we already know that most of his assets are not in this country. When it's probated, his estate here will probably amount to less than three quarters of a million, and he left the whole lot to a cancer charity. Trying to buy his way into heaven, I suspect. His major assets must be gathering interest elsewhere.'

'But he presumably laundered the proceeds of his crimes? He could well have needed professional assistance to do that effectively, especially if it's all abroad.'

'Possibly. Follow it up, Wendy. Shouldn't be too difficult to identify Duffy's accountant or Gus Grayling's. Companies House will have the details.'

Hood turned off the A14 on to Warren Hill. Passing the crematorium on his left, he drove on to Rothwell Road.

'We must be fairly close now,' he said.

'I think this is the hospital coming up, on the right, sir. At least we don't need to go into the town. I'm not sure where the mortuary is, but you know what these places are like. A veritable labyrinth, I suspect.'

Hood nodded. 'I've never been to this hospital before. It looks bigger than I thought.'

He drove into the first entrance he came to, the barrier lifting automatically, then found a parking place as close to the hospital as possible.

'I hate these places,' he murmured. 'Come on, let's get this over with.'

He and Knight walked through the automatic doors and headed towards the reception desk. Hood produced his warrant card and asked for directions to the mortuary. The receptionist, a middle-aged woman with a helpful disposition, looked at the clock behind her then pointed towards the stairs. 'It's a bit late,' she said. 'I'm not sure if anyone will still be there at this time.'

'Professor Romney is expecting us,' said Hood.

The woman nodded and directed Hood to go down to the lower ground floor and follow the signs. Hood thanked her then he and Knight walked towards the stairs.

'Have you noticed,' Hood whispered to the detective sergeant, 'mortuaries always seem to be on the lower ground floor?'

Knight did not respond. She was keeping her eyes on the overhead signs. Eventually, they found their destination at the end of a corridor and walked into a pleasant reception area. There was no one about. Hood called out and a few moments later, Guy Romney appeared from an adjacent room, notes in hand.

'Hello, Harry,' he said. Hood acknowledged the pathologist and introduced Wendy Knight. Romney smiled. 'I take it you don't want to see the corpse? He's still here, under refrigeration. But I think I can tell you everything you need to know.'

Hood looked relieved and nodded. 'Not unless you think it necessary. He was alive and kicking when I saw him on Wednesday afternoon.'

Romney got down to business. 'Well, he certainly isn't now. Shall we take a seat? By the way, Maurice Kingston has had to go. He'd been waiting for some time but was required back at Campbell Square in Northampton. Bit of a flap on. He's given me the benefit of his inquiries so far and he informed me of a possible motive for foul play to have taken place. The deceased had some sort of file lodged with a firm of solicitors in Leicester, I believe.'

'That's certainly the case. The contents was thought to be very damaging to a major O.C.G.'

'That's what Maurice told me. I know nothing about that but I should be able to let you have a fairly complete picture of how Duffy died.' He gave Hood a look which was anything but encouraging.

'I'm sorry we are a bit on the late side,' said the chief inspector, taking a seat opposite Romney. 'Trying to fit too much into the working day. We've been to see the deceased's daughter. She's being held at HMP Brampton Hall, just outside Market Harborough. She's firmly of the view her father didn't take his own life. Are there any indications this was not suicide?'

Romney's expression remained fixed. 'I can only tell you what I found, and what I didn't find. It didn't help that he had been cut down before I got to him. The officer who found him couldn't be sure he was dead. He cut him down and attempted CPR before sounding the alarm.

He was then rushed here, but it was too late, far too late. He'd been dead for several hours in my opinion and letting him down did interfere somewhat with my examination. I would certainly have liked to have seen him *in situ*.' Romney looked at his notes. 'The ligature – his bed sheet – had been removed, but the pattern it made on the neck was still visible. A knot had been tied in the sheet which would have presumably been placed behind his neck from what I can see. There was an obvious bruise at that precise spot.'

Hood hesitated. He knew from previous cases that Romney was not one for being too specific about time of death. 'There was a bit of a riot at Woodborough at lockup, around eight-thirty, I believe. Was he still alive then?'

'He could well have been,' replied Romney, 'but he was certainly dead well before midnight. Before ten, I'd say. You see, Harry, where a body has been left hanging for some time, as in this case, the post-mortem lividity settles in the legs, feet, hands and forearms. It's a well-established phenomenon.'

Hood grimaced. 'But if he died well before midnight, it does raise a number of problems.'

'I don't follow you,' said Romney.

'The burglary at the solicitors which Maurice told you about probably hadn't taken place by then – we're assuming for the moment there was a burglary – the object being to steal Duffy's file. The solicitor's office building seems to have been entered either late on Thursday night or in the early hours of this morning. If Duffy were already dead by then, I suppose it lends some support to his having taken his own life. This O.C.G. would not have risked killing him before they had got hold of his file.' He glanced towards Knight before continuing. 'Any sign at all of third-party involvement?'

Romney shook his head. 'Not that I found, and I took a long time over my examination given the circumstances and the deceased's background. As I said, I had a detailed report from Maurice Kingston about a possible motive for murder, but could find no indication of foul play; no sign at all of his hands or wrists being bound or held in any way, and, of some significance in my view, no scratch marks or other injuries around where the bedsheet pressed on his throat. You sometimes get that where the deceased has attempted to remove the ligature or tried to place his fingers underneath it. Sometimes the poor bugger panics. He thinks better of it and changes his mind, usually when it's too late, unfortunately.'

Hood sighed. 'Cause of death?'

'Asphyxia. I found deep grooving in the neck and bruising of the underlying tissues. Clear signs of asphyxia. The hyoid bone was fractured, which is a commonplace in cases like this. According to the officer who found him, he was slumped down with buckled knees, his feet almost touching the ground. He used the top of a bookcase to fix the ligature. There was nothing else available, so he must have bent his knees to keep his feet off the floor. He was five feet eleven tall and fifty-nine years of age. I measured the bookcase when I visited the cell. It was two inches shorter than him so he would have had to raise his feet from the floor in order to place pressure on his neck. Had he had second thoughts, it would have been perfectly simple for him to have put his feet on the ground and release the pressure.' He gave Hood a sympathetic look. 'I'm sorry if it undermines your theory, Harry, but there is every indication that this was a deliberate act of suicide. I can't find anything that suggests otherwise. And nearly all hangings in my experience turn out to be suicides. It's not the easiest way of killing someone who resists.'

'Any underlying physical problems?'

'Not that played a part in his death, no. He was obviously a heavy smoker – real smoker's lungs – and there were distinct signs of ischaemic heart disease developing. There were tiny atheromatous plaques in the large epicardial coronary arteries partially restricting blood flow. That would have caused him very real problems in future, but there's no doubt in my mind that he died of asphyxia.'

'But no note of any kind? Nothing to explain his actions?'

'Not that has been reported to me, no. You don't always get a note with a suicide, though. A lot would depend on his state of mind at the time.'

'He was fully clothed was he?'

'Yes. Tee shirt and jogging bottoms, boxer shorts. This was certainly not an auto-erotic hanging gone wrong.' The consultant forensic pathologist tried but failed to supress a cynical smile.

'He would have taken some time to die, presumably? Not like an execution where the neck is broken?'

'Correct. As I said, it would have taken some effort on his part initially to keep his feet off the ground. No drop of any kind involved here. You'll presumably be having a look at the cell where it happened?' Hood nodded. 'If he were being forced, there would have been clear evidence of a struggle. I found none. It looks like he really intended to end his life.' Romney paused for a moment then looked directly at Hood. 'Maurice tells me you were pretty sure he'd been murdered?'

The chief inspector nodded. 'I was, yes. I saw him on Wednesday at the prison. He was showing no sign of wanting to take his own life, quite the contrary. He had every reason to live. He wanted to help his daughter to try and get early parole.'

'Well, we have followed procedure to the letter; I can assure you of that. The bedsheet has been sent to the lab and SOCO have examined the whole cell in detail. They'll check the sheet for DNA, of course, but the prison officer who found him will have touched it repeatedly while getting him down.' The pathologist glanced at his notes. 'Prison Officer Logan found him at six-twenty this morning.'

'Nothing then to indicate this was a deliberate killing dressed up to look like suicide?'

'No, quite the opposite. It was deliberate all right, I'm sure of it. But self-inflicted.' He let out a lengthy sigh. 'I'm sorry, Harry, but I found nothing which would support the suggestion that Duffy was murdered.' He noted the look of disappointment on Hood's face. 'I've also taken samples from the body to be sent to toxicology in order to exclude the remote possibility that he was drugged. I know of one case years ago when a hanging occurred with no signs of a struggle, but it was later discovered that the true cause of death was a diamorphine overdose. The deceased was heavily tattooed and the injection mark was missed at the PM. Not that I think that happened here. I've been extra careful in examining the body and the deceased had no tattoos.' He looked at his notes. 'But given the unusual circumstances, I've arranged for a second forensic pathologist to take a look. Professor Lovell from Leicester is coming over first thing tomorrow. I know it's a Saturday, but you're welcome to attend if you wish.'

Hood was never one for attending post-mortem examinations. He much preferred to wait for the pathologist's report and usually delegated attendance to others. 'I think I'll give that a miss. I've arranged to see the governor at Woodborough Prison tomorrow morning. I need to see where this happened and speak to this prison officer, what was his name again, Logan?' Romney nodded. 'I don't want to interfere with the forensic aspects of the death. This is Maurice Kingston's patch, but I'll look forward to receiving both reports in due course.'

'As soon as they're ready, you'll have them. And we mustn't overlook that the cell was locked. Apparently, there was a special procedure to go through at Woodborough in order to obtain the key to the deceased's cell because of the threats to which he'd been subjected. The governor was insistent when I spoke to him that no one could have gained access to the cell during the night. I checked the record while I was there and Maurice has examined the duty rota. No indication that the keys were removed from the key-safe after lockup and before Officer Logan opened up in the morning. The riot seems to have been merely a coincidence. Oh, and there's something else of significance. There's a CCTV camera in the corridor that leads to his cell. You'll see that for yourself when you go there. Maurice has had it checked. No one entered the cell overnight, not until Logan opened up in the morning.'

Hood stood up and let out a lengthy sigh. 'I'm grateful to you, Guy. I'll check the key situation for myself tomorrow and have words with Logan, but it's beginning to look like I shall have to accept that Duffy did take his own life after all. I'll have a look at the CCTV too, but if no one went into the cell before the next morning, that puts my little theory out of court completely.'

CHAPTER 22

Hood visited Woodborough Prison on Saturday morning. He inspected the cell where Duffy had died, taking his time and looking for anything even remotely suspicious. He noticed the strong smell of tobacco which still lingered in the air. The governor, Patrick Rawlins, was in attendance. He pointed out that everything had been done to make sure there was nothing in the cell from which an inmate could fix a ligature. There was no bunk, just a single bed which appeared not to have been slept in, and no hooks or protrusions anywhere. The governor further pointed out that the bookcase had been deliberately selected because it was not as tall as Duffy. As Guy Romney had said, it would have taken real determination on Duffy's part to use it as the attachment for a ligature as his feet would have touched the floor unless he bent his knees. Hood and the governor then walked to the wing office, watched some of the CCTV, then spoke at length. The governor took the chief inspector through the duty rota in some detail. Hood noted that Brian Logan was the prison officer most frequently in contact with the deceased.

'Duffy liked it that way,' explained the governor. 'He was isolated and I had to monitor his mental health. He was under considerable pressure and in my view those pressures were beginning to make a significant impact on his wellbeing. That's why I was in the course of organising a further move. On this occasion, I was considering having him assessed with a view to transferring him to a medium secure unit in a mental health hospital.'

'Really? Things had got that bad?'

'I'm afraid so. I was growing increasingly concerned. Following my last meeting with him ten days ago, I formed the view that he would not be able to take much more. He was particularly upset about his daughter. She was always the main subject of conversation. She's serving a very long sentence and Duffy seemed to feel responsible for her present circumstances. That's why I arranged to have him assessed by a consultant psychiatrist.'

'Was he aware of that? Had you discussed it with him?'

'No, I hadn't. He wouldn't have had a clue, not until he was seen by Dr Jameson and that wouldn't have happened until next month. I had to get clearance from the Home Office before a transfer could be made and we were at a very early stage in the process. Dr Jameson had been sent a confidential file about Duffy; that's as far as we had got. If you need to speak to him you'll find him at St Andrew's in Northampton. Jameson hadn't seen Duffy yet. I don't even know if he'd got round to reading the papers. The Secretary of State could only authorise a transfer if Jameson advised it was necessary for Duffy to have treatment in hospital and that such treatment was in his best interests. We have to comply with the law, you know.'

'Would Logan or any other officer have known about this proposed transfer?'

'No. I'm sure about that. He may have anticipated a switch to a different prison as may Duffy, given his history. This is, I think, the fifth prison he's been in since his arrest last year, but the possibility of moving him to a hospital was known to me and my deputy only, and to Dr Jameson, of course. By the way, I suspect Jameson will be giving evidence at the inquest. He'll have read the file by then.'

'And his physical health?'

'He wasn't due a physical for some weeks, but he was a heavy smoker and had been advised to cut down, not that he did. And he took very little exercise.'

'The pathologist told me there were signs he was developing ischaemic heart disease.'

'Doesn't exactly surprise me. He was nearly sixty and his lifestyle here was hardly of the best. Then there's the cigarettes. Well over forty a day. That can't have helped.'

Hood reflected on what he had been told. 'Was it sensible to have the same officer dealing with him for much of the time? They could have built up a relationship of some kind, a relationship that could have led to difficulties or breaches of security.'

'I doubt it. I didn't see any harm in allowing him some say in which officers supervised him. He liked Logan, and Brian is an experienced officer. Been in the job for over fifteen years. Logan was not the only one, of course, but he did spend a significant portion of his shift in that section of the prison on the day Duffy died. And there wasn't that much contact with Duffy anyway. He spent most of his time alone in his cell, as was his wish. Apart from an hour's exercise, which he took separately from the other inmates around lunchtime, he remained there reading or listening to music and smoking. He never associated with the other prisoners. That's why I was growing increasingly concerned about him. Such isolation can have an adverse effect on any of us and Duffy was no exception.'

'And you have some dangerous men in here, of course.'

'You can say that again. That's the reason for the higher than usual staff ratio. Mind you, we are losing a few of our more violent prisoners. Several of them are in the course of being transferred to Whitemoor.'

'Do you know what sparked the disturbance on Thursday?'

'Not yet. But I'll get to the bottom of it, eventually. Someone will say something, if only to avoid being moved to Whitemoor.' He smiled.

'When I saw Duffy on Wednesday, Logan was one of the officers who brought him to the room where I interviewed him.'

'Yes,' acknowledged Rawlins. 'Logan and Fletcher were tasked to supervise him that afternoon. I believe it was Logan who returned him to his cell after you had finished with him.'

'So, he must have had possession of the keys?'

'Agreed. But if you look at the log, he returned the keys almost immediately.'

Hood glanced at it. 'Then obtained them again forty-five minutes later.'

'Yes. Duffy phoned his solicitor then his daughter just before eighteen hundred hours. For safety reasons the calls were made from the wing office. We can't risk him using any of the phones on the adjoining wing, not while the other inmates are out of their cells. And there's usually a queue anyway. Logan took Duffy back to his cell at eighteen-sixteen hours and returned the keys to the key-safe. The log shows they remained there until six-thirteen the following morning. There is no evidence they went anywhere during the trouble which broke out on Thursday evening. No one entered the wing office where the keys are kept. The disturbance broke out in D wing and was mainly confined to that area of the prison.'

'And the CCTV near the wing office covers only the entrance to Duffy's cell and a few feet of the corridor?'

'It does, but anyone entering the cell is bound to be recorded. Logan is the last person to appear on the CCTV until he returned just after six-fifteen on Friday morning.'

Hood let out a prolonged sigh. 'Is it normal for someone who was working after six in the evening to be on the early shift the next day?'

'Of course. It happens regularly. He changed from late to earlies over that period. He would normally have had a day off in between, but we've had a flu bug going around and we're short staffed. He volunteered to change over without taking time off between shifts.'

'Did he? Where is Logan now?' asked Hood.

'He was very upset at finding Duffy dead. I've given him a couple of days' compassionate leave in the circumstances.'

'Despite being short staffed?'

'I didn't think I had much option, and we've had four staff moved here this morning from Long Lartin following the disturbances on Thursday night. Brian Logan's already made a statement to Superintendent Kingston. No doubt you have seen it?' Hood nodded. 'He will be back on duty on Tuesday, early shift.' Hood resolved to question him when he returned to work.

'Were any of the telephone calls Duffy made recorded if they were made from the wing office?'

'The system has been extended to the wing office, but no recordings were made on Wednesday. We don't record all telephone calls made by inmates. As the notices by the phones on the wings state, recordings are random, and we never record calls made to their legal representatives. Solicitor-client privilege, you understand? We'd be in serious trouble if we did that. According to Logan, Duffy called his solicitor, then almost immediately called his daughter. That was at a pre-arranged time and it was a very short call. No longer than five minutes. We have recordings of previous calls between the two of them. Superintendent Kingston has copies. I've listened to them myself, three in number while he's been here. Nothing struck me as out of the ordinary.'

'Logan doesn't say in his statement that he overheard anything during either call.'

'Doesn't surprise me. The call to the solicitor would have been confidential and he seems to have allowed Duffy to speak to his daughter on a similar basis.'

'Can you explain why it took him over five minutes from when he obtained the keys to Duffy's cell on Friday morning to his sounding the alarm. It takes less than a minute to walk from this office to Duffy's cell. I timed it earlier.'

The governor frowned. 'He had to sign for the keys of course and he probably wasn't in too much of a hurry. He was slightly earlier than usual and he probably didn't want to wake Duffy. I'm not sure whether he pressed the alarm before or after he attempted CPR. No doubt you'll be able to ask him for yourself when you see him on Tuesday.'

'He should have pressed the alarm first, shouldn't he?'

'He should. That's what they're trained to do. But theory and practice in a real life-threatening situation do not always coincide.'

'Had he come on duty very early?'

'Not particularly. Duffy was usually checked at six-thirty every morning. Because of my concerns about him, I had introduced more regular visits to his cell. He should have been checked at mid-day and at twenty-two hundred hours on Thursday, but the disturbance in D wing required all the officers on duty to attend there. I regret to say that the twenty-two hundred check was never made.'

'And according to Professor Romney, he was probably dead by then.'

'I'm aware of that, as is the Home Office. No doubt there will be consequences.'

'Who should have checked on him at ten o'clock?'

The governor looked at the rota. 'Prison Officer Clough. He's the officer who sustained the most serious injuries. He's still in Kettering Hospital. I believe he's being discharged later today, but he's been signed off for a fortnight. Hardly his fault he didn't carry out the check. He was despatched into D wing after the trouble broke out.'

'And D wing is adjacent to where Duffy was lodged?'

'Yes. The cell you've just come from is one of four solitary confinement cells for D wing, but the three other cells on this corridor are not used. And there are two locked doors between that corridor and the wing. I was instructed by the Home Office that no other inmates were to be lodged on the same corridor as Duffy.'

'Were those doors opened during the riot?'

'Only for the officers in the wing office to get through to assist their colleagues after the trouble broke out. I'm assured they were locked again before they got involved with the inmates causing the disturbance.'

'And one of those officers was Clough?'

'Yes, I suppose it was. He was certainly one of those attempting to regain order.'

'I noticed when we were in the corridor, that one could hear the sound of the inmates on the adjoining wing.'

Governor Rawlins glanced at his watch. 'Yes, they're always a bit noisy on a Saturday. They don't work on Saturdays apart from a few volunteers. And several of them are confined to their cells because of what happened on Thursday night. Some of them have been very noisy. They don't fancy being moved to Whitemoor.'

'Not everyone took part then?'

'No. Only a minority.'

'I see from the records that one of the inmates on D wing is Haydon Connolly.'

'Yes. You know him?' Hood nodded. 'He was in the thick of it. He's ready to be transferred to Whitemoor later today, not that he knows it yet. And he's been charged with causing grievous bodily harm to Prison Officer Clough. We have him on CCTV punching the officer in the face, more than once. Clough's jaw was fractured.'

'Knowing what I do about Connolly, he could well have been the ringleader.'

'He probably was, but he has said nothing so far.'

'Must have been quite a party if Haydon was involved. And it's highly likely that Duffy would have heard the noise made by the rioters.'

The governor flinched at Hood's use of the word "rioters." He preferred to describe the incident as a disturbance.

'I think that must follow.'

Hood made for the door, then turned and addressed Rawlins. 'I have only one other question. What's the system here regarding written communications by inmates to the outside?'

The governor appeared relieved that the subject had changed. 'All incoming mail is opened, unless it's obviously from a prisoner's legal representatives. We ask solicitors to make sure the envelope and the letter is appropriately marked. Sometimes they fail to do that and the letters are opened but not read when it becomes clear it is privileged. Outgoing mail is subject to a similar process.'

'Easy for a prison officer to circumvent security, though, by posting a letter for a prisoner outside the prison?'

'Such things do happen, no doubt, but it is a serious disciplinary offence. Anyone caught doing anything like that would be dismissed. No question. And random searches of officers do take place, both entering and leaving the prison. They all know the consequences if they are caught. I haven't come across such an incident in the two years I have been here. Only one officer has been dismissed in my time and he was complicit in bringing in drugs. He was summarily dismissed for gross misconduct and prosecuted. He ended up in prison himself. Three and a half years was his sentence as I recall.'

'Has Duffy written any letters to his daughter since he came here?'

'Only a couple, that I know of, and that was some time ago when she was in the Stafford Unit. Superintendent Kingston has copies. Again, nothing out of the ordinary although Duffy was blaming himself for her incarceration. He said he was prepared to do anything he could to help her.'

'Including taking his own life?'

The governor did not reply.

CHAPTER 23

On Monday morning, Hood held a briefing for the whole *Operation Trent* team. PC Henshaw, who had found the discharged 9mm cartridge north of Cromwell Lock, was invited to join the team and given the temporary rank of detective constable. Hood was very keen to highlight the importance of officers being resolute and persistent. 'Miss a clue in the circumstances of this case and the evidence is gone forever,' he told them as he introduced Henshaw. The young officer had gone the extra mile when others were on the point of giving up the search and now received his due reward.

'Listen up,' said Hood. 'I assume you have all read the briefing I prepared over the week-end? I want to move this investigation forward this week. And I want to find Doyle. That is the priority. It doesn't look like he's still in the Midlands, but I'm convinced he hasn't left the UK.'

'Any feedback from the phone number, sir?' asked Craddock.

'Nothing helpful so far, no, but Andrew has prepared a "Written Sequence of Events" based upon the evidence we have at the moment. You all have a copy. Read it. I hope to be able to add to it significantly by the end of the week. Contrary to my initial view, it's now looking very likely that Duffy did hang himself. As you see from my briefing notes, there is no evidence of any third-party involvement. The CCTV in the corridor where Duffy's cell was situated shows nothing of relevance. I haven't checked all of it, but one of Superintendent Kingston's men has. I'm getting a copy sent here. I want Raymond to have a look at it, just to be on the safe side.'

Craddock groaned audibly. 'Thank you, sir. I'll look forward to that.'

Hood continued. 'Both pathologists who examined the body agree. No sign of foul play. We should have their written reports by the close of play today or early tomorrow. They'll be advising the coroner that the evidence is all one way; that Duffy took his own life. But why he chose to do what he did when he did still needs investigating.'

'What about toxicology?' asked Wendy Knight.

'That will be a few days yet,' said Hood.

'And still no note?' added Knight.

Hood shook his head. 'But you don't always find a note in cases of suicide. And the pathological evidence makes one other thing clear. Duffy hanged himself well before any burglary at the solicitors could have taken place, which again militates against his being murdered. Why would the O.C.G. risk killing him before they got their hands on his file?'

'But it doesn't explain why he chose to hang himself at that particular moment, does it?' persisted Knight. 'Why on Thursday night?'

'It doesn't, no,' agreed Hood. 'It also seems pretty clear that the riot, which was mainly confined to the immediately adjoining wing, broke out at about the same time. What do we think? Is the timing of the riot of any significance?'

'It could have been a contributory factor,' suggested Hooper. 'According to the briefing notes, which I helped put together, Duffy was depressed and had been under threat for some months. Living as he did must have taken its toll. If he heard what was happening on the adjacent wing – which must have been pretty obvious – he could well have thought that the rioters were coming for him. And that could explain why he took his own life at that particular time.'

'That's a possibility, I suppose,' said Hood. 'He told me when I saw him on Wednesday there were a few prisoners in Woodborough who wouldn't think twice about slitting his throat if they got the opportunity.'

'And rather than leaving a note in his cell which might have been interfered with by the rioters, he could have sent a letter to his daughter in advance of his actions explaining why he intended to commit suicide?'

Knight interrupted. 'But that would mean he must have planned to take his own life well before Thursday night. Before the DCI saw him on Wednesday. Any letter he'd written must have left the prison well before then.'

Hooper nodded. 'True. But he could have been planning to kill himself for some time and brought matters forward because of what he heard happening on the wing?'

Knight frowned. 'I suppose that might be the case, and Kelly Maguire did tell us that one of the officers at Woodborough was on the take. Her father had told her as much. This officer could well have smuggled something out.'

'But his daughter would be the obvious recipient of such a note, wouldn't she?' said Craddock. 'And anything sent to her would have been checked by the prison authorities at Brampton Hall, surely?'

'Not necessarily,' said Hood. 'Although any direct communication from Woodborough to Brampton would certainly have been opened and read, probably before it was sent, Duffy and his daughter could easily have worked their way round that. There are always ways to circumvent these security measures. For example, she could have persuaded another inmate to accept a letter from her father to avoid it being checked. At Brampton, unless a letter comes directly from another prison, they are not opened. It's all part of their current philosophy. They want to engender trust, not suspicion, in their charges. I don't want to appear over cynical, but we all know what that can mean. It wouldn't be difficult for both Duffy and his daughter to take advantage of such a system.'

'But Kelly never mentioned receiving a letter from her father when we spoke to her on Friday,' said Knight. 'She insisted Duffy didn't kill himself. She thought he'd been murdered. I must say, sir, she seemed pretty genuine in her belief.'

Hood shook his head. 'We have to be careful in accepting what she says. She could well have her own agenda. She's obviously been in discussions with her father. If she has received a letter from him she could have chosen not to reveal it to us, especially if the contents indicated he was thinking of killing himself. She may have her own reasons for wanting his death to look like murder.' Hood then brought the discussion of Duffy's apparent suicide to an end. He had other more immediate matters to raise.

'Raymond. You've found additional CCTV, I believe in respect of the Mercedes?'

'Yes, sir. I've set it up so we can all see it.' Craddock moved to the front of the room and switched on the equipment he had assembled. The CCTV was from a council camera in the centre of Leicester. Everyone watched in silence as a Mercedes appeared on the screen and parked outside the premises of the car rental firm in King Richard's Road. The driver could clearly be seen getting out of the vehicle and posting something through the letter box.

'That's Doyle, isn't it?' said Hooper.

'It is,' replied Hood. 'Can't be anyone else.'

'What time is this?'

'Twenty-two-fifty-five on the Sunday night,' said Craddock. 'And this is the Merc that was hired in Doyle's name. He's parked it exactly where we recovered it last Monday.'

'Could you pause on the bit where we can see his face?' asked Hood.

Craddock complied. 'It's not brilliant quality, but it looks like Doyle has been involved in a fight.' He pressed a button which magnified the image. 'That looks like swelling around his mouth.'

'Might just be a shadow,' said Hooper. 'The lighting is pretty poor.'

Hood took up the commentary. 'It certainly fits with our theory that Doyle was taken to Cromwell where an attempt was made to kill him which he survived, then he drove to Leicester and left the Merc outside the rental firm's office. He'd be familiar with where the business is because he's hired cars from them before.'

'After he'd had it valeted, of course,' Knight pointed out. 'There can't be many valeting places open on a Sunday night.'

'More than you think,' contradicted Craddock. 'There's one open until after midnight on the Melton Road and Doyle could well have come into the city that way. I've already checked it out, but they don't keep a record of their clients. Cash only. No one remembered this Mercedes. No one remembers anything. They were very reluctant to speak to me at all.'

'If he dropped the Merc off just before eleven o'clock, the incident with Kruger must have taken place about a couple of hours earlier,' said Knight.

'Allowing time for the valeting.'

'That's right,' said Hood. 'She was pulled out of the Trent by the jogger at about six-fifty the next morning, so she'd been in the water for under twelve hours, like Dr Waters suspected.'

'He's not dressed in motorcycle gear, though,' added Hooper, referring to the CCTV. 'And we know from our previous investigation of him that he rides a bike. Have we checked the system for a bike in his name?'

'Of course,' said Craddock. 'Nothing shown. If he has a bike it's not registered to him. And he must have it stored somewhere close if he abandoned the Merc in Leicester.'

Hood nodded. 'We never got anywhere investigating a motorcycle in the Charnwood inquiry, but he must have some sort of transport. I can't see him travelling everywhere by taxi. Any results from checking taxis?'

'Nothing,' replied Hooper.

'I wonder why he didn't leave the car round the back. The firm provide parking there for late returns,' added Craddock.

'Because of the CCTV camera on the main road,' suggested Knight. 'He probably wanted his returning the Merc to be recorded. He made himself pretty obvious didn't he?'

'You're probably right about that,' agreed Hood. 'Carry on with this, Raymond. You've done well so far. Henshaw can give you a hand. I take it there's a lot more CCTV to get through apart from the recording from Woodborough Prison?'

'Masses, sir.' He glanced towards Henshaw, who merely smiled.

'Moving on,' said Hood. 'Next item. The neighbour in Thrussington. Did you catch up with her over the week-end, Wendy?'

'I did. She told me that someone dressed as a priest called at the cottage on Wednesday, afternoon, looking for Michael Doyle.'

'A priest!' exclaimed Craddock, with a grin. 'Come to give him the last rites had he?'

'I don't think so,' replied Knight. 'He came to give Doyle a message about his mother. She's been very ill, apparently.'

'Did you get a description?' asked Hood.

'Very vague. All she can really remember is he was tall with dark brown hair, dressed in a black suit and wore a clerical collar. Irish accent. Said he was from Dublin. One thing did strike her as odd. He was driving a very flash BMW. She thinks it was a series six, but she's not sure. She didn't get the number either.'

'Did she get a name?'

'Father Gerry O'Brien. I looked the name up. As you might expect, there are several priests named O'Brien, none of which could be this man. There's even a Gerry O'Brien.' She smiled. 'But he's eighty-seven and gets around with a Zimmer frame! Lives in a monastery in County Limerick.'

'I don't think this man was a priest,' said Hooper. 'I'd bet my pension he was the assassin. Clever disguise when you think about it. You were closer than you thought, Ray. If this fellow caught up with Doyle, he'd need a priest to read the last rites. At least we have some idea now who we're looking for. We need to get the neighbour in and show her some photographs and get a facial composite and a photo-fit done.'

'Already arranged. She's coming in on Wednesday. I've sorted the artist too. I've also liaised with Dublin. They'll lend us all the assistance they can in identifying this man.'

'Always assuming he came over from Ireland,' said Hooper, cynically. 'But if he's allowed himself to be spotted dressed as a priest, chances are he'll have adopted a different disguise by now.'

Hood was quick to make the obvious observation. 'The fact that this assassin has been sighted here looking for Doyle confirms our view that he's is still around. Let's find him.'

The chief inspector said nothing further about the priest/assassin. He cast a glance at the officers assembled in front of him then continued. 'I want to move on now to this burglary at the solicitor's office in Leicester, if indeed there was a burglary. I've asked DS Smith to look into it and I'd value your take on what he has discovered. You can switch off your equipment now, Raymond. Sean, the floor is yours.'

DS Smith had remained silent throughout the earlier discussions. He waited until Craddock had switched off the CCTV equipment and returned to his seat before saying anything. He was not in the best of moods. Sheffield Wednesday, a team he had passionately supported since boyhood, had lost again over the week-end and were headed for relegation from the Premier Division. But he cast such considerations aside and concentrated on the issue in hand as he stood then moved to the front of the room.

'I've been looking at the evidence in respect of this so-called burglary,' he said, solemnly. 'I hate to adopt a controversial position, but I'm by no means sure that a burglary in the traditional sense ever took place.'

The atmosphere in the room altered significantly as he continued. 'Let me explain. We have proceeded on the basis that the damage caused in the street outside the solicitor's office was a blind, to cover up an unlawful entry and the placing of the bug under Worth's desk. We have then assumed, understandably, that the O.C.G. behind all this overheard the conversation between the DCI and Worth, got into the premises on Thursday night or early Friday morning, and stole Duffy's file from the private safe in Worth's own office.'

'You think there's a problem with that theory?' said Hooper.

'I do. Especially if Duffy was already dead by the time this burglary was supposed to have taken place. If there was nothing much in the file, as Kelly Maguire suggests, Duffy's death means they'd no longer have access to the one person who could have told them where the information, assuming it actually exists, is really stashed.'

Hooper answered him. 'But that's why we are now proceeding on the basis that Duffy took his own life. As you say, the O.C.G. would have been foolish in the extreme to despatch him before they got hold of his file. They probably had nothing to do with his death other than terrifying him to the extent he hanged himself to get away from it all.'

Smith continued. 'But that's my point. When you look at the evidence in the round, there's a much more likely explanation for how the file disappeared.'

All eyes were now on the detective sergeant from South Yorkshire with an upper-second class honours degree in forensic science from Nottingham Trent University.

'First of all, we have no idea how the alarm system was circumvented. We do know that it did not go off and we have, perhaps, paid far too much of a compliment to the O.C.G. by assuming their technical ability was such that they got in and out without tripping it. SOCO have found no evidence of the alarm being interfered with at all, and it's a very sophisticated system linked directly to Leicester Central Police Station.'

'Perhaps it wasn't switched on,' suggested Craddock. That comment earned a severe rebuke from DS Smith.

'We know it was. An automatic record is created every time it's switched on and off.' The DS looked at his notes. 'That record shows it was switched on at nineteen-thirty-seven hours on Thursday evening – which is when Mr Worth left the office after his extended meeting with a client. It was switched off about two hours later when Mrs Benedict, Worth's secretary, came in briefly to get some papers at twenty-one-forty-two hours. She'd been at the dentists during the afternoon having a wisdom tooth removed. According to her statement, she came in to collect some urgent confidential papers which needed typing from Worth's meeting that afternoon. She says she was there for just over half an hour which is confirmed by the record which shows the alarm being switched on again at twenty-two-oh-seven. It wasn't switched off until seven-ten on Friday morning when Mr Farmer came in. He comes in early to let the cleaners in.'

'Did Mrs Benedict go into Worth's office during the half-hour she was there?' inquired Knight. 'Did it really take her half an hour just to pick up some papers?'

'No, she didn't, not according to what she told me. The papers were left by Worth on her desk in her office opposite his. It's just across the corridor. That has been confirmed by Mr Worth. She typed up the urgent documents before she left. She didn't come in the next day. She'd been given the day off.'

'So, she's unable to say whether the safe in Worth's office had already been attacked by the time she came in on Thursday evening?'

'She says she didn't hear anything out of the ordinary while she was there. The impression she had was that she was the only person in the place. She typed up the essential papers then left. She never went into Worth's office.'

Hooper remained unconvinced. 'But it's still a possibility that the O.C.G. gained entry later without tripping the alarm. There were clear signs of attempts being made to force the side entrance door, which is where the alarm system control box is located. And if Worth left, as he says, at nineteen-thirty-seven and she arrived at twenty-one-forty-two, it didn't give them that much time to break into the safe.'

'Long enough.'

'Did the secretary say why she came in so late?' persisted Hooper.

'She'd needed time to get over the extraction, or so she said, but she knew the papers had to be typed up. She thought it preferable to coming in the next day.'

'And we mustn't overlook that the bug that was recovered from underneath the desk was bang up to date, top of the range,' added Hooper. 'They could have had some sort of gadget which prevented the alarm from sounding.'

Smith responded with a cynical look. 'Ah, yes, the bug. We mustn't forget the bug.' He paused at length, a cynical look crossing his face. 'Do we really think professional criminals operating at this level, whoever they are, would have been so stupid as to leave part of a bug behind?'

'Anyone can make a mistake,' ventured Knight.

'Not these people,' insisted Smith. 'These are real professionals. They don't make elementary mistakes like that.'

'Which entrance did Mrs Benedict use?' asked Knight.

'The side entrance, but that's the entrance the staff are told to use if they come in or leave outside usual working hours. As Andrew has said, the control panel is situated by that door. And the major points for tripping the alarm system are positioned at the entrances and as you approach the strongroom.'

'Perhaps she didn't close the door properly,' suggested Craddock.

'Or she allowed someone to come in with her,' said Knight. 'That's much more likely.'

'These are all matters which we need to follow up,' said Hood. 'But I don't think Sean has finished yet, have you Sean?'

'Thank you, sir. I think we also need to consider the method of entry into Mr Worth's private safe. His office door was not locked, but the safe, of course, was. Brute force. That's how they got into it. The external wooden door was broken off and the internal steel door forced open, using some sort of drill. Must have made quite a lot of noise. The report from SOCO makes that abundantly clear. So, for some reason, having got into the premises twice without causing any damage or tripping the alarm, these highly sophisticated criminals were reduced to literally smashing open a tiny safe? Something doesn't add up. They could have taken the whole thing with them. It's not that heavy. A hundred and twenty kilos, according to the report.'

'But they'd have had to wrench it off the wall to remove it which would have taken time. And they didn't steal anything other than the file.' It was Craddock again who spoke.

'Exactly. There was nearly three hundred pounds in there. Very odd burglars who would leave that much cash behind when it was there for the taking.'

Knight glanced towards Hood who had a smile on his face. DS Smith had obviously discussed his theory with the DCI. And the more she thought about it, the more it sounded the most likely explanation. That it might have been an inside job had already occurred to her but she was by no means sure how it had been accomplished.

'What are you saying then, Sean?' she asked.

'I'm not ruling out that a burglary in the traditional sense took place. All I'm saying is that we shouldn't jump to conclusions. Suppose there never was a burglary? Suppose the damage in the street wasn't just a blind but a double blind? The bug could have been left there in order to throw us off course; to divert us, to remove any suspicion that it was an inside job.'

Hood intervened. 'And we mustn't overlook the sheer coincidence of the file being in Worth's safe overnight rather than in the strongroom where it was normally kept; it would have been totally secure in there. I don't like coincidences like that.'

'But who knew about this file?' asked Hooper. 'Apart from Worth, no one was supposed to know about it, never mind where it was on Thursday night. And if it was an inside job and had been successfully completed before Mrs Benedict left, Duffy hadn't done himself in by then, had he?'

'The pathologist reckons he was probably dead by the time the rioting really got going, which was before the time Mrs Benedict left,' said Hood. 'But insufficient time had passed for whatever was in the file to be studied and then for someone to be instructed to despatch Duffy. Order wasn't restored until just before twenty-two-hundred hours. I don't think there's any point in trying to undermine the pathologist's opinion that his death was by his own hand.'

'Is Mr Worth now to be treated as a suspect?' asked Hooper. He could not resist grinning. 'The DCC won't like that.'

Hood was firm in his reply. 'With all due respect to the DCC, she is not investigating this case; we are. Worth is not the only suspect. His son and his secretary knew about this personal safe and they, or others, could well have picked up something from talk in the office about this file. Remember, anyone removing anything from the main strongroom was required to sign for it. Mr Worth went to the trouble of going down to the strongroom himself to get the file after I made my appointment with him. He didn't send his secretary like he usually did. Nor did he ask Mr Farmer or one of Farmer's clerks to bring it up to him. And despite the fact he's the senior partner, he signed for it in accordance with the established procedure.'

'He obviously didn't want it generally known he'd removed Duffy's file from the strongroom,' said Craddock.

'Perhaps. But Farmer and his clerks would have known if they cared to check the record that this particular file had been removed by Mr Worth. And anyone looking at the record, or signing out something else would know too.'

'Yes,' replied Hooper, 'but it doesn't follow they'd know what was in it.'

'I agree,' said Hood, 'but gossip is just as prevalent in a law office as it is here. We simply don't know if anyone knew or suspected what was in that file. Even Worth claims he didn't know. And if this were an inside job, it wouldn't be necessary for them to know the contents; all they'd have to do is identify which file was Duffy's and to remove it.'

'But they'd have to know it was in Worth's private safe,' said Hooper.

Hood indicated his agreement. 'Someone in that office plainly knew. There can't be any another explanation.'

'What do you want us to do, sir?' asked Wendy Knight.

'I propose to speak to Mr Worth myself. I must confess I am not presently inclined to the view that he has gone in with this O.C.G.' He smiled broadly. 'But his secretary and his son will need to be looked at, and possibly Farmer. We know how these criminal organisations work. They discover something about someone and having identified a particular weakness, apply pressure; pressure that eventually causes the individual to do their bidding. DS Smith has already carried out some informal inquiries into the secretary and the son at my request. I shall ask him in a moment to disclose what he has discovered, but there's more that needs to be done, a lot more. I propose to assemble two small teams to carry out discreet – and I mean very discreet – investigation of the son and the secretary to begin with. We'll look at Farmer and his clerks later. He must be due to retire soon and, you never know, he might have wanted to add to his pension. But on no account are any of them to be directly approached, understand? Not yet. Discretion at all times. I don't want the DCC finding out what we are doing. As things stand, she's more than happy to accept that a burglary took place. I don't want anyone suggesting the contrary. This aspect of the inquiry is to be kept confidential within the team. No leaks.'

'And the rest of the staff?' asked Knight.

'They are to be left alone for the moment. If we go in there heavy-handed that could prove highly counter-productive. We'll concentrate on the two for the time being. I'll decide if and when they are to be approached and questioned. Sean, what do you have for us, on the secretary first?'

Smith referred to his notes, then cleared his throat. 'Vivienne Kathleen Benedict, forty-two, divorced, lives with her mother in the Stoneygate/Oadby area. She's worked for the firm for nearly nineteen years, starting off as a typist and working her way up to becoming Worth's confidential secretary. She initially worked for another firm of solicitors after she left school. I don't know of any relationships at the moment, other than that she's a member of a book circle and a bridge club. I also checked with the Land Registry. The house she lives in is jointly owned by her and her mother. It's mortgage free and at today's values is worth a cool quarter of a million. No evidence that she's short of money. No evidence of an extravagant lifestyle, quite the contrary.'

'What about her mother?' asked Knight.

'Very little known. Agnes Brennan. She's seventy-six years of age. A widow. Her husband died seven years ago. He was a quantity surveyor. Worked for the city council. His death coincided with his daughter's divorce and it looks like she and her mother bought their present house together shortly afterwards. The mother has some physical disability but I'm not sure what it is, but she certainly uses a wheelchair on occasions. I saw the wheelchair in the back of Vivienne Benedict's car when it was parked on their driveway yesterday.'

'Any siblings?' asked Knight.

'I believe she has a brother and a sister, but they don't live in the area. The brother is in his early fifties. I don't know anything about the sister at the moment other than she's three years older than Vivienne. That's something that needs further research.'

'Do we know anything about the divorced husband?' asked Hooper.

'He's one Carl Benedict. Remarried with two children. Lives in Ratby. Works for the city council too, in the environment department. No form. I don't think he can have any involvement. They have no contact nowadays.'

'Anyone at the solicitors with any previous?' asked Craddock.

'No, none of the staff at the firm has any form, apart from a couple of convictions or fixed penalties for driving offences, speeding in the main, which is hardly surprising. I've checked them all out on the PNC.'

'You have been busy. And Worth Junior?' asked Knight.

Smith glanced at his notes again. 'Paul Anthony Ryman Worth, thirty-one, a graduate of Leicester University. Calls himself Tony. He was admitted as a solicitor in nineteen ninety-five. Married, no children. His wife is also a solicitor, but she works in Loughborough for a different firm. Tony Worth specialises in take-overs, mergers and other commercial work. He's highly thought of, apparently, but I picked up that his marriage might be in difficulties. He's a keen sportsman too. Had a trial for Leicester Tigers when he was younger, but now concentrates on golf, squash and, in winter, skiing. He's been known to take holidays separately from his wife. She has no interest in skiing, according to what I was told.'

'How did you find out all this so quickly?' asked Craddock.

'He was away from the office when I was there, in London at some meeting. His secretary, who seems to me to be in awe of him, told me all about him.'

'Any sign of a girlfriend?' asked Knight, displaying a keen interest in the younger Worth, 'other than his secretary, I mean.' Craddock and Henshaw laughed.

'No one I can identify, but I spent most of last Friday in Worth's office investigating this so-called burglary. I picked up some vibes that young Tony has a bit of reputation as a ladies' man. His secretary seemed almost jealous, not of his wife, I hasten to add, but of someone else she refused to name.'

'Do we know anything about his finances?' asked Hooper.

'Not at the moment, no. He and his wife have a large house in Rothley which is heavily mortgaged but with both of them working full-time, that shouldn't be too much of a problem. And they take expensive holidays, both together and separately, according to his secretary.'

'She's not very discreet, for a secretary,' said Hooper, 'telling you all this. But it doesn't look too hopeful.' Hooper had not yet jettisoned the idea that a genuine burglary had taken place. He remained far from convinced that this was an inside job. 'Nothing to suggest that either of them would have gone in with what's left of Grayling's mob.'

'Not so far,' agreed Smith. 'But I've hardly scratched the surface yet.'

'Worth's secretary seems the more likely of the two,' observed Knight. 'At least we know she was in the office after hours on the Thursday. And wasn't she the one who first raised the possibility that someone had been in the offices overnight on Wednesday?'

'She was,' agreed Hood. 'She didn't say very much though. Described it as a feeling prompted by the damage in the street when she arrived for work.'

'She also had a feeling it was the main strongroom was the focus of any intruder,' said Knight. 'And there's no evidence that anyone got into there. Farmer spent over an hour checking the contents. If it were an inside job, she must be the favourite.'

'Insufficient evidence at the moment, Wendy,' said Hood. 'We mustn't rush to judgement. And we can't rule anyone or anything out, not yet. I want Andrew to look into Tony Worth, and you and Sean to see what more we can discover about Mrs Benedict. As I said, I shall speak to Worth Senior myself.'

'What about Doyle?' inquired Craddock. 'It doesn't look like he's going to surrender himself.'

'As I said, he remains our number one priority,' replied Hood. 'If this assassin gets to him before we do, that will really upset the apple cart. Keep your eyes and ears open. He's obviously keeping in the shadows. Someone, somewhere must know where he is. He's bound to emerge, eventually. Any information about him is to come directly to me. We are monitoring his bank account. So far, he's not drawn out any money, so he must be in funds from another source. He lost most of his assets as a result of the confiscation proceedings. Then there were his back taxes to pay.'

'But he's not exactly skint, is he?' said Knight.

'Not by a long shot,' replied Hood. 'Now, let's get on with it.'

CHAPTER 24

Michael Doyle spent five nights at the B&B in Hopwas before deciding to move on towards his destination in North Wales. Five long and boring days and nights and, what was worse, no word from Jules. No calls, no text messages, nothing. He appreciated she had promised to call him when she and Grayling set off for Holyhead, but that would not be until the coming week-end. He'd thought she could have managed to call him at least once from Dublin before then, desperate as he was to hear from her. She must surely have had several opportunities when Grayling was otherwise engaged? With little to do, other than listen to Mrs Ramsdale's stories, all of which he'd heard before, and ponder on his immediate future, he had allowed his thoughts to become almost dominated by Jules. He couldn't get her out of his head. His frustration increased when he remembered how she had ended their liaison early in 1999, while he was on remand in Leicester Prison, just when he needed her support the most. The shock of her departure had devastated him, causing him to spend two days in the prison hospital wing. Then he recalled the exhilaration and overwhelming relief when he received the coded message via his solicitor that told him the rupture in their relationship was all part of her plan to make sure he was not convicted of the Charnwood robbery. It would never have occurred to him to blackmail a judge into directing his acquittal; only Jules could have thought up such a wild idea. It had not come off, but that was no fault of hers. What was more important, it proved to him that she still loved him and would do anything for him, even risking imprisonment herself. But he was once more plunged into despondency when he thought of Jules' child, the son he wanted to have with her, the son fathered, it seemed, by Michael Grayling. Why had she got herself entangled with such a man? Doyle was no angel; he fully appreciated that, but for her to get involved with the son of Gus Grayling exasperated him. Tears formed in his eyes as he remembered pleading with her to come away with him when they'd met at Barnard House following her acquittal and his release from prison. He didn't care about the paternity of the boy. He wanted her. He wanted to be with her. He needed her. He simply could not imagine life without her. He obtained a little consolation in convincing himself that her going in with Grayling was solely down to her desperate need to avoid conviction and imprisonment. Doyle realised he could do nothing for her, locked away as he was, serving a lengthy sentence. Grayling had the means to rescue her and the resources he was able to command had seemingly done the trick. Doyle had read about Hanlon's escape from Mansfield Shirebrook and how this had played into the hands of the defence, undermining his evidence and blowing the prosecution's case against Jules out of the water. He was grateful to Grayling for that, but not for what followed. Not for taking her off to Portugal along with her son. But still the doubts persisted. Did Jules really want to escape from Grayling as she had told him, or was she allowing herself to be used in order to draw Doyle into a confrontation that could only result in his demise? As he headed to the B&B in North Wales recommended by Mrs Ramsdale his thoughts were only of Jules. Would he ever get to see her again? And if he did, would he live to regret it?

CHAPTER 25

Hood received a telephone call from the governor of Woodborough Prison on Tuesday morning. Brian Logan had not reported for work. Calls to his landline and his mobile phone had gone unanswered. A visit to his modest home just outside Wellingborough by Detective Superintendent Maurice Kingston revealed he was not there. A neighbour reported him leaving with two suitcases early on Saturday afternoon. His car registration was circulated and two detectives from Kingston's team were tasked with finding him. Hood would be informed immediately he was located.

After making his now almost daily visit to ACC Gaunt at HQ, Hood called at the offices of Worth, Ambler and Partners. He had telephoned Mr Worth in advance and the senior partner, still anxious to cooperate, agreed to make himself available, cancelling an appointment with a client in order to do so. He and Hood met in the boardroom.

'Is this where you met with your client on Thursday afternoon?' asked Hood.

'It is. There were several people in attendance. My own office was hardly large enough. That's why we had this room constructed. It's only about three years old.'

'Very impressive,' said Hood, looking at the walnut panelling and a carefully lit oil painting by a minor Florentine artist.

'Yes it is. But our commercial clients expect a degree of pampering.' Worth smiled in an attempt to disguise his anxiety. Why did Hood want to see him again? And why had he asked for the meeting to take place in the boardroom? His own office was available and no longer designated a crime scene.

'Are there any unused offices in this part of the building?' asked Hood.

The senior partner appeared puzzled by the question but went on to explain how the firm's office accommodation was increasing in size. 'We merged with the firm next door two years ago in order to acquire more space. There are still some rooms that we have not yet refurbished. It's an ongoing if gradual expansion. Next-door's offices were not up to scratch, not for the sort of work we do. It's been an expensive business bringing everything up to date. By the way, Mr Hood, would you like some coffee or tea? I can easily get something organised.'

Hood shook his head and politely declined. He didn't have time to waste. He quickly pushed on. 'I don't expect you to breach professional confidentiality, Mr Worth, but could I ask what it was that caused you to work so late last Thursday?'

Worth smiled. 'You sound like my wife. That's a question she repeatedly asks, but it's not exactly unusual in the work we do, Mr Hood. Our clients are very demanding and expect things to be done almost immediately. Thursday was no exception.'

'The meeting began before lunchtime, did it?'

'Yes. About forty minutes after you left. A couple of the attendees were a little late. I was kept waiting for some time.'

'Was there a break for lunch?'

'Yes, but only for about half an hour, around one-thirty. My secretary got in some sandwiches, so I remained with my client in this room. The others left the building but they all returned later. I don't know what arrangements they made for lunch.'

'And your secretary's dental appointment was known before the meeting started, was it?'

'Oh, yes. She'd been on a course of antibiotics for some days. The appointment with her dentist had been made the Friday before. She left mid-afternoon, at about half-past three. Her appointment was at four o'clock and she had to get up to New Walk were the dental surgery is situated. I had booked a taxi to make sure she was there on time.'

'And she had the tooth removed?'

'Yes. It was very good of her to come in later to type up some essential documents. They were required urgently and I'd given her the following day off, you see, by way of an inducement.' He smiled. 'I had a wisdom tooth removed myself a couple of years ago and I took a little time to get over the experience. I was grateful she was prepared to come in when she did.'

'Could I ask if it was known by those who attended the meeting that Mrs Benedict had a dental appointment that afternoon?'

'I believe it was mentioned just before she left, yes – to explain why she was leaving the meeting early. I remember because I had to take notes myself after she had gone. My client was anxious that the documents we were drafting should be typed up ready for signature in the morning. That was why Vivienne volunteered to come in during the evening despite having had a wisdom tooth removed – to make sure they were ready when the client came in to sign them the following day. She'd had a few hours to recover from the extraction before she returned.'

'So, all those present knew about the appointment and that Mrs Benedict would be coming in that evening to finish the typing?'

'Yes. There were one or two comments when she left, of encouragement. Is it significant that her appointment was mentioned?'

Hood pressed on without answering Worth's question. 'And she did what she promised, did she?'

'She did. I found the papers ready for signature in the tray in her room on Friday morning.'

'And the client came in to sign them as planned?'

Worth shook his head. 'Actually, he didn't. I had a phone call from him on Friday morning, shortly after I discovered that my safe had been broken into. He told me that the proposed investor was pulling out. I wasn't entirely surprised. There were areas of disagreement which had not been fully resolved. When they left the previous evening, they were intending to have dinner in one of the client's restaurants. So discussions probably continued in my absence. I was invited to go with them, but I'd had enough for one day and wanted to get home.'

'This client of yours, was he well known to you?'

'Riyad Malik? Yes. We've acted for him for several years. He owns a manufacturing business and two or three Indian restaurants in the city.

You've probably eaten one of his curries. He supplies a number of the big retailers with ready-prepared meals.'

'And the meeting on Thursday? You say there were some issues which remained unresolved? I don't like to pry, but I'd be grateful for anything you feel able to disclose.'

Worth sighed. 'I suppose I can tell you this much. Malik is eyeing retirement. He wanted to expand the manufacturing business and was looking for investors to come in to provide finance for the extension and modernisation of his factory. He already owns the site but he wants to update the whole operation and increase the profitability of his business before handing it on to his sons. He's had this expansion in mind for many months and this was not the first investor he'd considered.'

'Would it be breaching client confidentiality to tell me who attended the meeting on Thursday afternoon?'

Worth sighed. 'I think I might have to speak to Riyad Malik first, Chief Inspector. Do you think this has something to do with the theft of the file? I can't see how.'

Hood pressed on. 'Let me ask you this, Mr Worth. Did anyone other than Mrs Benedict leave the meeting before it was concluded?'

A worried frown creased Worth's forehead. 'As a matter of fact they did. A representative of the proposed investor and her associate left just before six o'clock; that's when the office usually closes. She had childcare responsibilities apparently.'

'Her name?'

Worth hesitated. 'I don't suppose there's any harm in telling you her name; Rebecca Johnson. She's a business consultant, or so I was informed. I'd never met her before although I had heard of her.'

'And her associate?'

'A younger man. He introduced himself as John Rigby. He didn't seem to participate much. Rebecca told me he was still learning the trade, as she put it.'

'Did you see them leave?'

'I saw them leave this room, but I continued with the meeting.

Rebecca said they would have no difficulty finding their way out. I presume they left through the main entrance. Only the staff use the side door.'

'And that left how many still in this room?'

'Apart from myself, Mr Maddison and the proposed investor, a Mr Peter Hegarty, and Mr Malik, of course. We had a short comfort break then continued our discussions.'

'Mr Maddison?'

'Francis Maddison. He's an accountant with a practice in Kettering.'

'And you have no doubts about who he says he is?'

'None at all. My firm has dealt with him before. I also did a due diligence check on him at the specific request of Mr Malik. I was given notice that he would be coming to the meeting. His firm is not large, but well established and with a good reputation. Knowing Malik as I do, I assumed he would have already run a few checks on the proposed investor.'

'Who is this Hegarty fellow?'

'Never met him before, but that's hardly unusual. He possessed all the trappings of wealth. I saw him leave with Malik and the accountant. As I said, they were having dinner together later. They all went off in Hegarty's Bentley after the meeting ended. I noticed he'd parked it on the yellow lines outside the office. No doubt if he receives a fixed penalty it will be of little consequence for someone with his money.' Worth gave Hood a curious look. 'What is this all about, Chief Inspector?'

Hood remained enigmatic then sat back in his chair and almost smiled. 'I'm not quite sure, Mr Worth. But tell me, why was it necessary to have so many people at this meeting?'

'Not for me to say. I expected Malik would have someone with him, one of his sons perhaps, but I must confess, I got the impression that the others were all in the proposed investor's corner. Malik seemed to be wholly reliant on me. Why Hegarty had two advisers and Rigby with him, I couldn't say. Maddison was brought in to look at the accounts and advise on potential future profitability and the various methods of holding shares in the new company. I suspect Hegarty is particularly cautious before making an investment of the size Malik required, which is understandable.'

'What do you know about Hegarty?'

'Very little. Mr Malik seemed satisfied with him; he'd obviously heard of him, but I intended to carry out a detailed check on him before any final decision was made. But I already know he's very wealthy. He appears in the local "rich list" regularly.'

'So these papers typed up by Mrs Benedict did not amount to a final agreement?'

'Oh, no. Preliminary and non-binding but necessary for the appropriate checks to be carried out. But as the proposed investment has been abandoned, no longer required.'

'But you still have them?'

'Yes, but they are and will remain confidential.' He gave the chief inspector a knowing look.

Hood nodded. 'I understand. Did Malik give any reason for the proposal being abandoned?'

'Mutually agreed was all I was told. But these things happen, Mr Hood. Both parties slept on it and subsequently changed their minds. As I said, it was a considerable investment that Malik was seeking. Well into the millions.' He paused and looked directly at Hood. 'I have to be careful what I say, but we shouldn't have too much trouble finding an alternative source of funding. Malik's business is basically sound but he lacks the capital to expand it on the scale he wishes. Neither was I altogether surprised that things didn't work out. The meeting went on longer than I thought because Maddison was asking a lengthy series of questions about likely future profits and how the shares would be held. He certainly knows his stuff. Very professional.'

'Was there a particular area of disagreement?'

Worth nodded. 'Again, I must be discreet. But I think I can say that Malik was firm on one matter only. He insisted on retaining control of the overall business. It was that which seemed to cause conflict. Maddison suggested the possibility of a golden share, but Hegarty was not having that at all. I hoped they would come to some arrangement when they had dinner together, but it was not to be.'

Hood hardly dared disclose what he was thinking. He decided to keep his thoughts to himself and asked Worth if he could inspect the other offices in the vicinity of the boardroom. Worth shrugged his shoulders.

'Of course, Chief Inspector. But I can't think how that will help you. Some are still undergoing refurbishment. Most of the work is done at week-ends to avoid disturbance during office hours. There's not much activity during the working week. But please, look for yourself.'

The two men vacated the boardroom and walked along the corridor. The rooms that had been completed were locked. Two others, where work was still underway, were open. Hood looked around them briefly, noticing that both rooms had ensuite facilities behind internal doors. He and Worth then returned to the boardroom.

'Were any of the people responsible for the refurbishment working in the building on Thursday?' he asked.

'No, as I said, they come in at week-ends. The architect pops in now and again, but that's all. What are you thinking, Mr Hood? You don't seriously think the meeting on Thursday had something to do with the burglary?'

'I don't know, Mr Worth. But I've had more than a passing thought that with careful planning there was a way your safe could have been attacked without the general alarm being sounded.'

'But the alarm would be triggered if anyone forced an entry into the premises; that has already been established.'

'Yes, but suppose they were already in the building?'

'I don't follow you.'

'Suppose this Rebecca Johnson and her associate didn't leave when you thought they did, but hid in one of the vacant offices in this part of the building? Those two rooms you've just shown me are in the course of having ensuite facilities installed behind an additional closed door. Not difficult for someone to hide there for a couple of hours.'

Worth appeared astonished. 'Why on earth would they do that?

How would they know about the rooms? And they couldn't have known for certain whether other members of staff might still be in the building. Not everyone leaves on the dot at six o'clock.'

'Was anyone left in the building when you departed?'

'I don't believe so, no. I stayed on for about half an hour after they had all left. I would not have set the alarm as I did if another member of staff was working late. The board at the side entrance indicated I was the only one still in the office. Staff who stay late are asked to indicate when they leave, but the system is far from infallible.'

'There you are then. I think it's possible one or other or both waited until you left and had set the alarm, then attacked your safe. As I understand it, there is nothing that would trigger the alarm in the corridor between this part of the building and your office? And no alarm either in your office or controlling your private safe.'

'That's right. The system will be extended and brought into operation when the refurbishment of this section of the building is completed. But if they did as you say, they would be bound to trigger the alarm when they left. How could they know the code in order to reset the system?'

'Would they need to know the code? You've already confirmed that everyone at the meeting was aware that Mrs Benedict was returning after office hours. All they had to do after breaking open your safe was wait for her to arrive and disarm the system in the usual way, then out they could go. No one would be any the wiser. When Mrs Benedict had completed her typing, she would then have reset the alarm before she left. Quite simple when you think about it.'

'That would explain why the alarm was not triggered, but I simply can't believe that's what happened. And how would they unlock the side door?'

'They wouldn't need to. Think about it. Mrs Benedict didn't lock the door behind her using the mortice key when she arrived. She simply closed it, which automatically engages the Yale lock. Easy enough to open from the inside. She only double locked the door with the mortice key when she departed having reset the alarm.'

'But how would anyone know the file was in my private safe?'

'A good question. And I can't provide an answer to that at this stage. I shall need to speak to the others who attended the meeting. Can you let me have their details?' Worth sighed then nodded. 'And please, don't say anything to anyone about what I have told you. And I mean anyone.'

'I give you my word,' promised Worth.

Hood smiled his appreciation. 'Was anything said about Vivienne Benedict's dental appointment before the break for lunch?'

'I'm not sure. It might have been mentioned, I suppose. There was quite a bit of inconsequential chatter before we got down to business. There always is. It was certainly mentioned later, more than once.'

'Thank you. Oh, one final question. Do you know who brought the parties together? Who suggested that Hegarty might be interested in making an investment in Malik's business?'

Worth swallowed hard. His eyes told all. 'It was my son, Tony. He knew Rebecca Johnson from his golf club. She plays there regularly, apparently. And he was aware she did work for Hegarty on occasions. It is well known in certain circles that Hegarty is always looking for investment opportunities. She suggested he might be interested in Malik's business. But I'm sure my son had no idea it might have been part of a ploy to steal Duffy's file. He wouldn't be party to anything like that. Not knowingly. And he had no knowledge of the file, as far as I'm aware.'

'Good looking woman is she?' asked Hood, raising his eyebrows and recalling Tony Worth's reputation as a bit of a ladies' man.

'Very. Very attractive indeed.'

CHAPTER 26

DCI Hood returned to West Bridgford where he found DS Wendy Knight alone and concentrating on her computer screen.

'Where is everyone?' he asked.

'Sean is visiting the dentist in Leicester where Vivienne Benedict supposedly had her wisdom tooth removed last Thursday. Ray and Graham are going through more CCTV. The stuff from Woodborough has arrived. I haven't seen Andrew Hooper this morning.'

'He's looking into something for me.' Hood leant on the edge of Knight's desk. 'By the way, I don't think there's any doubt that Mrs Benedict visited her dentist. It seems to have been known by everyone in the office. Mr Worth even organised a taxi for her.'

'You've been there again, have you, sir?'

'Yes. On my way back from HQ.' He half-smiled. 'Poor old Worth. He's falling over himself to help us. He still feels responsible for the theft of Duffy's file. But from what he's told me, I think I may have worked out how it was stolen without the alarm being triggered.'

Knight looked up. 'You have?'

'Yes, and it involves Mrs Benedict's visit to the dentist and her returning to the office after hours.'

Hood explained his theory in detail. As usual, Knight looked for logical flaws.

'But if this was planned as you say – and it must have been very carefully planned – how would they know about Mrs Benedict's visit to the dentist and her intention of returning to the office in the evening *before* the meeting took place? Learning about it during the meeting would be too late to organise anything.'

'I don't think it was a secret within the office that Mrs Benedict had an appointment with her dentist well before the meeting on Thursday.

She'd been on antibiotics for five days. And the meeting broke up for half an hour or so for lunch. It could have been mentioned before then.'

'Not much time to organise a plan of this nature.'

'I agree. And if they didn't know she was intending to come back in the evening beforehand, that does create a potential difficulty. But Worth and the other professionals present must have appreciated that the necessary documents would have to be typed up as a matter of urgency. She'd also been given the following day off, as a sort of inducement, so a return to the office that evening might have been anticipated.'

'But supposing the meeting had concluded by the time Mrs Benedict's appointment came around? How could anyone have foreseen the meeting would drag on as long as it did?'

'According to Worth, there's nothing unusual about such meetings going on until the evening. On this occasion, it was down to the proposed investor's accountant. He was very thorough, a real details man. Insisted that everything was gone into very carefully which extended the length of the meeting well past six o'clock when the office usually closed.'

'And I suppose Farmer and his clerks would have gone home by then? No chance for Worth to put the file back in the strongroom until the next morning.'

'That could well be the explanation, Wendy. By keeping the meeting running well after the office usually closed, it created the opportunity to steal the file from Worth's less secure safe. That could well be the reason Maddison was dragging things out. And it was Maddison who suggested the idea of a golden share to ensure that Malik – the business owner – retained control. That seems to have been the stumbling block for the investor. Gave him an easy way out.'

Knight interrupted. 'Maddison? Francis Maddison?'

'Yes, have you heard of him?'

Knight smiled broadly. 'I most certainly have. Francis Maddison was Duffy's accountant. That's who I've been looking into this morning.'

Hood, too, broke into a smile. 'And if Kelly Maguire was telling the truth, he was also Grayling's accountant.'

'His firm certainly audited Grayling's companies for the last few years. The firm's name appears in the accounts. I've checked.'

'And there he was large as life in Worth's office!'

'Yes, sir. I think there might be something in your theory after all. It's just too much of a coincidence otherwise, although there could be no guarantee that everything would fall into place. Worth could have returned the file to the strongroom before the meeting started.'

Hood was thinking rapidly. 'I suppose he could, but we know that he didn't. And I don't believe the people we are dealing with rely too much on chance. I still think someone in that office must have revealed where the file was.'

'Over seventy suspects for that, sir.'

'I know.'

'You'll want to speak to Maddison, I suppose?'

'I shall, and quickly. Then there's the investor who didn't in the event proceed. A man called Hegarty. He's undoubtedly a wealthy individual from what little I know about him. He could well be entirely innocent but he'll need checking out all the same. Then there's his business advisor, a woman by the name of Rebecca Johnson. Interestingly, she's a member of the golf club where Worth's son plays. Another link that tells against this meeting being wholly coincidental. They know each other pretty well, I suspect, because young Worth seems to have been pivotal in bringing about the connection between Malik and Hegarty. She's very easy on the eye, apparently, and Tony Worth does have a bit of a reputation in that department.' He gave Knight a shrewd look. 'I want you to trace her and establish exactly why she was at the meeting last Thursday. And Wendy, see what you can discover about any childcare responsibilities she may have had. That was the reason she gave for leaving the meeting when she did.'

'What about Hegarty?'

'I'll check him out on the PNC then make an appointment to see him after I have visited Maddison. You have Maddison's details? I believe his office is in Kettering.'

'Yes, sir. I'll write down his address and telephone number for you. And Tony Worth?'

'Leave him to me. I'll speak to him after I've had words with Mr Hegarty and Worth's client, Malik. I also need to speak to Andrew to see what he's found out about him.'

'You think they could all be involved?'

'I don't know, Wendy. I don't think Malik has anything to do with it and Hegarty may just have been used. On the other hand, this meeting could have been set up in Worth's office specifically to gain an opportunity to steal the file.' He smiled. 'One other thing, before I forget, you have everything set up for the photo-fit tomorrow?'

'Yes, sir. The neighbour is coming in at eleven o'clock.'

'Good. When it's all complete, make sure any sketches and photo-fits are brought to me. I don't want anyone else seeing them until I have studied them, understand?'

Knight appeared puzzled. 'Whatever you say, sir. I'll let you have then as soon as they're completed.'

CHAPTER 27

'Is that you, Hegarty?'

'Yes. What do you want now? I did what you asked but that's it. No more favours.'

'Have I asked you to do anything else for me?'

'You haven't, not yet. And before you do, the answer will be no. I'm not getting involved in any more of your little schemes. I only did this because I owed your father.'

'I only want to know how it went. Have there been any comebacks?'

'Not so far. And that accountant of yours managed my withdrawal expertly. There was no way I was going to allow Malik to hold a golden share. A good man is Maddison. He's the sort of fellow I could use myself. He certainly knows his stuff.'

'How did you leave it with Malik?'

'I told him that having slept on it, it wasn't the sort of investment that interested me. He wanted to keep control of the whole outfit. I'm not one for putting in the sort of money he was looking for unless I get control. Mind you, it wasn't a bad deal overall. Perhaps you should put some of your ill-gotten gains into his business?'

'I might just do that, but not at the moment. I presume if any questions arise about the meeting last Thursday, you'll be able to deal with them?'

'Why should any questions arise? Who'd be interested in a business deal that didn't come off?'

'There's a police officer poking his nose into my affairs – a DCI by the name of Hood. He's already telephoned Maddison and arranged to see him. That is a bit of a concern. I thought I'd let you know so you can firm up your version of events.'

'I don't have a version of events. How does he know I was at this meeting?'

'I told you, he's an interfering pest.' He paused and cleared his throat before continuing. 'There's an outside possibility that he's worked out the real reason for the meeting, not that he'll be able to prove anything.'

'The real reason? Look, as far as I was concerned this was a genuine business opportunity. All I did was agree to use this accountant of yours. If there was some underlying purpose, that's not something I know anything about, and I don't want to know either.'

'I think you need to understand the basics.' He paused before continuing. 'A file was removed from the lawyer's office. A file I needed to get hold of.'

'What file? I know nothing about any file.'

'A file your old friend Duffy had placed with the solicitors.'

'Duffy? Number one, he wasn't my friend. Number two, he's dead, isn't he? Word is he killed himself. Why would a file of his be of any interest to you?'

'It was a file that could have caused me, and possibly you, no end of trouble.'

'Me? What was in this file that was so important?'

'Do you really want to know?'

Hegarty paused for a moment. 'No, I don't think I do. I hope to God I wasn't mentioned. I used to know Duffy pretty well although he used a different name. It was your old man who told me his real name.'

'No worries. You weren't named.'

'So, you've seen this file?'

'It's been looked at on my behalf, yes.'

'Is this something to do with Rebecca and her associate leaving before the meeting finished? I wasn't very happy about that and said so at the time. She gave me no warning she was intending to leave before the meeting was done.'

'She hasn't said anything to you?'

'No, she hasn't.'

'I wouldn't ask her if I were you.' He laughed.

'Now listen, Michael, Rebecca works for me, not for you. I don't like my people moonlighting on behalf of someone else in my time. Are you telling me she removed this file from the office?'

'I'm not telling you anything. Just a little favour she did for me – in her own time.'

'I want nothing to do with it. I know nothing about any file disappearing during that meeting.'

'You needn't worry then. Nothing disappeared during the meeting. I give you my word about that. And you have nothing to worry about because you don't know anything. Best we keep it that way, don't you think? Just make sure you can explain why you were there and have the figures available as to why you decided not to proceed with the investment.'

'I don't like the sound of this. If this DCI wants to speak to me, he's bound to want to speak to Rebecca.'

'He probably will. But she can look after herself. I've told you, there's nothing for you to worry about. As far as you were concerned, this was a normal business meeting. Just remember not to mention me if I come up. You don't know me; you've never heard of me or my old man. Understand, mate?'

Hegarty sighed. 'If only that was true. I'll certainly stick to that line. And what makes you think you'll come up in any conversation? And by the way, I'm not your mate!'

'Fair enough. I'm just covering all my bases. Nothing will probably come of it.'

'But I may be vulnerable when it comes to questions about Duffy. I knew him but he was using the name Lafferty. What will I say?'

'That's up to you. That you invested in Duffy's haulage business is hardly a secret. Just make sure you refer to him as Lafferty if he's mentioned. Make out that you've never heard of Duffy.'

'I only made the investment because your old man asked me to and I sold all my shares to Lafferty years ago. The business became successful very quickly.'

'As I said, if he comes up, it's up to you how you deal with it.'

'It won't have a good look though. Bit of a coincidence that I was once briefly in business with him and there I am sitting in his solicitor's office when his file disappears. You've put me in a difficult situation, Michael. I should have been told.'

'Just a coincidence. You didn't need to know. And I've told you, it didn't disappear while you were there.'

'I don't like coincidences, Michael. Especially when they involve me. And I don't like being used. I wish I'd never got involved with this.' Hegarty made no attempt to disguise his anger.

'Just get your story in order.'

'Don't you worry, I will. Oh, Michael, just to be clear. I don't want to hear from you again, understand?'

Michael Grayling did not reply. He simply terminated the call.

Hegarty looked at his mobile phone then quickly deleted all references to Michael Grayling. He stood up and walked to his office door, opened it and spoke quietly to his secretary. 'Get hold of Rebecca. Tell her I want to see her, urgently.'

CHAPTER 28

DS Knight and Acting Inspector Andrew Hooper were alone in the incident room early on Thursday morning. Wendy Knight looked up as she completed her report on her meeting with Rebecca Johnson. Andrew Hooper continued typing away as she spoke.

'Do you still think there's something going on in the background, Andrew? Something we aren't being told about?'

Hooper said nothing for several seconds, then stood up and walked over to Wendy's desk. 'I don't know, but I think Harry knows more than he's letting on. I've never been involved in an investigation before where the SIO makes almost daily visits to the ACC. He doesn't just phone him; he drives over to HQ almost every morning which I would have thought is both inconvenient and time-consuming. I wouldn't mind betting you that's where he is now.'

'What was it he asked you to do for him?'

'I've been in contact with the Australian police – in Sydney. Harry wanted me to look into Grayling's son again. The team received an anonymous call on the incident number suggesting it was Michael Grayling who was after killing Doyle. A similar message was left on Crimestoppers.'

Knight appeared surprised. 'Harry never mentioned Australia to me, but I suppose I was otherwise engaged, trying to locate this Johnson woman. It took me most of yesterday afternoon to find her.' She frowned. 'We checked out Michael Grayling when he didn't appear at his father's funeral last year. We were assured he was still in Australia.'

'Well, he may well have been back then, but it seems no one knows where he is at the moment. No joy from his office in Sydney either. I've been speaking with an Inspector Kevin Stilwell of the SOC.'

'The SOC?'

'Special Operations Contingent.'

'Sounds very high-powered.'

'Not really. Just a bunch of detectives as far as I can make out. Stilwell instructed a local ranger to visit Michael Grayling's home last week in what they call the Southern Highlands. Apparently he owns a large vinery there – it's a good hour-and-a-half from central Sydney. He wasn't there and the ranger had no joy in getting anything useful from his wife. She said he was away on business but she wasn't sure where.'

Knight did a double take. 'Grayling has a wife?'

'So it seems.'

'Well, that's come as something of a shock. And he's still in Australia?'

'According to his wife, yes. And she produced his passport to the Ranger which suggested he was still in the country. But she doesn't know where. He doesn't always tell her where he's going on his business trips. Sometimes he's away for weeks at a time. They appear to have what I believe is called nowadays an open marriage.'

'When did she last see him?'

'Three weeks ago, she says, but whether she's telling the truth about that I've no idea. But Border Security has no evidence anyone called Grayling has left the country in the last six months. Mind you, I got the distinct impression that Michael Grayling is a person of interest to the Sydney police quite independently of our interest in him.'

'Did you find out why they're interested in him?'

'Not definitely, no. They were very circumspect, but Stillwell paid close attention when I queried whether he'd left Australia and come to the UK. They had no evidence that he had, but they'd obviously like to know where he is. I got the impression it might concern illicit drugs. Apparently, there's a lot of Chinese heroin coming into Australia.'

'I thought Australian border control was pretty efficient?'

'That's what they tell me. But as we know to our cost, these mega-dealers always seem to find a way to get their stuff in whatever precautions are taken.'

'But Gus Grayling never had any truck with drugs.'

'Perhaps his son is different?'

Knight frowned. 'But we'd know if he came into the UK, wouldn't we?'

'It's always possible he's left Australia on a fake passport.' He stretched his arms and suppressed a yawn before continuing. 'You were not around these parts a few years ago when we had a really massive mortgage fraud to investigate. Before Harry's time, too. I was a humble DC back then. Many of the mortgages were taken out using fake passports – the banks and building societies insisted on passports being produced as evidence of identity. We reckoned that old man Grayling had a hand in providing them. If I remember correctly, he was interviewed twice under caution, but we were never able to prove anything, not against him. Several passports were recovered, though, which proved to be fraudulent. The CPS eventually dropped the whole case because of some serious non-disclosure by the reviewing lawyer and the SIO. Didn't do the SIO's career any harm though. He's about to retire as a Detective Superintendent.'

'Is he, indeed? What's his name?'

'Superintendent Bertie Woolmer. I haven't come across him for years. He's over at HQ now; works mainly in administration. Winding down. He's due to retire at the end of June.'

'I don't know him, but there's no reason why I should. You think that Grayling Junior might have carried on the family tradition and got hold of a false passport and used it to leave Australia?'

'It's a possibility. It's not that difficult to obtain a passport in a false name if you have the necessary paperwork, although I believe things have tightened up recently. And he is a British citizen, despite having lived in Australia since his teens. And if the New South Wales police can't locate him, it becomes even more probable that he's left the country. He could well have taken over from his old man after all. I'm sure Harry's now working on that basis.'

'Remind me, what name was used when Julia Hamilton and her companion flew from Coventry Airport after her trial?'

'Haynes, Ronald Haynes. That was the name on the man's passport. It was probably a fake. We checked it out at the time. Never managed to trace the guy. But it was definitely a British passport and seemed legit. And there are dozens of men of that name who hold genuine passports. Hamilton used her own passport. And she did arrive in Portugal as did the man using the name Haynes. That all checked out.'

'Where is Haynes now?'

'Presumably in Portugal. Hamilton has not left there either, as far as we know.'

'So, if they do leave Portugal using the same passports we will know about it?'

'We should do; there's an alert out in both names, but it doesn't follow they'll used the same identities. If this man is Grayling, you can guarantee he won't be using his real name and he'll probably not risk using the name Haynes again. He'll be too savvy for that.'

Wendy Knight nodded her agreement. 'And there was me thinking he and his father had fallen out big time. That's what we were told last year. And if he's married, what would he be doing with Julia Hamilton? Harry is convinced that Gus Grayling's successor is the person who's got Hamilton in tow in Portugal.'

'It must be him then. Perhaps he has his own reasons for being with her, or he and his wife might have fallen out or split up?'

Knight gave Hooper a cheeky grin. 'Or it could be one of these modern open marriages you mentioned.' She closed down her computer after printing off her report and emailing a copy to the DCI. She then had a sudden thought. 'You don't think Michael Grayling could have taken up with Hamilton simply to use her as bait?'

'Bait? What do you mean?'

'Think about it, Andrew. Whoever paid Maxine Kruger to kill Doyle now knows she failed. Let's assume for a moment that it was Grayling and he's hired this assassin to find Doyle, obviously to finish the job. But as we know, Doyle has gone to ground somewhere in the UK. No one knows where he is. If Hamilton is with Michael Grayling in Portugal or wherever, and Doyle is trying to find her, Grayling could be taking advantage of Doyle's obsession with her in order to locate him. Using her to get at him, if you understand my meaning? If anything will get Doyle out of the shadows, a chance to meet up again with Julia Hamilton must be top of the list. We haven't found him and neither has this hit-man, as far as we know. If Doyle were already dead, we'd have heard about it.'

Hooper reflected on what Knight had said. 'You might be on to something there, Wendy. If she is with Grayling, someone went to a hell of a lot of trouble to make sure she was acquitted of the charges she faced. And only this O.C.G. would have the necessary resources.' He paused and gave Knight a thoughtful look. 'You don't think he had this in mind all along? Getting her off so he could use her to draw Doyle out should the necessity arise?'

'Could be? Could also be that he fancies her like mad, of course. She's quite a looker in her own way. And don't forget, we know for sure that Doyle was at Barnard House near Hungarton, as was Hamilton. That must be why Doyle went there – to see her. And according to Harry, previous attempts had been made to finish Doyle off while he was inside but they all failed. It was because he went to Barnard House that whoever is behind all this was able to send him off with Kruger. The object, again, was to kill him then dump him in the Trent.'

'And, as we know, Kruger failed.'

'Yes. If the son has taken over the O.C.G. and he's with Hamilton, he could be using her again to flush Doyle out.'

'Then his assassin, whoever he is, finishes him off.'

'Exactly!'

Hooper let out a lengthy sigh. 'But if Doyle is still in the UK it would mean Julia Hamilton would have to be here too. She can hardly act as bait if she's still in Portugal with Grayling. She'd need to be here.'

'Perhaps the two of them are headed here?'

'Or Doyle means to go to Portugal?'

'But Harry is convinced he's still here. And if he is, Grayling and Hamilton would have to come here together. Grayling wouldn't want to allow Julia out of his sight, not with Doyle around, especially if he's obsessed with her too. And he'll want to make sure there are no mistakes this time.'

Knight hesitated. 'It's always possible, I suppose, that Hamilton could be being used to get at Doyle without her realising it.'

Hooper scoffed. 'I doubt it. If she's thrown her lot in with someone like Grayling she must know what he's about. She must have turned against Doyle and gone in with Grayling. Dole obviously had no joy in persuading her to stick with him when he saw her at Hungarton.' He narrowed his eyes. 'Have you said anything along these lines to Harry?'

'No, it's only just occurred to me. You think I should?'

'It's certainly worth raising with him. In fact, the more I think about it, it makes perfect sense. Perhaps we should both have a word with him, in private?'

'Let's not do anything prematurely, Andrew. Let's think about it first. If Harry is keeping something from us, he must have a good reason.'

Hooper nodded and changed the subject. 'I suppose you're right. Did you get anywhere with the Johnson woman?'

Knight smiled. 'I saw her last night, having located her at her apartment in Nottingham. Lovely view of the Trent, by the way.' She grinned. 'She was more than happy to cooperate. But she really is a piece of work. Arrogant in the extreme. Very attractive and doesn't she know it! She admitted leaving the meeting last Thursday at about ten to six, but I think we'll be in difficulties in proving she hid somewhere in the office until everyone had left.' She gave Hooper a languid look. 'She has a near perfect alibi, unfortunately. Her childcare responsibilities related to her sister's twelve-year-old daughter. The sister was in London on business and she had agreed to pick up young Alison from school – at six-twenty. By all accounts she did just that. I checked with the school myself. She was a few minutes late and a teacher was waiting with the child. There's no doubt about it. Her car appears on the school's CCTV leaving the premises at precisely six twenty-seven.'

'Bit late to be finishing school, isn't it?'

'One of the advantages of attending a fee-paying school, I suppose. After-school activities stretch the length of the school day which must be attractive to many working parents.'

'So she can't have been responsible for the theft of the file? The school is some distance from the city centre, is it?'

'Yes, just off the A6. South of the city. And she bored me rigid explaining the technical details why Hegarty didn't proceed with the investment in Malik's business.'

'So, perhaps the boss's theory isn't as water-tight as he thinks?' Hooper smiled more broadly. He had never quite abandoned the idea that a burglary involving a forced entry had taken place.

'There's always her assistant, John Rigby,' countered Knight. 'He could have stayed behind and he did have a bag with him. Might have contained the necessary tools? And he had no childcare responsibilities. Why did he leave with her?'

'What do we know about him?'

'Very little. He's twenty-six. No form and intelligence has nothing on him.'

'What did Johnson say about him?'

'He left with her, or so she says. But she separated from him outside the office to drive to the school to pick up her niece. Oh, and there's no doubt she had a car with her. She picked up a parking ticket for overstaying on the limited parking farther up Castleton Street.' She checked her notebook. 'The ticket was issued at seventeen twenty-nine hours.'

'I bet she left the car there deliberately to get a ticket. But what about Rigby? Why did he leave? Where did he go? Did he corroborate her account?'

'Haven't spoken to him. He's on vacation in Fuerteventura of all places. He left early Saturday. Won't be back for another two weeks, according to Johnson.'

'How very convenient. No CCTV in Castleton Street, either. Did anyone see them leave?'

'No. The receptionist had already gone. No one else seems to have seen them. Mr Farmer was last to leave, apart from Mr Worth, and he saw no one.'

'Not looking good then? And Hegarty?'

'Harry's seeing him this morning. He'll no doubt tell us if he's discovered anything of interest at the briefing later.' She looked at her watch. 'In about an hour and a half.'

'And Maddison, the accountant from Kettering?'

'Harry was seeing him yesterday evening. I'm especially looking forward to hearing what he made of him. He seems to have been responsible for the meeting on Thursday lasting as long as it did.'

'So, he's under suspicion too is he?'

'I would think so. But it won't be easy to prove anything.'

'By the way, how did the photo-fit session go yesterday morning? I haven't noticed anything going up on the whiteboard.'

Knight sighed. 'Harry's got it. Not that it will help overmuch. Could be anybody. All the witness can really remember is the dog collar and a black suit. Can't really help with the facial features. And how many men are there who are six feet tall with dark hair?'

Hooper smiled. 'Thousands. That's why he was dressed as he was. Most people would remember the collar but little else. Still, odd, don't you think, that it's not been put up on the whiteboard? I wonder why?'

CHAPTER 29

Peter Hegarty led Hood into his large and expensively furnished office. Sitting behind his huge rosewood desk, he exuded an aura of self-satisfied omnipotence. Slightly overweight, he was wearing a well-tailored suit but no tie. His obviously dyed hair was carefully combed. He didn't look the type to be easily intimidated. Hood had already run a check on him on the PNC and unearthed the old police file which showed he had a conviction twenty-one years before for fraudulent trading. That had resulted in a twelve-month prison sentence, suspended for two years, and a large order for costs and compensation. But the wealthy businessman betrayed no nerves at all as he invited Hood to take a seat. Hood proffered his card. Hegarty glanced at it then placed it on his desk.

'What can I do for you, Detective Chief Inspector?' he asked. 'I'm a very busy man.' He then offered Hood a coffee, which was immediately but politely declined. 'Something stronger?' He pointed to a well-stocked cabinet against the wall.

Hood shook his head. 'No thank you. Not when I'm on duty. I am making inquiries, Mr Hegarty, into two murders…'

Hegarty interrupted. 'Two murders? I don't think I can help you about any murders, Mr Hood. Who has been murdered? Anyone I know?'

If Hood thought highlighting the killings he was investigating would cause Hegarty to become unsettled, he was about to be sorely disappointed. Hegarty almost smiled, the expression on his face hardly changing as Hood gave further details. 'Two bodies were pulled out of the River Trent nearly two weeks ago. A man called Dudley Manning and a woman by the name of Maxine Kruger.'

Hegarty nodded but showed no real concern. 'I read about that somewhere or saw it on the TV news but what has it got to do with me? I've never heard of either of them other than what I read in the newspapers. And I don't usually read the tabloids. This is my journal of record which keeps me up to date with what is happening in the business world. Nothing else really interests me.'

Hegarty pointed to a copy of the *Financial Times* lying on the desk, but the chief inspector was not diverted. He pressed on. 'I believe you recently considered investing in a business owned by a man called Riyad Malik and attended the offices of a firm of solicitors in Castleton Street last Thursday?'

Hegarty raised an eyebrow. 'What if I did? I do that sort of thing all the time. Malik runs a food manufacturing business and a couple of restaurants. Was he involved? If he was, I'm glad I didn't pursue the matter.'

Hood shook his head. 'Not in the killings, no. But I am interested in why you and he were at the solicitors on that particular day.'

Hegarty narrowed his eyes. 'I can't think why you should be. It was all organised by my associate, Rebecca Johnson. I'm always on the lookout for local businesses which are expanding. I have a large amount of capital languishing in my bank accounts at the moment. Malik's business seemed worthy of consideration.'

'May I ask how long you'd had his business under consideration?'

Hegarty smiled. 'You may. In fact, I can do better than that. I can show you our analysis which we started some time ago, well before these murders you're investigating took place.' He opened a drawer and produced a bound bundle and passed it over to Hood. 'Look through it at your leisure. I decided against it, so it's no longer of any use to me.'

Hood flicked through the bundle, trying hard to conceal his disappointment. 'It appears you went into this business opportunity in some detail?'

'I always do, Mr Hood. That's why I'm still around. I don't throw my money about, you know. Rebecca did most of the analysis. That's why I use her. She's got a good business brain.'

'Was there a particular reason why you decided not to proceed?'

'Thought better of it. I'd only met Malik on one previous occasion, I believe. Rebecca introduced us at some business lunch. I didn't really take to him and he was resistant to my taking a controlling interest in the business. I'm very careful where I invest. There was a lot of money at stake. The business seemed sound enough. Rebecca had an accountant she knows, a man called Maddison, look into it in some detail, but the final decision was down to me. Three and a half million is a big investment, even for me.'

'That's what Malik needed?'

'Yes. He was investing a further half-million himself, four million was what was needed to rebuild his factory and modernise it. His company already owns the site.'

'But you pulled out, despite the attractions?'

Hegarty smiled. 'I thought I could persuade Malik to let me have a controlling interest, but he wouldn't be moved. I suspect he was thinking of his family. He has two sons who already work in the business and he wants them to take over eventually. I reckon he was thinking of retiring in the near future.' Hegarty adjusted his position in his seat. 'Mind you, I don't think he'll have a problem in finding an alternative source of funds. As I said, the business is basically sound and has decent future prospects, but I don't like it when family considerations interfere with what should be a purely business decision. Can lead to trouble in the long run, you know. You have no idea of the number of small-to-medium family businesses that hit the buffers when they take their eyes off the ball. I'm purely a numbers man myself. No time for sentiment of any kind. The bottom line should be the sole consideration in any business decision.'

'Do you always look to have control before investing?'

'Not always. Depends on the circumstances. Sometimes I go in to get a failing business back on its feet then pull out, providing there's a real prospect of getting a decent return on my investment, of course. I'm not a charity.'

'I believe you invested a few years ago in a haulage business in South Wales?' Was that a flicker of concern passing over Hegarty's face? 'A business owned by a man called Duffy?'

Hegarty paused at length before replying. 'Duffy? For some reason that name does ring a bell. Ah, I remember now. I invested in a fairly new haulage business in Wales owned by someone called, what was his name? Lafferty, that's it, Patrick Lafferty. Not Duffy. Back in ninety-five or ninety-six, I believe. Didn't I read somewhere he got himself arrested?'

'He did. His real name turned out to be Duffy, Derick Duffy.'

'That's it. Duffy. But I sold all my shares in that business, what, two years ago? Made a nice profit, too, as I recall.'

'You knew him as Lafferty?'

'Yes, although most of my dealings were with his manager. Bright young chap. Can't remember his name though. I could check if you like?'

'What caused you to invest in his business?'

'I'd have to look at my records. It was well before Rebecca's time, so I must have just come across it. I have a large number of investments, Chief Inspector. And I have feelers out all over the place.' He looked at his watch. 'Time is money you know.'

Hood ignored the remark. He was in no hurry. 'But why Wales? It's hardly local.'

Hegarty smiled. 'I've got business interests all over the country, Mr Hood. South Wales is hardly the other side of the moon, is it?'

'How long were you involved with Lafferty's business?'

'Again, I'd have to check, but not more than eighteen to twenty-four months, I believe. I sold my shares back in early ninety-eight. My accountants will have the details.'

'Maddison is your accountant?'

Hegarty shook his head. 'No, I'd never met the fellow before last week. It was Rebecca who decided to use him. I use one of the big firms for my annual returns. Costs me a small fortune. You need to speak to Rebecca about Francis Maddison.'

'She's been spoken to by a colleague. Has she not mentioned it?'

'No, as a matter of fact she hasn't. But I haven't seen her for a couple of days. We're not joined at the hip, you know.'

'How long have you employed her?'

'Now let me make it clear, Mr Hood. I don't exactly employ her. She's self-employed. She runs her own consultancy, but I use her to analyse some of the business opportunities that come my way. It was she who put me on to Malik, she and Malik's solicitor.'

'Mr Worth?'

'Not the old man; his son, Tony. He and Rebecca know each other very well, if you know what I mean?' He raised an eyebrow and gave Hood a knowing look.

'But he wasn't at the meeting on Thursday?'

'No, he couldn't make it. Urgent business elsewhere, or so he said. It was Worth Senior who handled the matter. Took longer than I thought it would. Dragged on until the early evening.'

'So I understand. Did anyone leave before the meeting ended?'

'I was there until the bitter end, then I went for a meal with Malik in one of his restaurants on the Melton Road. Bit of PR, although I'd almost decided not to go ahead with the investment. Waste of my time really. I couldn't budge him on giving up control although I did try. It was Rebecca and her associate who left around six o'clock. I wasn't very happy about that, I can tell you. She had to pick her niece up from school, apparently. Left me with Maddison and Malik. Didn't really get on with either of them.'

'Tell me about Rebecca's associate.'

'John Rigby? Nothing to do with me. He's Rebecca's man. She said he was still learning the ropes, but I don't really know him. He was here on a couple of occasions when she took me through her report. She should be able to tell you what you want to know.'

'You didn't know Maddison at all before last Thursday?'

'No, I didn't. A real cold fish, but I can't fault his knowledge or his professionalism. He certainly knows his stuff. Rebecca told me about him. Some of the analysis in that report you're holding originated with him.' Hegarty sat back in his chair and gave Hood an impatient look. 'What has all this to do with these murders you're investigating? I can't see how my business dealings have any relevance at all to two people

I've never heard of drowning in the Trent.'

'They weren't drowned, Mr Hegarty; they were both shot, with the same nine-millimetre Baretta.'

Hegarty seemed shaken. 'I didn't realise that. I have nothing to do with firearms, I can assure you. Scare the living daylights out of me, they do.'

'I'm not suggesting you were involved in the shootings, Mr Hegarty.' Hood hesitated. 'I'm interested in discounting, if I can, a number of unusual coincidences.'

'Coincidences? What coincidences?'

'You invested some years ago in Duffy's business – although you say you knew him as Lafferty.'

'So did everyone else, as far as I was aware. That was his name. I remember, I played golf with him on one occasion with a senior police officer, a local business man and the local MP. Everyone called him Lafferty.'

'Did you ever meet his daughter, Kelly Maguire?'

Hegarty shrugged his shoulders. 'Didn't even know he had a daughter. He never mentioned her, not to me.'

'The meeting you attended last Thursday does raise a question or two.' He paused for effect. 'The accountant, this man Maddison, who you say you didn't know, he has a link with Duffy, you see. He was Duffy's accountant too.'

'Was he? Must be a coincidence. I expect like most accountants he has several clients. News to me he acted for Lafferty. I left most of my dealings with the haulage business to my staff. I only went there twice, I believe, and once was to play golf. I'd just taken it up as a form of relaxation.' He smiled. 'My doctor recommended it. Didn't last though, I'm afraid. Takes up too much time and is hardly relaxing if taken seriously. And most of those who play regularly seem to take it deadly seriously. I can't for the life of me understand why.'

'You had no other dealings with Maddison?'

'Not that I recall.'

'Wouldn't his name or the firm's name have appeared in the

company accounts?'

'I suppose it would, but it would have meant nothing to me. I form my own judgement when reading a balance sheet. I told you, I never met him before last Thursday.'

'Ever heard of a man called Grayling?'

Hegarty shook his head. 'No, is he involved in this too?'

Hood did not reply. He flicked through the bundle again. 'Do you mind if I take this away with me?'

'Not at all. As I said, it's no longer of any interest to me. You can keep it as far as I'm concerned.'

Hood deliberated before he asked his next question but he really needed to know the answer. It occurred to him that like Doyle, Hegarty might have been given a helping hand by Gus Grayling and like Doyle might prefer to conceal it. That he had invested in Duffy's business seemed too much of a coincidence. After all, it was Gus Grayling who had set it up. 'Might I ask where you initially obtained your capital?' He hesitated. 'You see I've run a check on you, Mr Hegarty. You have a conviction over twenty-one years ago for fraudulent trading.'

Hegarty took a deep breath and nodded his head. 'So, that's why you're here. Can't a man live down a mistake he made decades ago?'

'I know the details of the case, Mr Hegarty. Not what I would describe as merely a mistake. We still have the file. You were lucky to get a suspended sentence from what I've read.'

Hegarty growled his response. 'I had a good barrister.' He paused then broke into a smile before continuing. 'I suppose I could tell you my success was all due to hard work and natural talent, but I'd be lying.' He looked directly at Hood. 'I've told very few people this before and I'd be grateful if you would keep it to yourself.' He smiled more broadly. 'I told you, I'm a numbers man. Six numbers, in my case, Mr Hood. That's when things took off for me. I'd only scraped a living before then.'

'Six numbers?'

'Yes, I won the lottery back in nineteen ninety-five. I still have a copy of the winning ticket, if you doubt my word. A double rollover! Kept it to myself, of course. Madness to tell everybody you have that sort of money, don't you think? Can't understand why big winners go on TV and tell the world what they've won. The lottery people are keen that you should, of course. Good advertising for them. I resisted the temptation. No publicity. That's what I plumped for. But in just five years I've multiplied what I won several times over through shrewd investments. I didn't fritter it all away like some do. Never won much again though, and I use the same numbers every draw. I'm still hoping they'll come up again.'

Hood let out a lengthy sigh. That was not the answer he was hoping for. 'I read somewhere you have a better chance of being murdered than winning the lottery jackpot,' he grumbled, giving Hegarty a derisive look. Hegarty was no longer smiling as Hood took his leave. 'Thank you, Mr Hegarty, I think that will be all – for the time being.'

Hegarty stood up, thrust his hands in his pockets and walked from behind his desk. 'Glad to have helped, if I have, Chief Inspector. Don't hesitate to contact me again if you think I can assist you further. My secretary will show you out.'

CHAPTER 30

Acting Inspector Andrew Hooper and Detective Sergeant Knight left DCI Hood's room at West Bridgford Police Station more than a little perplexed. The earlier briefing had gone as well as could be expected. Hood had formally announced that the investigation would proceed on the assumption that Michael Grayling was now running the O.C.G. and was responsible for the death of Dudley Manning, having directed Maxine Kruger to kill him. Hood also thought it highly likely that he had hired the hit-man to find and kill Doyle. But he also cautioned the team that Grayling was not to be arrested if sighted. He was to be watched and kept under surveillance until otherwise instructed. There was every reason to believe he would return to the UK at some point with Julia Hamilton in order to make sure Doyle was eliminated. He had, surprisingly, then suggested that searching for Doyle was no longer the number one priority. No progress had been made locating him and resources should now be concentrated on the theft of Duffy's file. He had gone into considerable detail as to the method he believed had been employed to steal it. Francis Maddison and Rebecca Johnson were knowingly involved, he thought, but the actual theft must have been carried out by the missing John Rigby. Rigby was to be arrested when he surfaced after his holiday in the Canaries. Hood was prepared to concede that Peter Hegarty had probably been used; his interest in investing in Malik's business having preceded by some weeks the events in the solicitor's office. Riyad Malik had confirmed that it was his refusal to allow Hegarty a controlling interest that had caused the wealthy businessman to walk away.

Hegarty had been prepared to allow Malik's family to retain control of his restaurants but insisted on having control of the manufacturing business before he was prepared to invest the considerable sum required. Hood had yet to speak to Tony Worth, who had made himself suspiciously unavailable, but he was prepared to discount for the time being any participation by Vivienne Benedict. The discreet inquiries Knight and DS Smith had made into her personal life had revealed nothing incriminating. No links with organised crime and no evidence of any sort of secret life. Hood directed that efforts were to continue to find evidence linking Maddison and Johnson to the theft. He agreed with Knight that Johnson's association with Tony Worth was more than coincidental. Hooper was instructed to find and interview the young solicitor. The briefing was then brought to a rapid conclusion with Hood observing that there were matters which had recently come to light that he was unable to discuss with his team; ACC Gaunt's instructions were that they were to remain confidential for the moment. Despite several questions, Hood remained firm in his refusal to say anything further.

'What do you think Harry meant when he said he could say nothing more for operational reasons?' asked Hooper, as he and Knight shared a coffee back in the incident room. The other members of the team were absent.

'I'm not sure,' said Knight. 'I got the distinct impression we were not far off the mark in suggesting that Grayling might be using Julia Hamilton as bait to bring Doyle out of the shadows. The information from Australia is consistent with the anonymous calls we received. If Grayling is the individual who has taken out the contract on Doyle, it follows it must have been Grayling who was at Barnard House with Julia Hamilton shortly after her acquittal which means he managed to leave Australia without his departure being noted by the authorities.'

Hooper stirred his coffee and gave Knight a curious look. 'I've had one or two further thoughts about this hit-man.'

'Oh, yes?'

'Grayling must have taken the contract out on Doyle pretty smartish, don't you think?'

'What do you mean?'

'Well, Kruger only died on the Sunday night. This so-called priest was round at the cottage in Thrussington looking for Doyle only three or four days later. How did Grayling arrange things so quickly? He can't have known Kruger had failed much before the Monday. Her body was only pulled out of the river early that morning. And we didn't know for certain who she was before Wednesday.'

'Perhaps this assassin is a member of the O.C.G. and not under contract?'

'Either that, or he's used him before and he was already primed to go after Doyle if Kruger failed.'

Knight smiled. 'Now that's what I call backup!'

Hooper grinned. 'On the other hand, I suppose it would only have taken a phone call for someone with the right contacts, and Grayling will definitely have the right connections. No question about that. Do you think it's possible that he and Hamilton may already be back in the UK, or on their way here, using different identities? Harry definitely knows something that he's not prepared to reveal to us.'

'What operational reasons could there be?' asked Knight.

'I don't know. He is under orders from Bob Gaunt, of course.'

'That's as may be, but what reason could there be for not revealing the full facts to us about Grayling's likely location? We're supposed to be part of the same team. That's information that has to be shared.'

'Must be pretty serious. Perhaps someone's life is at risk?'

'You mean apart from Doyle?'

Hooper smiled. 'Yes, apart from Doyle.' He paused for a second or two as if something had occurred to him. 'Could Harry or the ACC be in contact with Doyle, do you think? Is that why he doesn't seem as keen on finding him? Locating Doyle has been the number one priority until now, but all of a sudden it's been downgraded.'

Knight shook her head. 'I doubt if that's the reason for the secrecy. Harry is not one for going outside established procedures. Doyle is wanted for questioning in respect of Maxine Kruger's death. It would be highly improper to use someone in those circumstances as an informant. It must be something else.' She sipped at her coffee then put the mug down sharply on the table. 'Got it!'

'What?' asked Hooper.

'It's not Doyle who's at risk – any more than he always has been, anyway.' She looked around to double-check no one was in the room before continuing and dropping her voice. 'Harry's got someone on the inside. Someone on the inside of Grayling's organisation is in contact with Harry or the ACC. That's why he can't say anything. It would put whoever it is very much at risk if it got out. Grayling wouldn't hesitate to kill someone he discovered was in contact with us.'

Hooper's eyes widened. 'It must be pretty recent then. If he'd had someone on the inside from the outset, a lot of the work we've being doing would have been unnecessary. Perhaps we really are speculating too much?' Hooper then smiled. 'But if you're right… who do you think it could be?'

'No idea. It could be someone who's looking to displace Grayling as boss of the O.C.G., I suppose?'

'But surely, we should be arresting such a person, not using him to obtain information about Grayling?'

'Could be that Harry or Gaunt don't know who it is? The information could be coming anonymously.'

'Possibly, and if that's the case, it might explain one or two other things. He still wants us to obtain sufficient evidence to implicate Johnson, Rigby and Maddison in the theft of the file, but if he and Gaunt are receiving information directly from someone on the inside of the O.C.G., Duffy's file and his missing tape are largely irrelevant. We already know who's taken over.' He paused before continuing. 'You don't think he's side-lining us?'

Knight responded with a cynical grin. 'I don't think so. The file and the tape are still important. Certainly to Kelly Maguire. She's hoping the tape will bring her early parole. Mind you, she had her chance to tell us who's running the O.C.G. and she blew it. If it has been confirmed from another source that Grayling has taken over from his father, she might well find she's run out of road. Too late to gain any advantage now.'

Hooper mused on the situation. 'So, if we are right about this, bang goes her parole. Do you think we should say something to Harry? To let him know we've worked out what's happening?' His expression suddenly changed. 'My god, I've just had another thought that might well explain why finding Doyle is no longer a priority.'

'What do you mean?'

'Think about it. If you're right that Harry has someone on the inside of the O.C.G., he and Gaunt won't want Doyle taken into custody.'

'Why not?'

'If the informant is trustworthy and is providing regular intelligence about the plan to kill Doyle, our finding Doyle and taking him into protective custody could ruin everything. Doyle has to be free for their plan to succeed.'

Knight grasped the point immediately. 'Of course, that's it! Grayling is using Hamilton as bait to bring Doyle out of hiding. Harry and the ACC need him out there so that he'll walk into the trap they've set to seize Grayling. Without Doyle being at liberty, there'd be no point to any of it.'

Hooper's face was a picture as he nodded his agreement. 'It's putting Doyle at tremendous risk, though. I mean it's not as if he's agreed to play such a role. He's being used, presumably without his knowledge?' He smiled. 'No *Osman* warning for him.'

'I don't know about that, Andrew. He's simply being allowed to do what he wants to do; to meet up with Hamilton. An *Osman* warning would be pointless. Doyle already knows that Grayling is intent on killing him.'

'I suppose he does. But if Grayling is with Hamilton, there can only be one outcome if he and Doyle actually meet up. Someone will get hurt or worse. This is one high-risk strategy Harry is pursuing.'

'Unless someone intervenes?'

Hooper nodded. 'But why keep us out of the loop? Who's going to be able to intervene if not us? I really think we need to speak to Harry again.'

Knight did not answer immediately. When she did she shook her head. 'No, Andrew. Let's keep this to ourselves. I suspect this individual, whoever he is, has only just revealed himself. He will certainly be putting his life on the line and Harry could still be judging whether he can be trusted. It's always possible that Grayling has tasked someone to give misleading information under the guise of being an informant. I wouldn't put anything past him.'

Hooper shook his head. 'I don't think so. Whoever it is would hardly try and mislead us by lying about Grayling taking over the O.C.G. What would he gain by doing that? It must be genuine information. Someone is really putting himself at risk and putting Doyle in danger too.' He frowned. 'This gets more complicated and risky by the minute.'

Knight was forced to agree. 'You know what Harry's like. He doesn't jump in without carefully assessing the circumstances, always assuming he knows the full picture. But I think we should expect things to move rapidly from now on.' She picked up her coffee mug and looked out of the window. 'Look, he's heading for his car.' Knight pointed and continued sympathetically. 'He looked thoroughly exhausted to me at the briefing. Let's hope he has a chance to relax this week-end.'

CHAPTER 31

Kelly Maguire waited patiently in a room in the main building at HMP Brampton Hall. She had agreed to see Francis Maddison whose ostensible purpose in visiting was to explain the present position and profitability of her late father's haulage business in South Wales of which she was now the principal owner. The governor had granted permission for the visit thinking it might take Kelly's mind off the death of her father. Duffy's manager, who had effectively run the business for several years, still held twenty percent of the share capital which had come to him gradually over the years by way of bonuses in recognition of his work. Given Kelly's present predicament and the lengthy sentence to which she was subject, his continuing management of the business was essential. Hopefully, he would agree to carry on and ensure it remained profitable.

Maddison, unlike Hood, was not permitted to visit Kelly in her room. He was obliged to see her in the area of the prison set aside for domestic visits although the governor had agreed the meeting could take place on Saturday morning outside the usual visiting hours, thus providing a degree of privacy. The file he brought with him was given a casual check and he was searched before he was allowed into the room. Neither he nor Kelly gave any indication that they knew or recognised each other. They shook hands rather formally, then took a seat opposite each other. A solitary prison officer positioned herself at the other end of the room, well out of earshot.

Maddison began by making quite a show of taking Kelly through the company's latest balance sheet, drawing her attention to the details of the previous years' accounts. It seemed the business was thriving and providing a significant return on the capital originally invested. Kelly's shares were valued, he told her, at roughly one hundred thousand pounds. He added that the manager had expressed a keen interest in immediately acquiring another twenty-five percent of the share capital if Kelly was prepared to sell some of her stock. Maddison advised against such a course until Duffy's will had been probated and any tax due established and paid. Then, after probate, the manager's offer might well be worth considering. Indeed, transferring the entire business to him was probably worth attention. She was, presently, in no position to take part in the running of the business whilst a serving prisoner and if her future plans materialised would have other interests to pursue. Maddison eyed the prison officer who seemed more interested in her paperback novel than the details of the haulage business.

But apprising Kelly of the present-day value of the business was not, of course, the real object of the visit. As the prison officer turned the pages of her novel, more salient matters surfaced.

'Where are the tapes now?' whispered Kelly, as she pretended to study the balance sheet.

'Safe enough, where no one will find them.'

'And you've listened to them?'

'Of course. Both of them. Just to check I wasn't given a mention. You know me; I trust no one.'

Kelly sniggered. 'Duffy would never have given you away. Not with you being the contact with those controlling the foreign assets.'

'And neither will you, of course.' Maddison gave her a severe look. 'That would be most unwise.'

'That's a given. You have nothing to worry about on that score.'

Maddison nodded his approval.

'And you've spoken to that bastard Grayling, have you?' continued Kelly.

'I have. He believes the tape I told him about is genuine and he thinks you have control of it.'

She smiled. 'He has no idea you have it?'

'No, of course not. And no idea there are two tapes, either. He naturally thinks that your father will have exposed the whole of the organisation's links. He's definitely worried and appreciates he'll have to help you out of here if he's to get access.'

'You didn't lay it on too thick, I hope? He's a suspicious son of a bitch is Michael Grayling. My father never trusted him and he only met him once in recent years, although he knew him as a teenager.'

'I don't think I said too much. Just enough to retain his interest.' He chuckled to himself. 'Of course, the last thing we want to do is to reveal the contents of the real tape to the police. Not if we are to get you out of here. Very wise of your father to produce two tapes.'

'And the real one contains everything there is to know about the organisation, including those in high places who do their bidding. Nothing about the syndicate though, as far as I remember.'

'No mention of them or me, I'm pleased to say. He suspected I wanted out.'

She frowned. 'Like I want out of here. What about Doyle? Did you say anything to Grayling about him?'

Maddison glanced towards the prison officer before he replied. She seemed engrossed in her novel and hardly looked up. 'As we agreed, I told him that your father had written Doyle's name on the back of the note that was found in the file. It certainly threw him.' He smiled indulgently. 'I wrote it, of course. I'm very familiar with your father's handwriting and it seemed the obvious way of keeping Junior's attention fixed on finding Doyle. He's become utterly obsessed with locating him. We need to encourage him in his endeavours.' He smiled, knowingly.

'So, he's still after killing Doyle, is he?'

'He is, just like your father predicted. He also speculated there's an outside chance that Doyle has the tape, though I poured lots of cold water on that idea. I think, on balance, he believes you have it stashed somewhere safe but he'll probably want to check it out with Doyle before he has him eliminated.'

'He's taking a bit of a risk, isn't he, getting so close to Doyle? Maxine didn't do too well, did she, when she tried to kill him? I still can't believe she's gone. How someone like Doyle got the better of her I simply can't understand. She was such a cool professional.'

Maddison nodded. 'Well, he must have managed it somehow.'

'I can appreciate how Grayling feels about it. She'll be a real loss to him and the organisation. It will make quite a difference. She'll be difficult to replace.'

'Impossible I would say, certainly in the short term. And all because of his fixation with killing Doyle. A sensible person would give up on it. Doyle's no threat in reality. He knows nothing. But I'm afraid Junior doesn't have either the brains or the self-control his old man demonstrated. Gus would never have allowed a personal issue like this to interfere with business, not when it came to it. There are better ways of dealing with turncoats than killing them. Look how he handled Doyle's treachery. That's the intelligent way of dealing with such matters. It didn't quite work out because Doyle managed to get early parole. And we know how, don't we? Grassing up your father!'

'That's why I don't really care if he lives or dies. He must have known the score when he turned informer. But he couldn't have known about the Retford job, could he?'

'I don't see how he could have. I didn't, until you were all arrested.'

'Could Gus have grassed us up?'

Maddison shook his head. 'No, he would never have done that. It would have been against his somewhat idiosyncratic code. Doyle, on the other hand, put himself outside the code by his own actions in betraying his trust. But even then, Gus dealt with it using his brains. Unnecessary violence only attracts the attention of the police, unless it's done on the quiet, of course. Junior, on the other hand, has allowed his emotions to get the better of him. Just like he did with the Hamilton woman. When I think of the efforts we had to go to in order to get her acquitted so he could continue bedding her, it makes my blood boil. The favours we had to call in were endless and cost a small fortune. He'll tire of her, of course; he always does.'

'Do you think so?'

'Oh, yes. She's not the first, you know; he really fancies himself as some sort of Lothario. And him with a wife in Australia, too.' He moved closer. 'He now has an additional reason for eliminating Doyle because Doyle undoubtedly killed Maxine. Not a good omen for the future in my opinion. He's incapable of putting business first. That's another reason I want out.'

Kelly smiled. 'No one could have predicted that Doyle would have turned the tables on Maxine and killed her. Perhaps he'll do the same with Grayling?'

'Now that would be highly convenient, providing the timing is right. Grayling is determined to finish Doyle this time; he has hired some outside assassin to do the job. He doesn't want any more mistakes. But we need to take advantage of the situation while he's otherwise engaged.' He paused and glanced towards the officer again before continuing. 'DCI Hood called on me yesterday. He knows I was at the meeting last week at the solicitors but he didn't give anything away about the file. And neither did I. In fact, neither of us mentioned it. I'm hoping he thinks it was a coincidence I was there, but he's worked out your father used my firm as his accountants and that Gus's legitimate investments were audited by us too.'

'So, he's put two and two together and made four, has he?'

'He thinks he has, but those accounts I prepared are bomb-proof. Whatever he suspects, he won't be able to prove anything, and I suspect he knows it.'

'Did he ask you about Michael Grayling?'

'Of course.'

'And you told him what we agreed?'

'I did, although I also made it clear that I'd had no direct contact with him here in the UK. As far as I was concerned he was still in Australia.' He smiled. 'And I had a letter to prove it. The letter he sent me after I informed him of Gus's death, clearly post-marked New South Wales. Hood already knows that Gus had left nearly all of his UK estate to charity. All his other financial assets are located abroad and can't be directly connected with me or my firm. He seemed to realise that, but I'm sure he doesn't understand the full implications.'

He paused and glanced towards the prison officer, still engrossed in her novel. 'Our American friends are not happy with Junior's obsession with Doyle. Like me, they don't like publicity. They wouldn't have cared if Doyle had been despatched quietly, but they'll be thinking hard about what should be done now. They won't like it if it puts their latest venture with the Australians at risk.'

'You mean the, eh, merchandise from New South Wales?'

'Exactly. You need to bear in mind, Kelly, that the syndicate has the final say. They respected Gus, but I'm getting the impression they're having second thoughts about the son. Remember they take twenty percent of everything in return for managing the assets in the Caymans.'

'And Michael Grayling still thinks he will be the sole beneficiary after they've taken their cut?'

'Of course he does. Why wouldn't he? He doesn't know the alterations Gus directed before his death were never completed. Duffy was originally intended to take over from Gus which meant he'd receive the bulk of the foreign assets. That all changed when father and son were reconciled shortly before Gus's death. But the way the assets are held and shielded from the UK authorities is complicated and there wasn't sufficient time to alter everything in Junior's favour. As things stand, Duffy has about an equal share with him, which means about half will come to you when all the legal processes are completed. But that will take time. A very long time. But when it's done, there'll be an enormous amount of money coming your way, notwithstanding the syndicate's share.'

'Fat lot of good that will do me, stuck in here.'

'Patience, Kelly. It's all in hand. Grayling knows he will have to get you out of here if he wants to get hold of the tape. His boys are already working on it. Just be ready when you attend Duffy's funeral. With any luck you won't be coming back here afterwards.' He paused and leant closer. 'I take it you're not prepared to wait to see if Hood can do anything about getting you early parole?'

She narrowed her eyes. 'No, I'm not. There's no guarantee I'll get it. Not after the Doyle farrago. Even Hood thinks the powers that be won't be too keen on repeating the exercise and I doubt if what is on the tape I intended to hand over to him would be sufficient to get me early release, anyway. There's no way I'd let him have the real tape. I had to exaggerate quite a bit when I saw him, but I gave him the impression I was prepared to go down the parole route and I'll carry on doing that. I don't want them increasing my security too much. But I'm not prepared to wait for another ten years. No way! I've let Hood think I'll hand the tape over if early parole is granted, but our other plans will render that unnecessary, assuming everything works out.'

'We'll have to get the timing absolutely right though. Junior won't hesitate to have us both killed if he finds out what we are about. And there's no way I'm staying on with him running the show. Gus agreed I could retire after his death and that's exactly what I intend to do. I want as little as possible to do with Michael Grayling. Pursuing Doyle like he is, is pure madness, although I must admit, it's very convenient from our perspective. I've told him what the syndicate thinks about it, not that he'll take any notice. And I have the syndicate's permission to retire, whatever Junior my think. I've almost agreed a buyout of my accountancy firm with three members of my staff. I'll be all set to go within the month.'

'And you're sure we can get Michael Grayling arrested and imprisoned here in the UK? The syndicate won't object?'

'As I said, they've had enough of him. Getting him arrested is essential if our plan is to work but we have to get you out of here first. He won't do anything for you if he's in custody and we need his apparatchiks to organise your escape. As long as you're not transferred elsewhere, it shouldn't be a problem getting you out.' He looked about him. 'This place is hardly Alcatraz is it? But the funeral is the better plan. It will be simple enough getting you away during the ceremony.'

'But I'll be under escort.'

'That won't matter. All you have to do is to collapse while giving your brief eulogy. I'm sure you can manage that. They'll call an ambulance, but it will be Grayling's boys who'll arrive.' He leant forward. 'The funeral is fixed for Wednesday morning. The governor won't tell you until the night before for security reasons, so don't let on you know. Grayling's team has already done the basics. All you have to do is make sure you get permission to attend the funeral.'

'Always assuming the governor lets me go.'

'No reason why she shouldn't. You've told her you want to go, haven't you?'

'Yes, of course I have. But she hasn't given permission, not yet.'

'She will. This a category D prison. Category D prisoners are invariably allowed to attend family funerals and you are Duffy's only living relative. And I can't see the Home Office preventing it, but they'll probably have to okay it given the length of your sentence.' He grinned. 'They even let the Kray twins attend their mother's funeral and you hardly present the same level of risk. As you say, you'll be under escort of course, but that shouldn't pose a problem.'

'I hope you're right about this, Francis. I'm relying on you.'

'As I said, we'll have to get the timing absolutely right. Junior's coming to the UK this week-end, more fool him. He'll be arriving this evening. Anglesey of all places. As I said, I advised him against it but he won't listen. He never listens. He thinks he knows everything. He's completely obsessed with getting rid of Doyle.'

'Why Anglesey?'

'I don't know. He wouldn't risk coming back to the Midlands but I suspect he's checking routes for the merchandise that's coming in from Australia via Dublin.'

She whispered her response. 'Drugs? Gus never dealt in drugs.'

Maddison put his finger to his lips and looked about him. 'I know, but Junior's apparently up to his neck in Chinese heroin, along with some roughnecks in Australia. But the syndicate has okayed the operation. There's millions to be made and having lost out on the robberies, Junior feels he has no option but to go along with it. That's another reason I want out. I don't like dealing in that sort of merchandise.'

'We need to move things on and fast then. Do you know exactly where he'll be in Anglesey?'

Maddison smiled. 'I should do. I arranged where he's staying.'

'And you'll inform Hood where he is?'

'When I know he's arrived there, yes, but only after you're out of here. You never know, the idiot may get himself caught without us having to do anything. It's possible the local police have some intelligence about the, eh, merchandise.' He smiled and gave Kelly a knowing look.

'You mean someone might have said something to them?' She returned his smile. 'Surely, he'll have used his contacts to check that out?'

Maddison smiled more broadly. 'He should have done, but he's staying there for at least a week which is far too long. He'll attract attention to himself if he's not very careful.'

'Will you be able to contact him?'

'Yes. He's bound to ring me and if he doesn't, I have a mobile number for him. I'll arrange a call to Hood's team after the funeral. There's a phone number for members of the public to leave information anonymously which will suit us down to the ground.'

'And your family?'

'They know nothing, but my wife has always wanted to go and live in Canada. She's been nagging me about it for years. Both her brothers are already there. That's where we'll be headed. And my daughter has just secured a place at Toronto University. I have everything arranged.'

Neither said anything for some time. The officer looked up and called out. 'Finished, have you?'

'Just a few more minutes,' replied Maddison. 'Not long now.'

The officer scowled then returned to her book.

'I assume Hood asked you about the O.C.G?' whispered Kelly.

'He did. He thinks Gus was some kind of criminal mastermind which is not far off the mark when you think about it. He was certainly in a different league to his idiot son who thinks being utterly ruthless is all it takes.'

'What did you tell Hood?'

'I appeared shocked and pointed out that my client had no convictions and was considered by me and everyone I knew to be a businessman engaging in perfectly lawful commercial investments. And if he delves into Grayling's companies, he'll be hard put to prove anything. He was almost one hundred percent legit with his investments here at the time he died.'

'Then why did he organise the robbery near Retford? That's why I'm stuck in here.'

Maddison smiled. 'For old time's sake, I think. And when he heard about the five million in used notes, he couldn't resist having a go. He knew he wasn't long for this world. He wanted to go out in a blaze of glory.'

Kelly scowled. 'Well he certainly managed that. Pity about us going up with him.'

'That's how it appears, now. I never got involved in anything beyond laundering the proceeds of the old man's criminal activities, so I knew nothing about it.'

'Well, you were lucky. I wish I'd never gone on the job. It was Adam who persuaded me. Duffy advised me against it. I should have listened to him.'

Maddison sighed and sat back in his chair. 'Gus knew my limits, but his son is a different kettle of fish. He doesn't understand that there are some things I'm simply not prepared to do.'

'How did you get into the solicitor's office?'

'You don't really want to know, do you?'

She smiled and shook her head.

'Did Hood ask you about Duffy's death?'

'First thing he mentioned. But I feigned ignorance. I'd had no direct contact with your father, not after he was sentenced. All my dealings with the business were with the manager, David Lindsay, and I have a full record to prove it. I got the impression though, that they now believe Duffy killed himself, despite what you said to him.'

Kelly sighed and became tearful. 'I did my best when Hood came here to convince him that he was murdered by the O.C.G., but I knew the truth of it. Duffy had a letter smuggled here for me. He told me what he was planning to do, but I wasn't expecting him to act so quickly. I was hoping to stop him.'

'Did Hood believe you?'

'Of course he did. He wanted to believe the organisation did for Duffy. I merely told him what he wanted to hear. He's like most men in my experience. Tell them what they want to hear and they almost always believe you.'

'I'll remember that. But, it looks like the post mortem must have ruled out murder.'

'What if it has? I still blame Michael Grayling for what happened. My father may have hanged himself, but it was Grayling that forced his hand. He just couldn't take any more.' She bit her lip. 'He'll pay for that.'

Maddison nodded as he leant forward. 'He will, but don't repeat the mistake he's making over Doyle. He'll pay all right, but in a way you'll seem to have no part in. Don't get emotionally involved. I know it's difficult, but we need to keep clear heads. By the way, Junior wants to know what was in the letter.'

'He can whistle. It was highly personal. Just make something up, and make sure he knows I definitely have control of the tape. Doyle knows nothing.'

The prison officer stood up and looked at the clock on the wall. 'Time's up,' she called out, closing her book.

Maddison nodded. 'We've about finished.' He looked at Kelly and raised his voice so the officer could hear him. 'I'll write to you when I know anything more. I'll proceed on the basis you'll be allowed to attend your father's funeral, whenever it is.' He looked towards the officer who had joined them at the table.

'Not up to me,' she said. 'You'll have to speak to the governor about that. But I shouldn't think there'll be a problem.'

'Someone will do that,' said Maddison, addressing Kelly. 'William Worth and you are the named executors of your father's will. Mr Worth will no doubt be in touch.' He gave her a knowing smile.

CHAPTER 32

The ferry from Dublin pulled into the harbour at Holyhead on Saturday evening, about fifteen minutes behind schedule. Another twenty minutes went by before Michael Grayling and Julia Hamilton were able to disembark. Only a cursory inspection of their passports took place and their two suitcases were not examined in any meaningful way. Grayling was careful to keep the fraudulent Irish passports in his possession after retrieving them from the border official. Julia had merely been informed that for the purposes of this trip she was to use the name Julia Challinor. Grayling, purporting to be her husband, was travelling under the name of Matthew Challinor whose place of birth was stated to be Limerick in Eire. He wisely did not attempt an Irish accent.

A genuine Scot met them in the car park. Jamie Wallace had been waiting for them for over an hour. The Range Rover was parked nearby. He had taken the precaution of installing a baby seat in the rear for young Michael who was showing acute signs of weariness. His crying further irritated an already out of sorts Grayling whose demeanour matched the foul weather which greeted them. They hurried to where the Range Rover was parked and Julia was ordered into the back seat with the child while Grayling took his place in the front.

'How was the crossing, boss?' asked Jamie, after he placed the suitcases in the boot and climbed into the driver's seat.

'A bit rough in the middle. Upset little Michael. But he'll be OK. Any news? Any sign of Doyle?'

'Nae, boss. Nothing to report. Where to?'

'To the house. You know where it is, I presume?'

'Aye, I do. I've already been there. Not as remote as I thought, but well away from any neighbouring property. I've had a good scout around the immediate area too. It's not overlooked and has quite a large garden. And it's not too far away. It took me just over an hour and ten to get here.'

'I'm not surprised the way you drive. We'll adopt a more measured pace on the return trip. I've looked at the map. We don't want to draw attention to ourselves.'

Little Michael was now wailing intermittently. Grayling turned and spoke sharply to Julia. 'Can't you shut that child up? He's doing my head in.'

'I don't think he's very well,' replied Julia. She sounded genuinely concerned. 'The crossing seems to have made him worse. And he had a bit of a temperature before we left Dublin. He might need a doctor.'

'No, he won't. He'll be fine when we get him to the house and he's fed and watered. We don't want to get involved with any doctors while we are here. And remember, you have a phone call to make. I want Doyle to know precisely where you'll be on Monday morning.'

He laughed and returned to his conversation with the driver, glancing occasionally in her direction. 'Julia is my bait, you see, Jamie. Doyle is bound to try and make contact with her again and my man will be waiting. As will we, won't we Julia?' He turned fully and grinned at the mother and her child, the child now crying unconsolably. Julia did not reply.

'Me too, boss?'

'Yes, you too. I need to find out what he knows about this tape and there's an outside chance he knows where it is; he might even have it himself.'

'If it exists?' replied Jamie. He sounded sceptical. 'Duffy could have been bluffing. He was bluffing about his file. Hardly anything in it.'

'You've brought it with you?'

'The file? In the boot. I got it off the accountant yesterday.' He hesitated, glanced at Julia briefly, then continued, his voice just above a whisper. 'Francis seems to me to be getting a wee bit nervous. I had to remind him where his interests lay.' He grinned, revealing his recent dental work, then continued. 'But I didn't tell him that you have changed where we are staying. He still thinks we'll be at the house near Abersoch.'

Grayling chuckled to himself. 'Good. Francis wants to retire, you know. I've told him that isn't going to happen, not for a while anyway, but like you I've started to have the odd doubt about him. He did a good job at the solicitors but I don't trust him like I used to. He did very well for himself under my old man. It's time for him to step up to the plate. He needs to appreciate that.'

'He agreed to visit Kelly in prison, although he wasn't keen. He thinks it might draw him to the attention of the polis. He's certain any visit he makes will be recorded somewhere and the information passed to Hood.'

Grayling scowled at the mention of the detective chief inspector. 'Hood is becoming more than a nuisance. I really think the time has come to put a warning shot across his bows. I've told Francis that visiting Kelly shouldn't raise any real suspicions. He's the ideal person to see her. He was her father's accountant. She's inheriting most of the shares in his haulage business. What could be more natural than for the business's accountant to visit the new owner?'

'Well, he wasn't at all enthusiastic about it. Not since he was visited by Hood who knows he was present in Worth's office. But he'll do as he's told. He was supposed to be seeing her this morning.'

'I haven't heard from him, yet. I'll phone him later. I need to know what he said to Hood and how Kelly reacted to his visit. The police have obviously made the connection, but that was always on the cards. Francis should have been able to talk himself out of it. You might have to have another word with him, though, Jamie. Stiffen him up. The syndicate controls my old man's assets in the Caymans and they trust Francis implicitly. I don't want him going shaky on me, not now.'

'He won't. I'll see to that.' There was that grin again.

'And it's in his interests as well as mine that we find that tape. I suppose Kelly's more likely to know where it is than Doyle, but we can't take any chances.'

'Francis reckons Kelly has it hidden somewhere. I think Duffy put Doyle's name on the back of the note to mislead us. It'll be the daughter who knows where it is. Get her out of Brampton and we get the tape.'

'My thoughts, exactly,' said Grayling. 'You've spoken to Logan, have you? He's another one who needs stiffening up.'

Jamie hesitated before replying. 'I called on him again just before I set out for Wales. No sign of him where he stays. A neighbour told me he'd gone away. She said he's taken a few days off. He wasn't there when I called last week either.'

'You don't think he's done a runner?'

'No. Compassionate leave, the neighbour said. He'd told her all about finding Duffy's body. I haven't seen him since we first recruited him.'

'You phoned him on the mobile we gave him?'

'I did. No reply. I didn't risk leaving a message.'

'So, he's keeping himself hidden and we still don't know what was in the letter Duffy sent to his daughter?'

'No, we don't. Not yet. Francis was supposed to try and find out from Kelly. She's bound to know. It was intended for her.'

Grayling sighed. 'I think we are going to have to lose Logan. He could talk. And I don't want any loose ends. Time for you to arrange a little accident for him.'

Jamie smiled, nodded and looked in the wing mirror. 'Perhaps he just needs a little reminder?'

Grayling was adamant. 'No. Lose him. He's no use to us any longer, now that Duffy's dead.'

'And Kelly? She'll not hand over the tape, if she has it, not while she's still inside. It's the only card she has left to play. She's no divvy.'

'She'll be given temporary parole to attend her father's funeral. Just make sure she doesn't go back. Find somewhere safe to keep her until I have a word. Francis should be able to get hold of the details of the funeral arrangements.'

'Looks like I'm going to be busy.' Jamie smiled more broadly. 'I've already got a couple of lads lined up.'

'Sensible ones, I hope?'

'They know what to do; let's hope Kelly plays her part as required.'

'And they know where to take her?'

'It's all arranged. You'll be able to meet up with her after we've sorted things with Jessop.'

'Jessop. That's another thing. What do you think of him? Do you reckon he's up for what we require?'

'He's the top broker in Anglesey and he's never been pulled by the polis and keeps well out of the actual dealing. He seems to know what he's doing. I don't think he'd have lasted as long as he has if he took unnecessary risks.'

'But can we trust him? It will be very easy for him to take a bigger cut for himself than we've agreed. Always the same when everything is in cash. That's why my old man kept out of the drugs business. I'd rather have stayed out of it too, but the syndicate thinks otherwise. All that Chinese heroin will make us a fortune; that's what they reckon. And the Australians are pushing it with the syndicate too. The old man always said you could trust no one, no one at all in that game. Half the dealers are crackheads themselves. And any losses will come out of my share of the profits. The syndicate will want its full cut, no matter what. I'd rather we'd kept out of it.'

'But the syndicate is all for it?'

'Take a wild guess. They're only interested in results – and money. They never get their hands dirty. They just take their commissions. We don't have much option but to do as we are told.' He smiled. 'But whatever happens, we'll be as rich as Croesus once we get established.'

'But not as rich as the syndicate?' Do you have any idea who these people in the States are?'

Grayling scoffed. 'No, mate, no one does. They never show themselves. Even my old man never found out who's running things in New Jersey. Perhaps I should go out there sometime.'

Jamie laughed. 'That would put the wind up them.' He returned to more immediate matters. 'If Jessop doesn't play ball, we'll have to learn him, won't we?'

He glanced in the mirror again. He didn't notice the motorcycle a couple of hundred yards behind the Range Rover, partially hidden as it was by a black Mercedes Sprinter van. The heavy rain that lashed down unceasingly made visibility poor on the winding road. The rest of the journey passed without incident. The Range Rover eventually pulled into the driveway of a fairly modest house, much smaller than the property outside Abersoch. Jamie drew the vehicle to a halt outside the front porch. The van and the motorcycle passed the gates without slowing down. The front door was opened by a tall, slim man, casually dressed and smoking a cigarette.

'That's Ian Dewhurst,' said Jamie. 'He's been keeping an eye on the place. He's solid. You can trust him. He's my girl's brother. I'll vouch for him anytime. He only knows about the business with Jessop. He knows nothing about Doyle.'

'Let's keep it that way. Anyone else here?'

'No, boss. I followed your instructions to the letter and kept our people to a minimum. I can easily call on a few others if it becomes necessary.'

'Good. The fewer who know about events here the better. Anyone nosing around the place?'

'Not a problem. There's nothing between here and Aberdaron except a B&B and it's closed until after Easter. Not many tourists about this time of year, especially in this weather. It's a dreich night and cauld with it.'

'And the coast?' Grayling glanced towards the back of the vehicle and observed Julia trying but failing to comfort the child.

'In the other direction. Porth Ysgo, they call it. I'm not sure how it's pronounced, mind you. Easy walking distance. Looks ideal for our purposes. I'll check it out fully in the morning.'

'You've done well, Jamie, mate. Let's get inside. I can't think with this racket going on.' He glared at Julia. 'You deal with the boy, and for God's sake, shut him up!'

Grayling opened the passenger door and looked up at the darkened sky. 'Does it ever stop raining in this country?' he muttered but didn't wait for an answer. He launched himself from the Range Rover and rushed towards the house, acknowledging the man standing by the door as he raced for shelter, leaving Julia and little Michael in the car. Julia was tired and the child was still restless, his crying now reduced to occasional whimpering. Jamie followed Grayling, first opening the boot and removing Duffy's file then directing Ian Dewhurst to deal with the luggage. Julia, now alone in the car with her son, exhaled loudly in frustration and opened the rear passenger door. She'd just about had enough of Grayling. She'd noticed a distinct change in his attitude towards her during their time in Dublin. He'd also stopped bothering her for sex, which she regarded with relief but also concern. She'd realised for some time that it was the sexual act alone that drove his physical demands. He had no more regard for her than she now had for him. Their lovemaking had become completely mechanical. Once he was satisfied, he simply pushed her aside. He was no longer interested in her needs and the tenderness he had once exhibited had disappeared completely. But what would happen to her if he no longer had any use for her?

It took her over half a minute to remove the distressed child from the restraints of his seat as the rain poured down. She then followed the silent Dewhurst into the house. She had been unable to call Doyle from the ferry as Grayling had taken possession of her mobile phone. Now they had arrived at their destination she'd hopefully be able to contact him without Grayling listening in. But where were they? This was not the address she had given Doyle. She understood that much. Why had Grayling changed where they were staying? She'd attempted to read the road signs once they had passed the road to Abersoch but had no idea of their journey's end. All she knew was that they were within walking distance of the coast and she only picked that up that because she'd heard Jamie say as much before he got out of the Range Rover. Dripping wet, her hair bedraggled and her temper far from benign, she followed Dewhurst upstairs into the front bedroom. It was with some relief she noticed there was a telephone by the double bed. Perhaps she would have the opportunity of calling Doyle?

Downstairs, Jamie led his boss into a tiny study. Grayling sat down at the desk, eyeing the telephone. Was he waiting for Julia to make a call? He turned and spoke to Jamie.

'This place is cramped but no worse for that. Doyle couldn't get in here without being spotted and we're in walking distance of the coast. You did well to find it, Jamie.'

Jamie shrugged his shoulders. 'I thought the other place was more suitable. And that's where Doyle thinks we'll be. Julia gave him the address, didn't she?'

'On my instructions, yes. And that's the reason for the last-minute change. I don't want him finding us. I mean for him to meet with Julia on the coast on Monday. And I don't trust her; not anymore. I think she's still carrying a bit of a torch for that fuckwit. You keep an eye on her.'

Jamie nodded. 'And the Tinkerman?'

'He'll be phoning later. It was his idea to have the meet on this beach. It's very isolated, apparently, and there's plenty of cover.'

'It's certainly remote. Plenty of hiding places, if this hit-man doesn't want to be seen. Do we know who he is?'

Grayling shook his head. 'Not our concern, providing he does what I'm paying him to do. No need for us to know anything about him. He's a professional; he'll do what is required.'

'And he can be trusted, can he?'

'He'd better be.'

'Why does he not want to be seen?'

'Think about it, Jamie, mate. Would you want anyone to be able to identify you if you were a professional assassin? Stands to reason, don't you think? And I checked him out for myself when I was in Dublin. He has a fearsome reputation and has never failed. No worries on that score.'

'Did you check him out with the syndicate contact?'

Grayling's mood suddenly changed, a look of controlled anger crossing his face. 'They know nothing about this and it stays that way, understand? My business with Doyle is not their business. There's no reason why they need to know about him. It doesn't affect them.'

Jamie sighed. 'Will he turn up though? He's no dafty is Doyle.'

'What is this, Jamie? Why are you being so negative? He'll be there, all right. He won't be able to resist seeing Julia. That's his weakness. And that's what I shall exploit. He's obsessed with the bitch. But he won't see either of us, not until I choose to reveal myself. It will just be Julia and the boy as far as he's concerned. When I'm good and ready, the Tinkerman will then do his stuff. And I want to be there when he does. I want to look into that bastard's eyes as he dies and I want her to see it too. Our man will have to make an appearance when he shoots Doyle close up; but he'll be wearing a mask of some kind. As I said, he's very particular about anyone seeing him, and I'm paying him a fucking fortune. I'd be worried if he wasn't in some sort of disguise. He'd kill anyone he thought could identify him, no exceptions. So let's not get too curious, shall we?'

'And he'll recognise Doyle will he?'

'He will. His photo was all over the papers a week or two ago. And we'll be there to point him out should it prove necessary.'

'Do we really need to speak to Doyle, though? Francis should be letting us know whether Kelly has the tape. Much easier to despatch Doyle as soon as he appears. And what if he has a weapon? He's not that stupid. He'll have something with him. She's already told him about the hit-man.'

'Do keep up, Jamie, mate. That was so he'd think she was trying to help him. When she next speaks to him she'll be telling him the hit is off; that I've changed my mind; that I'm here on business that doesn't concern him. She'll tell him she will be able to see him on the sly.'

'Will she tell him that, though? She might not believe you. She seems to have changed from when I last saw her. Reminds me of my ex just before we broke up.'

'I don't care whether she believes me or not. She'll do as I say.'

Jamie sighed. 'It still worries me that Doyle might have a weapon or someone looking out for him.'

'He told Julia that he didn't keep Maxine's gun. He threw it in the river. The police have recovered it. My source at Mid-Shires has confirmed it. And remember, he'll think he's only meeting Julia. He's obsessed with her. He walked straight into the trap we laid for him at

Hungarton. He'll do the same here. There'll be no one with him. And just in case he has any reservations, she's going to tell him the truth about the boy. That's all he'll be thinking about once he hears the boy isn't mine.'

Jamie appeared shocked. 'You mean little Michael? But I thought the wee barra was yours. He is, isn't he? Julia certainly thinks he is.'

Grayling laughed. 'I don't think so. Keep it to yourself, but I had a vasectomy three years ago. And I don't believe in miracles. He must be Doyle's. He's certainly not mine. That DNA result was faked, to convince Julia that Doyle was not the father.'

'But I thought he had a low sperm count?'

'Perhaps he has; I don't know and I don't care.' He grinned. 'The tests were all faked, including that one. I had the fake result sent to him while he was inside at Colchester.'

'But he'd know if he had such a test done, wouldn't he?'

'Oh, he had the test done all right, after Julia told him the boy was not his. What he doesn't yet know is that the letter he received from the hospital was, how should I put it, eh, inaccurate. It was rigged.'

'Does she know about this?'

'No, not yet, but she's about to find out. Are you with me?' He grinned and stood up. 'Get her down here. Time for her to call him. And tell her to leave the boy upstairs.'

Jamie was still trying to get his head around Grayling's revelation. 'But why bother with the DNA if you knew the boy wasn't yours?'

Grayling sighed before explaining. 'When I discovered Julia was pregnant, I lost interest in her at first, because I knew it wasn't me who'd put her in the club. We'd had a good time for a few weeks after she first came to Hastings to see my old man, but I never intended it to amount to anything. I have a wife down under you know, not that we get on. Then my old man died and I did have a thought or two about adopting Julia's child providing it turned out to be a boy, of course.' His voice grew weaker and his facial expression changed. 'You see, Jamie mate, I had a son once, but he died not long after he was born. Two and a half years ago now. It's not something I like to talk about.

Unfortunately, I'd already had the vasectomy and I didn't fancy going through the process of having it reversed.' He paused for a moment then sighed deeply before continuing. 'That's all water under the bridge now. I don't want to be tied down, not with someone like Julia. She's disloyal, and I can't be having that. I don't trust her. She's a good lay, I grant you that, but I've done with her.' He let out a longer sigh. 'I did think at one time that if she saw Doyle dead she'd come round to my way of thinking, but she'll never change. I know that now. It will always be Doyle with her. But she'll do as I say this one last time or live with the consequences.'

'But suppose she tells Doyle?'

Grayling shook his head and smiled. 'That's precisely what I want her to do and what she will do. But she'll not be able to speak to him again afterwards. I'll make sure of that. He's still using Maxine's phone. I will cut it off immediately after their next conversation. I'm still paying the bill, remember? I can close it down any time. He'll want to speak to her again, of course. He'll be absolutely desperate to get in touch, but that won't be possible when he finds the phone is dead, so he'll have to meet up with her on the coast because that is where she'll be. He'll have no option. I have it all carefully worked out, Jamie. Nothing has been left to chance.'

'I don't know why you didn't let me deal with Doyle in the first place. I could have finished him off at Hungarton. Using Maxine didn't work out, did it? Why bring in this assassin?'

'I had my reasons. I was hoping at first he'd find Doyle and kill him, without my assistance, but he went to ground, so we had to use Julia as bait again.' His tone changed. 'Anyway, I told you, I want to see into his eyes as my man pulls the trigger and I want her to see it too.'

'I don't like it. It's too risky. Taking him out on the beach in front of Julia. How will she react?'

'I don't care how she reacts.'

Jamie sighed. 'What will you do with her after Doyle's dead? If she's still got a thing for him, she could do anything. She could even go to the polis.'

Grayling smiled. 'You know me, Jamie. I don't like loose ends.' He paused before continuing. There was pure hate in his eyes. 'She'll have to go too. She's been poking her nose into things that don't concern her. I don't want her interfering with our business here in Wales.'

'She knows about the merchandise? I wondered why you mentioned that while we were driving here.'

'Yes. She knows I'm meeting with our new partner on Wednesday in Pwllheli, well away from here.'

'How did she find that out?'

'Listening in to my phone conversation late at night. I caught her. She tried to tell me some ridiculous story as to why she was doing it. She'll have to go.'

'Did she hear who he is?'

'We never used names.'

'Does she know you know she knows.'

'Of course she does. I caught her red handed. And in view of what will be happening to her, it hardly matters. That's why I wasn't worried about raising it in the car.'

Jamie nodded his understanding. 'The hit-man will see to her too, will he?'

'He will. It's all arranged.'

'So, two bodies for me to dispose of then?' He cackled.

'Shouldn't be a problem. There's at least one deep mineshaft available. No one will find them down there, not for ages.'

'And the boy?'

Grayling let out a lengthy sigh. 'There could be a bit of a problem with him, Jamie. Our friend says he doesn't kill children, not at any price. That's where you come in.'

'Me?' Jamie looked horrified. 'I don't know about that, boss. Doyle yes, Julia even. I always said I'd have no worries doing for them, but a bairn?' He shook his head. 'I don't know if I could live with myself if I killed a child, I really don't. We all have to draw the line somewhere.' He shook his head again, this time more vigorously.

Grayling's eyes drilled into him. 'Now don't you be going shaky on me, too, Jamie.' He paused then drew in his breath as Jamie looked down. 'Perhaps you're right. I suppose we could just leave him somewhere.' He smiled and poked Jamie in the ribs. 'He can hardly give evidence against us, can he? He's not nine months old yet. There must be a hospital or something around here where we can leave him.'

The dour Scot appeared relieved as he looked up. 'Why not leave the boy here when Julia goes down to the beach?' he suggested. 'He'll only get in the way. We can dump him somewhere afterwards, somewhere where he's bound to be found. If anything goes wrong on the beach, he could get hurt.'

Grayling narrowed his eyes. 'What makes you think anything will go wrong? This isn't like you, Jamie. Do you know something I don't? Have you heard something about Julia? If you have, you'd better spit it out, mate.'

Jamie replied immediately. 'No, boss. I don't know anything, honest, but I don't think either Julia or Doyle are as stupid as we think. Doyle's not going to walk on to this beach without taking some precautions, is he?'

'Like arming himself, you mean? It'll do him no good if he does. He will want to see the boy and Julia after she's spoken to him. He'll be like a kid waiting for Christmas. It's all he'll be thinking about. That's why she has to have the boy with her when they meet or it'll look suspicious. Now, get her down here. She needs to make that call.'

CHAPTER 33

'Harry, Harry, wake up.'

Hood started to drift from sleep as his wife gripped him firmly by the arm and shook him.

'What time is it?' he asked, wearily.

'Quarter past six; you need to get up.'

Hood pulled the duvet over his head. 'Quarter past six? Come on, Sarah, it's Sunday. I was hoping to have a bit of a lie-in. I'm shattered.'

Sarah pulled at the duvet. 'Bob Gaunt is on the phone. He needs to speak to you urgently.'

'Bob Gaunt?' Hood sat up. He was now fully awake. 'What can he want?'

'I suggest you find out.' She thrust the phone into his hands.

'Sorry to bother you so early, and on a Sunday, Harry,' said Gaunt. 'Things are moving rapidly. Grayling has been spotted arriving in Anglesey in North Wales. You were right about him. He obviously isn't in Australia or Portugal. There was a woman and a child with him. Must be Julia Hamilton. They were caught on CCTV, but I haven't seen it yet.'

'Anglesey?' repeated Hood.

'Yes. They arrived on the ferry at Holyhead from Dublin – with false passports. They're using the name Challinor. Border Control sent a message late last night.'

'What's he doing sneaking into the country via Holyhead?'

'As I said, things are moving quickly. I want you to be ready to come with me to North Wales. I'll pick you up in thirty-minutes. Bring an overnight bag with you. I'll tell you more on the way.'

'Yes, sir. I'll be ready.' He returned the phone to his wife.

'Ready for what?' asked Sarah. 'We were supposed to be going to my mother's for lunch today, remember? It's her birthday.'

'I'm sorry, darling. But this is important. No reason why you and the kids shouldn't go. You know how your mother looks forward to seeing them. Don't cancel on my behalf.'

Sarah sighed. 'I have no intention of cancelling. What did Bob Gaunt want?'

Hood repeated what ACC Gaunt had said to him.

'So, you're off to Wales, are you? I suppose you want me to pack a bag for you?'

Hood smiled. 'If you would, love. I need to take a shower. He'll be here shortly.'

'Must be something big if ACC Gaunt is getting out of bed this early on a Sunday morning. I thought you told me he hardly ever gets personally involved in an investigation. This must be big.'

Hood smiled. 'It is big, very big. This may be our chance to smash this O.C.G. once and for all.'

'Be careful, Harry. These people sound dangerous.'

'Don't worry. I'm sure the ACC has everything in hand.'

'I've heard that before. You take care.'

She sat on the bed and took him in her arms, pushing her face against his. 'That hit-man you told me about is still at large, isn't he?'

'He is.'

She sat back and looked at her husband. 'No heroics then, Harry. Safety first, understand?'

'Yes, ma'am. Now I must take that shower.'

'I'll make you something to eat. Will a bacon sandwich do?'

* * *

'Are we going all the way by car?' asked Hood as he climbed into the rear of the unmarked Jaguar which had pulled onto his drive. ACC Gaunt, dressed casually, greeted him. Harry had hardly seen him before other than in uniform. He somehow seemed much less intimidating. A glass screen separated him from the uniformed driver. 'It will take some time to get to North Wales from here,' continued Hood as he placed his seat belt in position.

'No,' replied Gaunt. 'We're driving to the airfield at Gartree Road.

There's a police helicopter waiting for us there.'

'A helicopter. Things must be moving fast. Where are we headed?'

'North Wales police HQ. The Deputy Chief – Gareth Collins – is waiting for us. He and I go back a long way. This remains our operation but given the circumstances, North Wales will be assisting. They have an interest in this O.C.G. too.'

'They do?'

'Yes. They've noticed an increase in heroin on the streets, particularly in Anglesey. Chinese heroin. It looks like the O.C.G. we are investigating may be responsible for it coming in via the Irish Republic. They've been watching arrivals at Holyhead for some weeks now.'

'There must be someone on the ground in Wales doing the distribution.'

'I believe they have their eye on a probable broker, but no actual evidence at present.'

'But old Gus never dealt in drugs. He was dead against them.'

Gaunt leant closer. 'The drugs side of this is very hush-hush, Harry. I don't know the strength of their intelligence, but it wouldn't surprise me if this O.C.G. is expanding its operations since Gus died. There is some evidence the heroin is being transported to Ireland from Australia then brought to Anglesey.'

'Australia? That's a hell of a long way. And Michael Grayling has been based there for several years. That can't be a coincidence.'

'Exactly. There's a global connection; I'm sure of it. If Grayling is involved he'll be one link in a very long chain.'

'So he may have another reason for coming here? Not just to finish off Doyle?'

'That's how it seems.'

'Bit risky, mixing the drugs business with murder. Very foolish in fact.'

'I agree, but not uncommon. We have yet to get a handle on Michael Grayling. If he has taken over from his father as we believe, he could be using his contacts in Sydney to maximise distribution and the O.C.G.'s profits. And if he's doing business at this level with merchandise shipped from Australia, the international aspects are worrying. It's always possible he isn't in absolute control of this part of the organisation's activities. He could well be under an obligation to others. As I said, a link in a very long chain.'

'To whom?'

'No idea. But this thing could be bigger than even you thought.'

'But why Wales? The old man's main area of activity was the south coast with occasional forays into the Midlands.'

'Don't overlook he set up Duffy in Wales.'

'That was in the south, though.'

Gaunt nodded. 'True, but the ferry route from Dublin to Holyhead is obviously what attracts them. We need to leave the drugs matter to North Wales for them to deal with. Our task is to concentrate on Doyle. I want him kept alive. We were taking a bit of a risk leaving him at large.'

'I agree, sir. But if we'd brought him in, it would have undermined the operation entirely. Not that we'd got very far trying to find him. And there can only be one reason Grayling has brought the Hamilton woman with him.'

The assistant chief constable paused at length before replying. 'You're right, Harry. Like you suggested the other day, he's using her as bait. To bring Doyle out into the open. Like us, he's obviously been unable to unearth him.'

Hood smiled. 'So, my team really were on to something? DS Knight raised that very thing with me after the last briefing.'

'Bright girl, DS Knight,' replied Gaunt. 'Did she make any other comments?'

'She and Hooper confronted me on Friday evening. They both expressed the view, not only that Grayling was using Hamilton as bait but it had crossed their minds that we might have someone on the inside, passing intelligence to us. And neither of them got that from me, I assure you.'

The ACC smiled. 'As I said, a bright girl Wendy Knight. She'll go far.'

'And Hooper's not far behind.'

Gaunt made no comment about Hooper. 'What was your reaction?'

'Well, sir, you'd only confirmed on Wednesday morning that there was a source inside the O.C.G. and I'd received strict instructions it was to go no further, so I said nothing.'

Gaunt frowned. 'That will only have encouraged them to speculate some more.'

'Perhaps, but I told them that for operational reasons, some aspects of the investigation had to remain confidential. They seemed to accept that. And, of course, they know nothing about this trip to Wales, or about the drugs.'

'Not yet, no. They'll have plenty to do establishing who was involved in the theft of Duffy's file. That should serve as a sufficient distraction. I'm pretty sure your theory about how it was lifted is right, but proving it? That's not going to be easy.' He smiled. 'You, of course, had worked out for yourself we had a source inside the O.C.G.'

'Yes, sir. I had, and well before either of them. It seemed the only explanation for what you told me at our earlier meetings. I confess, however, I hadn't appreciated he was passing information on a regular basis. I'd thought it was just a one-off.'

'I can tell you this much, Harry. He's been in contact almost since the beginning, but he must remain unidentified for the moment, even to you. My hands are tied. He's putting himself in a highly vulnerable position. If Grayling discovered what he's about, this whole operation would collapse and his safety compromised.'

'But whoever he is, he has confirmed that Grayling has taken over the O.C.G. in the UK?'

'He has. You were right about that too. Our source is certainly putting his life on the line keeping us informed.'

Silence.

Hood then spoke. 'And it's a he, is it?' He grinned. 'So it isn't Hamilton?'

'I can confirm that much, but no more.'

'And it can't be Doyle. He wouldn't survive five minutes inside the O.C.G.'

'As you say, it isn't Doyle. The main reason for Grayling coming here is to find Doyle and to make sure he's killed. And he wants Hamilton to witness it. But I can't say any more. I have to follow orders too, you know. Hopefully, all will be revealed in due course.'

'I understand, sir. But I take it you know who the source is?'

Gaunt smiled. 'No comment.'

The Jaguar pulled into the airstrip off Gartree Road and the two men headed quickly towards the waiting helicopter. Once aboard, the noise from the engine made conversation almost impossible. Hood tried to relax and settled himself for the journey. He had never been keen on travelling by helicopter, but he could hardly believe how little time passed before they landed at Heddlu Gogledd Cymru in Colwyn Bay where they were met by Deputy Chief Constable Gareth Collins. The two senior officers greeted each other like old friends before ACC Gaunt introduced Harry.

'Gareth and I were at Hendon together, a long time ago. We've kept in touch over the years.'

'Must be, what, twelve years since we met at Hendon?' replied the DCC, shaking Hood by the hand. 'Come up to my office. The tactical firearms commander has already arrived. We'll brief Chief Inspector Hood when we're all together.'

The mention of firearms caused Hood some unease. Although he wasn't surprised that the tactical firearms team was involved, he hoped the use of firearms could be avoided. As he followed his superiors inside, he immediately recalled what his wife had said to him before he left home. He was a qualified firearms officer himself, but loathed having anything to do with guns on a police operation. He prayed he would not have to be issued with a firearm.

DCC Collins' office was spacious and traditionally furnished. He had sensibly provided coffee and sandwiches for his guests which now included Chief Inspector Richard Beddoe and Sergeant Owen Tudor Evans from the North Wales specialist firearms team. After refreshments had been taken, DCC Collins checked the corridor outside his office, closing his door firmly. He then explained the events in which Hood would, it seemed, be little more than a bystander. The

DCC uncovered a detailed plan and photographs of the beach at a place called Porth Ysgo on the Llŷn Peninsula. Gaunt had previously instructed Hood not to ask any questions as the briefing got underway. The ACC did not know how much information had been passed to the firearms team commander, but understood that the full background was known only to himself and the deputy chief constable. Collins began in serious mode, nodding towards Gaunt as he spoke.

'This will remain a Mid-Shires-led operation, but given the location and the necessity of employing armed officers, immediate operational authority at the scene will lie with Chief Inspector Beddoe. ACC Bob Gaunt will, however, retain overall control.' He paused and looked towards Chief Inspector Beddoe before continuing. 'We also have an interest in this O.C.G. It may well be responsible for the recent upsurge in Chinese heroin flooding our streets. In a perfect world, we would simply observe and let these individuals lead us to the main distributer.' He heaved a sigh. 'But we have to give priority to preserving life. And there is reason to believe that the individual behind the supply of the heroin is the same person in whom Mid-Shires has an interest. The information we have is that a determined attempt will be made to kill someone tomorrow on the coast at Porth Ysgo.'

'And this killing is connected with the drugs, is it?' asked Beddoe. 'I know that the problem caused by illicit drugs in Anglesey is worse than anywhere else in Wales.'

'That's certainly true. Although the same individual may well be connected with the drugs and the intended killing, they are quite separate issues,' replied the DCC. 'From what we know, the killing sounds entirely personal.' He glanced towards Gaunt and indicated for him to take over.

The assistant chief constable cleared his throat before he spoke. 'Michael Grayling, who we believe has taken over this O.C.G. from his late father Gus, arrived in Anglesey yesterday evening via Dublin. We believe he's been in Dublin for about a week. He has a woman with him, Julia Hamilton, who is the former lover of a man by the name of Michael Doyle, himself recently paroled – extremely early – from a lengthy sentence for armed robbery.'

'Do we know why he was paroled so early, sir?' asked Beddoe.

'We do, but that must remain confidential. It has no relevance to events we anticipate will arise tomorrow.' He gave a knowing look to Hood then continued. 'Grayling has hired a hit-man with a view to having Doyle killed. His reasons hardly matter but it is connected with the woman Julia Hamilton and the death of a female assassin in the Midlands whom we believe worked for Grayling. We think the female assassin tried to kill Doyle but he turned the tables on her. She is now dead.' He paused briefly. 'As far as I am aware the issue between Grayling and Doyle has nothing to do with the drugs which have started flooding the streets of Anglesey and North Wales. As DCC Collins has said, the problem between these two is personal. Anticipating as we do, that Hamilton is being used to draw Doyle into the open, Grayling has arranged for her to meet up with him at Porth Ysgo tomorrow.'

'Why Porth Ysgo?' asked Beddoe. 'And how do we know all this?' The chief inspector, an experienced firearms officer in his late thirties, obviously physically fit and of slim, athletic build, did not try and hide his disquiet about the operation in which his team was apparently destined to play a leading role.

'That's where the attempt to kill Doyle will take place. We have it directly from our source.'

'Where is Grayling now?'

'He's rented a cottage close to the coast. The house where he and his associates are staying is under observation and has been since they arrived. It's only a few minutes' walk from the beach at Porth Ysgo. Any movement from the house will be communicated directly. We are satisfied Hamilton has had contact with Doyle on several occasions by phone. The hit-man will be waiting somewhere in the vicinity. With any luck – and a great deal of expertise from the firearms team – we should be able to prevent Doyle's death and hopefully detain Grayling and any others of his outfit who may be present.'

'How many of them are likely to be there?' asked Beddoe.

'Apart from the woman and her child, three men have been seen coming and going. One of them is definitely Grayling,' replied Gaunt.

'Hamilton has a child with her?'

'Yes, he's about eight or nine months old. She may well have him with her when she and Doyle meet up.'

Beddoe sighed. 'Do we have a time?'

'Eleven hundred hours or thereabouts.'

'This is getting more complicated and dangerous by the minute. There could be people about at that time. And the presence of a child increases the risks significantly.'

Gaunt could hardly disagree. He then handed over to the deputy chief constable who pointed to the detailed map pinned to a board at the side of his desk. 'The advantage of the beach at Port Ysgo – which, by the way, is a good hour and twenty-five minutes from here – is that it is very isolated and not frequented much at this time of year, not even by the bouldering community.' He glanced towards the window and noticed the rain had started up again. 'And if the weather there is anything like it has been here recently, the chances of any innocent members of the public being about tomorrow morning are very remote. In any event, and out of an abundance of caution, from about six hundred hours tomorrow, the road which leads to the beach will be closed. The barriers will be erected well before the cottage occupied by these criminals. The story will be that there's been a rock slippage.'

'We can be sure that our targets will be unaware of this, can we?' asked Beddoe.

'Yes. Slippages, even in bad weather, are very rare but the weather has been unusually wet recently. And the location chosen for this rendezvous assists from our point of view in providing a number of places where officers can be hidden. Apart from the old mine workings which are close enough for our purposes, there are boulders, rocks and crevices and other places of concealment. Fairly high grassed cliffs provide the backdrop.' He pointed to various photographs which set out the geographical features he had mentioned then continued. 'Our understanding is that Julia Hamilton,' he held up a photograph of her, 'will meet with Michael Doyle,' another photograph bearing Doyle's likeness was produced, 'at around eleven hundred hours tomorrow morning on or near this beach. Our information is that Grayling and one or two of his men will also be there but initially hidden, possibly on the beach itself.' He pointed to a large photograph of Michael Grayling taken from the CCTV obtained at Holyhead the day before then paused and looked directly at the firearms team commander. 'Copies of the photographs will be made available to you and your team, Richard. As ACC Gaunt has said, the assassin we believe Grayling has hired to kill Doyle will also be in attendance at some point. I understand he is likely to be wearing a face mask of some kind to avoid being identified, so there should be no difficulty spotting him. He presumably will be in the beach area if and when Michael Grayling makes himself known to Doyle. We understand that Grayling will speak to Doyle before the hit-man attempts to kill him.'

Beddoe frowned. 'What about the barriers? They might put Doyle off. There's only one road leading to this beach.'

'We believe he will be on a motorcycle, not driving car. He'll be able to pass through quite easily. And he'll be keen to do so. He'll be desperate to see Hamilton.'

'Suppose this hit-man shoots from a concealed location? How are my men supposed to prevent Doyle being killed if we can't see the shooter?'

Collins gave way to ACC Gaunt. 'The information we have strongly suggests that the hit-man will shoot from close up. He'll be using a handgun, not a rifle; that's what he's being paid to do. Grayling for whatever reason wants it that way.' Beddoe looked far from convinced as Gaunt paused briefly then looked at each person present as he emphasised the importance of the operation. 'This is our opportunity to crack open a major organised crime group which has caused havoc, particularly in the Midlands, and may well be causing mayhem here in Wales by importing vast quantities of Chinese heroin. I'm sorry if it may interfere somewhat with your drugs investigation, but if we can stop this lot in their tracks, the drugs problem will solve itself as Grayling will be going away for a very long time.'

'There's usually not much of an interregnum when it comes to class A,' grunted Beddoe. 'Even if we put Grayling away, someone else will step in; they usually do.'

'That doesn't follow in this case,' insisted Gaunt. 'Not this time. If Grayling is arrested, we believe the whole operation will be compromised, including the route through which the heroin is trafficked. Of course, it may start up again in the future, but not necessarily here in Wales.'

DCC Collins nodded his agreement and addressed the commander of the specialist firearms team directly. 'That means, Richard, that your men will have to be carefully positioned; you'll be limited as to the number you can place on the beach itself. We can't risk any of them being spotted. It should be pretty obvious when any individuals of interest arrive and you'll have a heads-up from the surveillance team watching the house. As you know, there is a rough wooden stairway down to the beach with over a hundred steps.'

'More like a hundred and fifty, sir. I've been up and down them more than once. Excellent training for my marathon running.'

Collins smiled. He was impressed with Beddoes's detailed knowledge of the area. 'One hundred and fifty, then. But it is unlikely that anyone will attempt an alternative route down. And your team will have to be in position by first light tomorrow. I know it will mean a long wait, but we can't take any chances on their being spotted. Your placement of Sergeant Evans will be crucial. He must have the widest possible view of the beach area. I will leave it to you where you position both him and the rest of your team but I need hardly add that this is a high-risk operation. Hopefully we can avoid any casualties.' He glanced towards Sergeant Evans. 'But it may prove necessary to take out the assassin if he fails to surrender when you require him to do so.'

'How can we be sure they'll go down to the beach, sir? What about the weather? If it's anything like today, I can't see anyone risking going down those steps.' Chief Inspector Beddoe sounded anything but enthusiastic.

'The weather forecast tomorrow is better. Rain early, but dry with some sun later is what is predicted. And we have information the action will definitely take place on the beach. The tide will also be well out by eleven.'

'May I ask another question, sir?' asked Beddoe who appeared decidedly lukewarm about the operation.

'Of course,' replied Collins, 'but bear in mind I may not be able to provide you with an answer.' He grinned.

The chief inspector persisted. 'How credible is the source of this information? We seem to be putting a great deal of faith in whoever it is. And suppose Doyle fails to turn up?'

Collins let out a lengthy sigh. 'In a phrase, rock solid. And we have every reason to believe that Doyle will appear. But if he doesn't, I'm pretty sure the others I have mentioned will. Our source has proved extremely reliable so far. The object of this meeting on the beach is for the assassin to kill Doyle. That's the only reason it's taking place, but Doyle's death has to be prevented at all costs. He will be needed as a witness. I can't emphasise that too much. We owe him – and the others – a duty of care. As the ACC has said, Hamilton is probably being used as bait in order to get Doyle to reveal himself. Whether she is complicit or acting under duress will be looked at after the event. The O.C.G. and its paid assassin have been unable to locate Doyle, as indeed has Mid-Shires Constabulary.' He looked towards Gaunt.

'That's right,' agreed the ACC. 'Doyle has been lying low, well out of sight. We have been able to establish some of his movements in the Midlands shortly after his release from custody, but he has not been sighted for some time. But as I said, we know he has been in contact with Hamilton. All the signs are that he is heading towards North Wales with a view to seeing her. He's obsessed with the woman. I don't think there's any doubt that he'll turn up if she asks him to. And she has done just that, according to our source.'

Beddoe continued to probe. 'With respect, sir. We are putting a great deal of reliance on this source. And bearing in mind the risks you mentioned, it would be helpful to my team to know if your source is likely to be present at Porth Ysgo. We don't want to shoot the wrong guy, should it come to firearms having to be used. I would also like to know if Doyle is likely to be armed.'

DCC Collins glanced towards Gaunt before dealing with Beddoe's question. 'You should certainly proceed on the basis that the source will be there. And like everyone else, is to be arrested. I hope it will not be necessary for any firearms to be discharged, but I asked Sergeant Evans to attend this briefing so he fully understands what is at stake so he will be able to carry out the specific instructions I have given him should the necessity arise. You will give him and the rest of your team a more detailed briefing later.' He looked at Evans. 'As I understand it, Tudor is your most experienced officer and an excellent shot.'

'He is, sir, yes. There's no one better. His record speaks for itself.'

Evans smiled, but said nothing as Collins continued.

'The absolute priority is to prevent the assassin from killing Doyle or Hamilton or anyone. Sergeant Evans is fully aware of the specific role he is to play.' He raised an eyebrow and glanced towards the firearms sergeant who maintained a poker face. 'As things stand, we have no information as to whether Doyle is likely to be armed. But I appreciate that will be a concern of yours. And I would certainly proceed on the basis that Grayling and anyone with him will be carrying weapons of some kind.'

'That certainly seems likely,' agreed Gaunt. 'Grayling will do almost anything to avoid arrest. I doubt if he'll come quietly unless he appreciates he has no option.'

'Then we'll have to make sure that he does appreciate he has no option,' said Beddoe with a grin. He suddenly seemed more confident.

'Good,' said Collins. 'Anyone else present must also be arrested, and I include Doyle and Hamilton. No exceptions. I don't want anyone getting away. A sufficient show of force at the right moment should ensure they all surrender. The last thing we want is this turning into a shoot-out. Timing will be everything.' He looked directly at Beddoe. 'Your team must familiarise themselves with the location. They won't all have your knowledge of the locality.'

'Yes, sir,' replied Beddoe. 'We'll be there at first light to check out the immediate area around the beach. As I said, I've been there before, so I know it pretty well. There are one or two potential difficulties, but we'll overcome them. My final briefing with my team will be at six-fifteen tomorrow at what passes as the car park you mentioned.'

Collins nodded in evident satisfaction. 'There's a bit of a walk between the car park and the steps, as I recall, but I don't believe there's much of a view of the beach from the car park itself.' Beddoe nodded his agreement as Collins continued. 'The placing of your team will be crucial, Richard. And I cannot overemphasise that no harm must come to Hamilton's child if she's got him with her. I'll never hear the end of it if it does.' He paused for effect. 'I mention the child because our latest information is that Grayling intends to dispose of Hamilton too. The assassin's contract has been extended.'

'This comes from the source, I suppose?'

Collins nodded.

'Does she know this?' continued Beddoe, his expression hardly seeking to disguise his concerns. 'This will certainly add to our problems.'

'I doubt if she does know,' replied Collins. 'Grayling has obviously tired of her. Our information is that he wants her to see Doyle dead before anything happens to her, so she will not be in immediate danger if everything proceeds as we hope. Prevent Doyle being killed and she should not come to any harm.'

Beddoe whistled silently through his teeth. 'And if it doesn't?'

'Let's not go there,' replied Collins, 'but if necessary you will have to adapt. Make sure your team are wise to every possibility.'

'And I have permission to inform my team of this, sir?'

'Yes, Richard. Everything I have disclosed at this briefing can be, must be, communicated to each member of your team. I have arranged for an ambulance and paramedics to be close by, just in case. Traffic officers will be staging a fake accident about half a mile from the coast on a nearby road so the presence of an ambulance and paramedics will not appear out of place. The officers and the paramedics will be under the impression it's an exercise. ACC Gaunt and myself will also be in attendance, but some yards back from the action. You will be in immediate overall command at the beach.'

'And the DCI from the Midlands?' Beddoe turned and looked at Hood.

'Chief Inspector Hood will be with you. He is very familiar with Hamilton and Doyle. Photographs are all very well, but in a case like this we need certainty. Harry's met both of them previously, on several occasions. He'll be able to confirm their presence.' He glanced towards Hood. 'Is that all right with you, Chief Inspector?'

Hood nodded. 'Yes, sir. I was beginning to wonder why I was here. Now I know.' He smiled.

'Is DCI Hood to be armed?' asked Beddoe. He didn't sound too happy.

'That should not be necessary. His sole task is to assist you in identifying the people on the beach, but he will be issued with the usual protection, as indeed will we all.'

'Thank you, sir,' said Hood.

'And I can proceed on the basis that the action will take place on the beach, not above it?' asked Beddoe.

'Yes, but every possibility must be considered. There's always the potential in an operation like this for the unexpected to occur.'

'I have limited the team to six, given the location, sir. More officers would risk the element of surprise being lost, but in view of what you have said, I would like four more officers as backup. Not at the beach but not too far away.'

'If you think that is necessary, Richard, go ahead. Organise it. Now, I suggest that ACC Gaunt and Chief Inspector Hood go downstairs and draw their protective clothing and check the accommodation we have provided for them, much nearer Porth Ysgo, than here. I hope it's comfortable enough. And a car will be at their disposal. We will rendezvous immediately near the car park at Porth Ysgo at six-fifteen tomorrow morning. No vehicles are to be left in the car park. The place must appear deserted.' He paused. 'Now, I want to have a final word with DCI Beddoe and Sergeant Evans. No need for me to detain anyone else.'

CHAPTER 34

Hood and Beddoe had been ensconced together on an elevated ridge hidden behind some boulders which gave them an excellent view of the grass and gravel car park at Porth Ysgo. They were well concealed, perhaps too well hidden. While they could see the top of the steps going down to the beach, they had only a partial view of the beach area itself. The early morning drizzle had almost ceased and there were signs of the sun breaking through the still overcast sky. The final briefing had taken place at twenty past six. Hood had then been given a brief tour of the area, including the flight of steps and the disused mine workings. Beddoe had pointed out the locations where his men would be positioned. Hood then further conferred with ACC Gaunt and DCC Collins in an unmarked police Range Rover well back from the parking area. Gaunt indicated he and the DCC would stay three hundred yards from the beach, hidden behind the remains of a ruined building, but would remain in touch with events using the same communication device that Hood was already sporting.

At half-past eight, all police vehicles were driven away. The car park appeared completely deserted as Hood and Beddoe took up their positions. The flask of coffee Hood had brought with him was quickly consumed and the ham and tomato sandwiches eaten. Officers with a view of the beach reported that the tide was gradually receding and stretches of the beach were being revealed little by little. No sign of an assassin, though. Perhaps he was yet to arrive?

'This is always the worst part,' moaned the firearms commander, 'waiting for something to happen.' He stretched his arms, being careful to make sure they did not protrude from behind the boulders.

'Well,' said Hood, 'I hope this information is as solid as the DCC and the ACC think it is.'

'I don't suppose they'd have gone to all this trouble, particularly for an outside force, if they didn't think it was worthwhile.' Beddoe narrowed his eyes. 'When did you become aware of this source?'

'I'd had my suspicions for a few days, but I didn't know for certain until Wednesday morning when the ACC informed me on a confidential basis. My team back in the Midlands knows nothing, although a couple of the brighter ones were starting to speculate that we might have had someone on the inside. I still don't know who it is though.'

'I just hope we aren't wasting our time. There's always a chance in operations like this that the villains we're after might have called the whole thing off. It does happen, especially if they suspect there's a traitor in their midst.' He laughed. 'I once spent over five hours stuck in a ditch waiting for some drug smugglers to turn up; they never did.' He looked at his watch. 'If anything is going to happen, it should be happening about now.' He adjusted his position and checked his firearm. As he laid it by his side, he received a message that three individuals had left the house that was under observation and were headed towards the beach, but not on foot. 'Did you all hear that?' Beddoe asked his team. He received affirmative answers. 'Game on!' he reported, smiling towards Hood. A few minutes later, a black Range Rover drew into the car park and two men and a woman got out. The woman was carrying a young child in her arms.

'That's Julia Hamilton,' whispered Hood. 'The taller man must be Grayling. Difficult to make out his face from here.'

Beddoe was already whispering instructions to his team, many of whom would not have a view of the car park area from their positions.

'And the other man?' Beddoe asked.

'No idea,' replied Hood. 'His face isn't covered, so he can't be the hit-man. And it definitely isn't Doyle. Perhaps he's the source?'

Beddoe whispered further instructions to his team and watched as the taller of the two men pointed Julia Hamilton in the direction of the steps. She seemed reluctant to comply until the man thought to be Grayling grabbed her by the arm and walked with her forcibly to the top of the steps, followed a few yards behind by the other broadly built individual who kept looking around him. As he reached the top of the steps, Grayling turned and waved to the other man, who returned to the Range Rover and climbed into the driver's seat, started it up and drove out of the car park. Grayling and Julia Hamilton then began their slow descent towards the beach, pausing repeatedly on the steps. Hood heard reports, always brief and to the point, as other members of the team hidden closer to the beach spotted their targets as they came into view. About half-way down the steps, Grayling took the child from Hamilton and pushed her forward. It took a considerable length of time for them to arrive at the bottom of the steps, Hamilton stumbling more than once. When they reached the still wet pebbles, Grayling handed the child back to her and pointed to the sandy centre of the beach. He then waited. About five minutes later, the driver of the Range Rover returned, jogging through the car park towards the steps.

'He's moved the four-by-four so that it won't be seen when Doyle turns up,' whispered Hood.

'If he turns up,' replied Beddoe.

The driver descended the steps and joined Grayling on the beach. Grayling then walked up to Hamilton, said something to her, then trotted with the driver to some rocks and boulders. Both men disappeared from view leaving Julia Hamilton isolated, the child still in her arms.

'Where, I wonder, is the hit-man?' asked Beddoe. 'And if he is lurking somewhere, how did he get here? No sign of a vehicle.'

Hood shook his head and checked his watch. It was seven minutes past eleven. 'Could he have got down there by another route?' he asked. 'There are a number of places he could have concealed himself.'

'Possibly,' replied Beddoe. 'Assuming he's agile enough. If he has, I hope to God he hasn't spotted us.' Was that a twinkle in the eyes of the firearms commander?

Ten minutes later, Hood heard the sound of a motorcycle approaching the parking area. 'That'll be Doyle,' said Hood. 'I always knew he had access to a motorbike, but I could never prove it.'

'Well, you can now,' said Beddoe.

Hood was correct. Dressed in his leathers and still wearing his helmet, Doyle rode into the car park, stopping at a point where he could not have seen down to the beach. He remained seated on his motorcycle for several seconds, then looked behind him then slowly climbed from the machine and walked around the car park. He pulled a mobile phone from his pocket. It was clear from his actions that he could not get a signal. His frustration obvious, he stuffed the phone back into his pocket then removed his helmet, placing it on the rear seat of the motorcycle.

'That's Doyle all right,' said Hood. 'He hadn't got that beard when I last saw him, but it's definitely him.'

Beddoe was already passing the information to his team as Doyle left the car park, picking up speed as he arrived at the flight of steps and noticed Julia Hamilton standing on the beach seemingly alone apart from the child she held in her arms. She spotted Doyle and waved. He then rushed down the steps towards her.

'Stand by,' ordered Beddoe as Doyle reached the beach. 'Game on.' Doyle ran towards Julia Hamilton and embraced her and the child. Taking the child from her, he raised him up, then handed him back and hugged both of them. Beddoe and Hood emerged from their hiding place and walked quickly towards the top of the steps, keeping as low a profile as possible. Grayling and the other man then made themselves visible and approached Doyle, whose arms were still enfolding Julia and the child. He seemed quite oblivious to Grayling's presence.

'Now isn't that lovely?' said Grayling, his tone heavy with sarcasm. He glanced at Wallace. 'What do you think of this, Jamie? Makes your heart leap, doesn't it?' Jamie looked away but said nothing. Grayling continued. 'Get your hands off her.' Despite the wind that had started to get up, his words were clearly audible to both Hood and Beddoe as they crouched at the top of the steps.

Doyle turned, but did not release his hold. 'What's he doing here?' he asked, looking directly at Julia Hamilton. But there was no sign of panic on Doyle's part as he pushed back his shoulders and adopted a provocative stance.

Julia's eyes filled with tears. 'Please, Michael, I couldn't do anything about it. I'm sorry, I really am.' She pulled away from Doyle and took a step towards Grayling, facing him head on, her son still nestling in her arms. 'You promised you wouldn't hurt him. You promised you would let him go. I don't care what you do to me, but let Michael walk away. I'll do anything if you let him go. Anything.'

Grayling scowled. 'I'm sure you would, you conniving little bitch. Promises made to the likes of you are meaningless. You want him, you can have him. As far as I'm concerned, the two of you can spend eternity together.'

Doyle grabbed Julia and pulled her towards him then stood directly in front of her and the now screeching child.

'Move away from her,' ordered Grayling.

Doyle held his ground.

'You're a dead man, Doyle,' shouted Grayling. 'You killed Maxine. You'll pay for that.' He looked to his left. A third man, about six feet tall and dressed entirely in black and wearing a dark face covering, emerged from the other side of the beach, pointing a handgun directly at Doyle as he approached.

'Go, go, go,' said Beddoe to his team.

Several firearms officers appeared as if from nowhere, some running from their hiding places on the beach, pointing their weapons at their targets. Red dots played about the clothing and faces of Grayling and Wallace, but none on either Doyle or Julia Hamilton. 'Armed police. Raise your hands and drop your weapons. Get on the ground. Now!'

Grayling, obviously shocked, looked at the several dots moving about his body, then turned towards the hit-man. 'Do it,' he screamed. 'Do it.' The hit-man took a step towards his target, his gun pointing directly at Doyle's head. A single shot rang out. But it was not Doyle who collapsed onto the wet sand. The hit-man's head jolted backwards; he dropped to his knees and fell forward onto the beach. Blood began seeping from his mouth and spreading over his face covering. His gun was still held loosely in his right hand. Grayling and Jamie Wallace, still stunned, sank to their knees, placing their hands behind their heads.

'What do we do now, boss?' whispered a panicking Wallace. 'The game's a bogie.'

Grayling, still shocked, told him to say nothing.

Sergeant Evans then appeared with a grave expression on his face. 'Sorry about that,' he said, 'but he was warned.' He approached the motionless assassin and kicked the handgun away from him, then bent down to retrieve it. Within seconds, Grayling and his sidekick were squirming on the sodden sand of the beach, their hands handcuffed behind their backs. They were quickly searched and a loaded handgun and a mobile phone removed from each of them. Doyle, seemingly incredulous that he was still alive, received similar treatment. 'Unarmed,' shouted the officer who searched him, removing what had been Maxine Kruger's phone from him. The child, still screaming loudly, was taken from a distraught Julia Hamilton and she, too, was handcuffed. Grayling, still struggling as he was dragged to his feet, bawled at her, his eyes flashing with anger.

'You traitorous bitch. This is your doing. I'll get you for this if it's the last thing I do.'

A dazed Julia did not reply. She began to weep, pleading for her son to be returned to her, but the child was now in the safe hands of a female firearms officer. Hood and Beddoe rushed down onto the beach, still wearing their protective clothing. The intermittent wailing of an ambulance siren could be heard drawing steadily closer. Hood approached Grayling and immediately arrested him on suspicion of the murder of Dudley Manning and conspiracy to murder Michael Doyle. Grayling was cautioned but made no reply. Beddoe confronted Jamie Wallace. 'Name?' he demanded.

Wallace remained silent. He was then arrested for the same offences and cautioned. He gave the firearms commander a surly look. 'I don't know what you're on about.'

ACC Gaunt then appeared. He strode over to the body of the hit-man, bent down and only partially removed his face covering. 'He's still alive – just about.' Addressing Sergeant Evans, he said, 'Get the paramedics down here, pronto.' He then looked directly at Doyle and

Julia Hamilton. 'And get these two off the beach.' Grayling, his face like thunder, noticed that no words of arrest were directed to either Doyle or Julia Hamilton as they were ushered towards the steps.

CHAPTER 35

The car park was now filled with police vehicles and two ambulances.

Grayling and Jamie Wallace were unceremoniously bundled into separate vans and driven away. Julia Hamilton continued to weep profusely. She and Doyle were then placed in different police cars and driven from the car park. It had not escaped Grayling's notice before he departed that both Julia and Doyle, though still in handcuffs, were being treated much more gently than he and Jamie Wallace, which only served to confirm his instantly formed conclusion that Julia Hamilton had betrayed him. 'The bitch has done for me,' he whispered to himself as he began the lengthy journey to North Wales Police Headquarters. The officer sitting next to him mentally noted what had been said. It never crossed Grayling's mind that the traitor might have been closer to him than he realised.

Back on the beach at Porth Ysgo, two paramedics carried the hit-man on a stretcher up the steps and into the nearest of the waiting ambulances. ACC Gaunt and Hood remained on the beach for a few minutes, eventually following the paramedics but keeping some distance behind them. Gaunt was now in possession of the hit-man's gun. Both he and Hood were breathing heavily by the time they reached the car park. Beddoe, who had almost sprinted up the steps in front of them, was waiting and indicated he intended to debrief his team on the morning's events before travelling back to HQ.

'Bloody good shot, sir, don't you think?' he said to Gaunt. 'I told you Evans was a crack marksman.' He was plainly delighted with the successful outcome of the operation. 'I'm surprised the hit-man is still alive, though. But I suppose it's early days yet. They usually don't get up once Tudor has put them down.' He turned so Hood could not see the expression on his face as the commander winked at the ACC.

Gaunt smiled as the three men started to walk towards the waiting ambulance. 'The whole operation went very smoothly, Chief Inspector. You and your team are to be congratulated, Evans in particular. I shall want to speak to him myself this afternoon. Please make him available. DCI Hood and I will go to the hospital with the would-be assassin. I shall certainly commend you and your team to your chief constable when we get back to HQ.'

'Thank you, sir. That's very good of you. What about the people we've arrested? Are you planning to interview them here in Wales?'

Gaunt paused then shook his head. 'I don't think so. They're being taken to pre-arranged and separate police stations in this area to await transportation to Nottingham. We may well speak to Grayling after he's been processed, but I suspect he'll have nothing to say. My team will organise interviews when we get them back to the Midlands.'

'Not for me to say, sir, but they'll be all lawyered up by the time you get them to Nottingham and they'll have had more than enough time to think something up.'

Hood nodded his agreement. 'I think Chief Inspector Beddoe may well have a point, sir.'

Gaunt smiled. 'Let me worry about that, Harry. I don't think there'll be any way out of this for Grayling. The third man who was still at the house has already been arrested and we have a search team going through everything. We shouldn't have too much difficulty finding their Range Rover either. It can't be far away.' He smiled broadly. 'Mind you, I shall certainly be interested in anything they might like to say to explain what we witnessed this morning. That will take some doing, don't you think? Trust me on this.'

Beddoe shrugged his shoulders and started on his way, signalling to his team who were chatting with each other at the far end of the car park, some of them smoking, all of them relieved that things had proceeded as smoothly as they had. A second ambulance, its presence no longer required, pulled out of the car park and went on its way. Gaunt waited until Beddoe was out of earshot then led Hood towards the ambulance into which the hit-man had been placed. 'Come with me, Harry. There's something I want to show you. Now that everything seems to have gone to plan, I can let you have the full story.'

'I suppose we'll have to refer the shooting to the Police Complaints Authority, sir?' said Hood.

'Ah, I don't think that will be necessary,' said Gaunt as he banged twice on the rear doors of the ambulance. They were opened by a smiling Gareth Collins. 'Well done, Bob,' he said, as Gaunt and Hood stepped inside the patient compartment. 'That was as smooth an outcome as we could have hoped for.'

'Apart from the hit-man,' observed Hood. 'He didn't come out of it at all well. Not from what I saw.' Hood was surprised that the ambulance did not immediately set off for the hospital so the man who'd been shot could receive treatment. The engine was not even running. He noticed someone lying flat out on the gurney and a paramedic sponging blood from his face. But no emergency treatment was taking place. The atmosphere seemed to be one of relief and general satisfaction. Not at all what Hood had anticipated.

'Shouldn't we be getting this man to hospital?' he urged.

Gaunt smiled. 'I don't think so.' He gently poked the man outstretched on the gurney, who slowly sat up, took the sponge from the paramedic and wiped the remaining bloodstains from his face.

'Let me introduce you, Harry. This is Inspector Ronan Garrity of the Dublin Garda, otherwise known as the Tinkerman.'

Hood could hardly believe what he was hearing and seeing. He sank into the seat behind him, unable at first to fully take in what he was being told. 'You mean the assassin is an undercover police officer?'

Garrity stretched out his hand towards Hood as he got to his feet and dropped the sponge. Hood automatically took it into his and the two men shook hands. Hood's expression was still one of disbelief. 'Is someone going to explain what is going on?' he asked.

'Ronan, the floor is yours,' said DCC Collins, 'but before we go any further, I want to make it clear that so far as anyone else is concerned, our hit-man died in the ambulance on the way to hospital. That's the story for the time being. In fact, we'd better get started.' He addressed a broadly built individual, who had just appeared from the driver's compartment. Like the female paramedic, he too was to turn out to be a police officer. 'Can you get us underway now, Martin? Blues and twos until we hit the main road. We'd better look and sound the part.'

Martin smiled and returned to the driver's compartment and started up the engine then drove slowly out of the car park, the siren making conversation difficult.

'Who else knows about this?' asked Hood.

'Apart from the five of us and now you, only Beddoe and Sergeant Tudor Evans. We had to include them in this little pantomime as Evans fired the shot. It was a blank, of course. Nice bit of acting by Ronan, don't you think?'

'He certainly fooled me,' sighed Hood. 'What about the blood?'

'Stage prop,' replied Ronan, grinning and revealing his red-stained teeth. 'I just bit on this capsule as I fell to the ground.' He held up the item in question in his right hand.

'What if Grayling had not surrendered?' continued Hood. He was still getting his head round what had happened on the beach.

Collins answered. 'Fortunately, he did surrender. Had he not, any bullets aimed in his direction would have been real enough. As we anticipated he was armed with a handgun. Fortunately, he was overwhelmed before he had the chance to draw it.'

Hood breathed in then let out a lengthy sigh as Ronan Garrity began to explain.

'The real would-be assassin is a man from County Meath by the name of Donal Tinkler, ex IRA. He set himself up in business as an occasional contract killer shortly after the Good Friday peace agreement. His regular job, believe it or not, is as a plumber. We've been after him for years, but couldn't prove anything, not during the troubles. We know he's murdered at least three individuals, one an ex-UDA commander in the north, and two others on the continent but he's always managed to scare off anyone who could have proved who he was. We set up a surveillance team to watch him twenty-four-seven about three months ago and eventually got a result. He was all set to kill some politician in the Dublin government when he was caught, some six weeks ago. When he realised what we had on him, he sang like the proverbial canary, so he did.'

'I hadn't read of such a person being captured,' interrupted Hood. 'Surely, it would have received substantial publicity, especially given his history as a terrorist.'

Garrity smiled. 'Well, normally it would, but it's been kept very quiet. Very quiet indeed. The government didn't want it getting out and still don't. You see, he gave us so much information, including his Swiss bank account details and his cell phone numbers, we thought it worthwhile to play along for a time, you know, to see if anyone contacted him. He never revealed his true identity to any of his clients, so no one knew he was a self-employed plumber working on the outskirts of Dublin.' He laughed. '"Donny Tinkler – Plumber and Assassin!" And he's agreed to give evidence against the individual who hired him to kill a certain prominent Dublin politician. He's in custody too, but not proving as cooperative.'

'In return for what?' asked Hood. 'He'll expect something having given you what he has.'

'Now, that has yet to be finalised, but he'll need protection once it comes out he's cooperating with the authorities as it's bound to do, eventually. So we can't risk him being held in an ordinary prison. These things always leak out in time. We have him in a safe place where no one can get at him.'

'And Grayling contacted him?'

'His cell phone, yes. We'd had our eye on Grayling after Maxine Kruger died in your neck of the woods. If you remember, your Inspector Hooper shared your theory with us about what had brought about her death. Turns out you were spot on. Grayling had instructed Kruger to kill Doyle but it all went wrong and she ended up dead rather than him. He hired Tinkler, who called himself the Tinkerman for assassination purposes, and it wasn't to have him fit a new central heating system, if you know what I mean.' He laughed, then became serious. For someone who had just laid his life on the line, Ronan Garrity seemed to have a robust sense of humour. 'Your man thought he was speaking to the real assassin.' He smiled again. 'But it was me who spoke with him.'

'Do you know where he was when he first got in touch with you?'

'His initial contact was from Portugal, thinking he was dealing with Tinkler, of course, although he didn't know his real name. We have recordings of all his conversations, including his specific instructions to kill Doyle. He even mentioned Kruger being killed to underline why Doyle had to die. His accomplice, who has just been arrested with him, provided her with the gun. That's on tape too. Doyle's photograph was all over the media when you issued the appeal for him to come in, so there was no problem in identifying him. My problem was locating him, until Grayling changed things. That's the reason why we were not too keen on you finding Doyle. He had to be at large for our plan to work.'

'That explains a few things,' murmured Hood.

'That's down to me, Harry,' said Gaunt. 'I was happy to let you and your team look for Doyle when the plan was to find him, arrest him and then give Grayling the impression he'd been killed in accordance with the contract. You have to appreciate that we were not sure that it was Grayling who had hired the hit-man until he appeared in Dublin. He never used his name in the initial calls to Tinkler's phone.'

'So, that's why you didn't want me going public with the photo-fit of the assassin?'

'Exactly. Not until I had seen it. Wasn't much of a resemblance to Ronan, so I gave it the OK after I'd inspected it.'

Ronan smiled as he continued. 'Grayling understandably wanted to meet up with Tinkler when he was in Dublin, but that invitation was declined, of course. I was a bit worried, so I was, when he asked for the meet-up, but he accepted that the Tinkerman never revealed himself to anyone.' He smiled. 'I suspect that's a basic rule if you're in the assassination game.'

'You were playing the part of the assassin throughout?' asked Hood.

'I was. He never spoke with Tinkler; it was always me. I told him I never met with clients for obvious reasons and I never revealed any details about myself to anyone. He could see the sense in that. All contact was by cell phone. I thought at one point he was close to calling the whole thing off; he was a bit on the late side transferring the money! But he was determined to finish off Doyle. It was like an obsession with him.'

'Very dangerous game you were playing, especially down on that beach this morning,' said Hood.

Ronan Garrity shrugged his shoulders. 'Someone had to do it and I had two of my team with me.' He smiled at the paramedic. 'Maureen here used to be a nurse before she joined the Garda and Mr Collins had a genuine ambulance on stand-by in case anything went wrong. By the way, Martin is my sergeant. We've worked together undercover before, but not in the UK.'

'And Grayling never cottoned on?'

'No, he didn't. I'm told he thinks that Julia Hamilton is our source, which suits me down to the ground, I can tell you. She was spotted in Dublin with him. I'm not sure what her role was other than he was obviously using her to draw Doyle out into the open.' He paused ominously. 'He also extended the contract to include her. I was to cop for another ten grand for finishing her off too.' He grinned.

'And the child?'

Garrity shook his head. 'I drew the line at that. Tinkler would never kill a child, not deliberately anyway. He was known for that, apparently. I had to stay in character. But we have Grayling on tape asking me to kill the child too.'

'And you pretended to be a priest? It was you that was seen at the Hamiltons' cottage in Thrussington?'

'It was. I also visited Doyle's former solicitor near Ashbourne in Derbyshire. I had to be seen to be searching for Doyle at first. I thought it quite a good disguise. I studied for the priesthood for nearly two years, so I knew the basics.'

'The flash BMW was a bit of a giveaway. Not many priests can afford a motor like that.'

Ronan smiled. 'Actually, that was a genuine upgrade by the hire company. Not much I could do about it. I take it the chap who met me at Stansted was one of your men?'

'He was,' said Gaunt. 'But he had no idea you were an undercover officer. He thought you were the real thing! Essential, in my view, to keep the thing realistic. He'll be told the true position in due course.'

'Was that really necessary?' asked Hood.

'Dublin insisted,' replied Gaunt, firmly. 'We had no choice in the matter. No one was to know that Ronan was one of us. The risk of it leaking out was too great.' He hesitated for a moment. 'There is some suspicion that this O.C.G. has a contact in the force.'

Hood continued his questioning. 'And the handgun. Did we provide that too?'

'We did,' replied Gaunt. 'And the mobile phone. The safe house too. The bullets were blanks of course.'

'What put you on to Parker, Doyle's former solicitor?'

'Me again,' interrupted Gaunt. The ACC was becoming slightly concerned by Hood's interrogation of Garrity. Can't we leave all this until later, Harry? We need to work out exactly how we present what has happened before we go public. The priority has to be to protect Ronan.'

'I don't mind,' said Ronan. 'Although I'm quite keen on the protection bit. We'll have to go through everything at some time. May as well make a start now. It'll take well over an hour to get to Colwyn Bay in this old bone-shaker.'

Gaunt indicated for Ronan to continue. 'Very well.' He shouted to Martin in the driver's seat. 'We can shut off the siren now.'

Ronan Garrity settled down in a seat opposite Hood and continued with his account. 'As Mr Gaunt has said, Grayling's initial instructions were to find Doyle and to kill him, but he changed his mind and ordered me to hold back until he'd had the chance to speak to him which meant they would have to meet up. I wasn't very happy about that; it complicated things. Our original plan was much simpler; to find Doyle, detain him, then report back to the man we now know was Grayling that he had been killed. Grayling would then have been arrested.'

'Once he was located,' interrupted Hood.

'Yes. But we had a good idea where to find him, once we had established it really was Grayling who was ordering Doyle's execution. We couldn't share that with you. It would have ruined everything if you'd pulled him in.'

'It would have helped us if we'd known that.'

'That, again, is down to me,' grunted Gaunt. He sounded almost apologetic. 'I was happy to let you and your team look for Doyle initially. But after the instructions changed we had to leave him at large. And I couldn't say anything to you or your team at that point. The agreement I made with Dublin was that no one, other than me and eventually DCC Collins, was to know about the undercover officer. Shall we let Ronan continue?'

Ronan nodded. 'Grayling, of course, thought he was calling the shots, so I felt I had to go along with what he wanted. That's why the meet on the beach was arranged. But he abandoned the requirement to speak to Doyle late last night when I phoned him to give him final instructions about the location. I don't know why. But he still insisted on being present when I despatched Doyle. It was his insistence on being there that complicated things.'

'Why did you choose this particular beach?'

'I didn't.' He looked at the DCC. 'Mr Collins chose it. And we didn't have much time to set it all up. It had to be in this area as Grayling was coming here to check up on his drug-dealing venture.'

'So you know about that too, do you?'

'We do. We've had our eye on a couple of Dublin characters for some time now and we knew that heroin was coming in from Australia. Grayling met with them when he was in Dublin. We had him under observation throughout his stay and the decision was made to let it run. Once it was known he'd be in Anglesey and specifically in the area of the Llŷn Peninsula, the choice was limited. As the paid assassin, I had the final say, so I insisted the deed had to be carried out where DCC Collins advised.'

Collins interrupted. 'I know this area pretty well and we needed a suitable location with sufficient hiding places for Beddoe's team. The adjoining beach, known locally as Hell's Mouth, might have an appropriate name, but is far too open. Quite unsuitable.' He laughed.

'And Beddoe knew all about this, too, did he?'

'On a need-to-know basis only. Neither he nor Evans know for certain who our source is; but they had to know that the so-called hit-man had not to be harmed.'

'Doesn't take too much working out, then,' said Hood.

'They obviously had to know the hit-man was an undercover officer; it doesn't follow they thought he was also our source.'

Hood had his doubts about that. 'Well, whatever the position, Beddoe never said a word to me.'

'Good,' replied Collins. 'He and Sergeant Evans had to know about the undercover officer and the blank cartridge, for obvious reasons, but neither he nor Evans know the full background. And they never will. The full story is known only to us at the moment. It has to be that way for now. Ronan here was putting himself at huge risk doing what he did.'

'You can say that again,' said Hood. 'He could easily have been shot by one of the other firearms officers.'

'They were all under instructions not to shoot the hit-man. Only Evans was authorised to take him out.'

Hood didn't hold back. He was becoming increasingly annoyed that he had not been told the true position while others had, especially as he was the SIO. 'Then unless Chief Inspector Beddoe's team have no imagination at all, or are particularly stupid, which I very much doubt, they've probably worked out for themselves why they were under such restrictions. They must have thought it decidedly odd they were ordered not to shoot the one man who, to them, must have represented the greatest risk. I also foresee disclosure problems at any trial if we try and keep all this all under wraps.'

Collins shook his head and intervened. 'I don't think so. ACC Gaunt took legal advice. Top man. I think you know him? Harold Cronshaw, QC.'

Hood nodded. 'I'm acquainted with him, yes. So, he's another who's in the know?'

Gaunt replied. 'He hasn't been given the full circumstances, not yet. He was asked to advise on a specific question concerning the protection of an undercover police officer operating on the perimeter of a criminal organisation.' He glanced towards the Irish inspector. 'Ronan has been very careful not to suggest anything to Grayling, merely to appear to accept instructions from him. According to Cronshaw, we should have no trouble getting a judge to agree to a public interest immunity certificate. But we can discuss what we release for public consumption when we get back to HQ. I agree that it will all have to come out eventually, apart from the identity of the hit-man, of course.' He nodded towards Garrity. 'That will remain wholly confidential, permanently.'

'Well, I hope Ronan stays safe,' replied Hood. 'We may have bagged Grayling and a couple of his associates, but this O.C.G. is much bigger than them. There'll be others out there, some we don't even know about, who'll be bound to take action once they discover Grayling has been apprehended. We may have him safely in custody, but that won't stop him directing affairs from inside. There's Joseph Hanlon for a start. We have no idea where he is.'

'These arrests will remain a secret until we have established precisely how much is to be put into the public domain,' said Collins. 'That is essential. Protecting Ronan is our number one priority.'

'Don't worry yourself on my behalf,' smiled Garrity. 'There's no reason why my identity should be divulged, none at all. But I agree, Hanlon is a concern. You know he and Kruger were thought to be an item? And that son of his, the one he told you about, he'll be in his late teens now.'

'So, he was telling the truth about that when I interviewed him at Whitemoor?' said Hood.

'It seems he was, although the boy's older than he told you and doesn't have any health problems, not that we know of. It took us some time to raise his birth certificate. His name is Rupert Barlow and he's now eighteen. Maxine Kruger was his mother, and we're pretty sure Hanlon is the father, although he didn't put his name forward when the birth was registered. Barlow is Hanlon's mother's maiden name. Too much of a coincidence that, don't you think? We have officers looking out for the two of them. Current information is that he and the boy are hiding out somewhere in County Kerry. We'll find them, eventually.'

'I hope you're right,' said Hood. 'I really do. Hanlon is a hard man and would think nothing of eliminating anyone who got in his way. He knows how to hold a grudge like no one else. He'll certainly blame Doyle for Kruger's death and will have influenced his son to take a similar view. He could also have been in touch with Grayling. He was certainly on very friendly terms with Grayling's old man. And he's bound to feel he owes Grayling something. It was Grayling's O.C.G. that planned and executed his escape.'

'Ronan should be safe enough,' insisted Gaunt. 'If he needs to give evidence, his real identity will not be revealed and he'll be able to do so remotely without being seen. It's been done before in similar cases. We'll anonymise his voice on the tapes too. Again, there are precedents.'

Hood began to relax. It appeared that everything had been carefully thought out. 'Just one more question. How did you get down to the beach this morning?'

'Same way as you, just a bit earlier. Pitch black when I took up my position behind the waterfall. But it proved worthwhile. By the way, my flask and blanket is still down there along with my torch.'

'SOCO will retrieve your things,' said Collins. 'They'll be inspecting and photographing the whole of the beach area.'

Hood smiled. 'I suppose given the amount of evidence we should be able to assemble, there's some prospect of both Grayling and Wallace pleading guilty!'

Everyone laughed.

CHAPTER 36

Hood decided to conduct a brief preliminary interview with Jamie Wallace before Grayling's enforcer was moved to Nottingham. Michael Grayling's right-hand man initially refused to say anything, but his identity was quickly established using the PNC. Fortunately, he had a conviction for unlawful wounding thirteen years before and his fingerprints were still on record. While he said very little and made no admissions, he quickly raised the prospect of doing a "deal." Nothing was promised. Hood and Gaunt wanted to question Grayling and assess the overall strength of the evidence before considering possible witness cooperation, not that they were expecting anything helpful would emerge from that conversation. Hood was confident Grayling would simply go "no comment."

It was much later on Monday afternoon when Hood met with his principal adversary in a secure interview room at a police station in Colwyn Bay well away from where Wallace was being held. Grayling had been given a meal and the opportunity to get some sleep but he remained in handcuffs as the interview began. ACC Gaunt watched the proceedings on a computer screen in an adjacent room. He decided that he should not be involved directly in interviewing any of the suspects, certainly not at this stage. Grayling was informed he was being denied access to a lawyer until he was transferred to Nottingham and indicated immediately that he had nothing to say. But the detective chief inspector had plenty to say to him as he switched on the tape machine and cautioned him. Although he intended that the main interview should be carried out in Nottingham, he and Gaunt thought it tactically wise to let Grayling know the strength of the evidence against him from the outset. He would then have plenty of time to contemplate the weakness of his position as he journeyed to the East

Midlands in a secure vehicle with an armed escort. He could have no answer to the available evidence. Nothing was being left to chance.

After taking the seat immediately opposite Grayling, Hood took a miniature tape recorder from his pocket and placed it on the table. He looked straight at Grayling who slumped in his chair on the other side of the table. He still appeared to be stunned at the turn of events, his eyes betraying what Hood took to be genuine fear. The chief inspector had every intention of taking full advantage. 'We know you hired a hit-man to kill Michael Doyle, your rival for Julia Hamilton,' he began.

Grayling, dressed in a white forensic paper suit, sat up in his seat and glared at Hood. 'No comment. Do I have to have these things on?' He held up his wrists secured as they still were by the handcuffs. Hood noticed that Grayling's left upper eyelid drooped over his eye just a little which gave him a somewhat sinister appearance.

'You do.'

Grayling scowled. 'I'll have a lawyer when we get to Nottingham, you know. He'll put a stop to this. And the clock is already running. You can't keep me in custody for ever.' He slammed his hands down on the table in frustration.

Hood ignored him, confident that the necessary extensions would be granted, although he appreciated he could not deny him legal representation permanently. Grayling realised he was in deep trouble but he didn't yet know the half of it. The chief inspector went straight to the heart of the matter. 'You were heard to order the assassin you hired to kill Doyle on the beach earlier today to do just that. "Do it, do it," remember? Seven police officers have made statements to that effect. Oh, by the way, I heard you too.' Grayling looked straight ahead but said nothing as Hood continued. 'You really were quite determined to see Doyle dead, weren't you? Despite the fact you were surrounded by armed police officers. Do you know, I can't think of a case where I've had better proof of an intention to commit murder. It's hardly commonplace to have more than half a dozen witnesses actually hearing the main man ordering the execution.'

'No comment.'

Hood continued, a wry smile on his face. 'And it looks like Ian Dewhurst is prepared to cooperate.' Grayling appeared surprised. 'Yes, we have him in custody too. He's already asking for a solicitor. He wants to help us as much as he can. I can understand why. He'll not want to be implicated in a conspiracy to murder.'

'No comment.'

'And the search of the house you rented has revealed some very useful material, including a file that was stolen recently from a solicitor's office in Leicester. A file entrusted to the solicitor by the late Derick Duffy. Heard of him, have you?' Grayling looked away. 'I'm told it's been given a good going through by someone. Apparently it's covered in fingerprints. Should be lots of DNA available too.'

Grayling turned and glared at Hood, the ptosis affecting his left eyelid seemingly exaggerated. 'No comment.'

'Then there's Jamie Wallace. He's beginning to see the sense in cooperating. He'll be up for a deal in due course, I'm sure of it. Not that he'll get one. We don't need him to prove what you've been up to.'

Grayling breathed out but maintained his cool. 'No comment.'

Hood then turned to the physical evidence which Grayling could hardly dispute. 'Would you like to explain why you were armed with a loaded handgun when you were arrested? You appreciate that it is an offence to be in possession of such an item in this country? Maximum sentence, ten years, and that's just for possession. Then there's the question of what you proposed doing with it?'

'No comment.'

'As you know, you're under arrest for the murder of Dudley Manning as well as conspiracy to murder Doyle *and* Julia Hamilton. That's not a mere ten years; that's life. We already know you had instructed Maxine Kruger to kill both Dudley and Doyle. Seems like Doyle turned the tables on her but not until after she'd shot poor Dudley on the banks of the Trent. That's why you hired the hit-man to kill Doyle, isn't it? Because she failed to do so and could hardly continue with your orders after she was accidently shot and killed.'

Grayling resisted asserting that he knew Doyle had killed Kruger and he didn't believe that her death was an accident either, but the mention of Julia Hamilton caused his eyes to narrow. How did Hood know that he'd extended the contract to include her? Was the hit-man still alive? What had Julia told them? 'No comment,' he replied, through clenched teeth, but what little self-assurance remained was on the wane.

Hood then switched on the small tape recorder. Grayling heard what was plainly his own voice giving instructions for Doyle to be killed.

'That's you, isn't it?' Hood then stopped the tape. He had no intention – not yet – of allowing Grayling to hear the voice of the other person in that conversation. It would no doubt have to be disclosed eventually, but only after Ronan Garrity's voice had been suitably modified to ensure it could not be recognised. Although Grayling replied, 'No comment,' he could hardly conceal his astonishment as he slowly started to realise that each and every conversation he had enjoyed with the contract killer must have been recorded. But how? Was someone monitoring his phone, even when he was in Portugal? He seemed to be ruminating on every possibility, with one notable exception. It was yet to occur to him that it was the hit-man he had hired who had betrayed him. Hood waited, then turned to the question of the illicit drugs.

'Two hours ago, a man by the name of Brandon Jessop was arrested just outside Pwllheli. He's now in custody. He appears to have had your contact details on his mobile, and the phone we recovered from you contains his details. Quite a coincidence, that, don't you think? You obviously know each other. It seems he had an appointment to meet you later this week. We'll get the full picture when both phones have been interrogated by experts. And I don't think Brandon will want to be associated with your attempt to kill Doyle, will he? I suspect you'll be sold down the river in no time.'

Grayling shifted in his seat. 'No comment. I'm saying nothing until I have full disclosure, nothing I tell you.' He turned away and stared at the blank wall.

'Very well,' replied Hood, picking up the small tape recorder and getting to his feet. 'We'll leave it there for the time being. I'll speak to you again when we get you back to the East Midlands. The North Wales police will want to interview you in due course about the importation of heroin. One of their drugs squad officers will be popping in shortly to arrest you for conspiracy to evade the prohibition on the importation of class A drugs. I foresee a very lengthy indictment. By the way, they've recovered over seventy kilos of what appears to be heroin from Brandon's garage premises on the Caernarfon Road. It was well hidden, but not so well that the drugs dog was unable to sniff it out. Jessop's obviously a main wholesaler rather than a mere street dealer. They've already taken some fingerprints from the plastic packaging. And they're not Brandon's. I wonder whose they can be? Good morning, Mr Grayling. I'll see you tomorrow, in Nottingham.' Hood bent down and switched off the recording machine. 'Interview terminated at seventeen fifty hours.'

'Just a minute,' said Grayling as Hood made for the door. 'This man who was shot on the beach this morning by your lot, is he still alive?'

Hood turned and smiled. 'No comment.'

CHAPTER 37

Michael Doyle sprawled on a chair in a separate interview room in a nearby police station. He, too, was dressed in a white forensic suit, mightily relieved that he was still alive. He couldn't quite believe how naive he had been, agreeing as he had to meet with Jules on the beach at Porth Ysgo. She'd assured him she would be quite alone, apart from their son. *Their son!* When she told him that little Michael was indeed his, he had thrown all caution to the wind. Now, he didn't know what to believe. Had she betrayed him into the hands of Grayling? And how did the police know about the meeting? It was clear to him that someone must have done, but who had informed them? Jules? Or were there other forces at work of which he knew nothing?

'Hello, Mr Hood,' he said, as the chief inspector walked into the room. 'I wasn't expecting to see you when I came to North Wales.'

Hood smiled. 'I go where the evidence leads me, as you should already appreciate.' He then cautioned Doyle fully after switching on the recording machine at the edge of the table and stating the time. Doyle immediately demanded an explanation for his detention, refusing the offer of legal representation.

'Why have I been arrested? I was the intended victim here. That bastard was about to blow my head off.'

Hood took things gently. 'We'll come to that presently, but first, there's the question of what happened to the woman who died on the banks of the River Trent at Cromwell. You were there, weren't you? You drove the Mercedes back to Leicester. We have you on CCTV leaving it outside the hire company's premises.'

'I thought you might. That's why I left it there. There's a camera right outside. I wanted it recorded.'

'You admit it then; you were at Cromwell?'

'I hadn't much choice, Mr Hood. I was taken there against my will. That woman, whoever she was, intended to kill me.'

'You don't know who she was?'

'No, someone connected with that bastard Grayling. That much is pretty obvious, don't you think?'

'Would you like to tell me what happened?'

'Am I under arrest, or what?' asked Doyle.

'You are under arrest at the moment for breaching your parole conditions. You haven't seen your probation officer for some time. I believe he's considering having you returned to prison.'

'Is he? Hardly my fault I didn't see him.'

'You could have phoned him.'

'Didn't have the time. Grayling wanted me dead. I had to lie low.' He sighed. 'You tell me what you believe happened at Cromwell and I'll think about whether I should say anything. I'll tell you this much, I had no idea where I was at first. I was semi-conscious for most of the journey, although I pretended I was completely out of it. If I hadn't put an act on, I'd have been a goner.'

'You certainly appear to have nine lives. If it hadn't been for our intervention, you could well have been killed on the beach this morning, one way or another.'

'I know. I'm very grateful. How did you know I was there?'

Hood grinned. 'You'll understand I can't go into that. It must remain confidential.'

Doyle let out a lengthy sigh. 'What do you reckon happened at Cromwell then? You must have worked it out by now. As I said, that woman was one of Grayling's creatures. I'd seen her at the house near Hungarton. He was with her. She must have driven me to Cromwell from there.'

Hood went through his theory of what had occurred at Cromwell, Doyle nodding as each detail was articulated. But he shook his head at the mention of the motorcycle discovered in the shed along Lock Lane.

'I didn't know anything about that,' he said. 'I never saw a bike.'

'But you must have thrown her motorcycle helmet into the river?

That's where it was found. And she was dressed in motorcycle leathers, wasn't she?'

'Was she? Can't say I noticed. It was dark, you know. I suppose I must have thrown the helmet into the river, but I never saw any bike. I thought that someone must have been picking her up after she'd put the Merc in the river with me inside it. That's why I didn't hang around.'

'And the gun went off by accident, did it?' Hood tried not to sound too cynical.

'Like you said, we were struggling to get control of it. She'd was about to put it in my hand and dump me in the river. Her finger was on the trigger. There was an almighty battle; we fell out of the car onto the wet ground. It just went off. You need to understand, I was fighting for my life.'

'She had a few other injuries.'

'So did I. I wasn't messing about, you know. I punched her, I pulled her hair, I did anything to stop her killing me. She was very strong for a woman. Punched me in the mouth and elbowed me in the stomach, she did. It was a close-run thing. I didn't intend to kill her. She left me with no choice but to fight. The gun just went off.'

'And afterwards, you threw it into the river?'

'I didn't want to be caught with it. She'd probably used it to kill Dudley.'

'Did she mention Dudley at all?'

'No, but she must have done for him. Can't be any other explanation. I read about him dying near Trent Bridge. He was shot twice, according to what I read. I've no idea why she killed him though. Dudley wouldn't hurt a fly.'

'Then you rolled her into the Trent, did you?'

Doyle was quite open about it. 'That's where she intended to put me.'

Hood almost smiled. 'I suppose I should arrest you for concealing a body.'

Doyle sniggered. 'Come on, Mr Hood. You'd have done the same. Anyway, it doesn't look like she was concealed for very long. Didn't I read in the paper she'd been pulled out, not far from where I put her in? I was quite surprised. I thought she'd be washed out to sea. The river was flowing very fast and had broken the bank. I got very wet.'

Hood had some sympathy for Doyle. He was quite prepared to accept he had acted purely in self-defence. 'I suppose it would be a bit harsh in the circumstances to prosecute you for that, but you could have come to us, you know, and explained what had happened. It would have made things easier for you.'

Doyle scowled. 'And you'd have believed me, would you? Of course you wouldn't. You'd have had me back inside in no time. I'm telling you she killed Dudley.' He paused and ran his hand through his hair. 'I was supposed to meet him the next day, you know, after I'd seen Jules at that place near Hungarton. They obviously didn't want him speaking to me, but I have no idea why. Grayling turned up there with that Scottish muscle of his. It was him who belted me on the side of the head and knocked me out.'

'Jamie Wallace?'

'That's him. Jules told me his name. They were trying to fit me up for Dudley's murder. That's what it was all about. I'm sure of it.'

Hood moved on. 'You had a few phone calls with Julia, didn't you? The phone you had with you was cut off sometime on Sunday, but we should still be able to get a full picture of when you were in contact with each other.'

Doyle heaved a sigh and looked away. 'It was the woman's phone. Mine was taken off me at Hungarton by Grayling. Looks like Jules was being used as bait to line me up so he could finish me off. And I thought she wanted me back. I'll never learn as far as she's concerned.' He shook his head and exhaled loudly.

Hood nodded. 'That's how it looks, but whether she was in on the plot or simply being used we have yet to discover. She may have had little choice in the matter.'

Doyle looked up. 'You think she didn't know Grayling and the hit-man were hiding on the beach?' Doyle was clutching at straws again.

Hood hesitated. 'I can understand why you'd like to think that, but the evidence suggests she was aware they were in the vicinity. How do you think she got there?'

'She told me she was going for a walk at about half-past ten and I was to meet her in the car park or down on the beach if the tide was out. She said Grayling would be busy. When I got there, there were no vehicles about, so I thought she would be on her own. Then I saw her down on the beach with little Michael and, I don't know why, but when I saw them I just raced down to her.' He laughed. 'I almost broke my neck rushing down those bloody steps.' He paused and swallowed hard before continuing. 'She'd told me the night before that Michael was my son, not Grayling's.' He paused again and shook his head. 'I suppose that was a lie, too.'

'I don't know,' replied Hood. 'She might have been telling you the truth about that. We have reason to believe that the tests that were done were all faked to get her to believe that Grayling was the father.'

Doyle's face lit up. 'So, he really could be my son?'

'I wouldn't get your hopes up too much, not yet, but it's certainly a possibility. Didn't you have a test done yourself?'

Doyle nodded. 'When I was in Colchester, yes. Jules had told me when I found out she was pregnant that he wasn't mine, so I had the test done when I was in hospital. Had to pay for it, too. I got a letter saying I had a low sperm count, whatever that means. I screwed it up and left it in my cell before I was released.' His eyes widened. 'Was that a fake too?'

'The test was genuine enough, as far as I know, but the letter you received might have been altered. It was retrieved from your cell. I eventually ran down the doctor who signed it off. He produced the copy from the hospital records. He'd been working abroad so it took some time to locate him. The hospital record stated your sperm count was within the normal bands.'

Doyle appeared to be delighted. He stood up and walked around the room, his excitement palpable. 'He is my son, then. That bastard Grayling must have got someone to alter the letter.'

'Could well have happened,' said Hood. 'We know he has contacts all over the place, including in some prisons.'

'Don't remind me. Attempts were made to do me in more than once. That's how I ended up in Colchester – for my own safety.'

'But not at Draycott Heath. There were no attempts on your life there, were there? That stabbing was a put-up job between you and Manning wasn't it?'

Doyle sat down and smiled. 'No comment.'

His excitement suddenly fell away and he began to lose heart as he contemplated Jules doing Grayling's bidding. 'I don't know why he bothered faking the results if he was intending to have me killed anyway.'

'I may be wrong, but I suspect this was all for Julia Hamilton's benefit. He needed to convince her that he was the father of her child. He must have wanted her to stay with him at that point. She's an attractive woman. Beautiful, some might think. Did you know he'd originally abandoned her when he found out she was pregnant?'

Doyle shook his head. 'No, I didn't. I lost contact with her while I was inside. After she told me the child she was expecting wasn't mine, I didn't hear from her again for months. She was inside herself by then. I still don't understand why she got involved with Grayling. But there was nothing I could do about it. I was refused bail, if you remember? Locked up in Leicester Prison.'

Hood smiled. 'I suppose that was down to me, but we didn't have much option. You'd have taken off if you hadn't been remanded.'

Doyle half-smiled. 'You can bet your life I would.'

Hood looked at Doyle sympathetically. 'You've got to face up to it, Michael. She must have got involved with Grayling when she did because she wanted to. No one forced her.'

A pained expression crossed Doyle's face. 'I suppose she must have. She got involved with that lawyer before too. The one who gave evidence at her trial. I read about it in the paper.'

Hood smiled. 'I don't think there was anything in that. She needed an alibi to cover her for when Judge Campion's wife and son were kidnapped. Who better than a new QC to give her a convincing alibi? Grayling, on the other hand, was different. She must have seen something in him. You were inside, looking at a lengthy sentence. Her little scheme to get you off the Charnwood robbery had backfired. Perhaps she was looking towards pastures new? Of course, when she was charged herself, his organisation proved very useful in manipulating the evidence and making sure she was acquitted.' He gave Doyle a knowing look. 'We both know she was as guilty as hell, don't we? She planned the whole thing.'

'Did she? No comment.'

'I bet she was involved in the Charnwood robbery too, wasn't she?'

Doyle grinned. 'Come off it, Mr Hood. We wouldn't have taken a woman on a job like that.'

'Wouldn't you? I'm not too sure about that.'

'But why did Grayling take her back when he did?'

'Isn't it obvious? To use her as bait so he could get his hands on you. I presume that's why you went to Hungarton – to see her? You didn't realise you were walking in to a trap?'

'I wasn't sure what to expect when I went there. That's why I left the message with the taxi-driver. She was on her own when I got there and she did warn me that her new man was on his way. I could have left, I suppose, but like a fool, I decided to confront him. Not that I knew who he was at the time, not until I saw him. Then I had a good idea he was Gus's son. I'd seen him years before when he was still in his teens. He hadn't changed that much. He definitely has a look of his old man.'

Hood gave him a curious look. 'Not very sensible, as things turned out, was it? Going there on your own? That's what surprises me. Having fallen for it once when you went to meet her at Barnard House, you fell for it again and risked meeting with her on a deserted beach in Wales of all places?'

Doyle sighed. 'When it comes to her everything else just goes out the window. I can't help it.' Tears filled his eyes. 'She told me the night before I met her on the beach that Grayling had changed his mind. He was no longer interested in doing me in. He'd told her that the boy was not his; that he had lost interest in her too. He'd told Jules I had to be the father 'cos he'd had a vasectomy years before.'

'And you believed her? She could have been lying.'

'I wanted to believe her and you've just said the tests might have been faked. So it could well be true.'

'Well, there's one way to find out for sure. We can arrange to get the tests done again.'

'And if he is mine?'

'I'm no expert, but you're down on the birth certificate as the boy's father. You'll have some rights in the matter, I should imagine, whoever the biological father may be. Especially if Julia is no longer able to care for him.'

Doyle seemed surprised for a moment, then nodded his head as he realised what Hood meant. 'You mean she's likely to be prosecuted?'

Hood nodded. 'Too early to say, but it's a distinct possibility.'

'And jailed?'

'I would think so, wouldn't you? Won't be a short sentence either. She got away with it in her last trial. This time will be different. She baited the trap to lead you to Grayling so you could be killed. She might well find herself being charged with conspiracy to murder.'

Doyle showed signs of acute distress. 'I don't think she wanted me dead. I think she believed him when he told her he'd lost interest in me. He must have tricked her. What does she say?'

'We haven't interviewed her yet. And when we do, anything she says will have to remain confidential, at least for the time being.' He hesitated before continuing. 'But I think you should know that she was observed arriving at the beach with Grayling and Jamie Wallace.'

Doyle slumped in his seat. There were tears in his eyes again. 'So she must have realised nothing had changed; that Grayling still wanted me dead.'

Hood shrugged his shoulders. 'Looks that way, yes.'

'But she did tell Grayling to leave me be. She was quite brave about it. You must have seen her.'

'I didn't hear that conversation, I'm afraid. The wind was getting up.'

'Well, I did. She definitely stood up to him. And if I get the chance, I'll say so too.' Doyle wiped his eyes and looked up. The conversation then turned to more mundane matters. 'What have you done with my bike?'

'Your bike? It's not registered to you. We've checked.'

'It's in a mate's name. But it's mine. I can prove it.'

'It's safe enough.'

Doyle had a sudden thought. 'You knew that Grayling was after me, didn't you?'

'We suspected someone was, but we didn't know who, not at the outset. That's why we asked you to come in.'

'And you let this whole thing play out, so you could arrest him? You were watching on that beach weren't you? Never mind what happened to me. Are you allowed to do that without warning me?'

'We couldn't find you. We didn't have any other option.'

'I could have been killed.'

'Yes, but you weren't.'

Doyle shook his head but said nothing for over a minute.

'Where's little Michael now?'

'Social services are looking after him.'

'And what about me? I was your patsy. You can't be thinking of prosecuting me, surely?'

Hood took a deep breath. 'That has yet to be decided. I need to speak to the CPS when we get back to Nottingham.' He paused. 'But I also need to ask you something before I do. Would you be willing to give evidence against Grayling if it came to it?'

Doyle hesitated then shook his head. 'I'd be a dead man if I did. You've just said, he has contacts everywhere.'

'You could go into a witness protection programme.'

'With Jules?'

'Ah, I don't know about that. As I said, too early to say.'

'But it's a possibility?'

'Perhaps? We'll just have to wait and see.'

CHAPTER 38

When Hood arrived back in Nottingham early on Tuesday morning he headed immediately to the CPS offices where Fiona Morrison, Regional Head of East Midlands CPS, was waiting with ACC Gaunt. It was obvious to Hood that the two of them had been in conversation well before he arrived. Gaunt had already drafted a note setting out how further investigations into the O.C.G. were to be conducted. Hood read it carefully before commenting. He was pleased to observe that his team were to be informed of the details of events in North Wales with the exception of the identity of the undercover police officer. Dublin, understandably, insisted that Ronan Garrity's name should remain strictly restricted to those who already knew it and not shared further. Only his sobriquet of "the Tinkerman" should be revealed and even that would not form part of the information to be disclosed to the public in a press release to be issued in both North Wales and Nottingham at 1pm the next day. Nothing was to be stated publicly until the press conferences.

Hood continued to peruse Gaunt's draft. The ACC proposed that DS Knight and DS Smith should be assigned to interview Julia Hamilton after they had been fully briefed, of course. Hood and Hooper were to interview both Grayling and Wallace. Ian Dewhurst, had already given a full account of everything he knew to officers from North Wales and had remained in custody while the drugs conspiracy continued to be investigated. When he realised that a murder charge was on the agenda, it proved almost impossible to stop him talking. But Fiona Morrison advised that there was, as yet, insufficient evidence to implicate him in the conspiracy to murder Doyle and no evidence that he had any involvement in the killing of Dudley Manning. She nevertheless suggested that any application for bail should be opposed.

He would be safer in custody, providing he was kept well away from Grayling and Wallace who should be remanded, she advised, to different high-security prisons. Morrison was wholly satisfied that there was already ample evidence to charge both with conspiracy to murder Doyle and Hamilton and the murder of Dudley Manning, but the risks to the undercover officer if a trial were to take place concerning events on the beach at Porth Ysgo remained a delicate and sensitive issue yet to be addressed.

'They should be given the opportunity to comment on the evidence before they are charged, but I wouldn't waste too much time on them. They'll probably clam up anyway. Where are they at the moment?'

Gaunt answered. 'Wallace is at the Bridewell, under close supervision; Grayling is in the high secure unit in Newark. No one else will be housed there until we get him to Mansfield Shirebrook.'

'That's where Hanlon escaped from, isn't it?' said Morrison, a look of apprehension crossing her brow.

'It is, but the building work has been completed. There is no prospect of another escape. The exercise area has a rigid net covering it. There'll be no more departures by helicopter from there.'

'All the same, I think I'd prefer him elsewhere,' said Morrison. 'How about moving him to Woodborough after he's been charged?'

'Woodborough, like Whitemoor, doesn't like accepting remand prisoners,' said Hood. 'He'll be safe enough at Shirebrook.'

Gaunt agreed with Morrison. 'Well, they may have to make an exception in this case, at least when we get them to trial. In any event, wherever they end up, I want them kept away from the other inmates and from each other. No contact. He's a slippery one is Grayling. He'll use any and every opportunity to plan his escape then disappear before we get him to trial.'

'On the evidence you've told me about, he ought to be pleading guilty,' said Morrison with a grin.

'That'll be the day,' replied Gaunt. 'The fact he has no defence won't inhibit him one iota. We already have experience of the resources this O.C.G. can call upon. Perhaps we should look into having his trial transferred to the court at Woolwich? There's a tunnel between Belmarsh Prison and the court there. We could move him to Belmarsh when we get a trial date.'

Morrison agreed. 'I'll see what I can do. We'll be instructing Harold Cronshaw to prosecute. I'm sure he'll look forward to having another go at Julia Hamilton.'

Hood looked up. 'Has it been decided to prosecute her?' he asked. 'She hasn't been interviewed yet.'

'It's certainly on the cards,' replied Morrison. 'I'll be seeking counsel's opinion before a final decision is made.'

Hood finished reading Gaunt's note. 'You don't want to sit in on the interviews, sir?'

Gaunt smiled. 'I think not. I'm a bit out of touch when it comes to interviewing major villains, Harry. I'll leave it to you and your team. I'll preside at the press conference tomorrow, though. I'll want you with me, of course.'

Hood was not in the least surprised at Gaunt's decision. As assistant chief constable, he would be quite happy to take the credit in front of the TV cameras for the success of the operation, but content to leave the heavy lifting to Hood and his team. Nothing changes. It was always thus. Hood turned again to the question of the prosecution of Julia Hamilton. He knew what Doyle's reaction would be. And he needed Doyle to cooperate. 'Is there enough to justify prosecuting her?' he queried. 'Doyle may have second thoughts about helping us if she's standing in the dock alongside Grayling and Wallace. And it would look decidedly odd, wouldn't it, prosecuting her for conspiracy to murder when she could well have been one of the potential victims? It's clear from what the undercover officer has told us that Grayling had extended the contract to include her.'

'It would be a novelty, I agree.' Morrison paused and considered the options. 'She could always be indicted separately and the charge limited to conspiracy to murder Doyle. And we may not need him as a witness if the undercover officer gives evidence.'

'Dublin has gone very cool on the officer giving evidence, whatever precautions are made,' said Gaunt. 'We are going to have to think about using him. Doyle may be the better option.'

'And Doyle is the only person who can speak to the conversations he had with Hamilton before the events on the beach yesterday,' said Hood. 'And I'm pretty sure about one thing. He won't agree to give evidence against her. He's still besotted with her, especially now he believes she's the mother of his son.'

Morrison was not so sure. 'If she knows what's good for her, she'll give us all that we need when she's interviewed under caution. Let's wait and see what she says when DS Smith and DS Knight interview her this afternoon.'

'What about Doyle? Do you anticipate any charges against him?' asked Hood. 'I'm pretty sure he's telling the truth about what happened at Cromwell Lock. He'd clearly been taken there against his will and would certainly have been killed if he hadn't fought back. I can't see a jury convicting him of anything. And charging him with concealing a body would seem a bit over the top in the circumstances. The O.C.G. was trying to fit him up for the killing of Dudley Manning. We can prove the same gun was used to kill Manning, and Doyle couldn't have been responsible for that. I reckon if he were to repeat what he's said to me before a jury, it would go a long way to proving Grayling's responsibility for Manning's murder.'

Morrison frowned. 'I'll think about it, Harry. I think it wise to take counsel's opinion before using Doyle as a witness. Duffy's evidence in Hamilton's trial didn't exactly turn out quite as we expected, did it? And that's without mentioning the disaster of calling Hanlon. Doyle could present us with similar problems.' She gave Hood a cynical look, but the chief inspector had his own firmly held view about what had gone wrong in Hamilton's trial.

'It was Hanlon's disappearance that did for us in that case, no doubt about it. That's certainly Harold Cronshaw's opinion. And he, remember, was opposed to calling Hanlon in the first place. That was all down to the attorney-general. I doubt if Doyle will do a vanishing act on us like Hanlon, not if we place him on a witness protection programme. He'd have to remain cooperative then, and he'll certainly require protection if he helps us to put Grayling away.'

'I don't think we'll have the problem of the attorney interfering this time round,' said Morrison.

'I'm waiting for a full transcript of the calls between Grayling and the undercover officer,' continued Hood. 'It'll take a little time to modify the officer's voice, so we can't play the full tapes in interview, and we need to get a move on. Twenty-four hours will have gone by shortly, although we already have an extension from the divisional superintendent in respect of all those we arrested. Grayling's already demanding to see a lawyer.'

Hood's mobile phone buzzed. Gaunt indicated for him to take the call. It was DS Knight. Hood smiled as he listened to what she had to say then reported to the others some further good news, thanking Knight and indicating he would see her shortly. 'Brian Logan has been located. He came in of his own accord. Walked into the police station in West Bridgford asking for me. In my absence DS Knight is dealing. He's frightened to death, apparently. Thinks the O.C.G. are out to kill him. And he could well be right about that.'

'Remind me who he is?' said Morrison. She had not yet had time to study the papers in depth.

'Prison officer at Woodborough. He found Duffy dead in his cell. The governor gave him a couple of days' compassionate leave but he vanished. Didn't return to work. He may have been the link between Duffy and the O.C.G. I think I'd better get over there and have a word with him.'

CHAPTER 39

'I know they're after me,' said Brian Logan as he and Hood spoke privately in an interview room at West Bridgford. 'My neighbour told me someone had been round and forced an entry into my house. She thought it was a burglar, but nothing was taken. It must have been one of them.'

'Who are "them"?' asked Hood.

'That's just it. I don't really know. I usually got my instructions by phone; a mobile they gave me. I've brought it with me, by the way. Your sergeant has it. I only met any of them once. The one with a strong Scottish accent turned up at my home. I'd spoken with him over the phone before but only saw him the once. I'll certainly never forget him. Built like the proverbial and nasty with it. That's why I took off after Duffy hanged himself. He really scared me.'

'Did you get his name?'

Logan shook his head. 'No, we never used names.'

'But you'd recognise him again if you saw him?'

'I would. I'm certain.'

'And you received money from them?'

Logan dropped his head. 'I'm ashamed to say I did, but I was desperate.' He looked up. 'I owe some rather unpleasant people quite a bit of money. Gambling debts for the most part. Can't resist a bet on the horses, that's my weakness. Nothing to do with this other lot, but it was made very plain that if I didn't find the money, something untoward would happen to me. I still owe them, but not as much as I did.'

'Where did you run to?'

'Fishing lodge near Ross-on-Wye. I go there to relax and to fish when I take time off, but I realised I couldn't stay there indefinitely, so I turned myself in. I had nowhere else to go.'

'How long have you been involved with Duffy's friends?' asked Hood.

Logan scoffed. 'I don't think they're his friends. He seemed to me to be getting increasingly worried about them. He was even becoming reluctant to go out for his exercise some days. You see, he had to walk through another section of the prison to get to the exercise area. There were usually one or two inmates about the place. He looked quite scared when he went past them.'

'And all this began when?'

'It only started a week or so after Duffy arrived at Woodborough.'

'How did they make contact with you?'

Logan frowned. 'A large envelope came through my door. I remember I'd just got back from Warwick races. I'd lost a packet. They must have been watching me and knew I was desperate for money.' He shook his head. 'Not a single favourite came in. You have occasional days like that. When I opened the envelope there was a mobile phone with a note. I eventually rang the number and it started from there. There was five hundred quid in twenties in the package too.'

'Quite an inducement?'

Logan nodded. 'I'd had a message at the racecourse from the bookie's heavy. He'd warned me I had to produce at least five hundred in the next forty-eight hours or suffer the consequences. So, I handed over the money from the package. I had no choice but to make the call after I'd done that.'

'How much have you received from them in total?'

Logan breathed out heavily. 'About two-and-a-half grand. It comes regular as clockwork, but I'll be no use to them anymore. I've already resigned from the prison service. I put my papers in on Friday. I didn't know what to do next, so I decided to come in. I knew from the assistant governor that you were in charge of the investigation.'

'What did you do for the money?'

'Not a lot. I think it was more what they'd want me to do in the future. In the main, I just reported back to them on how Duffy was doing.' He paused and dropped his voice to a whisper. 'I was told to search his cell for a tape just before I found him dead. I've no idea what sort of tape. I did what they asked but I found nothing.'

'And reported back to them?'

He nodded.

'Did you do anything for Duffy behind their backs?'

Logan nodded again. 'I'll be frank with you, Mr Hood. Yes, I smuggled a letter out for him to avoid it being seen by the prison authorities. He paid me forty quid cash for doing it.'

'Who was the letter for?'

'His daughter, I suppose. She'd just been moved to Brampton Hall, not that it was addressed to her. The arrangement was to address it to one of the other women held there who would hand it to the daughter. It's a well-practised dodge. I'm not the only one who's done it.'

'Name?'

'Can't really remember.'

'I think you can.'

Logan sighed. 'Louise Daley, or something like that. The first name was definitely Louise.'

'I don't suppose you happened to read it, did you?'

'I wasn't supposed to. Duffy paid me to keep it confidential, but I admit I had a quick shufty before I posted it. I was getting worried about the old boy. He was getting very depressed. I'd had a few long chats with him. For some reason, he liked talking to me. He didn't really have anyone else; he spent most of his time alone. I could tell he'd just about had enough, but I never thought he'd actually do himself in. That never really crossed my mind.'

'What did he talk about?'

'His daughter, in the main. He thought he was responsible for her being inside. He kept saying it was all his fault. Not that he went into much detail. I tried to reassure him, but it didn't do any good. He was getting more and more depressed. I remember him saying, not long after you'd seen him, that there was only one way he'd ever get peace. It never occurred to me that he meant to kill himself.'

'When did he give you the letter?'

'Ah, the Tuesday before he died. I was on lates that day. I posted it on my way home, so it would have caught the post Wednesday morning.'

'And he spoke to his daughter that evening?'

'On the Wednesday, yes. Not long after you'd seen him. He spoke with his lawyer first. He'd mentioned something about a file that his lawyer was holding for him. I asked him what was in it but he wouldn't say.'

'Did you hear any of the conversations?'

'No, I left him to it. It didn't take very long.'

'Did you tell the people who were paying you what was in the letter?'

Logan let out a lengthy sigh. 'No, I didn't.' He turned away for a moment. 'But I told them I'd smuggled a letter out for him, but not that I'd definitely read it. I thought I might screw some more cash out of them by hinting I had some idea what was in it.'

'This may be important. Are you sure you didn't tell anyone what was in the letter?'

'Positive. The Scotsman told me over the phone he would make me an offer if I found out what Duffy had written. He wanted to meet up with me on Saturday morning, but I lost my nerve and took off instead. I was worried something might happen to me now that Duffy was dead. I'd be no use to them anymore and Duffy had told me that they didn't like loose ends. I thought that's what I was – a loose end.'

'You say Duffy was very depressed. Was that confirmed by the contents of the letter?'

'I suppose it was, yes. He said he couldn't take anymore. He just wanted it to end. He told his daughter he might not be around much longer and that he'd made a will and left everything to her. He also mentioned something about money in the Cayman Islands. I'd no idea what that meant.'

'The Cayman Islands?'

'Yeh, I'm pretty sure that's what it said.'

'And he was threatening suicide?'

'I didn't read it like that at the time. I thought he was referring to his state of health. He wasn't very fit, you know. Quite breathless when he'd taken his exercise and he never did anything too demanding. You've got to believe me. I thought he was just fed up with all the restrictions and feeling sorry for himself. I never thought he'd actually do anything about it. It was only after I found him hanging there I put it all together.' He shook his head and looked away. 'We've had suicides in prison before, but that was the first time I'd ever found anyone who'd hanged himself like that. It really upset me.'

'What did you do about his depression? Did you report it?'

'That was part of my job, yes. I told the governor some weeks before that I thought Duffy was very low in mood, but I didn't say anything to anyone about what was in the letter. I thought it might get back to Duffy if I did. He used to talk to other officers occasionally.'

'Did the governor do anything?'

Logan nodded. 'Yes. He increased the checks on Duffy, just to be on the safe side. And each officer had to report on a daily basis any concerns they had about him. That was standard practice.'

'Did he have any other physical health problems?'

'I don't know. He smoked like a chimney and as I've already mentioned I'd noticed he was a bit breathless when he came back from his exercise period, but that's all I can recall. He didn't do much in the yard, just walked around the perimeter. And he never used the gym.'

'Did he mention moving to a different prison at all?'

'I'd asked him about getting early parole, but he said he was no longer interested. I know he'd moved about a lot in the prison estate, so I suppose that another move was on the cards. Everyone knew he'd grassed up some important people big time. One of the last things he said to me was to try and find out if the powers that be were planning to move him somewhere else.'

'And did you?'

'Never got the chance, not that the governor would have said anything if I'd asked him. Movements of prisoners are kept highly confidential, for obvious reasons.'

Hood nodded, stood up and walked slowly around the room, then addressed Logan further. 'Did you have anything to do with the riot that started on the night Duffy died?'

'No, nothing. That was down to Haydon Connolly. He's been nothing but trouble since he arrived. He was bent on demonstrating who ran the wing. He'd fallen out big time with another prisoner, a man called Danny Dixon. Danny had been the daddy for the last two years. He's serving a thirty-year sentence for attempted murder and they'd been rubbing each other up the wrong way since the get-go. I reckon it all kicked off when one of Dixon's crew stabbed one of Connelly's boys. It all got out of hand very quickly.'

'I looks like Duffy hanged himself while the rioting was going on. He must've heard the racket. His cell was pretty close to the wing where it all started.'

Logan nodded. 'I reckon that's what must have happened. You don't think he thought they were coming for him?'

Hood shrugged his shoulders. 'I don't know, but something must have triggered his decision to do what he did when he did.' Hood turned the conversation to Logan's immediate future. 'You realise you're likely to be charged with misconduct in public office?'

'I know. It'll mean a prison sentence as well. I've seen other prison officers go down for less.'

'You're probably right. But full cooperation will assist. I can make sure the judge is told you've been helpful. Are you prepared to make a witness statement? It may have to wait until after you've been charged and the CPS will have to look at things before then.'

'I'd rather do it now, if you don't mind. Get it over with.'

'I'll speak to the CPS and get back to you.'

'By the way, Mr Hood, I don't want bail. I want to stay on remand and serve as much time as I can before I'm sentenced. I won't be any bother. It's a relief to get it all off my chest.'

CHAPTER 40

The press conference was arranged at Police HQ in Leicester for one-fifteen on Wednesday afternoon, ACC Gaunt presiding. Hood was sitting alongside him, together with the uniformed divisional chief superintendent. Neither Grayling nor Wallace had said anything when interviewed at length the day before. Julia Hamilton, on the other hand, had given a full account of her time with Grayling and her conversations with Doyle. She'd admitted that Grayling had listened in to all of them but she asserted that he forced her to say what she had said to Doyle. When asked why she hadn't contacted the police herself, she burst into tears, insisting she was too scared to do otherwise. She emphasised that she was under constant scrutiny and had no doubt Grayling would have killed her had she said anything to anyone. The decision as to whether she should be prosecuted was deferred.

Grayling and Wallace had already been charged with the murder of Dudley Manning and conspiracy to murder Michael Doyle and Julia Hamilton before the press conference was convened, which meant that further interviews could not take place. That was not considered to be problematic as neither man was willing to say anything, although both had been in private discussions with their legal representatives for several hours. After a brief appearance before the Magistrates' court on Wednesday morning, they were remanded in custody to separate prisons to await trial. Both had been informed that further charges were likely to follow in respect of the importation of class A drugs into Anglesey in North Wales. Nothing had been finally decided about Doyle's position but serious charges seemed increasingly unlikely. He had reluctantly agreed to cooperate and made a lengthy witness statement in the presence of a solicitor. But he insisted he would say nothing to implicate Hamilton in the events he described. An urgent conference was arranged by Fiona Morrison with Harold Cronshaw QC, where the question of prosecuting Julia Hamilton would be thrashed out. In the interim, she found herself in a separate safe house, well away from Doyle. Her child remained in the care of social services but she was assured she would be granted supervised contact with him on a daily basis.

After outlining the charges preferred against Grayling and Wallace and describing - in brief - events in North Wales while carefully avoiding any mention of the role of the undercover officer from Dublin, Gaunt complimented Hood's team on the thoroughness of their investigation. He then threw the meeting open to questions, a decision he had cause quickly to regret. It became clear that some of the journalists present had already done some digging and were aware of features of the investigation and events in Wales that Gaunt would have preferred to have remained unsaid.

'What happened to the hit-man?' asked the journalist from the *Guardian*. 'Was he shot dead by a firearms officer?'

Gaunt looked at Hood before answering. How did they know about the hit-man? 'No one died on the beach at Porth Ysgo,' he answered. He declined to add further details.

'It was a set-up, was it?' continued the journalist. 'You were acting on information received? Who was your informant?'

The ACC hesitated before replying. 'This was a lengthy and difficult inquiry. Certain matters must remain confidential. I would have thought an experienced journalist like yourself would understand that. The fact remains we have arrested and charged the leaders of a major criminal organisation. Other arrests are likely to follow.'

'Michael Doyle was the intended victim, you say,' said another. 'Is it merely a coincidence that all this came about after he was released early from his prison sentence? Why was he released so early?'

Gaunt dodged the question as to why Doyle had been released early. 'No charges are presently anticipated against Doyle. But his position remains under review. Investigations are continuing. I can confirm that Michael Doyle was the major intended target of this conspiracy as the charges I have read out indicate.'

'What about Julia Hamilton? She and Doyle were lovers once, weren't they? That's what she said at her trial earlier this year. Were they in contact with each other after he was released and she was acquitted?'

Gaunt could hardly make himself heard as the proceedings rapidly started to get out of hand. Questions were shouted out, one after the other, leaving him no opportunity to provide answers had he wanted to. 'And the woman who was shot at Cromwell. Has her death something to do with all this? Was Michael Doyle the informant?'

After giving Hood a concerned look, Gaunt then brought the conference to a swift conclusion. 'That will be all for now, ladies and gentlemen. In the event of any further arrests, a statement will be released to you. Good afternoon.'

* * *

'That did not go quite as well as I anticipated,' Gaunt confided to Hood as they walked into the adjoining corridor, the pandemonium from the conference room fading as they approached the stairs to the fourth floor. Gaunt was anxious to get to the comparative peace of his office.

'No, sir, but we can never satisfy these people. Best sometimes to say as little as possible.'

If that comment were intended to convey Hood's disapproval of what had just taken place it went over the head of the ACC who started to climb the stairs, then turned and faced Hood. 'It looks like someone has been leaking information,' he said, testily. 'It wouldn't surprise me if Grayling is already passing stuff to the press. This solicitor of his, what do we know about him? I'm told he was seen speaking to reporters just before the press conference.'

'Grayling had a local solicitor to begin with. But he was dismissed smartish when Julian Enderby turned up from London. He's from the same firm which represented Gus Grayling when he was interviewed a few years ago, according to Andrew Hooper. Andrew was involved in a major fraud investigation back then. He remembers Enderby well. Sharp as a needle and he certainly knows his stuff. Brain the size of a planet by all accounts.'

'But bent as a corkscrew, presumably?'

'The jury is still out on that question. One thing is clear enough; he certainly knows how to make trouble. We'll have to be very careful with him.'

'That's just what we don't need,' grumbled Gaunt. 'Grayling's only chance is to create the impression that this was all a set-up. His lawyers will keep pressing for information about how we happened to be at the beach. It's essential nothing is disclosed about that, Harry. Make sure your team fully understand that. Any further briefings are to be passed to me before distribution. Do I make myself clear?'

'Yes, sir. But I don't think Grayling or Wallace will be able to undermine the evidence we have or talk themselves out of this one. The recordings speak for themselves. And they were caught in the act. I can't see even Julian Enderby getting them off.' He paused briefly before continuing. 'I'd better return to West Bridgford. I shall be there if you want me for anything.'

'Keep in touch,' said Gaunt. 'No need to keep travelling here. Not anymore. A phone call will do. By the way, I think you should attend the conference Fiona Morrison is arranging with counsel on Friday. You have a good grip of all aspects of the case. Your contribution will be invaluable. And Harry, make sure you keep an eye on this fellow Enderby. He probably has a close association with the organisation or they wouldn't be using him. There's no knowing what he and Grayling will be discussing in their confidential meetings.'

'And we never will know, sir,' replied Hood. 'Andrew is checking into Mr Enderby with the Law Society. He's a Canadian by birth, apparently, but qualified to practise in several jurisdictions. Grayling's being moved to Mansfield Shirebrook as we speak following his appearance before the Magistrates' court. We can't really stop Enderby seeing him.'

'Why would he want to see him again? Grayling's been charged but no papers have been served yet. And they won't be, not for some time.'

'Taking instructions, I suppose. That we haven't served any papers doesn't stop him seeing his client, I'm afraid. The governor knows that only too well. He can't risk any complaints being made in such a high-profile case.'

'You've taken appropriate precautions, I hope.'

'Of course. An armed escort is making sure he gets to Shirebrook safely. And the prison will be taking additional security precautions, especially when Enderby visits him. The governor will put time limits on his meetings. There's no question of Grayling doing a Hanlon. No chance at all.'

CHAPTER 41

When Hood returned to West Bridgford he was greeted by a stony-faced Wendy Knight.

'What's wrong, Wendy? Has something gone awry with Grayling's transfer to Shirebrook?'

'No, sir. He got there over an hour ago. He's securely locked up. I've just spoken to the deputy governor.' She paused and cleared her throat. 'It's Kelly Maguire.'

'What about her?'

'It was Duffy's funeral this morning.'

'I know.'

'She was given permission to attend.'

'I know, but she was under escort. The governor made that clear. And her security was supposed to have been upgraded. The Home Office insisted.'

'She was under escort and two officers from Northamptonshire were also in attendance.'

'What happened? Come on, Wendy. Out with it. There can't have been much of a congregation. She's Duffy's only living relative.'

'It appears that she collapsed as she was reading the eulogy she'd prepared about her father.'

'And?'

'The escort called an ambulance. It was there in double-quick time to take her to the local hospital. One of the escorting prison officers went with her, but the ambulance never arrived at the hospital. The two police officers went there directly in their own vehicle with the other prison officer; it's literally no more than five minutes away. No show. Apparently another ambulance turned up at the crematorium ten minutes later. The first one was obviously bogus.'

Hood was furious. 'What happened to the escorting officer who went with her in the ambulance?'

'She was duped, no doubt about it. They let her out of the ambulance on the M1, northbound. She made her way to an emergency phone and called for help, but it took some time for her to get assistance. They were well gone by the time a police car got to her.'

'I assume the police officers who attended reacted quickly?'

'Not as fast as they should, perhaps? The offenders had taken her identification and she wasn't instantly believed. She was also in civilian clothes at the time, presumably because of the funeral.'

'Didn't she have her mobile with her?'

'She had, but they relieved her of that too before they let her out. Raymond's already checking the CCTV from the motorway. No joy so far. Apparently the system was down on that stretch of the M1 but according to the escort, the ambulance continued northbound so it should have been picked up farther on.'

Hood shook his head. 'Do we know why the system was down?'

Knight shrugged her shoulders. 'No evidence it was interfered with. Just a fault, apparently.'

'I can't believe this. How the hell was this allowed to happen? Was she not handcuffed to the escort?'

'On the way to the crematorium, yes. But she was released from the cuffs in order to give the eulogy. She broke down in tears, then collapsed. Her pulse was weak, hence the call for assistance.'

'She must have taken something to induce that. Was anyone else there, at the crematorium I mean?'

'The manager of Duffy's haulage business.' She looked at her notebook. 'He's called David Lindsay. No suggestion he was involved.'

'Anyone else?'

'Apart from the undertaker and his assistant, a Mr and Mrs Henderson, an elderly couple – no relation to Duffy. There was no priest or minister. Duffy had no religious beliefs, apparently.'

'What were the Hendersons doing there? Who are they?'

'Regulars apparently. Bit of a hobby of theirs, it seems, attending other people's funerals. They sometimes get invited to the wake! Free lunch, I suppose.'

'No wake for Duffy, though.'

'No, sir. But they stayed on for the next one. Bit of a conveyor belt down at the crem. They might have struck lucky later on.' She suppressed a smile.

'I take it they've been required to make statements?'

'Yes, sir, as has David Lindsay. The Northamptonshire officers are dealing. The escort is very upset. But she's making a statement at Campbell Square as we speak.'

'Does Superintendent Kingston know about this cock-up?'

'Yes, sir. He's taking the escort's statement personally. The necessary actions have already been taken. Kelly Maguire's details are now in the system. Her escape has already gone public.' She paused for a moment before continuing. 'The vultures haven't yet linked it to Grayling's arrest.'

'That won't last. They'll make the connection soon enough. And I don't think we'll be seeing her again. Like Hanlon, she won't reappear any time soon.' He sighed in frustration. 'This must be down to the O.C.G. They can't have heard about Grayling and Wallace's arrests. They'll be after the tape she told us Duffy had made.'

'If it exists, sir.'

'Whether it exists or not it's served its purpose. No information about any arrests was released until Grayling and Wallace appeared before the court this morning. If it had been, they may have called this off. Grayling must have authorised it earlier.' He sighed more deeply. 'I can't imagine what the ACC will say when he hears about this.' Hood had a sudden thought. 'Has Maguire had any visitors since we saw her at Brampton?'

'Yes, sir, she has. Only one person.' She hesitated for a moment and checked her notebook. 'Francis Maddison. He went to see her to discuss Duffy's business last Saturday morning, according to the governor. As you know, she inherited Duffy's shares. She now has a controlling interest in the South Wales haulage business.'

'Francis Maddison? Him again? He didn't waste much time. This is too much of a coincidence. Get him in.'

'Superintendent Kingston's already on to it. He has officers looking for him. He's not been in the office this week.' She hesitated. 'Apparently, he's retiring and moving to Canada. That's what his secretary said. Three members of staff are buying him out and taking over the accountancy firm.'

Hood harrumphed. 'How very convenient. He never mentioned that to me when I saw him last week. I didn't get the impression he was thinking of retiring. He can't be much over fifty. Have they visited his home?'

'Yes, sir. No one there. Neighbours say the wife and daughter are visiting relations in Canada. But it doesn't look like they'll be returning. They left from Heathrow early on Monday. Superintendent Kingston has been on to Canada House to check their immigration status. And their house in West Hill Drive in Kettering is being put up for sale. Sounds very much like Maddison is intending to join them.'

'But he didn't go with them on Monday?'

'No, sir. He hasn't completed the disposal of his business yet and he was seen at the house yesterday, well after the rest of the family had left.'

'He'll have heard about Grayling's arrest. Enderby will have told him.'

'Perhaps the arrests have panicked him?'

Hood frowned. 'I doubt it. This must have been planned for some time and I didn't get the impression when I spoke to him last week that he's the panicking sort.'

'Do you think he was involved in Maguire's escape?'

'Probably. He must have acted as the go-between. But proving it. That won't be easy.'

'We need to find him first.'

'Exactly. Let's get on with it. I need to speak to Detective Superintendent Kingston as a matter of urgency.'

CHAPTER 42

A solemn-faced Julian Enderby sat across the table from Michael Grayling in the cramped room assigned for the conference between lawyer and client at Mansfield Shirebrook, well inside the prison complex. A prison officer was conspicuously stationed directly outside the room. Enderby had lost count of the number of locked doors he had passed through before coming across a somewhat dejected Grayling. That wasn't all. He and his briefcase had been searched, he had passed through an airport-type security gate and been obliged to place his right index finger onto some device which recorded his identity. He'd also had to submit to being photographed.

'You've got to get me out of here,' whispered Grayling. 'I can't risk going to trial, not with what they've got on me. I'll go down like a stone.' He looked around him. 'You don't think they have this room bugged, do you?'

Enderby remained relaxed. 'Calm down, Michael. This isn't America. You're not losing it are you?'

'That depends. What are you doing to get me out of here? I got Hanlon out. You can do the same for me.'

The lawyer sounded anything but sympathetic. 'No chance. I suspect I'll have trouble getting out of here myself. Security is as intense as I've ever seen it. You are going nowhere, I'm afraid, not at the moment.'

'When then?'

Enderby sighed. 'The syndicate is not pleased with you, Michael.'

'What do you mean?'

'You're in real danger of being written off. Going after Doyle as you did has caused ripples in the ocean which have extended as far as New Jersey and well beyond.'

Grayling scoffed. 'Doyle has nothing to do with the syndicate.'

'Oh, but he has when your obsession with eliminating him has put the Anglesey operation in jeopardy. You do realise the whole thing will have to be reorganised at huge expense, always assuming it's worth the effort? We've probably lost millions and the route for the merchandise has been permanently compromised. The entire operation has been undermined. Brandon Jessop has been arrested and has opened his big mouth because he doesn't want to be implicated in the Doyle farrago.' He paused ominously. 'You are not very popular in New Jersey, Michael. No one is going to put themselves out to help you, not at present.'

'I still have my own people; they'll do as I say.'

'Well, they'd better get on with it. And who have you got who can help you in this situation? Jamie Wallace is as deep in the shit as you are. And by the way, Kelly Maguire is now free.' Grayling's eyes widened. 'You hadn't heard? That little enterprise went very smoothly. She's already on her way out of the country and cooperating fully.'

Grayling recovered some of his composure. 'There you are then. That proves I can still organise things effectively. The syndicate will be pleased she's no longer a threat. She has a tape hidden somewhere that could have put everyone at risk, including the boys in New Jersey. Duffy knew about my contact.'

'She hasn't got a tape.'

Grayling appeared shocked. 'You mean she was bluffing? There is no tape?'

'There's a tape all right; in fact there are two but she doesn't have them.'

'Two? Where are they then?'

'Now? They're on their way to New Jersey. But they were closer to you than you thought.'

'What do you mean, closer than I thought?'

'Maddison had them; both of them. Duffy prepared one for his daughter to hand to the police and another with all the information that could have irretrievably damaged us. I'm afraid he wasn't very complimentary about you in either of them.' Enderby allowed himself a wry grin.

'Maddison had them all the time?' Grayling slammed his fists down on the table. 'I'll deal with that bastard personally when I get the opportunity. I knew he was getting nervous. Now, I know why.'

Enderby reacted sharply. 'You'll do no such thing. He was acting under orders from the syndicate. He warned you not to go after Doyle. You ignored his advice.'

'He told the syndicate about Doyle?'

'Don't be naïve, Michael. We knew what you were about from the beginning.' He sighed. 'I'm afraid you're not quite as nuanced in your actions as your father would have been. He could spot the main chance and take the necessary steps to gain the advantage. He never let anything interfere with business. Gus was admired for that. You're too emotional, Michael. That's what's been your undoing. Getting involved as you did with that Hamilton woman proves what I'm saying.'

'I was betrayed. Someone informed on me. The police were there waiting for us.'

'No one betrayed you.'

'What do you mean?'

'Using that hit-man was your biggest mistake. Why didn't you let Jamie deal with Doyle? No one would have been bothered if you hadn't turned the whole thing into such a public pantomime on the beach at Porth Ysgo.'

'I wanted to see the bastard die, close-up.'

'I'm sure Jamie wouldn't have objected to your presence while Doyle was despatched.'

'We couldn't find him. Not after he killed Maxine. I had to get to him before the police got hold of him. And I thought he might have had the tape. Anyway, the Tinkerman came highly recommended. I understood that the syndicate had used him before.'

Enderby let out a lengthy sigh. 'They have, but not the hit-man you employed. Not a good idea to use an assassin who's been compromised.'

'What are you getting at? I checked him out personally while I was in Dublin. He was already on the job by then.'

Enderby could not resist a scornful smile. 'The hit-man you hired was an undercover police officer. It was confirmed by my contact in Mid-Shires before I set out this morning. You were had, Michael.'

Grayling slumped in his seat. To say he was stunned hardly did justice to his reaction. 'I don't believe it.' He shook his head and exhaled noisily. 'So, it wasn't Julia who betrayed me?'

'No, she didn't. You are, in the opinion of the syndicate, the author of your own misfortune. There'll be no assistance from that quarter, I'm afraid. You'll be left to your own devices from now on. No one will be going out on a limb for you.'

'What about my money in the Cayman Islands?'

'That will be looked after for you, until you need it. We are not thieves, you know.' Enderby allowed himself a brief chuckle.

'Who is he, this undercover officer?'

'That, we don't know, and in the circumstances, there is no appetite to find out. The Dublin police have the real Tinkerman under lock and key somewhere in the wilds of Ireland. You were dealing throughout with a police officer. As I think you already know, everything you said was recorded. Whether he was Irish, English or from Timbuktu we have no idea, and, as I said, we have no intention of finding out. As far as the syndicate is concerned, the UK operation is over for the time being, finished. And you killed it off, Michael. You will not be easily forgiven for that.'

'If the syndicate knew about the undercover officer, why was I not informed?'

'They didn't know until after you were arrested. You didn't clear it with us as you should have done. The information has only just been received. For once the police kept matters very secure. Our contact in Mid-Shires never heard a thing, not until after you were arrested.'

'So the hit-man is still alive? He wasn't shot dead on the beach?'

'No, he wasn't. The police are not usually inclined to shoot their own men. Which means, of course, he'll be able to give evidence against you. Any argument you might have had about the lawfulness or otherwise of taping your telephone conversations without your consent will get nowhere now. You were heard to direct Doyle's killing on the beach and caught in possession of a lethal weapon. They also have the undercover officer available to give evidence about your conversations. They'll not have to rely on the tapes.'

'I'd swear he was Irish. I heard his voice several times.'

'Whether he's Irish or not, is of no account. And, Michael, just to be clear, you'll be needing a new solicitor. Unfortunately, I'm not able to represent you any longer. Orders from above. I seem to have discovered a conflict of interest!'

Grayling stood up and raised his voice. 'You can't abandon me. I could tell the police all about you and quite a bit about the syndicate.'

The lawyer remained seated but gave him a hard look. 'And do you think anyone will believe you? The police know nothing about the syndicate. As far as they are concerned, you run the organisation here, just like your father did before you. And if you try and cause trouble, we can leak lots of damaging material to the police that will prove you are the main man. They are already expecting you to come out with some fantasy but it will do you no good. You don't know who the actual members of the syndicate are and all of them are outside the jurisdiction of the English courts. And, just so you are fully in the picture, you mention me to the police other than in connection with my brilliance as a lawyer and you'll be dead within twenty-four hours, whatever precautions might be taken to protect you. Understand?'

Grayling glared at the lawyer. 'You wouldn't dare.' He retook his seat.

The lawyer stared back, then stood up. 'Just try me. Goodbye, Michael. I'm sorry things have turned out as they have. But, as you say, you have your own people to help you. They'd better get on with it.' He scoffed. 'I should consider offering a guilty plea if I were you.'

Enderby banged on the door. When it was opened, he turned, gave Grayling another smile, then departed without saying another word.

CHAPTER 43

'Is this true? Grayling is offering a plea deal?' Hood was going through a pile of papers on his desk having taken just over a week off from the investigation. His wife had insisted and ACC Gaunt had agreed.

'Yes, sir,' replied Andrew Hooper. 'He has a new solicitor, a Miss Diana Rhodes. He's offering to plead guilty to the murder of Dudley Manning and possession of a firearm with intent to endanger life on the beach in North Wales as well as conspiracy to pervert the course of justice. The CPS insisted on the last matter.'

'And the conspiracy to murder Doyle? He and Wallace were caught red-handed. And we have the evidence to prove it. The whole arrangement is on tape.'

'But that would involve calling the undercover officer, putting him at risk. Fiona Morrison thinks we should at least consider what's on offer. There never was any prospect of Doyle being shot by the undercover officer anyway and Grayling's bound to pick up a life sentence for the murder of Manning. We have him on tape admitting to the undercover officer that he had ordered Manning's shooting.'

'We can protect the identity of the officer,' insisted Hood. He looked up from the paperwork. 'And it's the agreement that amounts to the offence, not whether there was any real risk of it being carried out. No, I'm not in favour of a compromise. This whole idea stinks!'

'ACC Gaunt wants to discuss it with you and Fiona Morrison. From what I hear, Mr Cronshaw has concerns too. If the undercover officer never had any intention of carrying out the contract, can it be proved that there was ever a true agreement? Bit too technical for me, sir. Well above my pay grade.'

'Never mind the officer, Wallace and Grayling were clearly party to an agreement to murder Doyle and Hamilton. That the innocent undercover officer never had any intention of carrying out the plot is neither here nor there. It doesn't affect their intent or the agreement. I know enough law to understand that.' He paused, his frustration obvious. 'I'm not happy about this at all, Andrew.'

'There's another problem, sir. Diana Rhodes seems to know there was an undercover police officer involved. I've no idea how she found out but she's pushing for him to be identified.' He paused for a moment. 'I gained the impression that accepting the pleas offered will avoid putting the undercover officer at risk by having a trial.'

'Is Mr Cronshaw attending the meeting with the ACC tomorrow?'

'I'm not sure, sir. I understand he'll try and be there if he can.'

Hood reflected on the matter. His dinner date with Cronshaw had been postponed so he'd not had the opportunity of a private discussion, but he was pleased that the distinguished silk was prepared to include him in any talks about accepting the proposed pleas. 'I'm sure no judge would agree to disclosing the officer's identity. That would put him at colossal risk and would effectively finish his career as a police officer.' He hesitated, let out a lengthy sigh, then changed the subject. 'What happened to Julian Enderby? I read he's off the case. He went to see Grayling at Mansfield Shirebrook ten days ago, didn't he?'

'He did, but ceased to act for him almost immediately afterwards. Conflict of interest, apparently. Mind you, we were all surprised that he ended up with Diana Rhodes. She's from London – a new firm with a good reputation – but not very experienced. Only qualified five years ago.'

Hood almost chuckled. 'I wonder what the problem with Enderby was. Instructions from above, I suspect. There's clearly an international aspect to this organisation which we know very little about. Lots more work for us to get on with.'

'Perhaps Grayling has been thrown to the wolves by his masters, whoever they are.'

Hood grinned. 'We can only hope he has! What about Wallace?' He talked to me about a deal when we were still in North Wales, not that I gave him any encouragement.'

'He's put forward a similar package. Wallace accepts in his written basis of plea that he provided the gun to Kruger on Grayling's instructions. He also had a loaded gun with him on the beach at Port Ysgo – he can hardly deny that – and has offered to plead to possession with intent to endanger life.' Hooper dropped his voice. 'He's also offered to give us some information about the O.C.G., on the quiet, of course. He clearly knows all about the plan to murder Doyle at Cromwell.'

'Has he, indeed? That we must pursue. We mustn't overlook that there were two attempts on Doyle's life. Wallace could also help with whoever organised Maguire's escape. I wouldn't mind betting that he was responsible for setting it up on Grayling's instructions.'

Hooper nodded. 'He'll be taking a bit of a risk, won't he? Especially if Grayling finds out.'

'Up to him.' Hood went back to the paperwork in front of him.

'Could I ask what's happening about Maddison, sir?' asked Hooper.

Hood looked up. 'I've just heard from the CPS about him. They have reviewed the matter. Insufficient evidence to charge him with anything. He's been very careful. Typical bloody accountant.'

'But he must have been the link between Maguire and whoever sprung her. She didn't see anyone else. Perhaps Wallace will confirm that?'

'He might, I suppose. On the other hand, he may restrict his comments to what we already know – people in his position frequently do. Safer that way. Naming the accountant might just be a step too far, and we'd need some form of corroboration to take the matter further. You and I both suspect Maddison was in on it, but that isn't enough, not according to Fiona Morrison. Maguire could easily have received the necessary instructions from someone else. That stratagem used by Brian Logan could well have been adopted by someone on the inside of the organisation. It's a well-practised dodge. Or the idea could have been discussed between her and Duffy at any time before he died. She was obviously lying when she told me she thought he'd been murdered by the organisation. I think she knew all along that he'd taken his own life. And I wouldn't put it past Duffy that he killed himself just to give her the opportunity of escaping by attending his funeral. He really did blame himself for her being locked up and he probably realised he didn't have much of a future himself.'

'So, do we continue with Maddison's bail?'

'No, he was discharged from his bail conditions earlier today. The decision was the ACC's. He's free to join his family in Canada any time he chooses. And the sooner the better as far as I'm concerned. The buyout of his practice has been more or less completed. We need to concentrate again on Duffy's file. Someone in that law practice knew the file was in Worth's private safe.'

'Worth knew, of course.'

'It wasn't him; I'm pretty sure of that. Since we collared Grayling and Wallace, the ACC seems to have lost interest in how it was stolen and Rigby still hasn't been found. He didn't return from the Canaries when he should have done. But I'm convinced he broke open the safe and stole the file.'

'Johnson and some of the others must have been party to it then. Isn't there a circumstantial case against them and Maddison? The meeting was kept going until well after six o'clock deliberately.'

'Not enough, Andrew. Not unless we discover who revealed where the file was. Only someone on the inside of Worth's office could have been responsible for that. And from what Kelly Maguire said to me, someone must have leaked where Duffy's file was before he told me about it. That someone must be working at the solicitors. It simply can't have been anyone else. Maddison can't have known where it was unless someone working in the office told him.'

'We've recovered the file, of course.'

'We have. But only Grayling's and Wallace's prints on it. That doesn't take us much further. Whoever organised this leak took every precaution.'

'Sounds like an accountant, sir.' Hooper smiled.

Hood gave him a cynical look. 'That would not surprise me. And Mr Maddison had dealings with Worth's office on previous occasions, perfectly legitimate dealings, but that contact might have given him the opportunity to get close to someone who worked there. I think we should keep a careful eye on him until he leaves the country, always assuming he intends to join his wife in Canada. He was included in the original application for residence, wasn't he?'

'Yes, sir. He, his wife and daughter, but not his sons. They're established in this country. And it was put in months ago, not long after Gus Grayling died. Mrs Maddison has two brothers already living in Toronto. Both have families. When she was questioned briefly by the Canadian authorities she said she'd wanted to live in Canada for several years. She'd been trying to persuade her husband to retire for some time so they could move there.'

Hood nodded. 'Well, now's his chance. I'd still like to know, though, who leaked that the file was in Worth's personal safe. I thought his son was the prime candidate but he wasn't in the office on the day the meeting took place. He was in Birmingham at a business conference which went on even longer than the one his father chaired with Maddison.'

'Probably arranged to be out of the office deliberately if he'd previously told Rebecca Johnson about the private safe. She was in this up to her neck in my view.'

'I agree. But no charges against her either, not at the moment. Both have denied involvement. As has the prisoner Louise Daley at Brampton. In the absence of the letter *and* Kelly Maguire, we can't prove anything against her. Little point in depending on a prison officer who's facing charges himself. As for Tony Worth, he couldn't have known his father had placed the file in his private safe on the day of the meeting if he was in Birmingham. He didn't know of my appointment. Mind you, I strongly suspect you're right when you say he'd passed something on to Rebecca Johnson. They'd have to have known about the refurbishment of some of the rooms to carry out the theft. Rigby must have hidden somewhere.'

Hooper smiled broadly. 'There's definitely been something going on between Tony Worth and the Johnson woman. I understand his wife has given him his marching orders. It was all round the office when I went there yesterday. Worth junior was looking very bereft.'

'I heard the same,' smiled Hood.

'Serves him right, I say.' Hooper paused for a moment. 'What about the secretary? She certainly knew about the file and the private safe. And you made the appointment to see Worth through her.'

Hood shook his head. 'Worth Senior won't have a word said against her. He's actually very concerned for her. Apparently, she's thinking of going part-time. Her mother's health is deteriorating and she feels obliged to spend more time looking after her.'

Hooper shrugged his shoulders. 'Does it matter, that much, sir? We've got Grayling and Wallace banged to rights and the Welsh have broken up the heroin smuggling racket. And they wouldn't have managed that without our assistance. We've not done too badly, overall. The chief must be quite happy it's all been resolved before he retires.'

Hood did not reply immediately. When he did, he was still somewhat dissatisfied. 'He's not happy about Kelly Maguire disappearing. He's mentioned that to me more than once. He's always been a bit of a perfectionist.'

'Hardly down to us, sir. That was left to Northants to deal with. We can't be blamed for that.'

'But it should have been prevented.'

'I agree. But that apart, we've busted open a major criminal organisation. That's what's important.'

Hood nodded. 'I suppose we have. And there's some prospect of Grayling and Jamie Wallace being charged in respect of the drugs conspiracy. A decision has still to be made about Doyle and Hamilton, though. If these proposed pleas are accepted, we won't need either of them as witnesses.'

'Doyle still wants Hamilton, does he?' Hooper shook his head. 'He's certainly a glutton for punishment.'

'He does. He remains absolutely besotted with her, especially since the new DNA tests showed he is the boy's father.' He sighed. 'It's quite remarkable how little impact raw facts have on a man who is hopelessly in love.'

'And her?'

'She seems to be less self-centred nowadays, I suppose. The experience of spending so much time with Grayling, perhaps?'

* * *

The proposed pleas proved acceptable, despite Hood's protests. The DPP agreed with Fiona Morrison and Dublin that it was imperative that the undercover officer's identity should be protected at all costs. Harold Cronshaw also pointed to practical rather than legal difficulties in respect of succeeding on a conspiracy charge when one party to the agreement never had any intention of carrying it out. Despite his advice that there was no legal impediment to charging both Grayling and Wallace with conspiracy to murder Doyle and Hamilton, he advised it might still have the look of a set-up and juries could not always be relied on to convict in such circumstances.

Three months later, both Grayling and Wallace were sentenced to life imprisonment for the murder of Dudley Manning, the judge afterwards writing to the Home Secretary recommending minimum terms of thirty-two and twenty-seven years respectively before applications for parole could be submitted. A concurrent second life sentence was imposed on both men for the firearms offences together with a fourteen-year sentence for conspiracy to pervert the course of justice, that offence arising out of the attempt to implicate Doyle in the death of Dudley Manning. The theft of Duffy's file was not proceeded with. Jessop and Dewhurst had yet to be sentenced in Wales, but it was thought that both would benefit from the cooperation they had offered as the heroin smuggling operation was broken up. Hood was delighted to learn that both Grayling and Wallace would be subject to further charges when the investigation was completed.

Doyle and Hamilton were both released from their bail conditions. No charges were brought against them and Doyle's parole conditions were relaxed. Given the risks both continued to face from the remnants of the organised crime group, they were permitted to move temporarily to Scotland as part of a witness protection programme, their precise location and change of name being treated with the utmost secrecy. Hood wondered how they would cope living in the remote highland community to which they had been despatched, far from their usual haunts. A move abroad in a few months' time, probably to rural France, was contemplated.

It was early autumn when the telephone rang at the home of Vivienne Benedict in Oadby in Leicestershire. Was this yet another call sympathising with the recent death of her mother?'

'Hello Vivienne. It's me. I got the card about your mother. I'm very sorry.'

'Thank you, but it came as a bit of a relief to tell you the truth. She was not at all happy and she was deteriorating quite quickly. The end was very peaceful.'

'So, nothing to keep you in England any longer?'

'I suppose not. I've told Mr Worth I'm proposing to retire completely at the end of November. I've been working only part-time in recent months because of my mother. She needed me with her much more than before. He's had sufficient time to find a replacement. What about you?'

'My wife and I have already separated. It's been on the cards for some time. Do you know, I don't think she ever really liked me, although she knows nothing about you. We are intending to divorce, once the finances are settled. She's quite happy about it, and I'm not particularly taken with Canada. I always fancied somewhere warmer. Are you still keen on Rio?'

'Absolutely. My mother and I went there on holiday four years ago. It was fabulous. But would we have enough to live comfortably? It's terribly expensive I suspect in Ipanema. And I've set my heart on living there. And I can make a contribution. I can put my house up for sale and I inherited quite a bit from my mother.'

'That's entirely up to you, my darling. It might be better to let the house and give the impression you are taking an extended holiday. We'll have more than enough, even for Ipanema. There's no need to worry about money at all. I promise you, there'll be plenty. I'll start making the arrangements for about Christmas time, shall I?'

'Yes, Francis. You do that. I can't wait. We've been patient long enough. We have a lot of catching up to do.'

END

ALSO BY MICHAEL G T STOKES

Blackmail
A Private & Convenient Place
When Supper was ended…
The Harman Brief

Visit the Author's website:
michaelgtstokes.com

ABOUT THE AUTHOR

Michael Stokes has been involved with the law throughout his professional life. He practised as a barrister for many years, becoming a QC in 1994 (now a KC) before becoming a judge in 2001. He was the Recorder of Nottingham between 2007 and 2016 and serves as a Deputy Lieutenant for Nottinghamshire. Familiar as he is with the area where he has lived for many years, his novels always have a Midlands setting. *The Tinkerman* is the third novel in his Inspector Hood series (although published after the fourth, *When Supper was Ended.*) He is presently working on the fifth in the series, *Death of a Coroner*, to be published in 2024. Michael is married with two grown-up children and lives in Leicestershire and Brittany in France.

Printed in Great Britain
by Amazon

34131837R00216